The Ghosts of Apollo

by

John Madower

Publishing History
First Edition, 2025
Trade Paperback ISBN 978-1-5092-5858-1
Digital ISBN 978-1-5092-5859-8

Published in the United States of America

Dedication

This book is dedicated to those who protected us from the ravages of the global pandemic, both our frontline workers and those who enabled them.

You were courageous heroes who gave so much to keep us safe. Your steadfastness and grace in the face of overwhelming adversity continues to be inspirational.

****

A sincere thank you to all those who helped with the development of this novel, especially Caitlin A. Madower, Malcolm Madower, Pat and Anne Finn, Ron and Lyn Keeler, Mike and Marcella Kampman, Brian and Carolyn Buchanan, Sudipta Sinha, Morgan Wade, Tedd Reed, Wayne Mee, Kevin Yamashita, Christina Walker, Victoria Feygina, and Lea Schizas.

A very special thanks to my lovely wife Linda who not only was key to my success in life but challenged me to be a better writer and contributed so many ideas to the creation of this novel. I can never thank you enough.

Prologue

Powerful Machines in a Viciously Divided World
1968, Area 25, Nevada National Security Site

Twenty-eight-year-old Doug Regent stood motionless in the frigid darkness of the early morning. The sky was black and awash with millions of bright stars, while the surrounding hills were obscure and foreboding. He looked almost straight up to take in the heavens more fully. *It's hard to believe that the work we're doing here will soon make traveling out there so much easier.*

Doug was not normally up this early. However, with his boss traveling from Huntsville, Alabama to visit Area 25's Nuclear Rocket Development Station, sleep was elusive. Once the sun was fully up and the day started, it would be hot, dusty, and intense. But right now, it was calming just to drink in the serenity of the moment. Unconsciously, he shifted weight from one foot to another, trying to generate some body heat. The compact, stony desert crunched with the gentle shifting of each foot.

Although things still needed to be done before the visit, experience indicated it was okay to take time for some self-reflection. Months of preparation had gone into this event; everyone was more than ready for the crucial demonstration test planned for the boss later in the day. *Besides, it's exactly at moments like this, when I take time to reflect, that I remember things I forgot to do. It's strange how the subconscious works.* Doug slowly exhaled and tried to will his breathing and heart rate to slow. As the red and orange hues from the morning light started to seep over the horizon, his thoughts drifted.

A kaleidoscope of visions, many representing events that led to this culminating milestone, paraded through his mind like a series of newsreels. A short, bald, rotund man gave an impassioned speech at the United Nations General Assembly. Working up into a lather, he beat the lectern with a shoe for emphasis. "We will bury you!" the newspapers reported Nikita Khrushchev, Premier of the Soviet Union, shouting while admonishing the United States for imperialistic behavior.

Mistrust and treachery consumed a globe segregated into two armed camps, each ready to vaporize the other at a moment's notice with nuclear weapons so powerful they would end civilization. Only essential business and an abundance of propaganda were exchanged between the two sides. Leisure travel was out of the question. Western democracies, led by the United States and President Kennedy, were pitted against eastern totalitarian communist states directed by the Soviet Union. East and West saw the very survival of their way of life at stake. Atomic scientists fretted as they advanced the hands of the Doomsday Clock to just seven minutes to midnight in a desperate attempt to get mankind to see how close we were to self-annihilation.

As the leader of the East, Khrushchev was ruthless and dangerous, a bully. After the UN tirade, he tried to bring West Berlin under communist control by starving its citizens into submission. When that failed, the Missile Crisis followed later the same year with an attempt to base nuclear missiles in Cuba where they would reach targets in the United States with virtually no warning. Fear of imminent nuclear war permeated all levels of society. *Sadly, even school children are taught how to respond to atomic weapons detonating nearby.*

Visions of new destructive Soviet technologies designed to dominate the international order flashed through Doug's head. When it came to space, the Soviets were unrivaled. They launched the first intercontinental ballistic missile, the first satellite, the first animal into orbit, the first probe to the moon, and delivered the first televised images of the far side of the moon. The much-publicized US plan to put a human in space was upstaged when the Soviets launched a spacecraft carrying Yuri Gagarin a few weeks earlier. Gagarin made a full orbit of Earth while Alan Shepard from the US only made a sub-orbital flight. Nonetheless, Americans and the West celebrated success. However, Soviet mastery of space was universally recognized and the 35th President of the United States was obviously worried.

A huge grin slowly spread over Doug's face as he remembered Kennedy's appearance before the joint session of Congress. *In response to a clear, deliberate challenge, the president rallied the country and redoubled efforts to capture lost ground.* In retrospect, it's now easy to see the speech was far more nuanced than was appreciated at the time. Most people recall him setting forth the challenge of "landing a man on the moon and returning him safely to the Earth." However, Kennedy also called for the development of other urgently needed national capabilities, such as nuclear rockets and satellites.

Doug fondly recalled the president's sincere interest in everything they were doing during his December 1962 visit to the secret Nuclear Rocket Development Station. Back then, Doug was new to the program but often wondered what the president thought of the name Jackass Flats where the station was located. Given how the American space program struggled in those early days, Doug was sure the irony would not have been appreciated.

Although the president had been gone for almost five years now, Doug believed Kennedy would be happy with the incredible progress that had been made in such a short time. For example, who could not be impressed by the sheer brute power of the Saturn V rocket? When it fired, a monstrously sustained explosion shook everything to the core for miles around. Standing at 363 feet, or over 30 storeys, tall, and 33 feet in diameter, the six-and-a-half million-pound Saturn V burned 20 tons of rocket fuel every second to produce the seven-and-a-half million pounds of thrust needed to lift itself off the launch pad and accelerate faster than 5,000 miles per hour before the first stage was spent. This monster rocket could lift a payload of over 130 tons into orbit. The engineering behind such a machine was simply staggering, and it was hard to imagine what the astronauts, tightly strapped down inside, went through during launch.

Doug remembered when work originally started at the Nuclear Rocket Development Station—the thought was to design a thermal nuclear rocket engine drop-in replacement for the Saturn V upper stage engines. As requirements and likely applications were more closely considered, it was decided that an entirely new engine, solely for use beyond Earth's orbit, would be more appropriate. After many years, the highly classified work had finally resulted in a proof-of-concept engine that had been test-fired for many hours. Although difficult to engineer and produce, the theory behind these engines was pretty basic. Rather than generate hot gas and thrust from the combustion of liquid hydrogen and liquid oxygen, the ultra secret new engines created super-heated hydrogen by directing it through the core of a nuclear reactor. These engines could drive rockets faster, longer, and carry up to three times the payload compared to conventional propulsion. The nuclear reactors could also be harnessed to generate electricity for the spaceship.

Doug eventually shook himself from his reverie and returned to the Support Area Building to join other team members starting their day. The early morning disappeared quickly and soon an intensely yellow sun burned high in the clear blue sky. What had started so slowly became a flurry of last-minute, mostly inane, activities. *Jitters. The whole organization seems on edge.* Nonetheless, things quickly fell into place. By mid-morning, he was back outside, this time accompanied by the remainder of the team. After a brief wait, far off in the distance, barely visible, was a telltale dust cloud rising from the dirt road that led to the station.

"There's the boss," Doug announced to the team, pointing toward the horizon as his stomach tightened.

Everyone was gathered outside the Support Area Building. Conversations petered off as people directed their gaze and squinted toward the distance.

That approaching wisp of dust silently announced Bob Gillespie's arrival. He was supposed to be coming today to witness the final test firing of the new nuclear rocket engine prototype and then authorize the development of a production model. Though the itinerary had been carefully choreographed, now there were indications the visit had another, yet unknown, purpose.

Intently tracking the approaching cloud rising from the road, Doug grinned furtively. *Whatever he wants now, it's too late to worry about changing the program; we'll just adjust as needed.*

Doug was confident that the team would impress the boss with what they were going to show him and the advances they had made since the last visit. With one year to go before the US was scheduled to launch a man to the moon to fulfill Kennedy's public challenge, this new propulsion system was one of the key technologies that would usher in the next phase of the space program, the phase hidden from public view. It was vital to preserving the American way of life in an uncertain, volatile world. *I just wish I knew what the boss was up to now.*

****

Early Warning
November 1972, Moscow, Soviet Union
The still night abruptly shattered when the telephone on the bedstand sprang to life, ringing insistently. Startled, but not yet fully awake, Alexi Volniev rolled over and reached out in the dark for the

irritating device. By the time the handset was next to his ear, he was coherent but not happy about being forced from a deep sleep at 3:00 a.m. To add further insult, the cold air in the room instantly rushed beneath the now disturbed heavy covers.

"*Da.*"

"Comrade Directorate Chief," a gruff, but tentative voice responded, "I am sorry to disturb you. The report you were expecting from Amerika has just arrived."

Alexi was instantly filled with trepidation. There was no question what the call meant. He needed to go to the office immediately. This was not a matter to discuss over the phone. Although the report was indeed anticipated, its actual arrival was not expected so soon. More fully awake, and better able to think, Alexi reasoned that one way or another, the information from Amerika would either put an end to months of worry and suspicion, or it would confirm the absolute worst. Either way, it demanded immediate action.

"*Spasibo.*" Spasibo literally meant 'God save you' but was used ironically as 'thank you' in the religion-intolerant Soviet Union. *Perhaps God will need to save us all*.

With the handset re-cradled, he slipped out of the soft bed onto the cold hardwood floor.

Karolina reached out. "Work?" she asked sleepily.

"Yes," Alexi answered, trying to hide the guilt for placing duty ahead of her yet again.

Standing beside the bed, fully immersed in the cold, and with nothing more in mind to atone for hastily abandoning her, he silently dressed, kissed his wife on the cheek, and left.

Minutes later, Alexi was racing across the rainy,

dreary city toward Lubyanka Square and the massive yellow palatial building that served as the headquarters for the KGB, the Soviet Intelligence Service. Uncharacteristically, the frigid air penetrating his heavy woolen overcoat and causing his breath to vaporize in the car's interior did not bother him. There was a vital task ahead.

The city was devoid of people and traffic at that hour, so the journey to work was much quicker than normal. Entering the operations center dedicated to foreign intelligence, he was struck by the number of people already present. The thick smell of cigarettes and stale coffee permeated the air. Harsh artificial overhead lights made the windowless room seem more somber. Teletype machines clattered over subdued discussions. Conversations quieted as people noticed the Directorate Chief in their midst.

"Good morning, everyone," he said with forced enthusiasm while walking to the Duty Officer who was now standing at attention. By then, Alexi had been joined by both the Deputy and Operations Officer for the organization.

"Sir, here is your copy of the report. It just came in an hour ago," the Duty Officer reported.

Alexi took the sealed manila envelope and immediately proceeded toward his office, followed closely by the Deputy and Operations Officer. Agitated, he stopped them.

"Comrades! Please…"

Alexi feared the content of the field agent's report might require the highest officials in the Soviet Union to be alerted, so his recommendation had to be correct and withstand the utmost external examination. The perspectives of these two key subordinates were always appreciated, but for this important issue, it was prudent to develop his own initial thoughts.

In a more conciliatory tone, Alexi added, "Thank you for being here on short notice…but give me a few minutes to read this. Then, I would like us to meet in my office to discuss our response."

Alexi's utilitarian office was a sanctuary from the din of the operations room. He closed the door and hurriedly tore open the sealed envelope protecting the highly classified report from one of their agents who had penetrated NASA. Scanning the document carefully, Alexi seized on a phrase that read "…NASA's next rocket to be launched after the moon missions is currently being assembled; it contains secret components of unknown origin or purpose. These components were not developed by the Apollo Program." *What are the Amerikans up to?*

Alexi knew the moon missions were the only bright spot in the US space program and the Soviets were intent on re-capturing the initiative in space. *This new rocket potentially poses a threat to a resurgence of Soviet dominance. But what if it was more than that? What if it was an entirely new strategic threat?* Alexi took in a long, measured breath and closed his eyes. Purposefully, he placed the field agent report on the green blotter of the desk and began to carefully read from the beginning of the document.

The report confirmed much of what had already been learned about the future direction of the US space program. With the final moon landing scheduled to be completed next month, it reaffirmed NASA's intention to utilize Apollo Program expertise and equipment to further space exploration. They called it the Apollo Applications Program. The first project was to be a space station in Earth's orbit called Skylab. This was all public knowledge, but the report explained in detail that during the assembly of the rocket containing the space station, there were a number of components installed in such a way that they could not be examined, nor their purpose determined. Also, there was extra shielding and other precautions against radiation exposure. Even some of the engines test-fitted looked different from any used previously. *Were the Amerikans planning on secretly breaking international law by weaponizing space with a nuclear missile in orbit?*

Alexi reflected a bit, then signaled for his colleagues to enter by opening the office door. They all took their customary seats; this was Alexi's trusted inner circle to which he looked for advice.

The Deputy, hardly able to hold back, opened the discussion.

"I've never trusted the Amerikans. They claim NASA is purely a scientific organization, but they draw their cosmonauts from the military and often use military resources. Clearly, there is a military nexus to their efforts. They have a history of using technology to gain an advantage over other nations, particularly with atomic weapons. The secrecy about the equipment on-board the rocket currently being assembled indicates it is not for peaceful scientific, or exploratory, purposes."

****

As soon as the regular workday commenced, Alexi was standing with his superiors in KGB Chairman Yury Andropov's lavish third-floor office in the Lubyanka building.

"Chairman Andropov, this new rocket will place a space station over our heads with secret on-board technology that is not part of the Apollo Program. It can only have a military purpose. If it were scientific, it would be out in the open."

"I understand," the Chairman said, once additional details had been provided. "This is now the KGB's top priority. I want all our resources focused on it. And press the agent in NASA harder. We need to quickly find out what the Amerikans are up to with that spacecraft."

Chapter 1

Searching for Something More
02:30 hours 17 February 2018, Forward Operating Base (FOB), Khost, Afghanistan

The US Army Black Hawk helicopter from Kabul raced 150 miles to the southeast toward Khost City. Tess Shefford, the sole passenger on-board, strained against her seat harness to get a better view through a nearby window. It was a black abyss outside. Occasionally, she could make out faint lights revealing the location of a village far below, but mostly she was alone with her thoughts in the cramped, noisy aircraft cabin.

"Are you still with us back there?" a scratchy voice rose over the background hum of the intercom system.

Tess reached for her 'press-to-talk' button on a long cord attached to her headset.

"Yes, thank you. All good back here."

"This must be important…I mean…to spool up an aircraft in the middle of the night," the voice came back quickly.

Tess could see the two pilots ahead in the cockpit, crouched over the controls, eerily illuminated by the dim lights of the instrument panel. One pilot had his head half turned toward her.

"Uh-huh. I was thinking that too," Tess gently

deflected.

The smell of hydraulic fluid and engine exhaust hung in the air. Despite portraying an air of confidence, Tess could not help but feel uneasy about the mission ahead. Part of the angst was because she had no specifics about the impending operation. She was told there would be a detailed briefing upon arrival. Although confident in her abilities, adding to the discomfort was knowing this was also her first foray 'outside the wire.' She usually worked in far more secure locations, like protected compounds within well-guarded camps.

A crewman moved across the dark interior to open the cargo door on each side of the helicopter, interrupting Tess's contemplation about what might lie ahead.

"Please ensure you are securely fastened in back there," the voice from the cockpit cautioned over the ICS.

"Yes. All buckled up," Tess responded.

"Cabin check complete," the crewman announced while strapping in.

The Black Hawk immediately snapped over on its side and descended rapidly to avoid potential small arms fire from the ground during landing. After its aggressive tactical approach, the helicopter touched down on the taupe-colored, flat gravel with a thump and a slight bounce, causing dust to swirl everywhere. The instant they landed, the crewman jumped out onto the ground to assist Tess exit the loud, whirling machine. He helped her extract her duffle bag and backpack, and then they both crouched, walking out from under the helicopter's overhead rotor arc.

A tall, muscular, black Special Forces major met Tess at the edge of the landing zone.

"Welcome to Khost City. I'm Gavin Ross," the major, who looked to be in his mid-thirties, called into Tess's ear as the deafening helicopter departed, sand blasting everything in the near vicinity while it spiraled away overhead.

"Hi, Gavin. I'm Tess. Thanks for meeting me." Tess flashed a hurried smile.

"Thank you for coming on short notice," Gavin responded more casually now that the FOB was calm. "Our analyst was air evac'd yesterday with appendicitis and we had difficulty getting a replacement. We've got this really big show going down and specialist support is vital to success."

Tess was not a field operative, but rather a communications analyst with the National Security Agency. However, when the urgent call went out for assistance at the FOB, she immediately volunteered. It was not that she was cavalier about her safety and actively sought out danger, she was just resolute about wanting to make a real difference while she was in Afghanistan. She knew Khost Province was a hornet's nest and saw being there as the best way to contribute directly to the fight against cruel zealots. She also saw it as a way to honor her fiancé, who had been killed in operations in Kandahar two years earlier.

Grasping Tess's luggage, Gavin motioned for her to follow him toward the heart of the FOB.

"Come on, they're expecting us."

Tess was slim, with thick, long, straight, jet-black hair tied up in a bun for the helicopter flight. At five-foot-five, she had to walk with purpose to keep up with the major's long, effortless strides. Tess was driven by a strong sense of duty and hard work, qualities inherited from a hard-working Japanese-American mother and American father. Although she never considered her looks, she was incredibly attractive, and at thirty-one could easily pass for someone much younger.

"So, you're normally based out of Kabul?"

"Yes. I've been there since I got in country," Tess said as she looked around at the war-battered, spartan FOB.

During her time in Afghanistan, Tess had quickly earned a reputation for being a personable, focused professional who understood the complications at play in the country. She knew the Taliban stronghold in this region represented a microcosm of the larger challenges Afghanistan faced. Situated adjacent to the lawless Federally Administered Tribal Area in Pakistan, Khost was marked by poverty, numerous internally fighting factions, pervasive corruption, a weak central government, a porous border, and a neighboring country that pretended to be helpful but was determined to keep Afghanistan weak by actively fostering instability. Things were generally hard in this country, but they were really hard in the southernmost provinces of Khost, Kandahar, and Helmand.

While Gavin continued to lead the way through a tangled maze of brightly lit pathways, security gates, and check points, he explained that nominally the Afghans had assumed responsibility for this base, but due to its important location, the US still maintained a presence and continued to exert much influence here. As they pushed by shabby buildings, workshops, and shipping containers, Tess could feel another wave of uncertainty start to build, but she immediately tamped the emotions down. *You are in it now. There's no time for second thoughts.* She was determined to do her best no matter what lay ahead.

In front of a building Tess took to be their destination, Gavin abruptly stopped. Scanning the area, he slowly inhaled, and then looked directly at her. Tess felt the stare, like she was being examined.

"This is a once-in-a-generation operation. It'll be dangerous for our guys on the ground. We will all need to bring our best."

"I'm ready," Tess responded, but wondered if Gavin had somehow sensed her earlier unease.

He held her gaze for a moment, as if trying to gauge her ability.

"Great," was the only reply.

Then, turning abruptly, he hastily entered the secure briefing location with the bags. Tess quickly followed.

"Would you like a coffee or water before we go in to meet the Special Forces Commander?" Gavin asked, now seemingly calmer.

Tess pulled a water bottle from her backpack and shook her head.

"Thanks. I'm okay," she said, not wanting to delay the inevitable.

Tess was then hurriedly ushered into an adjacent conference room. The officer at the head of the table immediately stopped speaking. Tess was sure it was the commander because of his presence in the room. He looked about mid-forty, average height, thinning dark hair, but still rugged enough to look oddly out of place in a comfortable conference room. There were two disposable Styrofoam cups in front of him—one held coffee and the other was a spittoon for the wad of chewing tobacco held between his jaw and inner cheek, which bulged out. The six other people seated at the table turned in unison to face her and Gavin.

"Apologies, commander," Gavin said to the man who had just been speaking. "This is our comms analyst, Ms. Shefford."

"Ah, welcome," the commander said warmly with a smile. "We've been expecting you. How was your flight?"

"Fine, sir," Tess responded, more stiffly than she intended.

"Please, we're happy you could join us," the commander said, motioning her to one of two vacant chairs at the table.

"Good morning, everyone," Tess said, glancing around as she sat down and pulled out her notebook. Gavin placed her luggage against the wall and sat beside her.

After initial introductions, the commander, Lieutenant-Colonel Salazar, resumed the briefing. *The tobacco habit doesn't impair his speech. Oddly, it seems to force him to speak more slowly and deliberately.* Salazar explained that they had numerous intelligence sources indicating an impending gathering of regional Taliban leaders for a "*shura*", or consultation, in Khost. The Taliban Commander, who normally cowered in safety in the Tribal Area while his men fought and died on this side of the border, was expected to make a rare appearance at the meeting in order to coordinate activities for the upcoming fighting season. The Taliban Commander was the High Value

Target.

Through actions and speech, the Special Forces Commander telegraphed a feisty scrapper persona. *I wonder if this is an attempt to animate the team.* Behind all the bravado, it was obvious there was a thoughtful and intelligent man.

Adding more precision at the critical part of the brief, the commander said, "We've been getting lots of chatter through the net, indicating a meeting is imminent. Unlike some compound in the middle of nowhere that we can isolate, we believe they plan to gather in one of the busiest areas of Khost City, somewhere near the market. It will be easy for these leaders to slip in and out as part of the crowd, and you can bet they'll have sentries out to ensure they're not surprised during their discussions.

"By using a location like this, they prevent us from employing Predator or other air strikes for fear of collateral damage. So, we plan to breach the front door of their meeting location with a shoulder-fired Carl Gustav medium attack weapon. It's easy to move and packs a hell of a punch. Once the breach occurs, an assault team led by Major Ross will quickly move through the meeting location, fighting through, if necessary, with the objective of identifying, capturing, or if need be, killing the High Value Target. Every effort will be made to take him alive for intel exploitation.

"After the breach, a much larger support team will immediately establish a cordon around the meeting location and the entire market area. Nobody gets through this cordon until the HVT is confirmed in our custody, alive or dead. I want the market included in the cordon because it is an obvious escape route. They'll slip out of the meeting at the first sign of trouble, hide amongst the crowd doing their shopping, and disappear in the confusion. Major Levesque, you'll be leading the support team. There'll potentially be large, unruly crowds to manage, so prepare for that.

"Captain Naude, you have the Quick Reaction Force. You're in reserve. Be prepared to respond to any unforeseen eventualities.

"Using the Carl G to gain entry might seem a little heavy-handed, but we anticipate lots of security given the high-level attendees at the meeting. This particular group is known for their fortified entrances and booby traps, so we aren't taking any chances with our men– we're going to blow the front off the building."

The commander paused for a moment, seemingly to let this part of the plan sink in, then asked, "Questions?"

Tess waited to see if anyone else had a question, and when there were none, she proceeded.

"Commander, what do you need me to do?"

"Ah, yes, Ms. Shefford. I haven't forgotten you. I just wanted to get the broad-brush strokes on the table first, so we had a frame of reference. You are the key to this whole enterprise," he said, looking her directly in the eyes as if to emphasize the point. Tess flushed. "You'll be call sign Wizard. I need you to confirm the meeting location and that our HVT guest from Pakistan, code-named Geppetto, has arrived. The challenge is that we have no idea what Geppetto actually looks like."

The Commander continued. "This op is being jointly run with the CIA, but we cannot publicly divulge they are here. If anything goes wrong, even if it is their fault, we get the blame. They have been working the market for months and we are leveraging the eavesdropping equipment they had previously installed for other requirements. Like most markets in this country, it's like a watering hole on the Serengeti; it draws in everybody, the good and the bad.

"Although the place looks like it's right out of the fourteenth century, our Agency friends have literally wired it for sound. They've hacked into local comms towers and can 'ping' cell phones of interest if they are turned on. We've found most of the higher-level fighters in this region have pretty good security discipline by not carrying phones, or removing the SIM cards, but many of their low-level associates aren't so attentive. Therefore, it's a matter of knowing who consorts with whom in order to determine who might be around.

"In addition to tracking and monitoring cell phones, the Agency has placed parabolic microphones and video cameras to cover key gathering spots. These are disguised as local satellite TV dishes. It's amazing what people say when they don't think they're being overheard. Because the meeting will likely be held indoors, for this op our friends also brought in low-power infrared lasers to listen at a distance to conversations through the windows of suspect buildings and houses where the *shura* might take place. It's all run out of an office overlooking the market. We need you to take charge of this technology and cue us to anything suspicious. I cannot overstate your importance to the success of this operation. We've been trying to capture or eliminate Geppetto for years. We are looking to you to tell us where he is. Can you help us with that, Ms. Shefford?"

Tess could feel the eyes of everyone in the conference room as they all simultaneously turned to look at her.

"Yes, of course, commander. The sooner I can see my equipment, the better," she responded, immediately wondering if she might have projected too much confidence in what appeared to be a complex, high-risk mission.

After the briefing, Gavin escorted Tess to one of the shipping containers used by the CIA as an office. While they waited for the Agency contact, she noticed Gavin became increasingly quiet. *I wonder if he's mentally preparing for the operation, or just reflecting on the Commander's orders. Whatever it is, this is getting awkward.*

"I'm glad we had the opportunity to meet today," Gavin finally said.

"Yes, I really appreciate you looking out for me," Tess responded.

Then Gavin said something unexpected. "I knew Lincoln. We served together in Zangabad. He was an amazing guy. Words cannot say how sorry I am about what happened."

Tess was unsure of how to respond. "Thank you, Gavin," was all she could manage as a tear formed in her eye, and memories of happier times with her fiancé came flooding back.

Tess could see the sadness in Gavin's eyes, which now averted her gaze. Then, he reached into a pocket and thrust an envelope and a pistol toward her. "This is a savage place, Tess. People play for keeps here and from now on it's just going to be you and the Agency guy out there. This is a 9 millimeter SIG Sauer—just point and squeeze the trigger. The safety is built into the trigger pressure, so squeeze really hard the first time. There is a round in the chamber and ten more in the magazine." After a brief pause, in a very calm voice, he added, "Above all, you cannot be taken prisoner out there."

I know what you're trying to tell me, but right now I don't want to think about what I might have to do with my last bullet.

"And the envelope?"

"Two thousand dollars. In case something goes sideways, and you need to bribe your way home. Keep it with you—you never know when a situation might turn for the worse and you need to incentivize people. The greenback is accepted everywhere."

Just as Tess was thanking Gavin for the unanticipated kind words and thoughtfulness, Randy, the CIA operative, showed up in a dilapidated pickup. She loaded her kit into the truck, and they headed out of the FOB under the cover of darkness. As they continued into the city, Gavin's warning about how quickly things could change made Tess think of her grandfather. He had made a good living fishing off the coast of Seattle when the Second World War broke out. Overnight, everything was lost when the government confiscated his boat because they thought he could spy for the enemy. Then, the whole family was interned in a camp, simply because of their Japanese ancestry. One minute they were comfortably prosperous and the next they were enemies of the State. When it was all over, her grandfather moved the entire family to Chicago, as far away from the ocean as possible.

Tess also thought about Linc, who always warned about the need for contingencies in Afghanistan because of opportunists everywhere. She could still remember him saying, "You never quite know who you can trust." Tess allowed herself another spell of remorse, knowing no contingency could have saved him from the IED.

Passing through a safehouse and donning local clothing was transformative, Tess was all business now. She was spirited to the clandestine office in a low-rise building overlooking the dusty, vacant market that would be a hub of activity in about six hours. Her heart sank when she saw the state of the surveillance equipment. The job was half done. Some pieces of equipment were functioning, but the heart of the system appeared to be part of a nest of twisted cables and hardware piled in the middle of a table. Tess suddenly felt the entire weight of mission success in the pit of her stomach. She knew that for the operation to succeed, the equipment had to be fully up and running. It was a daunting task for an operator without any 'tech' support. However, she generally knew what needed to be done and how the system worked since it was similar to the one back in Kabul. Besides, there was no choice—she had to figure it out.

Methodically, piece by piece, Tess connected the remaining components of the surveillance system, testing each one as it was added to ensure the system worked properly. Just as the cold morning light sparkled into the room as if through a prism, Tess was completing her work. Triggers had been programmed into the computer that would automatically sound an alert in the presence of active cell phones used by local Taliban leaders or their associates, especially Geppetto's associates. Geppetto's voiceprint was set as a trigger so Tess would be signaled if he spoke, and it was picked up by any of the microphones or lasers. Finally, words likely to be used in his presence, like 'commander' would also result in the computer sounding an alarm in the surveillance office.

Tess rested her head on her forearm for a moment and gently held her eyes closed. In the distance, she could hear the muezzin call the faithful to prayers, the sixth such series of hypnotic chants since last sleeping, twenty-four hours ago. However, before even contemplating a brief rest, she texted the Tactical Operation Center controlling the operation using a secure phone.

—TOC, Wizard G2G. Ack— was all she sent.

Acknowledgment from the TOC that they knew she was 'good to go' came back instantly with a simple —Ack—.

With the equipment ready, Tess could fully relax, confident the computer would trip an alarm if it detected any of the triggers that had been established. The trap was set. She crawled into an inviting sleeping bag on the floor, closed her eyes, and slowly exhaled.

The door from the hallway crashed open and Tess woke with a start. It was Randy, sporting a grin and a casual style, which seemed at odds with the seriousness of their work. Now resembling an overloaded porter, he gingerly carried a piece of cardboard, used as a makeshift tray, into the room.

"What's all this?" Tess asked sleepily.

"Oh, just something from the market to get your

day started."

Then, noticing how high the sun was in the sky, Tess quickly checked her watch. She had been asleep three hours. While she had been concentrating on the surveillance equipment, Randy was flitting in and out of the office all night. With a dark tan and curly black hair, he easily passed for a local. Fragrant smells of hot tea, warm flatbread, and eggs now filled the air.

"Randy, this is lovely, thank you. I was so focused on setting up the equipment that I never really thought about food. I thought we'd be eating MREs."

With outstretched arms, Randy gently placed the culinary treasure on the desk in front of her and pulled up a couple of chairs. After breakfast, Tess started to double-check the surveillance gear. Echoing Gavin's earlier warning as she worked, Randy offered that in the field they did not always have the luxury of monitoring things remotely. Sometimes they had to physically intervene to ensure mission success. And sometimes, they were pulled into situations against their preference or better judgement. *It's as if he's trying to prepare me for the worst, or something unexpected.*

Things were quiet for the rest of the day and for subsequent days. Tess periodically re-checked the computer to ensure it was still working correctly. It was. The TOC reported that the chatter they had been monitoring had settled back down to normal levels. It was pointless to look at her watch again. It was like the digital display never changed. She and Randy had exhausted all small talk topics and, rather than get too personal, now they also added to the quiet. It was tedious. Eventually, the TOC signaled that higher HQ was contemplating calling off the whole thing. Tess tried to remain professional, to resist the tide of disappointment and frustration. This would not be the first canceled mission she experienced, but still; she could not help but think about all the time lost by everyone who had been preparing for action. The day continued to grind on.

Suddenly, the computer chirped softly, indicating a trigger had been detected. Was it an accident? Tess moved behind the keyboard to investigate. There it was. It was unmistakable, the cell phone of a low-level associate of a Taliban leader. Was it a coincidence the signal was picked up at the market or a sign the *shura* was about to begin?

Two hours later, the computer betrayed the presence of a phone belonging to another Taliban leader. Both signals quickly disappeared after detection and Tess was not able to localize their positions. She wondered if they had orders to dismantle their phones as they approached the meeting location. Later, the parabolic mic picked up Geppetto's voice in the market; it was not a long conversation, just a few words, but it was him! The crowd was too dense and congested for the video to pick out who had been speaking. Randy ran out to get a look at the microphone voice capture area from another angle, and to see if anyone stood out. Tess thought about Randy's earlier comments. *What would he do to ensure mission success if there was something obvious? Would Geppetto be summarily executed or just followed to the location of the shura?* As all this was happening, Tess was informing the TOC. There were lots of indications, but no clear picture. Still, it did not look as if the operation would be canceled just yet.

The computer alarm sounded again when the

system heard someone in the market say, "Commander, we have finally reached our destination."

Then nothing. Everything went quiet. The TOC pressed Tess for a location where the meeting was being held, but she was unable to provide the information the Special Forces Commander needed. A while later, the computer alarm sounded again. Through the window of a small dwelling in the far corner shadows of the market, a low-power infrared laser picked up the word "commander" several times. That had to be the location. Tess updated the TOC that she had a possible location but needed to confirm by tapping into the entire conversation captured by the laser. Impatient, the TOC had enough indicators and launched the assault team. They were convinced the *shura* location had been identified. As Tess continued to listen to the conversation through the laser and computer translator, she realized there were women and children inside the house. She knew the Taliban often used families as shields against attack. If an attack came, they made claims that Coalition Forces mistakenly killed a wedding party or some other family gathering. Blowing the front off the building would be a disaster.

"TOC, this is Wizard, recommend you stand down. Women and children present in *shura* location. We have to find another way."

"Wizard, it's too late. Trigger has already been pulled."

Randy came racing into the office. "What's going on?"

"Women and children are inside—it'll be a disaster," Tess responded quickly, and then added,

"Standard Taliban tactic." She might be new to frontline operations but had experience with dozens of similar events. While speaking, she looked out the window and quickly scanned the area where the dwelling in question was located. Nearby there were several large transport trucks at the edge of the market; they probably had carried the produce that was for sale. *I wonder if Randy or I could get one of those transport trucks in front of the shura location to block the gunner from having a clear shot.* Just as Tess was having that thought, the corner of the market exploded with a large concussion and fireball. It was too late; the attack was underway. People ran in all directions as debris and dust rained down everywhere in front of the targeted residence.

The assault team rushed into the building and past the carnage on the first floor, but as they tried to enter the basement where it appeared the men were meeting, they encountered resistance.

"TOC, this is Wizard, I'm getting reports of people fleeing the *shura* location through tunnels."

Major Ross's team quickly dispatched the fighters guarding the basement entrance and found this part of the building relatively unaffected by the blast. It appeared the men had all escaped through hidden underground passageways to adjacent buildings and once outside, they melded into the crowd. The assault was a bust, but hopefully, the security cordon established around the meeting location would keep the escapees bottled up. The QRF began a search of buildings adjacent to the meeting location to ensure no one was hiding inside. The cordon was a good idea if those attending the *shura* tried to fight their way through it because they would become identifiable. But, if the insurgents stayed hidden amongst the people in the market, the cordon would be ineffective.

Tess also warned the TOC that, because of the deference they were given in not being searched at checkpoints, Taliban fighters often covered themselves in women's burkas to slip through security lines. She suspected the TOC was already familiar with this tactic, but thought it best to offer the suggestion, just in case. Then she had an idea.

"TOC, this is Wizard, over."

"Go, Wizard."

"TOC, we can use the voice print of our High Value Target to identify him. We just need him to speak into a phone or radio to this location and the computer will identify if it's him. We'll need the support team to ensure no one leaves the cordon without being screened."

"Wizard, excellent idea. Set up your end! Out."

Exits to the cordon were established where, in order to leave, people needed to recite over a cell phone their name, where they lived, and why they came to the market. This was just a way to get them to speak, and if it did not trigger an alarm from Tess's computer, they were permitted to depart. Of course, explaining this unanticipated requirement to the tactical operators took some time, so it was a while before the cordon exits actually started to function. Tess got Randy to help her and together they had four cell phones feeding into the computer. Even with Randy's assistance, the screening process was slow. Crowds built up as hundreds of people pressed to leave the market area. It was difficult to maintain order, especially knowing ruthless militants were hiding amongst women and children.

Nerves frayed. A man and woman walked toward one of the exits. When they approached the guards, she cowered behind her husband. When one of the guards tried to speak to her, she pulled a scarf tighter over her face. The man became angry. Why did his wife need to speak into a phone? Why was the head of the household not trusted? Why were they disrespecting him as a husband and a man? He not only scolded the guards but also complained loudly to the others in line. The crowd started to become agitated. People hollered, waved their fists, pushed, and shoved. The line surged.

Bang!

The officer responsible for the checkpoint discharged a pistol in the air to quell the situation before it got out of hand. The man and woman at the head of the line eventually complied with the security team's direction. Even feigning a woman's voice, the computer recognized the burka-clad Geppetto.

As the security forces began to react, a man further back in the crowd behind Geppetto cried out, "*Allah akbar*," drew an AK-47 automatic weapon from under a blanket poncho, and managed to get off a few rounds, killing an American soldier and wounding another before being shot dead. Simultaneously, the sentries the Taliban had posted in the market made a rush for the crowd to create a distraction, AK-47s firing in the air, people screaming, and running. The Taliban tried to corral a large group of market-goers. A suicide bomber prepared to detonate himself to allow Geppetto to slip away in the confusion. The Taliban were masters of taking the initiative by hitting unprotected targets and then using media reporting as a vehicle to terrorize and coerce the population into compliance, but this was not their operation, and they did not have the initiative. This was a Special Forces operation, and the Taliban were reacting. Special Forces snipers on a nearby rooftop dropped the men firing AK-47s in their tracks, as well as the suicide bomber carrying an AK-47 and wearing an explosive-laden backpack. They were dead before they hit the ground. Operatives whisked Geppetto away to the FOB and the cordon was dissolved. The Special Forces disappeared as quickly as they had arrived.

Hours later, Tess and Gavin Ross stood at the edge of the helicopter landing zone inside FOB Khost.

"You were brilliant out there, Tess. The whole mission would have been lost if you hadn't taken the initiative you did, sorting out the surveillance equipment, helping to solve tactical problems when things started to roll. We would not have gotten Geppetto without you."

"Honestly, I just reacted and did what I thought was right. I know we did a good thing by taking out Geppetto, and our approach minimized the risk to our own forces, but it's still hard knowing a lot of women and children got caught in the crossfire."

Realizing the same result could have been achieved by tossing a few concussion grenades at the front door, scaring the fighters to vacate and catching them in the cordon, gnawed at Tess. But that was only with the benefit of hindsight. Who knew they had a back way out? Sometimes they did not have an alternate escape route and would fight to their deaths, in total disregard for the safety of their family members.

"You're right, it is a tough call," Gavin agreed.

Then quickly sounding more official, as if not wanting to forget, he added, "The commander insisted I pass along sincere regrets…for him not being able to personally see you off. He is extremely appreciative of what you did."

"Thank you, Gavin, for everything," Tess said, with a lump in her throat as she hugged Lincoln's big friend. She never liked goodbyes.

"You're welcome. Reach out if you're ever in need, I owe you one," Gavin said.

Just as she had arrived at the FOB, Tess helicoptered alone back to Kabul, unsure of what lay ahead. Although she was comfortable with her contribution to the Khost operation, she knew it was a very tactical and temporary victory. The Taliban would be unbalanced for a time and make mistakes that would hurt them, but eventually, Geppetto's successor would find his stride and there would be a resurgence of security concerns in the region again. Alone in the dark and noisy Black Hawk cabin, Tess could not help but be frustrated by the futility of it all. Rather than this intractable conflict, she wondered if she should focus her life on more vital, long-lasting outcomes.

Chapter 2

Secret Cargo
2019, Southern California

It was a typical sweltering hot summer day in Southern California. The heat waves radiated off the asphalt and concrete so intensely that FBI Supervisory Special Agent Caleb MacLeod did not have to look too hard to see them with the naked eye. The 32-year-old agent had lived here long enough to know the heat, just like that of a brick pizza oven, would continue to provide warmth to the urban areas, wanted or not, long after the blazing sun had set.

Driving along the ridge line of the southwestern San Gabriel Mountains, Caleb could easily make out Pasadena far below. Ten miles beyond, lay the heart of the great city of Los Angeles, but it was fully enveloped in the shimmering heat and haze that rendered it invisible on the horizon. High overhead, stark white fluffy cotton-ball clouds lazily drifted eastward from the ocean through a faint blue sky.

"The team is taking bets on what we're transporting," the driver said to Caleb. "Want in on the action?"

"It might be worth it…if there was ever a way to settle the wagers," Caleb responded without taking his eyes off the road ahead. "I don't think we're ever going to know what's inside the trunk."

"Maybe it's empty and this is all a big misdirection," the driver said, likewise scanning the road in front of them.

"Could be, but that's a bet I wouldn't make."

The two Toyota Highlanders Caleb's security team were using had worked their way up from the oppressive heat of the plain below by the serpentine switch-back two-lane road that led from Pasadena and the Deukmejian Wilderness Park. They were now in high country approaching the Angeles National Forest. Surrounded by nature, a steady breeze, and beautiful vistas, Caleb always found it more pleasant and cooler in the mountains. He quickly surveyed each of the three team members traveling in the vehicle with him. The driver deftly handled the steering wheel while continuing to intently eye the road ahead. Caleb twisted his six foot, one hundred and eighty-five-pound, athletic frame to see the two team members in the back seat.

"You okay, Jonesy?" Caleb asked. "You're being quiet. Late night?" he pressed, both a little concerned and annoyed.

"Naw. Never before a big job. It's this corkscrew road. It's killing me. Should've taken a Gravol this morning."

"Would it be better to sit up front in my place?"

"Thanks. It's fine, boss. I think we're through the worst of it now."

"All right. Let me know if you change your mind," Caleb said, adjusting the controls to blow more cool air toward the back.

As they quickly approached the next sharp twist in

the road, the driver abruptly applied the brakes, cranked the steering wheel hard around a tight turn, and accelerated again. Caleb resisted being pulled toward the center console when the SUV changed direction and then relaxed as the increasing speed pushed him back into his seat. The second vehicle in the convoy briefly caught up at the corner and completely filled the side-view mirror. Now it was slipping away again, its reflection becoming progressively smaller.

These two SUVs, traveling together and co-ordinating their every movement via radio, were identical in virtually every way. Both were armor-protected against IED blasts and small arms fire, and both carried a highly trained security detail. However, there were just enough subtle differences between the two Toyotas that would make a casual observer question if they were really traveling together or if it was just a coincidence. The lead vehicle was brown, while the second one was light blue. One sported a crucifix dangling on a thick chain from the rear-view mirror, and the second had a pair of small fuzzy dice. The lead vehicle carried a peace sign bumper sticker, whereas the rear truck sported a yellow and black 'baby on board' decal in the rear window. They both purposely carried a couple of weeks of old road dust.

"Good call on not taking those oversized, black Suburbans," the driver said, gently tapping a rhythm on the steering wheel while continuing to examine the road ahead. "They'd be junk on these turns."

"I was thinking more like they'd be screaming 'government security vehicles'," Caleb quipped with a half smile.

"Yeah. Best not to look like a target if you don't

want to be one," the driver said, succinctly expressing what they were all thinking.

Silence permeated the SUV once more. Normally security details protected VVIPs, but in this business, there always seemed to be an exception to every rule. Rather than a person, today Agent MacLeod and his team were transporting a very important package from NASA's JPL facility near Pasadena to the Palmdale Regional Airport, where NASA shared a highly secret facility with the United States Air Force's Plant 42. Caleb had no idea what was in the locked metal trunk firmly strapped to the cargo area floor of the SUV behind him. Whatever it was, it was important enough to fall into the FBI's second highest priority task of protecting American interests against foreign espionage and intelligence operations. Caleb was aware that NASA's Jet Propulsion Laboratory was responsible for interplanetary spacecraft and NASA's Deep Space Communication System but had no idea what occurred at the destination in Palmdale where the 'package' was to be delivered. None of that really mattered because, throughout a distinguished career, including military duty in the Middle East, he had gotten used to focusing on the job and not being distracted by things deemed beyond his need to know.

On the journey today, he and the security detail in the lead vehicle were responsible to clear any obstruction and provide a clear route, even if it was an escape route, for the team members carrying the cargo in the rear vehicle. If necessary, Caleb and his men would leave the protection of their armored Highlander to confront any assailants and ensure the safe passage of the second vehicle.

As they sped along, Caleb surveyed the steep, gray topography sparsely covered by large, determined pine and fir trees clinging to any available crag or outcrop. This was rough terrain and traveling cross-country on foot was not an option, so the only concern was with vehicle routes. Unlike the plethora of intersecting roads on the plain below where there was an endless number of potential avenues of approach and escape, up here there were only a handful. This was the primary reason Caleb selected this particular route.

"Nice to have Watch Master with us today," came a comment from the back seat.

Although no one had spotted the FBI Cessna surveillance aircraft, they knew it was with them. Fitted with a high-resolution electro-optical zoom camera that could also see the infrared spectrum and specialized communications equipment, this asset offered additional protection.

As the two-vehicle convoy continued along and rounded a curve, the road gently hugged the high ground to the left. To the right, Caleb noted a scenic look-off with enough parking space for several vehicles, but just two were present. An old sun-bleached station wagon that had seen better days and obviously belonged to a large family of tourists stretching their legs and admiring the view. The other vehicle, a big new white RAM four-door crew cab with a cap over its cargo bed, was ready to depart the rest stop. With its nose slightly out on the road and its turn signal blinking, the white pickup appeared eager for them to pass so it could pull out onto the highway in the same direction they were traveling. Immediately ahead, just beyond the look-off, the highway disappeared into the mountain. A huge yellow sign on the rock face warned of the fixed overhead dimensions of the half-circular highway tunnel cut through the stone in 1941. A 12-foot height at each edge of the road, arching to 15 feet in the center, was all that could be accommodated.

"Watch Master, this is Mobile 1. Approaching our potential radio blackout point. Talk to you on the other side. Over," Caleb's driver spoke into his mic.

"Copy that," the pilot responded in a mechanical, nonchalant tone. "Comms might be down Mobile One."

Cool darkness quickly enveloped the two closely spaced and fast-moving north-bound Highlanders as they passed under tons of rock above. At the tunnel's mid-point, they met a silver sedan heading in the opposite direction, followed at a distance by a large red tractor truck. The tractor truck was towing a flatbed trailer with a black tarp covering its load.

Caleb instinctively gasped as the silver sedan, without warning, swerved across the double yellow line; it instantly filled most of the windshield. Caleb's driver jerked the steering wheel to the right, desperate to avoid a collision. Anticipating a severe impact, Caleb's body automatically tensed, with teeth clenched, and eyes closed. A violent jolt accompanied the sedan as it plowed into the Toyota. Screeching tires, smashing metal and glass, and noisy rapidly expanding airbags all seemed to be a long way off in the distance, even though Caleb knew it was his vehicle being torn apart. With everything swirling, it was as if he were looking at himself in slow motion through someone else's eyes. Then, as the situation settled, it was hard to tell if the ringing noise was coming from inside his pounding head or somewhere inside the now twisted and battered vehicle. Smoke and steam seemed to be everywhere. *It's odd. The sedan looked like it didn't have a driver.*

Conduct security assessment! Caleb instinctively prodded himself to follow the immediate action checklist. Struggling to make sense of what was happening, he quickly scanned the interior of what remained of a badly damaged vehicle. Through a mirror, and obscured vision, the second Toyota in the convoy, the one with the secret cargo, could just be seen. The second SUV looked to be unaffected, but the driver must have been quick thinking and immediately applied the brakes to avoid colliding with Caleb's SUV because there was hardly any space between the two vehicles. There were no signs of impending danger to the cargo they were transporting. Acrid smoke now stung his nostrils as he pushed to maintain focus. *Radio in situation report*, Caleb thought even as his vision began to close in, and everything started to go dark. That was the last thing he remembered.

Chapter 3

Stealing the Key to the Future

Stanislav Tishchenko intently watched the accident scene play out before him through cool, gray eyes. He could see everything from the vantage point of the passenger seat in the red Kenworth 18-wheel flatbed tractor-trailer. The silver sedan crossed the double yellow line in the tunnel and crashed into the unsuspecting lead Toyota Highlander coming in the other direction. The driver of the second Toyota, with rapid, animated expressions, barely avoided rear-ending the now destroyed vehicle in front. Similarly, the white RAM pickup, accelerating to catch the two Toyota Highlanders, just managed to come to a stop and avoid running into the back end of the second Toyota. The undamaged second Toyota carrying the secret cargo was effectively blocked between the wrecked Toyota in front and the RAM behind. Trailing behind the silver sedan that had crossed over into on-coming traffic, the big red rig Stanislav was riding in also came to a screeching halt in the confined tunnel. The rig's driver and other passenger immediately dismounted, leaving Stanislav alone. There were shards of broken glass and bits of twisted metal and plastic strewn everywhere. Steam and the smell of boiling radiator fluid permeated the crash scene.

Sitting alone, Stanislav was transfixed by the situation but was fully prepared to intervene if necessary. Surveying the accident from the Kenworth's cab, he was an inconspicuous-looking relic from another age. At five-eight, with slicked-back white hair, the extra weight he carried was all in a distended stomach.

"Perfect. Just like clockwork," he said aloud to no one in particular, as if watching a football game on TV. "So far, so good."

He could see the individual in the second Highlander frantically speaking into a radio handset. *Probably trying to raise someone in the smashed vehicle ahead of him.* Then the FBI agent appeared to figure out the 'comms' did not function by the way he was fidgeting with the radio controls; he would not know it was because they were being jammed.

Stanislav's men had rehearsed this so many times that he was impatient for the FBI agents in the undamaged Toyota to conduct their rapid tactical assessments and then follow the path that had been set for them. They only had a fraction of a second to think of what to do, but Stanislav had been laying this trap for much longer. He was like a master puppeteer who had carefully scripted the entire scene.

"Come on, come on. You only have one play here," Stanislav said in a low tone, straining through gritted teeth. Now that the first action had been taken, the adrenalin flowed freely. *We are committed now.* "This is the vulnerable period," he said, as if expressing concerns aloud inside the Kenworth's cab might somehow keep misfortune at bay.

But Stanislav could not verbalize any internal

fears, even to himself; those were saved for his innermost thoughts. *If anything goes wrong, if it takes too much time, if we get outmaneuvered by the FBI or local law enforcement responding to this incident, we are in trouble. There is always some 'do-gooder' and a 911 call. We need to move smartly here.*

"Come on. Let's not drag this out too long," he murmured, teeth still clenched.

Stanislav Tishchenko had been in the espionage business a long time, and, despite an internal unease, carried himself with confidence and precision. Nothing was left to chance. He had carefully chosen this specific site along the highway for the interception to take place, choreographed to the smallest detail what would happen, and practiced it repeatedly for the past couple of days. Of course, there was a need to assemble a make-shift team and develop a plan in haste; he hardly had any notice that the FBI would be conducting this operation. Opportunities like this rarely occurred, so he kept telling himself to be bold. There was the potential to be a hero with his masters in Moscow, and he hoped they appreciated the risks that needed to be taken and the potential for something unforeseen to go wrong. Initially, the men were not happy with all the drills he put them through, but now they moved with lightning speed.

Stanislav knew to the second how long it took the specially equipped silver sedan and the lumbering Kenworth to travel the short two hundred feet from the Hidden Springs National Forest Picnic Area south to the highway tunnel. *I'm not sure why they call it a highway when, really, it's just a two-lane road. Americans always make everything sound so grand.* His intuition that the package would be moved through the forest had paid off, and the tunnel was the perfect place for an ambush.

As soon as the Toyota in the on-coming lane was identified through the glass camera lens mounted on the front of the autonomous silver sedan, it had a 'lock on' its intended target. The computer assessed the relative motion and performed the analysis to determine the optimal impact point to immediately render the Toyota non-drivable and severely disorient its unsuspecting occupants. It was easy for Stanislav's computer expert to hack past the security protocols and turn the driverless car into a weapon—she programmed the sedan to surge across the yellow lines at just the right moment, angle, and speed so the Toyota's passengers were not killed from the collision, but rather severely incapacitated through a vehicular-induced concussion. That way, the FBI agents could be more easily manipulated by the exacting, high-speed ruse unfolding around them. More importantly, the possibility of damaging the precious cargo carried by the second Highlander would be greatly reduced if the plan worked.

Stanislav was prepared to accept collateral damage through the injury of unsuspecting bystanders because, in his mind, there were no innocents in the United States. Ultimately, it was acceptable to use brute force tactics as a backup plan if needed, but why kill people or use firefighting rescue equipment to pry and torches to cut into steel if it were not necessary? It was not as if Stanislav had become soft after all these years, it just made much better operational sense to use a more elegant velvet glove approach instead of a sledgehammer if it would work. The longer the authorities took in the ensuing confusion to figure out they had been robbed, the more time there was to escape.

Everything now focused on the undamaged Toyota Highlander isolated in the middle of the highway tunnel. The leader of the security detail inside the vehicle had stopped trying to get his radio to work and now faced a dilemma. Stanislav continued his soliloquy commentary.

"Are you going to sit there, unable to move the SUV forward or backward, unable to use your radio to call for help while your comrades in the vehicle ahead are likely grievously injured, or…are you going to take a chance and break the cardinal rule by opening the door and potentially expose the cargo to danger?"

Stanislav was sure the agent would take a risk. *He has to. There's no choice. He's a man of action and can't simply sit there and do nothing. It would be against his nature.* Surely the surrounding tons of rock would be blamed for the communications challenges, and the idea of simply running back to the mouth of the tunnel to make a radio or cell phone call for help would be too enticing.

To induce the agent in the undamaged Toyota to react as desired, the driver and passenger of the RAM exited their vehicle and ran ahead to the wreckage. One carried a fire extinguisher and started to spray down what remained of the engine compartment of the badly damaged Highlander. A cloud of white fire fighting chemical began to envelop the accident scene. Surely the fear of a fire would encourage some action.

"And there he goes," Stanislav said, gleefully

watching the agent take off his seat belt in a flurry.

Clearly, the agent knew the danger. Pausing a moment to check the side mirror to ensure nobody was behind him, he then did it. He opened the door. Stanislav smiled. *Yes.*

What the agent did not know was that the RAM had been carrying four, not two, people. While the first two drew everyone's attention as they made their way to the wrecked vehicles, the other two simultaneously crept forward out of view and hid between the unharmed Toyota and the RAM. The hidden assailants sprang into action as soon as the door started to open. They rushed the FBI Agent from behind. Just at the awkward point of being half in and half out of the vehicle, the first assailant tased him. As he was losing consciousness, the second assailant tossed two stun grenades inside the unprotected Toyota.

Stanislav glanced back toward the flatbed to see the black tarp had been removed, exposing a brown and a light blue Toyota Highlander. These two SUVs now rolled down onto the road and headed out the north end of the tunnel in the same direction the FBI highlanders had been traveling. These were not the expensive, specially armored vehicles; they were just a couple of regular production trucks, one that was recently spray painted in the Hidden Springs National Forest Picnic Area parking lot. Stanislav had a stakeout team watching JPL for days; they radioed him the colors earlier when the two armored vehicles arrived at the facility and again later to confirm which one was leading the convoy when they left the facility.

Now that they had ceased jamming and had activated signal boosters at either end of the tunnel,

Stanislav could hear the transmissions from the FBI surveillance plane using a personal communication device lifted from the tased agent.

"Mobile One, there you are—got eyes on you now. I thought you'd never come out of that tunnel!" called the pilot to the convoy below. With no response provided, a more formal attempt followed.

"Mobile One, this is Watch Master, over."

After a moment of silence, the Cessna pilot called again.

"Mobile Two, this is Watch Master, over." The transmission was followed up with, "Nothing heard, out."

After numerous attempts to re-establish comms with the two Toyotas below, Stanislav anticipated the pilot would invoke the standard 'loss of comms' protocol. This was better than having him detect a new voice on the radio net coming from the two decoy Highlanders now speeding along the Angeles Forest Highway.

About ten minutes later, Stanislav heard the pilot call out on the radio again to the convoy below. "Not sure if you guys can hear me, but you got through the tunnel just in time. I'm hearing from Highway Patrol that the whole thing is now completely blocked by a bad accident. Just giving you a heads-up that you may encounter responding emergency vehicles along your route."

By then, Stanislav Tishchenko and his crew had jumped into the RAM pickup and executed a tight 'U-turn' to depart the tunnel, heading back toward the look-off. Some of the team rode in the cab, while others rode in the cargo area with the trunk removed from the undamaged Toyota. The traffic was backed up for a quarter mile in the opposite lane leading to the tunnel. They successfully wound their way back down from the mountains and were safely lost amongst the myriad of roads and traffic on the hot, hazy plain below. Relieved, Stanislav laughed as pandemonium erupted over the radio net.

"What do you mean those aren't our trucks you are flying top cover for?!" the FBI air dispatcher blurted out. "How can they not be our trucks?"

"They aren't our trucks. There's no bumper sticker or decal in the window. No wonder they weren't responding. I'm returning to the tunnel," the pilot reported in rapid succession. "Call out the cavalry to intercept these guys, whoever they are."

Stanislav imagined the FBI plane banking sharply and racing back to the tunnel where the last communication with the Highlander convoy occurred. He knew they would not find anything.

"Report," the air dispatcher demanded.

"I can't see anything. Just a long line of stopped traffic leading to the tunnel, and an eighteen-wheel flatbed completely ablaze in the opposite lane heading down the mountain."

Stanislav smiled as the drama was now successfully ending. Using a cell phone, one of the team members described what was transpiring as the two decoy Highlanders approached the hastily erected Highway Patrol blockade near the junction with California State Route 14.

"Light them up," Tishchenko said.

He could hear the explosion through an earpiece when the person, watching from a point partway up a nearby mountain, flipped the detonator switch. The two vehicles and the unsuspecting drivers, locals just trying to make a few bucks, were incinerated. That was the way Stanislav wanted it. No loose ends.

Chapter 4

Passing the Torch
2019, NASA's Marshall Space Flight Center, Redstone Arsenal, Huntsville, Alabama

Tess was always excited when she started a new job–especially one that promised intrigue and was so strategically important for the country. In accepting this new position with NASA, she was looking for a positive change; however, this new responsibility promised to be even more fascinating than initially anticipated.

Her new position required the highest security clearance, Top Secret–Sensitive Compartmented Information, commonly known as Special Access, which she possessed. Although the NASA mission had been running for many years, they were modernizing it by adding a dedicated signal and computer protection focus in response to potential hackers who now had much more capable tools, and posed a significantly higher risk, than when the mission was launched. They said she was the top pick to ensure communication contact with the clandestine spacecraft was always maintained, especially during a modern cyber attack. NASA even had NSA and DoD endorsements to hire her. *How could I say no?* Still, it was not immediately clear this was the right move. It was Doug Regent who convinced Tess it was the smart thing to do.

"I'll confess," he said, almost sounding father-like. "After the Cold War ended in the early 1990s, there were many who thought continuing this covert post-Apollo mission was no longer required, and as a result, there were some pretty lean years. However, concerns about strategic existential threats to the country not only resurfaced, but they became more numerous and complex than ever. In addition to Russian and Chinese nuclear, bacteriological, and chemical warfare threats, now we were faced with vulnerabilities from global natural disasters like pandemics and emerging concerns about where such things as artificial intelligence and machine learning would lead. This convinced everyone, from the White House down, that this mission was more essential than ever."

That cinched it for Tess.

"No, I was not even looking," she confided to Zoe Kirkwell, her one close friend at the NSA.

"Are you sure you're not being a bit rash? I mean, you just got back from Afghanistan. It takes a while to get settled back in."

"I know. It might be easier if we had the same support coming back that others, like the military, have, but that's not it. I feel I need to be making a difference, contributing to something more critical than what I've been doing, something lasting," Tess insisted. Then added, "And NASA's unsolicited overture was too interesting to ignore. It's what got me to look into this in the first place."

"It sounds like your mind's made up."

"I'm surprising myself, even as I say it, but I've decided to do this."

"I'm going to miss you," Zoe responded. "Promise me you'll stay in touch."

"I promise."

The very next week, Tess found herself in the small, hot, northeastern Alabama city of Huntsville, which is neatly nestled in the Tennessee River Valley. She immediately began to be 'read in' as they say in the trade, with the view of making her an expert as quickly as possible on a mission that was still hard to imagine was real. Given time, it would seem more routine, so for now, she just marveled at the refreshing newness of it all.

Tess's early training sessions confirmed that Doug Regent was a gentleman who took leadership and mentoring responsibilities very seriously. His steel-gray wool suit with sharply pressed creases accentuated a tall, wiry stature. Today he provided some context about the program and how it started back in the 1960s.

"I always thought there was something ironic, even irreverent, about conducting our work at a place called Jackass Flats. I mean, here we were, performing ultra secret tests for a clandestine NASA mission; you would think the test site would have had a more suitable name, one that reflected the historical significance of the work. Perhaps it was part of the cover story, or maybe it would have raised too many questions to re-name a patch of ground off US Route 95 in the middle of nowhere. Anyway, naming geography was 'not my part ship' as we used to say in the Navy. As the Space Vehicle System Engineering Manager, I had many more pressing and important things to think about. We were on an extremely tight schedule and the White House continuously monitored our progress."

Doug explained that Jackass Flats was hidden within the government's sprawling, top secret Area 25 test location, which formed part of the Nevada National Security Site.

Tess pegged Doug to be in his late seventies, but with enthusiasm and strong calloused hands, revealing a robust zest for life often absent in others that age. There was an air of civility and self-reliance about him. He looked Tess straight in the eye when speaking and used plain language that was impossible to misconstrue. Doug was a problem solver, but not the bureaucratic kind who could just figure out what needed to be done and then would require someone else to do the real work. A man of action—if something was required, he just got on with it. When the professor responsible for teaching orbital mechanics had to cancel her lecture at the last minute, Doug just rummaged through the computer, found the course material, and stepped in. He even helped Tess through the optional test material to ensure a solid understanding of this important subject.

Since their first meeting, Tess thought Doug might be an aerospace engineer, but now the Jackass Flats connection made more sense knowing there was a Navy connection. In preparation for this new job, she had done some homework and discovered NASA and the Atomic Energy Commission had secretly collaborated there as far back as the 1960s. Now it looked more like Doug might be one of Admiral Hyman Rickover's hand-picked nuclear engineers. She learned Rickover was considered the father of the nuclear navy because of a dogged focus to develop reactors small enough to drive warships.

It was impressive that after all these years, Doug

clearly still had a passion for work, and seemed especially excited about finally starting to pass the torch of knowledge and responsibility for this mission to a new generation. After everything that had been done for the country, he had earned the right to retire long ago, but Tess understood why he had stayed on.

Perhaps that'll be me in the future; I'm not sure. It's just an honor to be considered for this important position.

Given the gravity of his responsibilities, Tess was convinced Doug felt he was carrying a huge burden and it would be a well-deserved relief to finally entrust others with some of those duties. *I hope I am up to the task...and that I can maintain an unblemished record like Doug.*

Following the initial weeks, which largely focused on the foundational elements of the program, Doug then examined Tess's intended role with more granularity.

"As we've previously covered, you'll be responsible for all communication contact with the spacecraft. The part we haven't yet discussed is that you'll be partnered with Mike Bandy. Mike's a smart fellow; he'll be responsible for the craft itself and the operation of its systems. Although the division of responsibility is clear, we expect you two to work as a team and support each other. Mike has worked for me for the past ten years. You'll meet him tomorrow and you'll see that he's very knowledgeable."

Tess was not surprised by Doug's revelation. She had fully anticipated working as part of a closely-knit group.

"If I've learned anything over the years, it's that you need to work together to succeed. I'm definitely a team player," she reassured Doug. Then followed with, "And you seem to be answering my questions, even before I get a chance to ask them!"

"Glad to hear it. The work is complex enough, we need to make it easy when we can," Doug quipped with a hint of a grin.

The weeks that followed were replete with expert guest lecturers who immersed Tess in the engineering details of every piece of communication hardware and software used in the program. To do her job, she needed an intimate understanding of the systems, and how they interfaced, to prevent viruses from worming their way into the operation. As this final phase of indoctrination was drawing to a close, Tess noted a more familiar rapport starting to develop with colleagues and hoped this was a good sign. Still, Doug managed to surprise her. Midway through the second last week of the training syllabus, she noticed him uncharacteristically, pensively staring at the far reaches of the small conference room they had been using in the Marshall Space Flight Center. Not wanting to break his concentration, she waited. Finally, he spoke.

"Tess, I want you to know that NASA was extremely lucky to have found you. As we look to the future, you will be an excellent addition to our team."

"Thank you, Doug…it's very flattering…but I am sure there were lots of people available with the necessary skills."

"Well, I am not so sure," Doug responded. "You were very carefully screened. Your work for the National Security Agency in Afghanistan came to our attention through highly placed DoD connections."

He continued to scroll through the laptop,

atypically looking more at the screen than at her.

"I've read these reports before, but each time I look at them, I can't help but be impressed. They say you made your mark monitoring Taliban, Haqqani, and other terrorist and criminal organizations fighting us and our allies. From what I read before," he said, briefly glancing at her, "I got the impression you found the signals of these organizations relatively easy to intercept and exploit in order to guide Coalition attack missions or help to thwart impending danger to US or allied troops."

When Tess sensed where the conversation was going, a twinge of angst washed over her. She knew Doug had the necessary security clearance to review all her records on file, but without a 'need to know,' discussing any classified mission details was prohibited. That was how the security system worked. You had to have both the clearance and a need to know before you were permitted access to certain knowledge.

Surely, he knows this.

Regardless, she hoped the conversation would not reach a point where it became evident that she was being evasive with her new boss.

Perhaps he's testing me…to see if I can be trusted to protect the classified information I've been learning about this program.

Bending slightly toward the screen and squinting, Doug continued, "The notes go on to indicate that you especially excelled in exploiting the more sophisticated, encrypted communications of the Pakistani ISI and even the Russian Embassy's communications with Moscow."

To avoid divulging any classified information, Tess

resolved to keep any answers short and superficial.

"Well, during the war, it seemed even those who might be helping you had mixed loyalties and agendas, so it was always wise to keep close tabs on everyone."

"I also note you and your small team of analysts were often a critical element of any important mission, and you became very proficient in advising the four-star Marine commander and key staff on how best to prepare for missions from a signals and computer intelligence point of view."

"Yes, it was convenient that we were co-located in the headquarters in Kabul, so we participated in all the critical operations. There were many high-value enemy leadership take-downs, but for me, the most rewarding missions were those involving hostage rescues," Tess said, remembering the welling of emotion people often displayed when they realized they were free.

Doug deftly continued working the laptop mouse while Tess wondered what information was being accessed now. As she waited, a little anxiously, it was impossible not to observe that, unlike his decisive nature, Doug's thick unruly hair seemed it could not make up its mind about the color it wanted to be, ranging from deep dark hues of gray to bright silver. And although the thick glasses with metal frames were perhaps a decade out of style, somehow, they suited him.

"Very impressive," Doug concluded with a final click of the mouse. "From everything I read, you performed expertly during your time in Afghanistan. No matter how hectic or complex the mission, they say you always had a calm, laser-focused approach to your duties. They indicate you are exceptionally bright, and you always came extremely well prepared."

Tess could feel her cheeks redden.

Doug continued. "This brilliant, meticulous, hard-working approach to ensure you were always ready in Afghanistan is what NASA needs from you in your new position. Even more than in Southwest Asia, we can leave nothing to chance. Our mission is too important. As your training is coming to a close, I need you to always remember that."

"I understand," Tess said, finally letting go of the inner tension now that Doug had gotten to the point. Thankfully, there was no awkwardness about protecting classified information.

Tess also realized the discomfort with Doug's conversation transcended security issues. Compared to most, she was an intensely private person and did not like to talk about herself. It was just the way she was raised. Perhaps the feelings about privacy were reinforced by previous work with the NSA, monitoring people from afar, secretly eavesdropping on them with remote sensing equipment, aircraft, and drones. Or perhaps it was because men always commented on how attractive she was and showed unwanted attention. Maybe it was a combination of the two. Tess had only ever opened up to Lincoln, and he was taken away. Her reaction was to bury the pain by throwing herself into work. She actively tried to be personable and supportive with teammates and colleagues, but always kept them at a professional distance.

At the next lunch break, Tess picked up on a previous conversation with Doug.

"How are your horses doing? I mean, it's been long days, so you probably haven't been able to ride them much these past few months," she ventured.

"True, not as much as I'd like, but Jill's been able to pick up the slack. My wife is an incredible rider, so she's been keeping them well exercised."

"It must be great to have a country place close by where you can escape the city."

"Well, we've been going there a long time; it's truly a second home." Doug poured Tess and himself a coffee. The aroma from the hot beverage quickly enveloped the break area. "Whenever I'm not at work here at Redstone, Jill and I try to get away. There's something gentle and uncomplicated about horses, it's a great way to unwind."

Doug took a careful sip of hot coffee.

"Tess, I remember you telling me your dad was a motorcycle police officer, and he introduced you to riding motorbikes."

"Yes, much to my mother's angst."

"Well, if you're comfortable with that kind of riding, you'll do fine on a horse. Jill and I'll have you out to the farm sometime when all this is done."

"I'd like that. I'm a city girl, but I'm always game for something new."

"We were lucky to find our country place," Doug said, peering down at a now half-empty coffee cup. "Land is not as available, or as inexpensive, as it once was."

Doug went on to explain that his farm bordered on several large hills, forming part of the Appalachian Mountain region of the state.

From briefings earlier in her training, Tess knew this was a very isolated part of Alabama in the 1940s and '50s. That was one of the main reasons why the government established America's rocket program here at the Redstone Arsenal after World War II. Of course, things evolved from those early days. The massively powerful Saturn family of heavy lift rockets for the Apollo Program was developed here. Then other classified programs followed, like the one she recently joined. The Space Shuttle was also developed at the Arsenal, and, today, the establishment supported the International Space Station.

Just then, an authoritative knock reverberated through the small conference room and after a moment, the door quickly opened.

"Mr. Regent, the administrator needs to speak to you on the phone right away," an officious-looking woman stated.

"Thank you. Excuse me, please," Doug said and immediately left the room.

Minutes later, he returned crestfallen and ashen-faced.

"There's been an attack in California. We have to go to work."

Chapter 5

Assessing the Damage
2019, Mary W. Jackson Building, NASA Headquarters, Washington, DC

Tess had been with NASA for almost three months and had fully anticipated meeting the administrator as part of her duties, but she did not expect it to be so soon or under these circumstances.

To keep a low profile for security reasons, she and Doug had traveled from Huntsville to NASA's Headquarters in Washington via separate routes. She drove to Birmingham and flew from there while he flew directly from Huntsville. They had arrived independently at one of the few conference rooms cleared for classified briefings and discussions.

"They indicated the administrator would be with us in a few minutes," Doug said.

"That's okay. I'm sure he's fighting lots of fires right now," Tess replied. "He's smart, though…to ask for a personal update on the California situation. There is only so much you can say in a classified message."

"There's that. But he also has enough experience to know that initial reports provided up the chain can often be misleading, or not entirely accurate, simply because there are usually more questions than answers in the early stages of a crisis," Doug, always the mentor, said.

"Now that a couple of days have passed since the incident, he hopes more detailed information will be available, especially since an update to the president is required."

Tess was concerned the administrator's expectations might still be too high. Although they had been working virtually around the clock since the event, it was still very early in the process, and many unanswered questions remained.

As they waited, Tess reflected upon the abundance of detailed initial briefings Doug had provided during her early weeks at NASA. Even for someone with an extensive NSA background, she had thought the emphasis placed on security was a little over the top. Now, of course, after all that had happened, it was clear this was not the case. As such, she doubled her resolve to follow all of Doug's counsel to the letter–even if it might seem a bit excessive. From a security perspective, the briefings had been clear. Members of the team were never to be seen together in public. This way, it would be much more difficult for anyone trying to get information on the program to determine who was involved if the team never connected in the community, not even through a normal phone call. They were to socialize at the Arsenal and if they had to speak after hours, they were to use a secure mobile phone, which scrambled the phone number being used as well as the conversation. In that regard, her and Doug's individual trips to Washington fully satisfied a protocol established years before.

"Because of our extreme focus on security, I wonder how those responsible for the California incident even knew about the armored convoy and its cargo," Tess wondered aloud.

Before contemplating this question further, or Doug could comment, the door to the conference room burst open. A mountain of a man, devoid of any entourage, stood before them. It was Administrator Dwight Jacobs. Tess recognized him from photos, which somehow did not convey his big-boned, oversized six-foot-five frame, massive hands, and large head topped with graying, wavy hair. He had a reputation for being a good administrator, although today he seemed to be carrying the weight of the world on his shoulders and appeared more than a little agitated.

"Administrator," Doug said sharply, as if on the parade ground. Still the naval officer, Doug quickly stood as a mark of deference and respect when Mr. Jacobs entered the room. Tess took Doug's cues and followed suit.

"Doug, I am always happy to see you, but I must confess that I wish it were under different circumstances. You are the last person I have to tell what kind of a disaster we could be potentially facing here."

Jacobs' careful enunciation of every word communicated a preoccupation with precision. Before Doug could respond, Jacobs shifted his gaze and smiled. "You must be Tess," he said. "Welcome to the team. I have heard lots of good things about you."

"Thank you, Administrator Jacobs, it's a privilege to be here," Tess replied, wondering if he might actually think she was at fault for what had happened.

"Doug, I read the Significant Incident Reports you have been sending, and we've spoken by secure videoconference a few times, but take it from the beginning," Jacobs asked. "Recap what happened, what threat this poses to the most complex, secret, and important spacecraft this country has ever launched, and finally, what we are doing about it."

Tess suspected Jacobs was going to use this interaction as a rehearsal for his presentation to the White House.

The barb about the importance of the program was a bit much. Everyone is frustrated and under a lot of pressure.

After a brief pause, Doug cleared his throat and responded slowly and deliberately to the necessary, but uncomfortable questions.

"You are correct, sir, this is the most serious and direct security threat to Helios since it left the launch pad in 1973, and in the worst-case scenario, it has the potential to eliminate the strategic advantage we have all worked so hard to maintain since then. We are doing everything in our power to prevent that from happening."

Tess was sure Doug chose his words specifically to convey to the administrator, and through him to the president, that the gravity of the current situation was fully appreciated.

Doug continued. "The stolen component is a Jam-Resistant Encryption Cube, or JREC," Doug pronouncing the acronym as "Jay-Wreck" and then continued the description for the administrator. "This is more Tess's area of specialty than mine, but in essence, JREC is an encryption device that also parses any message we send to the Helios spacecraft by randomly varying the frequencies and transmission pattern. We can get into the technical details if you like, sir, but really, it was one of the early applications of secure, frequency-hopping communications. It was cutting-edge technology at the time. There were only four JRECs produced. We use one in Huntsville to create the messages which are then passed to JPL for transmission through the Deep Space Network. A primary and a backup JREC were installed in the Helios space vehicle so it could decrypt the coded transmissions, respond to commands, and reply as necessary. The final JREC, the one stolen, was a spare that is normally held inside a safe at JPL. It is an off-site emergency backup in case we ever needed to generate a message and Huntsville was out of action for some reason. We in Huntsville are the only ones with the combination to the safe."

"So, what was it doing unprotected out in the middle of the Angeles National Forest?"

"The Cube was being transported from JPL to our secure facility co-located with the Air Force's Plant 42 in Palmdale by a highly trained security detail from the FBI's National Security Branch–there is no one better qualified for the task. From Palmdale we were going to fly it to the NSA at Fort Meade where it was going to be examined to determine the best way to enhance the security of the device by bringing it up to more modern standards. Of course, the changes that could be made are limited to what we could do remotely to upgrade the equipment already fitted in the spacecraft, but we believe this is an important area to be examined."

"Sir, it was my idea to enlist the services of Fort Meade. This is what I was hired for, to modernize and enhance communications security," Tess added. "This is why the Cube was being moved." Tess wanted to be clear about her role in setting this whole thing in motion.

Doug was quick to note that Tess sought full approval before anything was actually done.

"With only four made, this equipment is unique to your program?"

"Yes, sir," Doug replied. "And given the nature of the incident, we need to assume this was a state sponsored attack by one of our rivals, likely Russia or possibly China, with the intent of eliminating the strategic advantage we have held since the 1970s. No one else has the intelligence network and resources required to plan and execute an operation this sophisticated. This is pure conjecture on my part, but this attack has all the signature markings of the Russian SRV, their Spetsnaz special forces, or Chinese equivalents."

"If you had to guess, who do you think it was?"

"Sir, I'd have to say the Russians. We know KGB Chairman Yury Andropov personally identified the Helios Program as a Soviet intelligence priority even before the core spacecraft was carried into orbit by a Saturn rocket in 1973. Then, after many years, the probing eventually stopped, and things went quiet, or went undetected. The only recent indication we had of any kind of potential surveillance on our program by foreign agents was when I was followed last year in Copenhagen. We redoubled our security protocols as a result." Doug paused to think. "It has to be someone who has been watching the program for a long time and someone who has the capability to pull this off. My money is on the SRV."

"That kind of makes sense. They are the KGB's

successors," Jacobs added.

"Sir, in a perverse sense, it was fortuitous this incident occurred. Now we know there is a gaping hole in our security and hopefully, we can perform damage control fast enough to mitigate any real harm to the program."

"Okay, tell me. How easy would it be for someone to exploit this device, now that they have it, whoever they are?"

"The good thing is this device is highly tamper-proof because of the way it was constructed. It has lead shielding built into it so it cannot be X-rayed, and the circuit boards are so integrated and fused together; they would be physically destroyed if anyone tried to disassemble it."

"So, what good would it be to anyone?"

Doug continued. "Well, as you know, communications with virtually all our spacecraft are only protected by limiting and compartmentalizing knowledge of the vehicle's trajectory and location…"

"So, someone wishing to interfere would not know where to point their transmitter," the administrator interjected.

"Right, and you are aware that we limit knowledge of the precise frequency or frequencies being used, and the specific message protocol used to control the spacecraft. For many of the pure science missions, this is sufficient, but obviously not in our case. In addition to normal NASA precautions, we use the JREC in all communications with Helios. Although it is unlikely anyone could disassemble a JREC to see how it works, if they have been capturing and saving our messages to and from the spacecraft over the years, they could now decrypt them and likely figure out the communication protocol." Then, looking at Administrator Jacobs directly in the eyes, Doug added, "If they know its location and the protocols, it is possible they could hijack it."

Tess watched Jacobs absorb what Doug had said with a stone face. Snapping out of his funk, the administrator asked, "What is your intended course of action?"

"We plan to follow a two-pronged approach," Doug responded calmly. Tess could see he was clearly telegraphing that all was not lost. "First, we are working on altering the communication protocol the spacecraft will accept. In the long history of Helios, this has only ever been done twice because it involves a lot of programming. Also, it is like changing the combination of a lock, it is complicated and if you mess it up, you will never have access again. So, we need to be extremely careful and methodical, but the team has already started to work on this. Secondly, we need to insert Tess into the FBI investigation as a technical advisor and Liaison Officer to help them quickly figure out who is behind this and what they are up to. Because of her background, she may see things the FBI does not notice. We'll need your help getting her embedded into the investigation."

Doug had briefly mentioned the possibility of going to California while they were waiting alone in the conference room for Administrator Jacobs, but it still surprised Tess to hear the words confidently articulated as part of a plan.

"Okay, is there anything else?" Jacobs asked, signaling the meeting was coming to a close.

Given what Doug had just said, Tess had one question that was posed in a way that either Doug or Jacobs could answer. "The FBI will want to know about our mission. How much do I tell them about Helios?"

Doug, glancing at Administrator Jacobs, thought a moment, and then answered. "Tess, we'll need to leave this to your discretion, which is the main reason for asking you to go to California. As a rule, the less you tell them, the better, but obviously, you'll need to tell them enough to keep things moving forward as smartly as possible. You can assess how much information will be helpful to them. We want to provide them with enough to facilitate capturing the perpetrators as quickly as possible, but at the same time, preserve as much secrecy as possible about our mission. It will need to be a judgement call on your part."

Administrator Jacobs thanked Doug and Tess while getting up to leave. They also rose to their feet, recognizing the meeting was now over.

"Neutralizing this threat to Helios is a national security priority. Let me know immediately if anything else develops, or if you need any additional resources to sort this out," Jacobs said before leaving as quickly as he had entered.

Doug then closed the conference room door and returned to his seat with a brooding face.

"How are your aliases coming along?" he asked.

"Fine. The one I like most is Theresa Wentzel, Tess for short. She is a computer and communications expert NASA has made available to the International Space Station support team, should they ever need assistance. To help with her back story, I have already had a few meetings with ISS colleagues at the Payload

Operations Center."

"Good," Doug responded automatically, as if thinking about something else.

Tess knew it was a good cover because, conveniently, the ISS team was located close to her work. It was natural to go to the Redstone Arsenal, but once on post, she had the option of going to the ISS support office or the highly classified Helios Program compound where she spent most of her time.

Then Doug said emphatically, "You need to use your alias the whole time you are in California."

"Even with the FBI?"

"Yes, and with everyone else, the hotel, car rental, restaurants, everything. When you are in California, you are Theresa Wentzel. There has been a security breach somewhere. For all we know, even the FBI could be infiltrated. Our aliases are robust, birth certificates, credit cards, the whole works. Use them with confidence."

After finishing their impromptu meeting, Doug and Tess went their separate ways. Doug headed back to Huntsville via a circuitous route. Like Doug, Tess departed NASA Headquarters by cab. Her ultimate destination was the airport to take a flight to Los Angeles, but given the recent attack, and mindful of the resolution about being ultra vigilant regarding security protocols, she wanted to ensure no one was following her. This was probably being overly cautious, but she still asked the cabbie to drop her in downtown Washington. She walked a few blocks to the high-end City Center DC Mall on H Street NW. It was convenient because she was traveling very light and needed to pick up a few articles for the unexpected trip west. All purchases were made in cash. Walking through the half-empty shopping center, Tess surmised it would be absolutely bustling later in the day. The subtle, yet intoxicating fragrances from the Dior boutique gently drifted out into the main thoroughfare.

Walking along inside the mall, Tess wondered how to interpret Doug's insistence that she be the Liaison Officer to the FBI. *I understand communication equipment was stolen, but still, as the new communications lead for the mission, shouldn't I be directing the effort to develop the new spacecraft communication protocols? Surely Mike Bandy would be a better choice than sending the new person to California. Perhaps it's Doug's way of protecting the mission. I can't inadvertently divulge as much as the others because I don't know as much as they do.* In the end, she had to trust Doug's judgement and resolved to do the best job possible.

After making her purchases and doubling back a few times to ensure no one was tracing her steps, she exited the mall and made her way a few blocks to Franklin Park. In the park, she took time to admire the precisely trimmed greenery lining the curved footpaths while again ensuring there was no one trailing her. Upon leaving, she took the park exit that led directly to the McPherson Square Metro Station, rode the train a few stops, and then caught a cab to Reagan National. In the taxi's backseat, she admired from afar the many sites this beautiful showcase capital had to offer. Tess loved Washington and looked forward to a more leisurely return.

It would be nice to linger in the Smithsonian or slowly wander down Pennsylvania Avenue.

Arriving at Reagan National, these thoughts were pushed out of her mind and replaced with a focus on getting a ticket, proceeding through security, and finding the gate as soon as possible. Then she could relax. Eventually easing into her assigned aisle seat of the Boeing 757 about to depart the terminal, she was confident about being alone on the journey to California but was not sure what awaited her there.

Chapter 6

The Crime Scene
2019, Southern California

Struggling to open his eyes, Caleb MacLeod was conscious someone else was in the room. *This can't be heaven because I feel so awful, but why is there a beautiful angel near my bed?* She had raven dark hair braided into a singular long thick ponytail that ran three-quarters of the way down her back. She wore slim blue jeans, black ankle boots with a big thick silver buckle on the side, and a form-fitting short-sleeved feminine white blouse. There were loose papers and a notebook on the small table in front of her; it looked as though she had been there a while. On another table was a helmet with a dark visor, a black leather jacket, and matching riding chaps. Somehow her presence even made the air in the stale hospital room smell nicer.

Caleb wanted to make a wisecrack about waking up in paradise, but never seemed to have any luck with one-line icebreakers. All he could muster was a scratchy voiced, "Hello, can I help you?"

"Oh, hello there. How are you feeling?"

Although just a few words, her intonation sounded genuine and caring.

"I've been worse, but it seems the more I lie in bed, the more tired I get. I've been drifting in and out of sleep all day. Maybe it's the drugs."

Caleb realized he should stop talking. It sounded like he was complaining, but it was not the case. He was banged up pretty good with cuts, bruises, and abrasions, not to mention the cast on his left wrist. *I came away basically unscathed. Unlike the last time in hospital.* The deep scars from those injuries, the kind where you can see the accompanying individual suture marks, still marked large tracts of his body. *Reminders of former military service.*

"I'm sorry, I didn't realize…" Caleb said, adjusting the blanket to better cover himself. "I don't get many visitors and after a while, you lose all bashfulness with the medical staff."

"No, I'm sorry. I didn't mean to intrude. I'm Tess, here from NASA to help with the investigation.

"They told me someone was coming, but I understood it was a guy, Doug something or other."

"Unfortunately, Doug can't make it, so you're stuck with me," Tess said, showing Caleb her official NASA identification.

"All right, Miss…Theresa Wentzel," Caleb said, taking a close look at the identification, "Pleased to meet you, I'm Caleb…Supervisory Special Agent Caleb MacLeod, FBI, at your service."

Caleb, now sitting up in bed and more alert, never thought rocket scientists could be so strikingly attractive. If she had also claimed to be a model, he would have believed it.

"I see you have your transportation sorted out…how about a place to stay?"

"Realistically. I thought it might be more than a few weeks, so I rented a one-room apartment not far from the Federal Building. It usually caters to businesspeople, so it'll be easy to extend my stay if needed. I thought it made the most sense, being so close to your office."

"Yes, it makes perfect sense."

"How about the case, what do we do now?" Tess asked, eager to get started.

Caleb knew she probably would not tell him, but asked anyway, "What were we transporting and why were we ambushed?"

"It was highly classified 'communication equipment' that is of the utmost importance to the United States. We think the equipment may have been stolen in order to hijack or co-opt one of our strategic satellites. So, time is critical."

"Let me guess, that's all you can tell me!"

"I'm sorry. Really, I am."

Embarrassed about letting the country down in a high-profile mission, Caleb's face burned. It was uncharacteristic; he was used to keeping emotions in check. Perhaps it was the realization of how helpless they were during the attack, or the frustration of not being able to strike back at the perpetrators, or maybe it was just the offence of being purposely kept in the dark by people who claimed to be on the same side. Caleb felt exposed and used.

"And you didn't think to tell me this before? You tied one of my hands behind my back by not giving me the full picture, not to mention the injuries inflicted on my team! My guys are pretty smashed up and some of them were at the total mercy of those...thugs. They could have even been executed."

At first, Tess did not say a thing; it was as if she

was thinking. Then, in a calm and measured voice, she responded. "Look, I'm not here to defend NASA, or explain why the equipment needed to be transported. I'm just here to help with the investigation. But, since you brought it up, you knew that you were transporting highly classified equipment. The specific type of equipment doesn't matter. You picked the route and the timings. Are you saying you would've changed your approach? Are you saying you didn't take all necessary precautions?" Silence filled the room. Then, seeming to extend an olive branch, Tess's voice softened. "Look, this is not productive. I'm here to help. We need to find the attackers quickly before they do even more serious damage!"

As quickly as his anger had built up, Caleb realized he was on the wrong side of the argument. She was no theoretical scientist lost in the real world; she was quick on her feet and would not be pushed over. She seemed invested in this issue, and obviously knew about operations too. He needed her assistance as much as she probably needed his. Now, he felt self-conscious about the outburst.

"You're right. In addition to everything else, clearly my ego is bashed up pretty good as well. Truce?"

And with that, he courteously shook Tess's hand very tenderly, not for her sake, but for his. He then gingerly swung his legs over the side of the bed and pulled the IV out of his arm.

"They were going to discharge me tomorrow anyway. Let's get to work," Caleb said, applying pressure with a finger where the needle had been. He quickly ducked into the bathroom to find a bandage and change out of the hospital gown into his clothes.

When Caleb unceremoniously discharged himself from the hospital, Head Nurse McBride pursued him right to the front door trying to get him to sign the official release paperwork. Caleb was polite but just kept walking as she determinedly marched after him, forms waving in one hand and a pen in the other.

"It'll just take a moment, Agent MacLeod," she said, trying to reason with him.

It was not that Caleb was displeased with the care. In fact, it was excellent, and the staff was tremendously professional. It was just that he had been there too long already, and it was time to get moving on the case. *Besides, the forms likely require me to substantiate why I'm leaving early or acknowledge I'm taking full responsibility for this decision.* He really was not in the mood for bureaucracy. This was uncharacteristic, he usually had the patience of a saint, but this case had gotten to him. Perhaps it was the fact that the attack was perpetrated on him and his team. This was not some crime where it was possible to be detached and clinically investigated in an arms-length manner; this was an investigation that directly touched close to home. He was angry with the attackers, knew it was affecting his behavior, and had to get it in check.

"Thank you, nurse, thank you very much," Caleb called back over a shoulder to the matronly lady dressed all in white who was now literally chasing him down the corridor.

Caleb's escape plan was to catch a cab and meet Tess at the Angeles National Forest Tunnel, but at the hospital entrance, he almost knocked over Daniel LeBlanc, head of the FBI L.A. Office forensic team, who was on the way to provide him another bedside update. As the designated lead for the investigation, Caleb had been guiding activity from his hospital room, which was another point of contention with Nurse McBride. He graciously accepted Daniel's offer of a lift.

Caleb was happy to finally be in fresh air, even if it meant returning to the site of the attack. Normally, the FBI would have given him more time to recover and assigned the investigation to someone else, but Caleb insisted. This was personal; it was his responsibility. His supervisors only relented when he agreed to report findings and intended lines of inquiry to a more senior agent on a weekly basis. They also made it clear there would be an independent examination of circumstances that led to the situation in the Angeles Forest, to confirm he and his team had conducted their work diligently. Caleb knew they were just preparing for the inevitable inter-agency finger-pointing likely to ensue. *With this added scrutiny, they're also putting me on notice. The investigation needs to be above reproach in all respects. As if that wouldn't be the case anyway.*

Daniel and Tess gathered with him at the look-off along the Angeles Forest Highway. While Caleb had been sidelined in the hospital with other members of the Close Protection Team, the forensic unit had poured over every inch of the various sites related to the attack, specifically the highway tunnel, the look-off just before the tunnel, the picnic area just after the tunnel, and the observation point up in the high ground where the two decoy trucks were monitored from a distance and ultimately dispatched to their destruction. Lastly, there was the abandoned lot in L.A.'s Wholesale District where the LAPD had discovered the burned-out carcasses of a RAM pickup and a Dodge Charger, which was also likely used in the get-a-way.

The forensic team had taken to referring to the tunnel as "crime scene central." Regrettably, these sites had yet to give up any obvious leads and, as if to highlight this point, Daniel painstakingly walked Caleb and Tess through what the team had pieced together.

Standing in the middle of the now taped-off look-off parking lot, Daniel explained, "It is evident that this was a very carefully planned and executed operation," he said to both Caleb and Tess. "We believe there was a spotter positioned in this parking lot, perhaps the fellows in the white RAM pickup, and another on the high ground above the tunnel who cued and possibly assisted with the timing of the driverless vehicle intended to immobilize your Highlander," Daniel said. Then, glancing toward the tunnel, before continuing. "The flatbed truck immediately followed the driverless car and launched the decoy vehicles out of the tunnel once the convoy was stopped. All these vehicles were prepared and staged out of the picnic area just on the other side of the tunnel. From the air, it would have looked like the convoy entered the tunnel and exited a minute or so later. Once the lead Highlander was halted, the RAM pickup blocked the second armored Highlander from reversing and carried the attackers who struck when the door of the vehicle was opened."

Daniel then led them up above the tunnel opening where there was more crime scene tape cordoning off the area. They could see where the ground had been disturbed as if someone were trying to make themselves comfortable while sitting or lying down. There were burn marks on the ground where cigarettes had been crushed out, but nothing else. No butts, no garbage, nothing. Someone had been mindful enough not to leave anything behind.

"From up here you have a good view of where the flatbed truck was set ablaze at the mouth of the tunnel. During the get-a-way, eyewitnesses watched it follow the RAM pickup out of the tunnel, then it stopped. A guy in black overalls and a balaclava jumped out of the Kenworth and ran to the RAM pickup, which then sped away down the mountain. Moments later, the flatbed truck was engulfed in flames. We think that had two purposes. Firstly, to block the lane behind the attackers as they made their escape down the mountainside. This would make it more difficult for them to be pursued, perhaps by someone in the undamaged Toyota, or by another vehicle coming through the tunnel. With one lane completely backed up with traffic leading to the accident, this served to completely close off the rest of the road. Secondly, when initial responders did arrive, the burning flatbed would be a beacon, temporarily distracting them from the more significant accident scene inside the tunnel."

Then Daniel, Caleb, and Tess slowly walked through the tunnel to the picnic area parking lot on the other side. Daniel's monologue continued.

"You can see the blue overspray on the asphalt. The perpetrators had temporarily screened off this small section of the parking lot to paint one of the decoy vehicles, but as with the other sites, this area has provided no further clues. The paint used was not exotic or remarkable in any way. And just like above the tunnel, we found evidence the ground at the hill overlooking the intersection of the Forest Highway and Route 4 had been similarly disturbed and burned by cigarettes, but there was nothing else there. It was a hunch that led us there because it had a line of sight to the intersection where the decoy Toyotas were blown up. It was the perfect point to command detonate explosives. We are still processing the burned-out flatbed truck and the vehicles found in L.A., but our expectations are not high.

Daniel exhaled loudly while referring to notes.

"We're running down nearby paint suppliers, checking with vehicle rental agencies, and going through dash cam video from the Highlanders and other vehicles at the accident scene. We're also combing through traffic cam photos in hopes of catching something. Finally, we've asked the M.E. to put a rush on the autopsies for the two individuals driving the decoy vehicles.

Then Daniel shifted his gaze to Caleb and Tess, alternating between the two of them.

Daniel continued. "From what we see, it's clear that the guys who carried out the attack were professionals. They were careful not to leave any clues behind. But that just means we'll need to work this hard until something pops. It will; it always does."

Caleb smiled. "Thank you, Dan. You know this is important to National Security, spare no resources. If there's something you need that you are not getting, let me know immediately." With this final encouragement, Daniel excused himself.

Tess pensively watched Daniel rejoin the forensic team and then looked back toward the highway tunnel.

"I'm sensing you were hoping we'd have more to

go on at this point," Caleb said.

"I know this is your domain, and intuitively I know crime scene analysis is a deliberate, methodical process, but I can't help thinking that the clock is ticking. The trail might grow cold before we can prevent the attackers from striking again. Somehow, I just feel there is something we should be doing to gain some initiative," she said.

"Tess, don't worry. This is normal. We're going to get these guys. Our people, they're experts. No matter how careful criminals are, there's always evidence, something left behind; our team will find it.

Caleb understood Tess's desire to see more rapid progress but knew from experience that it often took dogged, determined, hard work to produce results, especially at the beginning of an investigation. He was comfortable they had a good foundation and were stepping off on the right foot.

What Caleb did not know was that when he and the others were leaving the hospital to go up into the mountains to examine the crime scene, they were being watched. From a non-descript car parked on West California Boulevard, one of Stanislav Tishchenko's men monitored from a distance as Caleb and Daniel walked from the hospital toward Daniel's car. He also watched Tess ease her gracefully curved mat-black motorcycle out of the parking lot and down the central drive of Pasadena's Huntington Memorial Hospital. The overly rich green grass on the hospital grounds stood in bright contrast to the hospital's Spanish-inspired red-orange clay roof tiles and salmon and cream-colored exterior walls.

Tess drove past the excessive number of light

standards lining the main drive leading from the hospital, and then past the clump of palms standing sentry at both sides of the entrance to the grounds. Tishchenko's man continued to monitor Tess as she adjusted her posture to better mold with the bike, and then accelerated down West California Boulevard. No one noticed him, or the bug planted in the hospital room to listen in on Caleb's entire conversation with her. He entered Theresa (Tess) Wentzel into his cell phone.

Chapter 7

JPL Under the Spotlight

Caleb met Tess early the next morning at the Federal Building, located at 11000 Wilshire Boulevard, Los Angeles. This large utilitarian structure, situated almost midway between Santa Monica and Beverly Hills, hosts the offices of several Departments, the FBI's L.A. Field Office being just one of many. Caleb had previously arranged for Tess to park in the secure area for building occupants. Once she locked her helmet to the bike frame and stowed her riding gear in the saddle bags, she emerged in a dark business suit and low-heeled black pumps. Even dressed for the office, Caleb thought she looked stunning. He wore a lightweight charcoal-colored suit, crisp white shirt, and blood-red tie. Probably not ideal colors for the expected hot temperatures of the day, but he was pleased to be able to thread the cast through the jacket sleeve because he looked the best in these clothes. After getting a coffee to go, they departed immediately for JPL in Caleb's dark blue Chevrolet Impala work vehicle.

Since she had turned up at the hospital yesterday, they had covered a lot of ground–crime scene 101 he called it. Although they were together the entire previous day and into the evening, there was always someone else present. This was the first time they were alone and able to openly discuss what they thought about the case.

"In all my years doing this, I've never heard of the perfect crime," Caleb said. "I'm not saying this one was perfect, but the lack of any early clues is a sign itself. Clearly, it confirms your notion that these were highly trained professionals who knew about the communications equipment, knew it was being moved, and knew the details of the move," he continued, eager to entice further thoughts from Tess.

"Have you ever seen any other incidents similar to this?" she asked. "Incidents so expertly executed."

"Honestly. Thankfully, no. These guys knew too many important details. For instance, how did they know the equipment was in the second vehicle? Their whole ambush was designed to isolate the second vehicle in our convoy. To me, this has all the indications of an inside connection."

"Really? An inside person," Tess repeated.

"Unfortunately. Nothing surprises me anymore. I'm sure this points right back at NASA. It was too slick to have been executed without inside information. And the approach taken, resources used, and equipment stolen, also seems to confirm your initial assessment that this was probably the work of a foreign government."

Tess only said one thing in response to Caleb's analysis. She cautioned that it could be possible for someone in NASA to be a victim of remote surveillance without their knowledge.

"Organizations like the NSA, or their foreign equivalents, do that type of thing all the time."

"I wasn't thinking along those lines, but it's

something we need to keep an open mind about," Caleb conceded. *How would a NASA scientist know that kind of thing?*

As they headed southeast on the San Diego Freeway, Caleb thought that after all these years of being an FBI agent, he would have learned not to judge people by first impressions. Given her preferred mode of transport, it was logical to assume his new NASA colleague would have a hard edge, maybe even be a bit brash, but it was far from the case. Tess was obviously very intelligent, confident, and precise in her actions and comments, and she was also very demure, feminine, and considerate of those around her. She appeared to be a bit of an enigma though. She seemed very personable, yet skillfully evaded any personal discussion. She did not wear a ring. Out of politeness, there were some things Caleb felt uncomfortable asking directly. He did not know if the apprehension stemmed from a concern about learning something undesirable, like she was in a committed relationship, or that opening up such a personal discussion might eventually reveal his poor track record with the opposite gender, to include the long-term relationship a girlfriend of two years recently ended without warning. He was still stinging from the abrupt departure after she claimed it was not the right time to settle down.

As they made their way through the dense morning freeway traffic, Caleb thought a lighter subject might be better. "So why the bike?" he asked, trying to sound casual. "I mean, isn't it easier to rent a car?"

"Well, I didn't want to be dependent on anyone for transportation, this way I can come and go as I please without disturbing anyone. And there are some advantages to a bike, there are lots of places they can go where cars can't."

"Been riding long?"

"Yes, since I was a kid. Mom insisted that my brother and I swim and skate in the winter, and in the summer, we rode bicycles as a family. As I got older, I got into BMX and then transitioned to small motocross. My father was a Chicago Motorcycle Police Officer, so it seemed like a natural progression to gravitate from bicycles to motorcycles as soon as I was old enough. Mom was not too happy about it. In the spring her daughter would take a motorcycle to figure skating class."

"Did your brother figure skate as well?"

"Oh no, he was a hockey player. You know, rough and tumble. My poor parents, between the pool and the arena, they never got outside in winter. How about you? What did you do growing up?"

"Oh, I was like your brother. I played hockey. Being from Duluth, it was pretty much mandatory. I played from elementary school age until I graduated from university. Living in the Congdon Park area, we had great rivalries with clubs from other nearby neighborhoods. Each had their own outdoor rink, and everyone, parents, classmates, teachers, friends, all came out to cheer on their team. It seemed like every game you were defending your community's reputation; it brought out the best in everyone. There was a real sense of belonging, of comradery. Those were such formative years."

"That sounds nice."

"Yeah, as I look back, I realize just how fortunate I was to have had such great opportunities. In the summer I played competitive soccer, so I was outdoors a lot. The University of Minnesota had a Duluth campus, so I was able to maintain connections with friends right through to adulthood. Then I joined the Bureau. Since Quantico, I've been here in L.A. It's quite a change. I like the ocean and the beaches; the waves lapping on the shore seem to wash away all the stress. It reminds me of home and the beaches on Lake Superior."

"You miss home?" Tess asked.

"L.A.'s big. Everything is here, but I do miss friends and family. And four distinct seasons. But California's great too."

"And you? You're no longer living in Chicago?"

"Heavens, no. I left after high school. Right now, I'm living out of a suitcase, somewhere between Maryland, Huntsville, and here. But Chicago will always be home," Tess clarified.

"So, you have friends there still?"

"More like family."

"Oh."

"Sounds like your childhood was ideal, though," Tess observed.

"It was great. Although we didn't know it at the time, we were extremely privileged. We were encouraged and nurtured from our earliest days in elementary school onward to set our goals high. Historical figures who were adventurous, or had an entrepreneurial spirit, were greatly revered. For instance, the drinking fountains at school were all unique. Each one had a different hand-tiled mosaic of a famous explorer, like Christopher Columbus, or Marco Polo and the like. They were quite artistic. Every time I got a drink of water, I would think about the hardships those early explorers had to overcome, and I would wonder what my mark on the world would be. I know it was just a small thing, but it encouraged you to think big. I remember it like it was yesterday. Now I have friends who own their own medical clinics, practice law, are engineers, and belong to other great professions across the States. I never thought I would be chasing international villains though," Caleb said with a smile.

"Yeah, me too!"

As the conversation came back around to the investigation, Tess pointed out there were potentially one or two scenarios at play.

"Firstly, the communications equipment was stolen for a reason, likely to hack into NASA's deep space satellite," she said. "To make use of the classified equipment, the attackers would need to access a deep space communication system."

She explained that there were not many options, and the US and Russian systems were the best. China was developing a capability and India had a system with limited capacity. Japan and the European Space Agency also possessed this capability. This meant that if the stolen equipment was not moved out of the country, they would likely try to tap into the US Deep Space Network.

"Secondly, depending on how much knowledge the thieves have of previous NASA communications with the deep space satellite, they may need the services of a world-class cryptographer. If the equipment they took is still somewhere in the United States, it might be helpful to find out if any known cryptographers have recently entered the country and where they are. This could lead us to the equipment.

Casting the net wider, she also suggested US overseas intelligence resources be alerted to monitor foreign communication sites and known high-profile cryptographers for unusual activity.

"Those are great ideas, Tess. They are things that weren't even on my radar."

"Don't feel bad. This is sort of my area. I'm just trying to think of ways to get ahead of the attackers before they can benefit from their crime."

Caleb made a mental note to follow up on Tess's suggestions. As they rounded the curve heading southeast on the Foothill Freeway, the sun shone directly into their faces. Despite the intense glare, Caleb could still make out the 177-acre JPL campus nestled up in the heights. *It looks just like the photos.* Although it seemed the traffic had been heavy from the moment they departed the Federal Building, they had made good time. It was still early, and it was shaping up to be another hot day–just as Caleb had feared when selecting his suit. As they got closer to JPL, he started to think more about the upcoming interview.

"If required, I should play the bad cop and leave the good cop role to you. After all, you'll need to continue to work with these NASA colleagues long after this crisis has concluded."

"Thank you, Caleb. It could be helpful in the future."

From the Freeway they wound their way up Oak Grove Drive, found visitors parking, and walked toward the town-like campus where they were supposed to meet the director's executive assistant.

"Welcome to JPL," said a lady who was positioned to intercept anyone arriving from the parking area. Cradling a leather-bound agenda in one arm, she quickly extended her other hand to Caleb and Tess. "I'm Denise Urquhart, Director Coombs' assistant. You must be Agent MacLeod and Miss Wentzel. Thank you for texting me as you were arriving, it makes meeting our guests so much easier."

With a glance at her watch, she said "Follow me, please." She then spun about and marched off toward the maze of buildings ahead.

Caleb wondered how this middle-aged woman could walk so easily in such high heels and a tight-fitting skirt.

"I hope the traffic wasn't too bad this morning," she said, as they followed a route naturally leading to the main administration building. Inside she handed them each a pass that had been neatly tucked in her agenda.

"This way, our special guests avoid the security screening process, but I still need to confirm you left your cell phones and other electronics in the car."

"Yes, we did," Caleb said, looking at Tess.

After weaving through a few corridors, they arrived at an impressive set of double doors.

"Director Coombs is very much looking forward to meeting you," she announced as she shepherded them into a large, executive board room.

Two men deeply engaged in conversation around a large table rose to their feet. One immediately approached Caleb and Tess, offered his hand, and a big disarming smile.

"Welcome to JPL. I'm Director Coombs, and this

is George Sibley. George is responsible for our Deep Space Network."

"Thank you, Director, Mr. Sibley, I'm Supervisory Special Agent MacLeod and this is Ms. Tess Wentzel. I appreciate you seeing us on short notice. I know you are terribly busy," Caleb said, showing an official identification.

"Agent MacLeod, Miss Wentzel, please just let me say that I, and the entire JPL team, are at your disposal. We were deeply shocked by last week's events and if there is anything we can do to assist, just say the word."

"Thank you, Director, that's extremely helpful," Caleb said.

"Please, have a seat," Coombs said, motioning Tess and Caleb to the ample conference table. The director and George Sibley returned to the seats they had originally occupied. "This is a secure board room so please be comfortable to speak your mind."

Everyone politely declined the refreshments Denise Urquhart offered, and she discretely closed the door as she left.

"Thank you, Director, for your assistance," Caleb said. "Can you tell me who knew about the classified equipment being transported from JPL last week?"

Coombs stiffened a little in his chair, "Well, you need to understand. For as long as anyone can remember, there has been a safe here at JPL, but nobody knew what was in it. We don't even have the combination; it's held in Huntsville. Every year someone comes from Huntsville and checks inside, I assume to ensure everything is accounted for and in good working order. From our end, all we knew was that if it was needed, probably as a result of some emergency or something, we would be given the combination and instructed what to do with whatever was inside. That's why we were surprised when we were contacted four weeks ago and told the contents would be removed from JPL."

"So, before then, who would have known about the safe?"

"Not many people. There would have been me, George, and our immediate staff."

"Why did Mr. Sibley and the staff know about the safe if you didn't know what was inside? I mean why him instead of some other executive?" Caleb asked.

"Well, we didn't know, and we still don't know what the contents were, but we did know it had something to do with deep space communication. As I said, George is responsible for the DSN. Only he and I knew there was something pertaining to that capability in the safe. He was the backup emergency contact if for some reason I could not be reached in a crisis. We knew this pertained to national security and was on a need-to-know basis so the fact the safe was here was treated with the utmost discretion."

"Could I get a list of the people who would have known about the safe and who may have interacted with the Huntsville person during the annual visit, even if it was to greet him at the front door? I'll need that right away please." Caleb was being polite, but the tone indicated he was not asking.

"That'll be no problem. I think we can get it to you by the end of the day, or first thing tomorrow."

"Now, how about last week? Who would have known the contents of the safe were going to be moved?"

"Well, Agent MacLeod, the director was out of town for business, so I handled last week's activities," George Sibley said. "The people involved were kept to an absolute minimum, but I did need to bring in some additional assistance. The gentleman we have been dealing with the past few years from Huntsville was here to open the safe and I remember you, Agent MacLeod, were here to pick up the contents. But we needed to organize a dolly, clear corridors, and set up a security cordon, so naturally, this was an unusual occurrence bound to attract some attention–not that we advertised in any way, or told folks what was actually going on. We just said we were conducting a security drill; and when we asked folks to do things, we asked them to do what we needed done. We did not say why or explain what it was really for."

"Okay, thanks. That's helpful. I'll need a second list of folks who were involved in any way, even on the periphery, with the move. Some names may be duplicates from the first list."

"I understand," the director replied.

"Has there ever been anyone who has shown or expressed an unusual interest in the safe, or speculated as to its contents in a way that stands out?"

Coombs slowly leaned back in his chair. "No one comes to mind."

"How about from your team, Mr. Sibley?" Caleb pressed.

"No…no one stands out."

"Now, how about when the fellow from Huntsville showed up for the annual visit? Was it always the same person who met him, or assisted him?"

"It will be easy for us to check our security logs

and confirm," the director stated.

"Since the incident, have there been any unusual absences from anyone who might be on either of the two lists you will be preparing?"

"I'm not sure, I'll need to check to confirm, but I am not aware of anything out of the ordinary," said the director, adding to his notes. George Sibley nodded in agreement.

"I'll need you to indicate on the lists if anyone has missed any time at work since the incident."

"No problem."

"I would like an FBI National Security Branch team to sweep the phones and computers of anyone who will be on those two lists to check for listening devices, spyware, or malware of any kind."

Director Coombs inhaled sharply, then exhaled. "I understand the need for that, but this is delicate." Clearly, Caleb had touched a nerve. "There may be classified information on the computers, and even proprietary data owned by some of our contractors, so I would need assurances that no copies of any information will leave JPL and any disruptions to the network will be minimized. Could this be coordinated with our head of cyber security? Should I get him to contact you?"

"Yes, of course," Caleb said. "Can you show us the safe? I know I saw it a couple of times recently, for the pickup and also during the preparatory reconnaissance, but those visits were from a transportation perspective. I'd like to examine the safe itself, and its environment, more thoroughly now."

"Yes, we can go over whenever you like."

"We'd like to return tomorrow to start interviews

of those on your two lists. Would it be all right?" Again, this really was not a question Caleb was asking. "Would it be possible to have a private interview room where classified information could be discussed?"

"Absolutely, we can arrange it. Is there anything else?"

There was an extended moment of silence and just when the men were about to get up, Tess asked, "How confident are we in our transmission security?"

Caleb appreciated Tess waiting for him to finish before she took the discussion on an entirely new tack. He observed that she was both polite and considerate, but this did not dissuade her from pressing home uncomfortable questions.

"What do you mean?" George Sibley asked.

"How confident are we that only authorized transmissions go out over the DSN?" Tess asked more precisely. "What specific checks do we have in place to ensure each transmission has been reviewed and approved?"

There was another period of awkward silence, and then George Sibley spoke, "Messages are compartmentalized by program area, and there are protocols developed within each area identifying who can approve messages for transmission. Out of necessity, not all programs are the same. For instance, some might be in a more active phase because there may be spacecraft conducting surveys or performing experiments while others may be in a quiet phase because they are in transit in space and have not yet reached their destination. Only specified personnel in each program area are authorized to approve transmissions."

"Many vehicles use the same frequency bands, correct?" Tess said, leaning forward as if to further emphasize her point.

"Correct," George responded slowly, as if to signal it was not clear where this was all going.

"Would it be possible for a person authorized to approve transmissions for one program to actually release a message that impacts or is destined for a vehicle in another program?"

"But why would someone want to do that?"

"Do we have the procedures in place to prevent this?"

"Well, it would be hard for someone to do what you are proposing. In addition to the specific frequencies, they would need to know the access protocols for the spacecraft in the other program, and the vehicle's trajectory and location, which they should not know."

"But if they did."

"I suppose it could happen, but it would likely be caught. There would be a record and presumably, the team responsible for the craft would notice their vehicle reacting when they did not provide it any commands."

"So, it might be possible?"

"Yes, but not likely. This has never been an issue."

"How about if someone hacked into your system and sent out an unauthorized message, would you know?"

"Again, there would be a record of what went out."

"But is anyone cross-referencing what goes out to what has been actually authorized?"

"We've not ever had to do it in the past."

Adopting a very conciliatory, but factual tone, Tess

explained, "Director, Mr. Sibley, there is a strong possibility someone will use the stolen equipment to access the DSN. It may not have been needed in the past, but we must quickly put checks in place to ensure any transmissions that go out are legitimate. We also need to be prepared to quickly shut down any unauthorized outgoing messages. We need to assume our system may already be compromised, and we must be prepared to react instantly to anything unusual. If this occurs, I need to know immediately."

Sibley lifted his expensive pen off the table, only to place it down again slightly further away. "I understand the issue. I'll look into it."

"Thank you, sir. Could I ask you to advise me what new procedures you put in place as soon as you are ready?"

"Yes, of course."

Tess had one last question.

"Would it be possible to visit Goldstone and have someone walk me through how messages are formulated for specific programs and then transmitted?"

Caleb had no idea what Goldstone was, but assumed it was a signal to George Sibley about being knowledgeable in this field.

"No problem. I'll get you the contact details of someone on site who can walk you through the process as soon as you would like," Sibley replied, again repositioning his pen.

"Thank you, Mr. Sibley, it would be very helpful."

"Okay, is there anything else before we walk over to the safe?" Director Coombs asked.

Caleb and Tess looked at each other and then indicated they were ready to go. They both left their business cards with the two men, just in case they thought of anything else relevant, then they all departed the office together, Coombs leading. For his part, the director reiterated that he and George, and their staff, were at the FBI's complete disposal. He also invited them to contact Ms. Urquhart if they could not immediately get in touch.

After thoroughly examining the safe and its immediate proximity, Tess and Caleb bid the director and George Sibley farewell. They confirmed they would be back the next day to commence the interviews and security sweeps, and then made their own way out to the campus mall and walked to Caleb's car. As they drove back down Oak Grove Drive toward the freeway below, Caleb restated the suspicion that someone from JPL or Huntsville had to be the link to the attackers, wittingly or unwittingly. It only made sense. What, he kept to himself was the satisfaction NASA had seconded Tess to the investigation. She was bringing thoughts and perspectives the FBI would likely not have thought of otherwise.

Back at the Federal Building, Tess told Caleb that she had to head back to her apartment so as not to miss the daily call with Doug Regent, her boss. Planning a roundabout route home would provide the dual advantage of ensuring no one was following and allowing her to clear her head with a little highway speed. She said it was important to provide Doug a heads-up to expect a visit from the local FBI office in Huntsville about potential security leaks at Redstone, particularly related to the annual checks performed on the safe in California. Tess said she wanted to have the conversation with Doug using the encrypted telephone at the apartment. *I wonder if there's more to it. Why call from off-site? Is there something she's not telling me or doesn't want me to hear?* Despite these thoughts, he still had a good feeling about her.

After Tess departed, he was finally able to retreat to his office for a moment of solitude. Even at times like this, when searching for some quiet, the office door was usually slightly ajar. Otherwise, the door was fully open because it made him more accessible; it was only ever fully closed for confidential discussions. If work required concentration, he came in before most co-workers, or departed later. This was the most productive time of the day because it was truly his to control. Often, he exploited the quiet at the end of his shift to mentally consolidate actions that had occurred and to set priorities for the next day. That way, when he left the office, the work remained behind. The rap on the office door signaled he would not be going home just yet.

"Come in!" Caleb said, getting up from behind the desk. He was halfway to the door when it opened, and Daniel LeBlanc stepped in. "Hi, Dan, what's up?" Caleb said, trying not to sound perturbed.

"I am not sure if we should be considering this entirely a foreign attack," Dan said.

"What do you mean?"

"Early results from Lydia indicate the remains retrieved from the decoy vehicles were likely American."

"How does she know that?"

"You know our M.E., she's more than thorough. Although it's still unknown who they are, based upon the dental work and other tests, she's confident they are

American."

"Nothing else?"

"She is still completing her work, but I thought you should know right away."

"Okay, many thanks, Dan. This complicates things. If this was a foreign sponsored attack, then there were American accomplices, or involvement at least."

"Yeah. And there *is* one more thing," Dan said. "The plastic explosive used to detonate the decoy vehicles was military grade C4, manufactured in the United States."

Chapter 8

So You're the One

Tess was very strategic with her interim lodgings in L.A.

"I wanted to be close to work for an easy commute and also close to lots of green space," she explained during a scarce free moment over the phone to her close friend Zoe Kirkwell back in Maryland.

"It sounds ideal," Zoe agreed.

"It's perfect. It's an apartment in an area called Beachwood. It's adjacent to Griffith Park, and almost equidistant from the Fed Building on Wilshire, where the FBI office is located, and JPL. Sometimes after a long day, it's refreshing to walk the numerous footpaths in the park, wander by the zoo, or stroll along the pedestrian walks near the Los Angeles River."

Although Tess found the ideal location for her apartment, opportunities to enjoy the surroundings were becoming rarer. On the other hand, the commute was easy. The ride to the Fed Building was about 15 miles to the southwest. Normally she varied the timings and route to and from the office, always taking a long winding ride home to ensure no one followed, but it was less critical on the way to work.

Today she took a more direct path to the office by traveling southwest on a couple of main arteries, then picked up Santa Monica Boulevard, which flowed west, and finally took Interstate 405 north a short distance to the Wilshire exit. Although it would have been shorter to take Wilshire right from Santa Monica Boulevard, the short distance on the Interstate had the benefit of leading to the Fed Building from the west instead of the east where her apartment was, thereby throwing off anyone who might be monitoring her arrival. The few minutes of Interstate driving also reinforced how lucky it was not having a highway commute every day.

On arrival, she swung by the small shop in the lobby and picked up two coffees, one for her and one for Caleb. She remembered how genuinely happy he seemed by these small gestures of politeness. He grinned from ear to ear. After a week of working together, they were firmly established in the routine of meeting in his office early in the morning to plan their approach to the day, usually before most other people even arrived at work. Although they had a quick huddle at the end of each day as well, Tess's nightly phone call with her boss Doug Regent back in Huntsville often provided information that influenced the plan they had discussed the evening before. Today both Tess and Caleb decided it would be far more efficient for her to head directly to Goldstone to check things out while Caleb continued interviews at JPL. They would meet back in the office at the end of the day to compare notes.

Tess was not particularly looking forward to a three-hour motorcycle ride out of L.A. to the Mojave Desert but was very much looking forward to experiencing a different part of California. More importantly, she wanted to see firsthand the changes

George Sibley put in place to ensure only authorized messages were transmitted by the Deep Space Network. The team at JPL offered a briefing, but it was better to speak to someone at the coalface. Tess had the scars to prove that every now and again what high-level leaders and managers thought was happening was not actually the case.

After skirting the downtown core of Los Angeles, Tess was heading in the opposite direction to most of the traffic so the ride toward Goldstone was relatively straightforward and uneventful. Driving along, she reflected upon becoming more used to people using her alias, but there was still a twinge of guilt about it. Sometimes when people would call out for Tess Wentzel, Tess Shefford would wonder who they were looking for. With Caleb, however, it felt really awkward keeping her real name and the true information about the stolen communication equipment from him; perhaps it was because they worked so closely together and were supposed to be a team. She wanted to just clear the air and tell him about herself and that the highly classified satellite communications equipment they were desperately trying to retrieve was actually used to communicate with an ultra secret spacecraft called Helios in deep space. Lost in thought, Tess did not notice the vehicle that had been following her since the Federal Building; it was the same car that had been parked outside the hospital during her visit with Caleb.

Tess took a rest at the small town of Barstow, which was at the two-hour point in the journey. Besides being a great line in a Sheryl Crow ballad, Barstow was the last opportunity for gas, a snack, and a restroom break before Goldstone. The old Historic Harvey House was also home to NASA's visitor's center where displays explained the history and current missions of the Deep Space Network communications system.

In the center, Tess overheard one of the local guides explaining to a group of tourists, "NASA named its modern-day high-tech facility 'Goldstone' after an old, abandoned gold mining town nearby."

Tess already knew many of the other points the displays presented to the general public, but it was interesting nonetheless to hear the guide explain it to space enthusiasts.

"Now you might ask, why here? Well, it's not by happenstance. It turns out this area of the United States actually has some unique geographical formations, which make it ideal for receiving messages from space. Can anyone help me out by naming some of them?"

There was silence. Tess was tempted to chime in but resisted, letting the guide have fun with her guests.

"The facility itself is located far out in a desert that is surrounded by high hills and mountains, so Goldstone is isolated from the electromagnetic radio signal noise generated by surrounding built-up urban areas. This way the weak signals from far away spacecraft can be received with little interference."

"So, what is the furthest we have been able to communicate out into space?" someone asked.

"What a great question. Does anyone know? No. It's hard to imagine, but our Deep Space Network is still in communication with Voyager I which has now traveled completely outside our solar system."

There were positive sounds from the tourists as they moved along to other exhibits, obviously impressed by DSN capabilities. Tess knew the tour only touched the high notes but was surprised the guide did not explain that Goldstone was protected within the confines of the Fort Irwin Military Reservation located midway between Las Vegas and Los Angeles and it was one of three such facilities NASA operated worldwide. The others were in Spain and Australia. With equidistant separation around the globe, at least one of the three stations making up the network would be able to communicate with a distant spacecraft.

Tess arrived at the Fort Irwin gate at 11:15 a.m. and was happy to find her name was on the visitors' list. She was issued a temporary pass and instructed to follow the main road for about five miles, and then to turn left on NASA Road where there was another security check point. It was not until entering the confines of Fort Irwin, with much lower speed limits, that it fully registered how hot it was in the desert. Driving northwest along NASA Road, she could see a couple of large white radio telescopes far off to the left and evidence of a couple of deactivated sites in the distance to the right. *I'm sure they paint the antennas white to reflect the blistering Mojave heat.* Continuing to drive at a slower speed she wondered if there might be a market for white leather motorcycle gear.

The road bent in a long, gentle curve to the left where she could make out the dry bed of Goldstone Lake and a nearby airstrip. As the road wound its way further around some hills, the view finally opened up to expose the massive white 210-foot diameter parabolic radio telescope dish at the far end of the complex. Altogether, the Goldstone facility had five space communication antennas of various sizes that looked like large TV satellite dishes, but the 210-foot diameter antenna was more than twice as big as any of the others. This gigantic dish and its mount weighed over 8,000 tons and could communicate with a spacecraft over 10 billion miles from Earth. *Everything related to space seemed to come with staggering numbers.* Tess parked her bike in the visitor's spot near the Signals Processing Center. Inside, the building was a refuge from the oppressive heat, but she now shivered in the chilled air-conditioned environment, which was primarily intended to benefit the banks of computers that seemed to be everywhere. She was directed to the manager's office.

After a moment, he looked up from his desk.

"Ah, we've been expecting you. Ms.…Wen…?"

"Wentzel," Tess said.

"Yes, of course. Wentzel."

"Thank you for the opportunity to visit."

"Yes, yes. No problem. Just wait a minute," he said, reaching for the desk phone. "Mandy. Yes, she's here."

A moment later, a young blonde woman wearing an opened brown cardigan with the sleeves pulled over her hands appeared.

"Tess?"

"Yes," Tess said, looking at her, and then toward the manager.

"I'm Mandy Prokapowicz," the woman said, confidently shaking Tess's hand. "It's nice to meet you. I'll be your host."

"Oh, wonderful."

Tess thanked the manager again and then followed Mandy down the hall. Out of earshot, she whispered.

"He didn't seem too happy to see me. I hope this

isn't a bad time."

"Oh, no, don't worry about it. We get lots of visitors."

"Okay, good."

"He's just upset about the new security protocol business."

"Oh. Really?"

"Seriously, don't worry about it. I've been telling them for years something had to be done, but they continually blew me off. He just didn't like to hear from his boss there was a problem."

Tess spent the next two and a half hours with her host. Mandy was a grad from the UCLA Master of Science in Signals Processing and Communications Program and had worked at the site for almost four years. She was extremely professional and candid about how Goldstone and the other facilities in NASA's worldwide network functioned, both together and individually. Tess could tell immediately that Mandy was thorough and exacting. She liked the approach, and it was nice to meet another expert in her field. Without asking, Mandy walked Tess step by step through the approval procedure required before a transmission was made to one of the numerous spacecraft that DSN supported. The recent improvements George Sibley had put in place were also covered in detail, including being vigilant to shut down any unauthorized transmission that may have resulted from an external hack. Mandy carefully took her through the entire process to demonstrate the integrity of the system. After the tour, Tess was confident the DSN was tight as a drum.

Tess paid a courtesy visit to the facility manager's office and thanked him again for the opportunity to visit and for the comprehensive briefing on Goldstone activities and communication protocols. She noted how thorough and professional Mandy had been. The manager seemed genuinely happy, and Tess asked him to pass on her sincere appreciation to Mr. Sibley. The manager forced a smile, thanked her for her interest in their work, and said he would pass along the comments to *George* when they spoke next.

Exiting the building was like opening a blast furnace door. Tess could feel the super-heated air attack her lungs. She had grown accustomed to the cool air-conditioned environment which now made the outside late afternoon desert heat seem all the more oppressive.

Mandy followed Tess outside to say farewell.

"You have quite a ride home…on a motorcycle, I mean," Mandy said with a grin as Tess donned her leathers and helmet. "If you need anything else, don't be shy to give me a call, I'd be happy to help if I can," Mandy volunteered. "And if you are ever out this way, look me up. It is pretty quiet out here in the desert!"

"I sure will," Tess said, starting her bike with a rumble and easing it off its kickstand. "Mandy, I really appreciate the time you spent with me today. You truly went above and beyond." Then, feeling a little philosophical about the recent attacks, said, "I know we are going to be all right with professionals like you working here." Mandy seemed a bit surprised. *Maybe she doesn't know about the attack.* Tess certainly could not reveal any details of Helios or other secrets, though it was clear Mandy was touched by her comments. "Let me know if you are ever coming to the city," Tess said with a smile. "It would be nice to get together for some girl time!" Mandy waved as Tess slowly headed out of the parking lot and began to retrace her route heading southeast back toward the camp's main gate.

Tess could not help feeling satisfied when clearing the last gate of the Military Reservation. It had been a long, yet productive day. It was comforting to see how professionally the DSN was run. Now off the base, she could speed up a bit and generate some airflow to cool down. The road from Fort Irwin led directly south across barren desert and then linked with Interstate 15 to L.A. *If all goes well, I'll be back at the Fed Building around 6:00 p.m.* But Tess knew she needed to be careful near L.A. because of the drive directly into the setting sun and dense rush-hour traffic.

The first part of the route was across open, washed-out, tawny-colored, flat ground where the road was straight as an arrow and framed against an endless sky with low rounded mountains way off on the horizon. Three quarters of the way south the roadway reached some of those distant mountains and began to thread through the darkened valleys before the landscape would open out onto the familiar flat desert again. Soon after Tess entered the mountainous area and started to weave her way around the high ground, the road took a long swinging arc to the left. In the far distance, it looked as if a silver sedan had pulled over to the side of the road with its hood up and the four-way flashers going. One of the occupants was waving. Tess took in the scene while decelerating and got a little closer. There were three well-dressed men, all with sunglasses. *They aren't locals*. One man was in front of the car facing forward, another was by the trunk facing her, and the third was near the driver's door waving his arms at her.

John Madower

This doesn't feel right.
She slowed her bike further.

Chapter 9

A Desert Ride Like No Other

Ed Dale was a nervous driver. Everyone said he was very skilled behind the wheel, but this did not ease the discomfort, especially when it came to highway driving. In his own lane, everything was okay; but initially merging onto a busy highway, changing lanes, or driving at high speed on densely packed thoroughfares, especially on greater Los Angeles freeways, made him extremely anxious.

Normally he would avoid highways at all costs, preferring secondary roads where it was far more comfortable and easier to demonstrate driving competence. Today, however, was not a normal day. Ed was helping his son move from their family home in Flagstaff, Arizona to San Diego, where he had landed a lucrative computer programming job right out of university. Unfortunately for Ed, the distance and the route to the coast forced him to use some of the busiest Interstate Highways in the country. Adding to the unease was the traffic speed that pushed him to drive the rented U-Haul van well above the posted limit in order not to impede the flow of other vehicles. Ed was silently rehearsing to himself an explanation for breaking the law, in case he was pulled over by the California Highway Patrol, when suddenly there was the most disquieting, unrecognizable noise behind him and to the left. It sounded like nothing he had ever heard before, it literally hurt his ears. Just as he started to turn to glance over his shoulder out the driver's side window to see what was generating the screeching high-pitched whine, everything instantly went quiet, and 'whoosh' was all Ed heard as a motorcycle sped by in a blur so fast it made everything else on the highway look like it was standing still. Immediately after it passed, the strained motorcycle engine noise returned as it seemed to struggle to keep up with the racing two-wheeled machine ahead. The rider, dressed in black leather with a long, thick braided ponytail that hung down from her helmet and danced in the turbulent air, was determinedly perched on the bike.

"It's the craziest thing I have ever seen!" Ed exclaimed. "One second of inattention and she'll be wrapped around a light standard."

Ed had never witnessed anything with wheels move so fast. He imagined the pistons, gears, and other components of the motorcycle all being 'red-lined.' They sounded like they were about to burst out of their engine and transmission cases.

About thirty seconds later, a black, full-size, Chevy SUV sped by.

"These people are insane, driving like that," Ed barked out again. "I don't care if they write themselves off, but they're going to take some innocent bystander with them!"

Ed could feel his pulse quicken and grasped the steering wheel even tighter.

****

A little faster than walking speed now, Tess

continued to roll toward the silver sedan on the side of the road with its hazard lights flashing. *Strange…nobody is fussing over the engine even though the hood is up.* She continued to survey the sedan, and the men, for clues about what might really be happening.

Just as Tess slowed to almost a stop, the man by the driver's door started to move toward her and a gust of wind blew the flap of his jacket open. Then she saw it! He had a holstered handgun fitted with a sound suppressor! Gritting her teeth, she simultaneously released the brake, twisted the throttle, and accelerated through the intended ambush before any of the three men could react. *Legitimate security agents don't carry sound suppressors under suit jackets!* She sped up as quickly as possible before daring to look back to see what was happening with the sedan. Not far behind the car was already spinning its wheels as it kicked up a dust cloud before fully pulling onto the asphalt. She had a head start but would need to step it up to maintain it. Tess knew from her police officer dad that pistols only had an effective range of about 25 yards, or maybe 50 yards for an advanced shooter, so they would need to get close or be really lucky to harm her.

The road continued to twist left and right, up and down as it followed along the easiest path through the valleys and uneven ground. Racing, Tess used both sides of the road on the turns to increase the distance from the pursuers. The skyline hinted that this section of the route was almost through the mountains. *I can really open it up when I get back on the straight desert road.* Up ahead, a long black SUV was parked sideways across the road. It blocked both lanes. Tess hit the brakes and screeched to a halt. *Go forward or go back? Decide quickly. Neither option is good.* Just as the silver sedan sped around the corner into view, she decided on a completely different course of action–cross country. As a teenager, she rode motocross and the desert here was hard-packed, not soft sand. The Suzuki V-Strom was not ideal for this type of riding, but it would work if she were careful.

Negotiating down the steep side of the road was tricky, followed by the shallow ditch, and then it was out onto the desolate ground adjacent to the roadway. Starting the cross-country trek, Tess was immediately happy to have not accepted the heavy street bike the rental agency had suggested. *It would have been a problem with its low ground clearance.* Trying to recall details about nearby intersections, she thought about the next steps. *I need to connect with one of those side roads before the sedan and SUV can find the long way around.* Tess knew it was a gamble riding off-road, but there was no way the SUV or sedan could negotiate the ditch, and even if by chance they were able to get out onto the flat desert, they were much too heavy for the ground to support. They had to take the long route. Briefly stopping at a safe distance and pulling out a phone, she just took an instant to check the map. *I need to find a way back to the highway before I get bottled up by these guys.*

It was less than a quarter of a mile to one of the secondary side roads. It was rougher going than anticipated, but now back on a prepared roadway, she was able to pick up speed significantly. Sage-colored vegetation flapped from the lower portions of the motorcycle. This route took a back way into Barstow, across a bridge over the dry Mojave Riverbed and onto Interstate 15. On the highway, trying to be inconspicuous, Tess tucked into a long line of cars in the right-hand lane. Then everything that had happened hit and she started to shake. Why was someone targeting her? Had they followed all the way from the Fed Building?

While contemplating what to do, Tess realized with a start that the black SUV was up ahead, pulled over on the shoulder. Reacting immediately, she pulled into the passing lane and fully opened the throttle. The bike protested loudly with horrific whining noises, but Tess continued to press for maximum speed despite the mechanical complaints. *It'll be a while before they can work their way onto the highway, and I need to capitalize on my slim lead.* Pushing the bike as fast as it would physically go, she whizzed by cars in the right-hand lane so fast it looked like they were hardly moving. If cars in the passing lane were not going fast enough, she split the lane and threaded in-between the cars in the fast and slow lane. Every fiber of Tess's body was alive and tuned to the immediate task. *This is perilous. Stay focused or this could end really badly.* Her mind was hyper-alert. Things were happening so fast, 'snapshot' images flashed in her head. An older gentleman in a U-Haul van gave a strange look as she sped by.

It was crazy dangerous driving that could not be kept up for long. *I need to get off the highway. Coming up to Victorville now. There are several exits.* Palmdale Road exit ramp was too long—the occupants of the SUV could see her leaving the highway. The next exit was the same. The one after that looked okay. So, Tess sped down the Bear Valley Road exit ramp, turned right, passed a shopping mall, and then took a quick right into the large, busy parking lot. The mall blocked the view from the highway. *If they didn't see me take the exit, they won't know I'm here.* Waiting for what seemed like an eternity, her rib cage could hardly contain a heavily pounding heart; blood swooshed against her ear drums with each beat. Slowly, as time passed, and no SUV or sedan appeared, the breathing gradually became easier, and the pulse slackened. After about twenty minutes, she carefully drove through the parking lot, exited on the far side of the mall and followed Bear Valley Road west as far as it went. Now, halfway to Palmdale, there was no choice but to get on the four-lane California State Route 14 highway, which led west through the mountains to the greater Los Angeles area.

When Tess picked up Interstate 5 south, it was approximately 7:30 and much later than she had planned to be on the road. Still, her intention was to go to the Fed Building where Caleb would be working late and waiting. Another car on the side of the highway began to move just as Tess drove by. Coincidence? Was this paranoia, or just being extra careful? Following events earlier in the day, there would be no waiting around to find out. Unlike the previous race toward Victorville, this part of the city was intimately familiar. She quickly got into the far-left passing lane and throttled her steed to move as fast as it would go. When traffic slowed, she drove on the left shoulder. Briefly glancing in the rear-view mirrors, the white sedan stood out as it dodged through traffic, trying desperately to catch up.

Route 14 is one of only two possible highways leading from the Mojave. They were waiting for me. They knew that if I took the 14, this is where I'd need to join Interstate 5 to get back to the Fed Building. Tess remained vigilant while continuing to advance through the fast-moving traffic. Checking the mirrors again, it was easy to see the pursuing white sedan had also adopted the tactic of driving on the shoulder, even though there was barely enough room. It was gaining ground. The traffic was dense. *If I slow down to cross the highway to the exit lanes on the right, the sedan might get close enough for someone to take a shot.* So, rather than head for the safety of Fed Building as originally intended, she decided to continue south on Interstate 5.

The Interstate brushed the eastern edge of Griffith Park, which was near her apartment. Once beyond the zoo, and seeing all the green space to the right, Tess was in very really familiar surroundings. Near the southern end of Griffith Park, there was an opportunity to pull over to the right-hand lane. She immediately slowed her bike, and took it. The white sedan, not far behind, was still weaving through traffic. Maintaining a slightly reduced speed, Tess pulled over onto the right shoulder of the highway, so the pursuing car had a good view of her from a distance. Driving under a pedestrian walkway and bicycle bridge, she continued to bear right onto the Glendale Boulevard exit ramp. The exit continued to curve to the right in a quarter circle and came to a "T" junction on Riverside Drive, which ran parallel to the Interstate. Tess waited at the junction until the white sedan started down the ramp as well. She then turned right and slowly drove north about 700 feet, passing a busy community center on the right. The white sedan ran the light at the bottom of the ramp, forcing its way onto Riverside Drive in an obvious attempt to catch up.

Cars swerved to avoid collisions and horns honked to add to the commotion. As the white sedan got closer, Tess turned right off Riverside into the community center and picked up a recreation path that led to the narrow pedestrian walkway and bicycle bridge across the Interstate, which they had just passed under. On the other side of the highway, the path led to another bridge over the Los Angeles River with its reinforced concrete spillway. Now Tess had the advantage. Cars physically could not fit on these bridges purposely built for pedestrians and bicycles only. She moved quickly so it would be useless for anyone to try to follow on foot.

The car will need to exit the community center parking lot and drive either north or south on Riverside to find the next opportunity to cross the river. Hopefully, by then, I'll have long disappeared in traffic.

Miles away, Tess quietly pulled into a familiar multi-level shopping center parking garage and found an out-of-the-way spot for her much-abused motorcycle, and stowed her riding gear. She walked through the mall with purpose and crossed the street to the Museum of Neon Art located beside the Glendale library and Central Park.

****

An hour later, her taxi slowed to a stop at the corner of a quiet residential street.

"Here. Thanks, just let me out here."

"Here?"

"Yes…yes, this'll be fine."

Tess paid the fare in cash and added a generous tip. After the cab pulled away, she walked three blocks to a modest, neatly kept house in the nice, unassuming neighborhood. It was her first time being there; she had the address in case of an emergency. This was an emergency. She waited a few minutes, watching from a distance to ensure it was safe and that there was no one monitoring the residence from the street. Tess continued to watch the house for some time, looking for anything untoward. Not seeing anything amiss, she eventually plucked up enough courage and discreetly knocked on the side door.

Chapter 10

A Roman God and a Magician's Sleight of Hand
2008, NASA's Helios Facility, Redstone Arsenal, Huntsville, Alabama

"Tell me what you know about Skylab," Doug Regent, in his late sixties at the time, quizzed Mike Bandy. Mike was undergoing a series of extensive indoctrination briefings while being recruited into the Helios Program.

For the past twenty years, Mike served as a United States Air Force test pilot and systems engineer at Edwards Air Force Base before joining NASA's Dryden Flight Research Center. Heavy set and square featured, Mike's thick sandy blond hair was closely cropped in a brush cut. With fair complexion and piercing blue eyes, he was good-natured and confident enough to cut his own path in life. That is what made him so good at work.

Doug had been monitoring Mike's career for a long time and had actually wanted to invite him to join the program years before, but the timing was not right. When the Berlin Wall fell in 1989, and the Cold War finally drew to a close, everyone expected a new era of peace. Budgets for national strategic capabilities were severely constrained, and remained constrained, through most of the Mid-East war period, meaning both

Gulf Wars, 9/11, and Afghanistan. The economic recession of the early 2000s did not help either. However, it was now clear that Russia still posed an existential threat to America. Although a mere shadow of the former Soviet Union, and having only the economic strength of New York State, to re-assert itself on the world stage, Russia invested in niche weapons capabilities that could strategically threaten the United States and the West, often secretly violating various arms treaties in the process. China was also ascending. Once the reality of the new world order had become clear, Helios funding was secure for the foreseeable future and Doug brought forty-two-year-old Mike Bandy in as a potential successor.

Mike responded crisply and almost automatically to Doug's question, as if reading from a cue card.

"Skylab, America's first space station, was launched in 1973 following the Apollo moon program. It was the last use of the Saturn V heavy lift rocket. Once in orbit, three Saturn 1B rocket launches carried crews of three astronauts to the station in 1973 and 1974 to conduct near Earth experiments. Saturn 1B rockets were sufficient to deliver and recover the crews because they did not need to travel to the moon and back. Skylab was very large, about eighty-three feet long and twenty-two feet in diameter at the widest point. It was comprised of a crew living and working module, an airlock with EVA hatches for space walks, a docking component with the ability to simultaneously accommodate two Apollo Command and Service Module spacecraft, a large telescope capable of multi-spectral observation, and a large solar array."

"Okay. Good. What else can you tell me?" Doug

asked, gently pushing Mike further.

Now realizing Skylab was a more important topic than originally anticipated, Doug could see Mike's eyebrows furl with added focus. While Mike took a moment to reflect, Doug could not help but be impressed by Mike's performance to date. He was obviously working very hard, and Doug was also happy to see this new opportunity seemed to be good for Mike's family as well. Doug knew a stable family life was a key ingredient for this type of employment.

Earlier on in the interview and vetting process, Mike expressed sincere gratitude for being considered for such a prestigious position. He also said the opportunity was important for Claudia, his wife. She was thrilled to be back in the south and close to family in Tennessee after spending so much time in the desert in California. She wanted their teenage daughter and son to be close to their cousins as they grew older. Family was very important. She was an amazing partner who gave up a successful career in business to raise their two children. Mike confessed he was grateful for her incredible work in nurturing and guiding their kids over the years; they had become positive, out-going, well-adjusted teenagers as a result of Claudia's skill and success as a mother.

Mike went on to explain that this move to Huntsville was emotionally difficult for the children though. Like their mother, they were excited about living closer to grandma, grandpa, and cousins, but naturally, they did not want to give up their current friends. Mike and Claudia did everything they could to facilitate maintaining links back to California through long-distance phone calls, the internet, and Skype. It helped. They also enlisted the kids' assistance in picking a school and, from there, narrowing down the neighborhood and house they wanted to live in. As a family, they approached the move like a scientific study, and Mike was pleased with everyone's engagement. This way, everyone was invested in their new home in Alabama. The kids even picked out the sports teams they wanted to join when school started.

As far as the new job went, Mike reassured Doug there would be no problem simply telling Claudia he was working on a NASA 'black' program. She knew this meant it was classified and could not be discussed. As an Air Force wife of twenty years, she knew not to ask. Like many people, Claudia was aware Huntsville was an important NASA facility; it was the site where Werner Von Braun and the other World War II German scientists helped launch the US space program and today it supported the International Space Station.

Hardly missing a beat, Mike added to the previous Skylab response.

"Well, as I recall, the mission was almost doomed from the very beginning when the micro-meteor shield opened prematurely and was damaged, along with one of the solar arrays. Although repairs were made, the damaged station was never fully capable. It was abandoned after the initial three planned missions were complete and remained unused in low Earth orbit for years. As a result of an orbit that decayed sooner than expected, it re-entered the atmosphere in 1979 after five years of disuse. I believe some larger parts hit Australia."

"Excellent, it's a good summary of the public version of events," Doug happily stated. "We'll come back to what really happened in a few minutes. But first, what do you know about the Helios Program?"

"Not much really, just what you've told me."

"Good, then our security is working," Doug said lightly, but with an undertone of seriousness. "Okay, we've spoken in general terms about what we do here, but for context, we need to look back to the 1960s and 70s when this country actually pursued two space initiatives simultaneously, one public and one highly classified. Apollo was public while Helios was, and still remains, extremely secret; even the name can't be used openly because it could trigger digging for something we do not want found."

Doug went on to explain that the name of the secret program, Helios, was expressly selected to demonstrate the close connection to Apollo. According to Greek and Roman mythology, Helios means the personification of Apollo. So, Apollo, the god of the sun and light, becomes Helios when in human form.

"You'll see how appropriate the name is as you get exposed to more details. Let's start with the broad strokes." Doug paused, as if to gather his thoughts.

He had a sparkle in his eyes and a mischievous grin.

"At its peak," Doug continued, "NASA spent almost four and a half percent of the entire federal budget and employed more than four hundred thousand people, most of whom were contractors in many different companies. With such large resources and wide distribution of discrete work elements, it was easy to hide one program inside the other and to keep the true nature of Helios secret. Think of NASA's work at the time like an onion. Apollo was the outer layers while Helios was the inner core, a program within a program. Apollo was the moon-shot intended to capture everyone's imagination and attention while Helios was designed to remain in the shadows as Kennedy's Plan B in case things went really wrong during the Cold War.

"After seventeen Apollo missions, NASA had finely honed its capabilities; there was nothing we could not do," Doug concluded. "We could send a rocket to the moon and back and pinpoint exactly where it was going to splash down in the ocean. Prior to Apollo, we could not even hit the moon with our rockets. Heck, for the longest time, we could not even get rockets off the launch pad. On the heels of Apollo, Skylab was a smashing success, but at the time it was an undertaking more complex than anything we had ever previously considered. We needed to lay the groundwork in case we didn't succeed. And, if the mission was successful, which it was, we would still need to use our cover story about the space station being plagued with problems."

Doug knew he now had Mike's full attention. "Even before Skylab launched, our communications team planted the seeds that it was cobbled together in a makeshift manner with left-over Apollo components due to deep budget cuts, and that the effort was a final gasp of the current space program before it was re-tooled to deliver the Space Shuttle. Actually, we constructed two purpose-built Skylab spacecraft, a primary, which was successfully launched, and a complete spaceworthy backup, which now sits at the Kennedy Space Center. NASA budgets remained strong until after the four Skylab missions were completed.

"Granted, in comparison to the peak funding years,

the annual budget during the Skylab period represented a much lower percentage of the overall federal budget, but they were still significantly higher than anything we have seen since. The three crewed missions that visited Skylab were actually outfitting it for its deep space mission. Their work was extremely complex and required extensive Extra Vehicular Activity. This is why, for the first time ever, we had a rescue rocket ready to launch immediately in case something went wrong, which thankfully it did not. But if you look carefully, the work and experiments the public was told were occurring in orbit were quite benign and mostly internal to the space station; they would not have required a dedicated rescue craft ready for launch at a moment's notice. If there were any issues, the astronauts could have just returned to Earth using their own re-entry vehicle. The ISS doesn't have a rescue rocket on immediate standby. It was the danger of the EVA construction work the astronauts were really doing, including the transfer of highly volatile liquids for auxiliary propulsion and life support, that necessitated this unprecedented precaution. We were also working with nuclear propulsion rockets in space for the first time."

"So, Skylab was the public 'front' for the Helios Program," Mike finally said.

"Precisely. You cannot launch a six-and-a-half million-pound rocket without people asking questions. So, we gave them Skylab. Publicly it was a product of the Apollo Applications Program and a bridge to the near-Earth work the Space Shuttle was eventually going to be doing, but in reality, it was the nuclear rocket equipped deep space vehicle to accomplish the Helios mission," Doug said with a grin. "Once the spacecraft was ready, it continued in orbit for a couple of years to ensure it was functioning properly. That explains the period of disuse, but it was a nerve-wracking time because we feared someone would discover the significant modifications made in orbit. For example, when the first two work crews were launched to prepare Skylab for its mission, they each arrived with a highly modified Service Module and an Augmentation Module. These four additional modules were added to Skylab. The third crew also added an Augmentation Module, but its Service Module carried a large radar reflector, making it look like the unmodified Skylab. When the fully modified Skylab, now called Helios, departed Earth's orbit to secretly commence its deep space mission, which also silently marked America's bi-centennial year, the third Service Module remained as its decoy. Everyone thought Skylab was still in orbit. It was part of the Service Module that eventually crash-landed in Australia."

"That is brilliant!" Mike gasped, hardly able to contain his excitement. "You know, I never could get my head around the idea NASA would have let such an incredible investment simply burn up on re-entry. It was as if they gave up too easily. They had a reputation for being able to do anything and they let Skylab go without much effort. It never did seem right," Mike said. "I guess the irony is that while some people were looking to the moon landings trying to find a conspiracy, the Skylab sleight of hand was happening right under everyone's nose."

"Now you know," Doug said, almost in a whisper.

"And it is still out there…"

"…going strong," Doug said, finishing Mike's last thought.

Chapter 11

An Unyielding Foe
2019, Southern California

Stanislav Tishchenko woke with a start, covered in sweat. Mornings like this were terrible. *It must be the cold.* The crisp mountain air was the kind where you could see your breath in the early hours. Sometimes, days like this provoked dreams of a childhood in Mother Russia. Even as an old man they were unsettling. Now fully awake in the old safehouse used by Russian intelligence, he had difficulty recalling with clarity the patchwork of early memories that still vexed him.

Trying to remember, he could see himself as a child standing alone on a train station platform. Steam and the smell of burning coal permeated the air and enveloped him. People rushed everywhere.

"There you are," a woman said. "Come on, you're going to miss your train," as she took him by the hand and led him to a carriage.

In what seemed like a blur through the eyes of a young child still in shock from the death of a loved one, he was commuted from one state official to another in rapid succession. These people were strangers, and from their lack of personal interest, it was apparent he was just another mundane task in their overworked lives. Interaction with these minders was mechanical, transactional, and without any meaningful human contact. Still reeling from the loss of his mother and the treatment from cold-hearted officials, like he was just a commodity, made him miss her even more.

"Here's your ticket. Do not lose it. Someone from the orphanage will meet you at the other end."

A tear ran down his cheek.

"Come on. No time for that. Up you go."

A solitary journey delivered him to the State Orphanage at Ulyanovsk, about 440 miles east of Moscow. It was 1959. The father he never knew, had been sent to a Siberian work camp after being convicted for trading on the black market; and when his mother passed away from illness, Stanislav was suddenly all alone in the world at eight years of age. It was a scary and emotional period of life where he was vulnerable and learned quickly how harsh things could be. At that time, the Union of Soviet Socialist Republics had a system to deal with dispossessed children, and he immediately became a ward of the state.

Gilded by the late afternoon light, Stanislav remembered how idyllic the orphanage grounds looked on arrival. The sun hung high over the endless manicured green lawns and sports fields that flowed eastward to the shores of the Volga River, which was so wide at that point it looked like a lake. The colorful collection of farms and golden wheat fields were picturesque on the opposite shore as they rose gently to low, fertile, rolling hills. Snow-topped mountains provided a protective barrier to the west.

Everything changed when darkness fell. Exhausted from the journey, Stanislav recalled falling asleep immediately after being shown to his assigned bunk. Waking with a jolt in the middle of the night, older boys were crashing through his dormitory room. He could not see them because it was so dark, but they were there.

"Here he is," one of them said, as they approached his bed space.

Before he knew it, they had a blanket over his head, and they were hitting him all over. Their faces could not be seen, nor could he see when the blows from the fists were about to land. He screamed out in protest, but no one came to help. The experience made him want to lash out in retaliation to this very day.

"Hold him, hold him," a voice that seemed to be giving all the orders said. "I want his watch."

So, they pounced upon him, stole the watch, and beat him some more.

The last thing Stanislav heard before they left, laughing as they exited the room, was, "If you tell, we'll kill you."

He laid awake the whole night, afraid they might come back. The next morning, he was disappointed that none of the orphanage staff noticed the new injuries and bruises. There was no plan to tattle, but if someone had acknowledged the pain and hugged him, like his mother would have, it would have helped a little. There was nothing. The beating was not so bad, but the watch had been a gift from his mother. It was the only possession he had, and it was the only thing that linked him to the family he had lost. From that point onward, Stanislav found it hard to fall into a deep sleep at night. Of course, the cold did not help. He remembered laying in bed night after night, shivering under a single wool blanket, wondering if he would ever be warm, and hoping the roving groups of marauding boys seeking mischief would leave him alone.

He learned from other children that the steam plant was not scheduled to produce heat until mid-October, regardless of the temperature outside. Even if it was decided to turn the heat on early, it took several weeks to ready the plant, and for the hot steam to work its way through the web of pipes that fed the many government buildings in the vicinity as well as the massive dormitory and academic blocks of the orphanage complex. When the heat did finally come, it would clang and bang its way through the radiators of the enormous and unimaginatively square concrete block buildings of the orphanage that typified post-World War II Soviet architecture. It was as if the heating system was being beaten into compliance, like students who did not fully embrace the orphanage's strict curriculum that focused on stringent obedience and complete allegiance to the Communist Party.

He had a vivid memory of the Great Hall, where a thousand orphans were fed in an hour. Partway through the lunch meal, the senior boy got up and read administrative announcements. One day stood out as different because news was also reported.

"Demonstrating superior technical ability, earlier this week our air defense forces shot down an American U-2 spy plane flying deep over Soviet territory."

The dining hall erupted in cheers as orphans began to enthusiastically pound their fists on the table. China and cutlery clattered and danced across the heavy oak tables to add to the cacophony.

In a lull in the noise, the senior boy added, "Gary

Powers, the CIA pilot, has been captured and will stand trial for crimes against the USSR."

The Great Hall erupted again. There was something about stating the name in the announcement that made it all seem so real, like they were all involved in the operation.

"That will teach those Americans," one of the older boys at Stanislav's table said. "They are so arrogant. They didn't think our missiles could fly as high as their spy planes, so they just flew over our territory whenever they chose. Not anymore. How would they like it if we flew over the US whenever we liked?"

Of course, Stanislav was only nine years old at the time and remembers just copying the actions of the older boys, but becoming older, he could see for himself how aggrieved the Soviet Union actually was at the hands of the US. With the aid of school classes, he began to realize that there was a double standard in the world, that the Americans saw themselves on the top of the international order, and they twisted the rules for their own benefit to remain supreme. They were incensed when Khrushchev tried to deploy nuclear missiles to Cuba because it threatened the United States, but they had no qualms with American missiles in Turkey intended to intimidate and gain advantage over the USSR. Khrushchev was just trying to establish an even footing, but to the Americans that was unacceptable. It was always the same with their strategic weapons. The United States developed the atomic bomb during World War II in collaboration with the UK and Canada, but would not share information with the Soviet Union, their other ally at that time. After the war, when the Soviets developed their own atomic weapon, the US, always seeking advantage, immediately introduced the more powerful hydrogen super bomb.

As a younger boy, Stanislav never understood why other people, and other nations, seemed to be oblivious to the double standards that the US perpetuated. Perhaps they benefited by riding American coattails. Capitalists did not change. He also never understood why the USSR backed down over Cuba. It made them look weak on the world stage. That situation motivated him to adopt personal life goals by committing to a struggle against the capitalist West, especially its leader the United States. He appreciated that out of necessity the USSR had entered into an unholy alliance with the West during World War II. But the West must have taken advantage of the Soviet Union during that time, since they suffered well over eight and a half million military casualties while the West had only a fraction of that number. No one counted the civilian casualties, even though those losses were far greater. He felt that the West watched as the Soviets died in droves, not wanting to get their hands bloodied to provide relief. With the fascists eliminated, the capitalists would be next, and Stanislav wanted to help make that happen. Stanislav dedicated himself completely to his self-selected ambition and soon became a model Soviet ward.

Despite the brutal, authoritarian approach employed by the orphanage, Stanislav was intelligent and able to successfully navigate the harsh environment. While younger, he kept out of the crosshairs of the staff during the day and older boys bent on torturing others for fun at night. Growing older, he learned how to manipulate people without giving himself away. The orphanage provided both structure for life and expectations. Continuing to grow, he liked the environment even more because there were goals and objectives to work toward. In class, he demonstrated a particular zeal for politics and world issues. After class and at night, he now led the terror group instilling fear in the younger wards.

At sixteen, he transferred to the Suvorov Military School at Kazan, just over one hundred miles directly north of the orphanage. Two years later, he joined the relatively newly formed Strategic Rocket Forces.

At twenty-five, Stanislav had been recruited into the ranks of the KGB. A few years prior, Yury Andropov, the KGB Chairman, had expanded the teams targeting US missile and space programs. At that time, the failed American misadventure into Vietnam was winding to a close and nuclear weapons parity between the globe's only superpowers, the United States and Soviet Union, had been a reality for many years. Bombers from both sides were on constant alert, along with ballistic missiles deployed in submarines, fixed land bases, and mobile launchers. Minefields lined the Iron Curtain that divided Europe into the Eastern and Western camps. Both sides were spring-loaded for military action at a moment's notice. If the first salvo was launched, there would be enough nuclear armaments exchanged to obliterate the opposition many times over. The arsenals were so large, it was impossible for one superpower to use a pre-emptive strike to prevent the other from retaliating with enough force to eliminate the instigator.

An uneasy deadlock persisted where any strategic

nuclear action would have resulted in what was commonly referred to as Mutually Assured Destruction, or MAD. It was MAD to think even school children of the day were aware of this barbaric concept and accepted it as the way of a normal world. Atomic scientists continued to warn everyone of the danger we were all in by setting their fictitious Doomsday Clock closer and closer to midnight, which they denoted as the time when a self-inflicted catastrophic event would extinguish human life on Earth. They were not wrong. Any misstep would have initiated an unstoppable cataclysmic chain of events.

Stanislav remembered the uneasy tension at the time as both superpowers came to terms with the strategic nuclear arms equilibrium. It was as if neither party knew how to act. For a while, a policy of polite détente was pursued; it was intended to lead from mutual engagement, to better understanding, and eventually to acceptance of co-existence. In space the Soviet Soyuz and American Apollo capsules linked for almost two days as a visible gesture of the new era of cooperation. But everyone knew the Americans would never accept the Soviet Union as an equal. The Americans continued to refuse to agree to the Soviet proposal of a non-first use of nuclear weapons.

Yuri Andropov was convinced the Americans somehow planned to use Skylab to gain an advantage over the Soviet Union and directed the KGB to use all resources to find the evidence. Stanislav had first come to the United States as part of a team infiltrating the American space and strategic weapons programs. The work was great because, finally, he was able to contribute directly to helping the Soviet Union in the struggle with the United States, but every second in America was agonizing. He was surrounded by people swimming in consumer goods, who were oblivious to how difficult their government, and other so-called democracies, made life for the rest of the world. The decadence and opulence were pervasive, oppressive even, and afflicted every aspect of life. Simple things became needlessly complicated.

"All I wanted was toothpaste," Stanislav lamented to a colleague who was also stationed at the Soviet Embassy in Washington. "It's not simple like at home. Here you need to choose a brand from a half dozen different companies who all make toothpaste, each of them vying for your attention through fancy advertising and packaging, and all claiming to be better than their competitors. If that was not bad enough, each company makes several types of specialty toothpaste to satisfy specific consumer issues and likes. The excesses complicate every aspect of life. Analysis and decision making is required for every mundane thing you want to do. And then you need to decide which brand of gasoline to put in the car, the brand of cigarettes to smoke, the matches or lighter to use."

"The world is funny. It seems there are either too many choices, or not enough," the colleague observed.

"But it's never-ending here. Clothes, household goods, food, even deciding what store to shop at is difficult since they all sell the same goods."

Stanislav was constantly weighing options and trying to figure out the gimmick. There was always a ploy in the West. Nothing was clear, simple, and transparent. There was always something they were not telling you. He believed all this consumerism distracted soft and spoiled citizens from seeing what was really happening in the world and prevented them from focusing on the important issues. They were all mesmerized by sales and new colors available on products they did not need.

Happily, work was a reprieve from everyday living. The KGB tried everything to gain insight into the US secret strategic programs. They employed sleeper agents, tried to recruit Americans inside clandestine programs, used electronic equipment to eavesdrop on conversations, employed blackmail…the list went on. You name it, they tried it. American overreliance on contractors made it easy to penetrate some of their classified programs. Even though they insisted on strict security during the hiring and employment process, nobody followed up on employees let go when projects were completed or delivered. The KGB went as far as to scoop up ex-employees by hiring them to work in "front companies" that pretended to be part of the US defense-industrial complex. They would then give the former employees tasks similar to their previous work. It was amazing how many of them would simply repurpose what they had done in their previous jobs.

Although nothing was ever discovered about Skylab, a few years later, one of the initiatives they launched stumbled across unusual activity. NASA was periodically sending obscure coded messages out to space and Soviet agents could not correlate this communication to any known spacecraft. Had the US secured the ultimate high ground by placing a nuclear weapon in space, one beyond Soviet reach? Was this a modern Gary Powers U-2 operation? Stanislav would not have put it past them. Earlier Soviet intelligence work had revealed that in the late 1950s when the US was losing the space race, they had a Top Secret project to detonate a nuclear bomb on the moon in order to demonstrate their continued supremacy to the American people, and also serve to as a warning to the USSR. NASA's unexplained communications out into space re-oriented KGB efforts, but the shroud of secrecy was immense. The Soviets were convinced more than ever there was something incredibly important behind these strange signals.

From the calm of the safehouse, Stanislav recalled the foreboding cracks that started to appear in the international order just as espionage efforts towards NASA and the U.S. Air Force intensified. It should have been a warning of darker days to come. When the Communist government in Afghanistan asked for Soviet assistance to prevent collapse against a tide of religious zealots, the United States did everything in its power to aid the rebels. Then Ronald Reagan pushed for cruise missiles as a way around nuclear arms limitation treaties. Then came the production of neutron bombs designed to kill people but leave equipment and infrastructure relatively untouched. The Strategic Defense Initiative followed, the infamous Star Wars Program, designed to further upset the equilibrium paradigm by defeating any Soviet missile launched against the United States. Just as Khrushchev blinked during the Cuban Missile Crisis, Reagan's unanticipated armament push caught the Soviet Union off guard and forced Gorbachev to recognize American economic and military supremacy. Stanislav remembers being ashamed for the Soviet Union and wondered why it was cursed with weak leadership at critical junctures in history; it was as if the capitalists knew it and purposely took advantage. Regardless of strong feelings about those in power, he knew it would be his doom to ever show an ounce of disloyalty.

Rather than responding to the American challenge by refining areas in the Soviet system that may be deficient, Gorbachev became beguiled by the West and tried to emulate it. The radical changes initiated ultimately perpetrated the complete economic collapse of the Soviet Union in the 1990s. Stanislav detested Mikhail Gorbachev; his naivety, and lack of vision and determination led to the destruction of the USSR. The ideas of Glasnost and Perestroika contaminated the Communist system. The Union of Soviet Socialist Republics broke apart and many former republics and independent countries in the Eastern Camp and aligned to the USSR through the Warsaw Pact, the Soviet counterbalance to NATO, defected to the West. It was turbulent and unsettling.

When the USSR collapsed, Stanislav and fellow agents were recalled home. It was a scary time. It seemed everyone was on their own. In a world where the Soviet state had been everything, it simply crumbled away so quickly. Stanislav had felt like a vulnerable eight-year-old boy once again. He was married to his work and had no other family. For a second time in life, he felt completely exposed, but consoled himself and reasoned that he was luckier than most. Older people who relied on a state pension found the value of the money they received plummeted, while the costs of the necessities they required skyrocketed. It was like being in the middle of a stampede as everyone scrambled to look after themselves.

Russia's short experiment with democracy proved the system was not so great after all. Now the country was firmly in the grasp of a few extremely powerful and rich men, oligarchs, who satisfied their interests by making up their own rules and using force to get what they wanted. Most of these "*nouveaux riches*" made their fortunes by plundering what had rightfully belonged to the old Soviet Union and then Russia. Over time, the chaos began to slowly subside. Despite all the challenges of the past, and her economic near-death experience, Russia was now becoming stronger every day through tenacity and wisdom. Stanislav revered President Vladimir Putin, who demonstrated calm and resolve in re-establishing order and in standing up to the West. Evidently, the KGB was a good training ground to lead the nation. Putin was clearly interested in re-asserting Russia's presence on the world stage, and Stanislav admired the goal. Once again it could challenge the United States for world influence.

Stanislav quietly peered out the safehouse bedroom window, surveying the road and grounds below. Despite the unpleasant memories and everything that had happened, he was pleased to be back in the United States to continue important work after years of hiatus. Even though the team and resources now were minuscule, insufficient even, compared to what the Soviet Union had fielded, the prey was far less suspecting. The mission had not changed - to discover the purpose of those secret coded messages NASA still transmitted deep into space. He wondered how far away the spacecraft was that they were communicating with. They were still in contact with their Voyager 1 probe outside the solar system, so the secret craft, if it existed at all, could be anywhere. There was also a possibility this was just an elaborate 'spoof,' and these transmissions were designed to fool would-be foreign intelligence agents into thinking there was something out there. However, the stolen communications device seemed to indicate otherwise. It had proven impervious to X-ray, and to disassembly, but there were years of previous messages that had been intercepted, and they could now be decoded to learn what was going on.

Stanislav and his new team had another advantage over the old Soviet days. They had recently acquired a mole deep inside NASA. In fact, it was this insider who had tipped them off about the communication device being transported.

No specifics were provided, just the comment, "Something very unusual was going to happen at JPL in a couple of weeks."

This simple, innocuous indication was all Stanislav needed. By focusing other surveillance assets on JPL and aggregating the indications they received, he rapidly obtained a good sense of the plan to move the communications gear. Stanislav concluded, smiling to himself, that there would need to be some energy put into further developing the new asset inside NASA.

Lost deep in contemplation about the next steps, Stanislav recognized the uncomfortable cool of the morning, which seemed to cut right through to the bone, would soon give way to oppressive heat later in the day. For now, he silently reveled in the success of the brazen high-risk robbery while walking behind the house and barn of the high-country ranch safehouse near Millersville, just to the east of Bakersfield,

California.

Taking in the surrounding light brown mountains splotched with patches of dark green trees, he continued to consider the situation. They had just kicked over a hornet's nest and the Americans would mobilize all their resources to recover what had been taken. They had no idea his next move would take the legs right out from under them, and this would provide the breathing space to focus on discovering what was behind the secret equipment. If it was a weapon, Stanislav swore to himself that it would be used to threaten the US. If that were not possible, then it would be set on a trajectory to burn up in the sun or crash into a planet. At least that way, it could not be used to imperil his beloved homeland. This had been a long time in the making.

Chapter 12

Time To Regroup

It was a little past 10:00 p.m. and Tess wondered if Caleb was even home, or if so, would he even hear the knocks on the side door? After no response, she knocked again, this time with more determination. *Sounds like there's rustling inside.* Then the side light of the modest bungalow came on. The door opened ajar, just enough for Tess to see Caleb's troubled eyes. Not waiting for the door to fully open, she unexpectedly rushed in and hugged him. Tess even surprised herself. After being fierce and indomitable following repeated attempts on her life, seeing a familiar person in a safe place opened a flood of emotions. Embarrassed, she started to tear up. It felt so lonely and isolated in the desert being chased. This on top of a short-notice move to Huntsville, and then being sent to L.A. before even getting settled. She had been living out of a suitcase for months now, working a vitally important new job that was becoming increasingly problematic as time went on. Even Tess's mother did not understand the reason for taking a position in Alabama, prodding as to how she was ever going to meet anyone there. In an instant, all the stress and frustration, which had stoically been held back for weeks and weeks, came rushing out uncontrollably.

"It's okay, Tess, you're okay, I'm here with you," Caleb said, holding her firmly in his arms and gently stroking her hair.

Tess sobbed. She felt secure and protected in his embrace. He held her for a long time before she was able to recount what had happened. She told about narrowly escaping the ambush, getting away by racing through the desert, and thinking it was finally safe only to be chased again along the highway entering L.A.

Tess knew she was lucky to be alive, especially after pushing her bike so dangerously. *Speed was my only chance of escape. One moment of misjudgement and the assassins' work would have been done for them.*

"I was so worried," Caleb said, finally loosening his hold. "I'm just glad you're safe, it's all that matters."

Caleb described waiting at the office until after 8:45 p.m., the many calls to her phone with no answer, and how the contact at Goldstone said she left in the middle of the afternoon. There were no reports of motorcycle accidents along the route. He confessed how helpless and worried he had felt and how he regretted not insisting more strongly that she take his car. Finally, after alerting highway patrol, he said there was nothing else that could be done, so he reluctantly came home.

"After telling me what happened," Caleb continued, "I feel I abandoned you."

"But you were right. At the time, there was nothing you could have done. Who would have anticipated such an attack?"

"Well, it's now clear we're under surveillance. Our

phones may even be compromised. This is extremely unusual. Mostly, when a crime is committed, the perpetrators go into hiding, hoping not to get caught by drawing further attention to themselves. Obviously, there is something very different going on here," Caleb offered. "Perhaps the investigation is getting close, and this was an attempt to slow things down. Whoever these people are, they must be good if they know who you are."

Tess winced.

"What does all this mean? If it is unusual for criminals to behave this way, surely, we need to approach things differently," she said.

"Absolutely. These attacks are persistent, almost military in precision. Recognizing the tactics is the first step," Caleb said. His eyes met hers. "We're going to need to be careful and assume we're being watched at all times."

Drawing comfort from his confidence, she tried to relax a little, knowing it was okay for the moment.

"I'm sorry to ask, but would it be all right if I took a quick shower? I'm still covered with dust and sand from the desert. I must look a mess."

"No. You look fine. But the bathroom is down the hall, on the right. There are clean towels in the linen closet."

As the hot water flowed over her from head to toe, Tess could feel the fears and worries wash away. Standing still, absorbing the heat from the shower, she would not deny it had been a harrowing day. At the same time, she was proud of her reaction. When presented with the most challenging situation in her life, she did not fold, but rose to the occasion.

Tess toweled off and slipped into the tee-shirt, gym shorts, and bathrobe Caleb had neatly piled outside the door. She emerged from the bathroom, physically and mentally refreshed. Entering the kitchen, Caleb handed her a glass of wine.

"Feeling better?"

"Yes, one hundred percent. Thanks, I needed that."

"No worries. Dinner in five? I don't suppose you stopped to eat while you were speeding through the desert?"

"That sounds really nice. I didn't even think about food until I smelled your handiwork. If I knew you were such a good cook, I would have made an excuse to come over much sooner."

Tess smiled.

"Caleb, thank you for everything. I'm really sorry for showing up unannounced like this, I just didn't know where else to go or what to do."

She pulled the terrycloth tie more tightly around her waist, feeling self-conscious about standing in Caleb's kitchen wearing his clothes and bathrobe.

"Don't be silly, we're partners. You did exactly what you should have done."

Before long, Caleb had laid out dinner and the two of them sat down to eat. Tess was surprised at her hunger. For a time, they ate in silence, each immersed in their own thought.

"You must be an incredible analyst, otherwise NASA would not have sent you," Caleb finally said. "Tess, I deeply admire and respect what did out there…"

"I'm sensing a but."

"No. No buts. Just a consideration. I know you

have been very careful when leaving the Fed Building to ensure you're not followed home at the end of the day, but after what happened today, we need to assume we are being targeted. You should stay here tonight. The guest room down the hall is made up. Tomorrow I'd like to make arrangements for us to move to a safehouse. We know these guys are professionals, they clearly have lots of resources, and they're dangerous."

"I really don't want to give up the little piece of paradise I found in Beachwood," Tess responded, "but I agree."

After dinner, Caleb telephoned for a squad car to be stationed outside the house for the night. Tess felt relieved, and although it was now quite late, she wanted to know about his day and the investigation at JPL.

"Aren't you sleepy?" Caleb asked.

"Oh, no. I'm too wound up," Tess replied, as they both settled into comfortable chairs in the living room.

Caleb explained that while he conducted interviews, the FBI National Security Branch IT team continued checking phones and computers. They focused their efforts on those identified on the first list that JPL Director Coombs had compiled. Those were the people who knew of the safe, but perhaps not its contents, or had an association with Walter Poulin, who came from Huntsville every year to check on the secret communications equipment. Caleb put a priority on Poulin and those who interacted with him.

"I'm not sure if it's correct, but my instincts lead me in that direction."

"Well, Poulin was technically the only person who was supposed to know what was in the safe," Tess said. "So, your approach makes sense."

"Exactly," Caleb responded. "He would be a prime target for espionage if some country out there had NASA's space program under a microscope. And if it wasn't a matter of international intrigue, but something baser like prestige or money, Poulin still figures prominently as a central suspect."

"How's that?"

"Just imagine the safe," Caleb gently responded, repositioning himself to get more comfortable in the lounge chair. "Valuables or secrets are usually put inside, left, and often forgotten. However, in this case, along comes Poulin every year to remind folks he knows a secret that is right under their noses, but they can't be trusted with it. Naturally, they would be curious to find out what it was. And if they forgot about it, he would be back again the following year to remind them. The annual visits would continuously rejuvenate their interest, maybe play on their subconscious, and perhaps get them thinking about how they could possibly benefit from the secret."

"Okay, I see what you're thinking."

"I'm convinced this whole thing hinges on Poulin, or someone close to him. You know how people talk. The business with the safe could have easily been picked up by a foreign agent who had infiltrated JPL. It would just be a matter of time. Or maybe it wasn't a foreign agent in JPL, but someone in JPL being exploited by a foreign agent. In any event, it had to be a connection that was well-established. The idea of moving the communications equipment only occurred three weeks before the theft, and therefore it had to be someone who was watching, and interested, for a long time. I think the timing probably eliminates those on the second list, the people just involved in the move."

Caleb explained that for people on the second list, there would not have been sufficient time for a spy to learn about the safe, signal their handlers about the opportunity, get approval, and then commence preparations for the Angeles Forest Highway attack.

"It has to be someone who had routine, longstanding contact with Poulin, either as a foreign agent or connected to a foreign agent."

"What about Walter Poulin himself—any flags there?" Tess queried.

"The Huntsville FBI Field Office is doing a deep dive into his background, while I focus more on the people who connect to him here at JPL."

Caleb divulged that although Poulin was married, he had a girlfriend at JPL, Krista Maguire. Krista was part of George Sibley's administration staff and looked after organizing the California portion of Poulin's visits. He would perform the equipment inspection and then would visit his sister who lived in Borrego Springs, a small artist town of 1,500 people about a three-hour drive southeast of L.A. The town was known for its privacy, theater, art, and especially for oversized iron sculptures out in the surrounding desert. After visiting Borrego, Poulin and Krista, who were both in their early thirties, would often rent a vacation home for a week on the nearby Salton Sea.

Aside from the morality aspect, technically Poulin was not breaking any laws, but it still did not sit well with Caleb who remained suspicious; if a man lied to a loved one, then what else was he capable of lying about? The FBI was drilling into every aspect of Poulin and Krista's past and Caleb said he could not wait to see what the IT team was going to come up with. He concluded the summary of the day's events by stating that there were also a couple of other leads from interviews that needed to be rundown but likened it to Daniel LeBlanc and the forensic team's work; they were laying out the facts. Caleb said something was sure to eventually pop.

Tess acknowledged the progress being made, and while it was a long, frightening day, she was still not ready to retreat to her room. *Finally, I'm starting to unwind.*

"Tell me a story," Tess said with just a hint of a smile. "I really need something to take my mind off all this."

"Still trying to avoid sleep," Caleb countered. "You're going to be tired tomorrow, especially after the day you had."

"I know, just one story?"

"Okay, you're on. What would you like to hear about?"

"I don't know, something that takes place far from here. Something refreshingly different. You're a hockey guy. Tell me about…the greatest hockey game ever played."

"Well…the answer to that question could be in the eye of the beholder."

"So,…it's not clear which one is the greatest, or you're not sure?"

"Hey, those are fightin' words."

Tess grinned widely.

"If you really want to know, there's probably about half a dozen games that could be considered the greatest ever, including the Miracle on Ice.

"I've heard that expression before."

"Yeah, a bunch of unknown college players from all over the US came together for the 1980 Lake Placid Winter Olympics and defeated the reigning four-time Soviet gold medal champions."

"Yes. It sounds familiar."

"Then there's the 2002 Olympic Gold Medal Games at Salt Lake City, which featured the US and Canadian men's and women's teams, both vying for gold."

"So, sort of a two for one situation."

"Exactly. But, if I had to pick the greatest of all time, I would say it was the last game of the Summit Super Series played between Team Canada and the Soviet Red Army in Moscow in 1972."

"The Summit Super Series?"

"Yes, this was before my time, but I guess this series was decades in the making. Apparently, the whole of Canada held its breath during the last game and most Canadians my parents' age can tell you exactly where they were when the game was being played. Living close to the border, my dad was completely captivated. He paid a king's ransom for a VHS recording of the entire series; my brothers and I watched it time and again when we were growing up. My mom was furious. She thought it was expensive and frivolous. We loved it though. Watching this as a kid was electrifying, even without knowing the back story."

"You're really into this."

"Are you teasing me?"

"No. I've never heard this before. So, what makes this particular game so great compared to all the others?"

"Besides the exceptional playing, it's the decades of buildup to the series, the East—West Cold War tensions of the time, the professionals versus amateurs, the wrangling that went on behind the scenes to come to an agreed format, the dirty tricks that were played and the willingness of two nations to put their pride on the line for the whole world to judge. Ultimately, though, it's a story about never giving up. All together this makes the series incredible, and the best of all time, especially the last game."

"It really does sound fascinating," Tess admitted. Caleb gave her a look. "I'm serious. Tell me more."

"It's an amazing story and it goes beyond this series. My dad used to say it provided a window into the Cold War and the ruthless lengths and deception the Soviets applied to win at all costs, which applied to all facets of their international relations, not just hockey."

"Interesting," Tess said, leaning in. "Maybe it's something about the psyche. We see hints of the same behavior in modern-day Russia."

"And maybe we're seeing shades of this in our case, with the relentlessness and brutality."

"That would explain a lot."

A moment passed.

"So…the game," Tess gently prodded. "You've got me really curious now."

"Right. Well, I didn't know this, but apparently hockey is not native to Russia, or at the time, the Soviet Union. They played a game called bandy, which is like field hockey on ice with skates. Maybe that is why the Brits always say ice hockey instead of just hockey. Anyway, in the 1920s or '30s, the Soviets started to purposely transition to what was then known as

Canadian style hockey because it had been adopted at the international level as the standard for competition. Eventually, the Soviet intent, as in many sports, was to demonstrate the superiority of the communist system on the international stage, and to do so they focused their energies on developing skilled hockey players. Notwithstanding, the Canadians dominated the sport from the 1920s into the '50s where the Olympics served triple duty because they were also recognized as the European and World Championships.

"As the sport became more popular, the best Canadians joined professional leagues, especially the National Hockey League, and were precluded from playing in the Olympics. The Canadians protested that the Soviet Red Army were really professionals, since their only job was to play hockey and they got paid for it; but the Olympic governing committees took a narrow interpretation of what it was to be an amateur and ruled against the Canadians, who were then prevented from sending their best to the Olympics. That began the period of Soviet Red Army dominance in international hockey."

"How is it you know all this?"

"I don't know. I guess I'm a real fan of this series. Anyway, for decades, hockey fans around the world speculated on who was truly better, Canadian professionals or Soviet 'amateur' players, but there was no mechanism for them to compete against each other to find out. They also speculated on the two very different styles of play, the Canadian one being more freewheeling individual skill based, and much rougher, while the Soviet approach was rooted in strict disciplined team play. The debate about which was better raged for years. Then the Soviets floated the idea of a series to settle the dispute once and for all."

"Uh-oh. Beware."

"Exactly. In 1972 the two countries agreed to an eight-game series, but in retrospect, just like you, many people now think this was a Soviet setup to humiliate Western hockey and its professional players on the international stage. The NHL was mostly comprised of Canadian players, the majority of whom played for U.S. teams and were paid in U.S. dollars, so they were seen as the ultimate capitalist mercenaries by the communist regime."

"Were the Canadians suspicious at the time?"

"I'm not sure, but I think at the time there was great confidence they would prevail."

"So how did it go?"

"Well, the first four games of the series were played in various cities in Canada, and the last four in the Soviet Union. Because it was really a deal between Hockey Canada, the NHL and the Soviets, players who had signed with the newly formed World Hockey League, like Bobby Hull, or those in the midst of contract negotiations who had not fully committed to the NHL were not permitted to play. Right away, this eliminated four top-ranked Canadian players."

"There's always technicalities."

"The Soviets certainly squeezed out every advantage possible. There was also the issue of timing; the series started in September to minimize the impact on the NHL season. In those days, the professional players essentially took the summer off and used their team training camps to get back into shape for the next season, while the Soviets trained year-round. In advance of this series, the Soviets trained extra hard. Their coach even had players take boxing lessons to prepare for the fighting style of Canadian play. So, the scene was set."

"Exciting."

"In North America, there was no doubt that the professionals would quickly demonstrate their supremacy and to the delight of hockey fans across Canada, thirty seconds after the puck dropped in Montreal for the first game, Phil Esposito, Team Canada's unofficial Captain, drew first blood with a goal. However, by the time the game was over, the Red Army had won seven to three. A humiliating defeat. The Canadians soundly took the next game four to one in Toronto but tied in Winnipeg and lost again in Vancouver. The hometown Vancouver fans even 'booed' Team Canada. The Soviets complained about biased American referees but came away from the first part of the series on top with two wins and a tie versus one win and a tie for the Canadians. It was not looking like the cakewalk Canadians and everyone else in the West expected."

"Then…?"

"Well, then the series moved to Moscow, where all four of the next games would be played. The off ice dirty tricks really ratcheted up in an attempt to keep the Canadians off their stride."

"Like what kind of dirty tricks?"

"People called the rooms of the players in the middle of the night in order to break their sleep pattern. Food specifically flown over from North America for Team Canada disappeared between the airport and the hotel where they were staying, stuff like that."

"Huh."

"The Canadians gave a good showing in the first game, leading three to zero after two periods, but ultimately the Red Army prevailed five to four. Nonetheless, the three thousand rabid Canadian fans who followed their team to Moscow, boisterously cheered throughout the game and defiantly sang "O Canada" as their players left the ice. This type of raucous hockey fan behavior was new to the Soviets, and they were worried by the unruly crowd. But, despite the fan support, Canada was on the ropes. They needed to win the next three games straight in order to win the series. Against all odds, including some very obviously biased officiating on behalf of a pair of East German referees who clearly favored the Soviets, the Canadians won the next two games.

"In Game Six, for example, the Canadians were handed thirty-one minutes in penalties compared to four minutes for the Red Army. The Canadians got their revenge though, scoring three goals in the space of a minute and a half. Also, by this point in the series, they had skated themselves back into top physical condition. It all came down to Game Eight. Then things really got crazy."

"Oh, my goodness, how much crazier could things get?"

"Oh, it got really crazy. It seems the Soviets, who must have been embarrassed at how openly biased the two East German refs were, had already agreed to take them out of the lineup for future games, but for Game Eight they tried to re-insert them into the roster. The Canadians refused to play if those referees were going to officiate the game. The Soviets relented and a compromise was struck where one of the two was permitted to officiate, but as a further slight, the Soviets canceled a pre-game ceremony where the Canadians were going to present a totem pole as a gift to the Soviet Union to mark the historic matchup. The Canadians politely informed their hosts that despite the itinerary change, the totem pole would be carried to center ice as planned and the Soviets could choose to either accept it or skate around it during the game. Of course, the game was televised worldwide so the Soviets were backed into a corner."

"Emotions must have been high."

"They must have been. Finally, the game started. There were some very poor calls made by the refs against the Canadians. One Canadian player got so angry about the obvious bias from the official that the Soviets got reinserted into the game, he threatened to swing a hockey stick at the official's head. When he got tossed out of the game, the Canadian coach threw a chair out onto the ice in protest. At one point in the first period, there were two Canadian players in the penalty box. Then, things seemed to settle down and the refereeing was pretty reasonable for the remainder of the match. The two sides focused on playing the game. The first period was tense but ended in a two-two tie."

"And how did the rest of the game go? I'm dying from anticipation."

"So, in the second period, the Soviets pulled ahead five to three, but by the end, the Canadians had scored another goal. They were down one going into the final period of the game and the series. With about ten minutes left in the game, the Canadian coach noticed the Soviets had changed their style. They were now playing very defensively, trying to protect their lead. This was a big mistake because the Canadians were mostly an offensive team. Yvan Cournoyer, nicknamed the roadrunner because nobody could catch him, scored to tie up the game. But the Soviet goal judge refused to turn on the goal light. Allan Eagleson, the head of the Canadian delegation, charged toward the goal judge and was intercepted by police who roughed him up so hard he had the bruises the next day to prove it; the police were intent on dragging him out of the arena. Meanwhile, the quick-thinking Canadian coach cleared the bench and sent the players out on the ice to celebrate the goal to embarrass the Soviets into acknowledging publicly the game was now tied up. The judge relented and turned on the goal light. Then, some Canadian players out on the ice realized the peril Eagleson was in, hopped the boards, climbed up into the stands in their skates, and beat the police back with their sticks. For protection, they then escorted Eagleson out onto the ice and to the safety of their bench."

"That's insane."

"I know, totally wild. It looked like the series might end in a tie, but the Soviets then announced that if it did, they would claim victory because according to international rules for breaking ties, the total goals scored were counted and they had scored one more goal in the series than the Canadians."

"It seems it's never-ending with them."

"Exactly. You could feel the electricity in the air. Soldiers with guns were dispatched throughout the arena to keep the raucous crowd in check. With less than a minute remaining, Cournoyer sped down the wing and shot. Paul Henderson, near the Soviet goal, took a wild swing to try and redirect Cournoyer's shot but missed and fell behind the net as the play moved on. Henderson jumped to his feet while Esposito got the puck and fired. The Soviet goalie made the save but by this time Henderson was all alone in front of the net. Henderson recovered Esposito's rebound and shot, it too was blocked, but he recovered the rebound again, and with thirty-four seconds left in the game, he sunk the puck deep into the Soviet net. All mayhem broke out. Against all expectations, the Canadians had refused to concede. They played through all the conniving and trickery and returned home victorious."

"That's incredible. It's the most amazing sports story I've ever heard."

"You should see the video. They were mobbed by thousands of crazed fans when they landed back at the Montreal airport. Phil Esposito, the informal Canadian leader, who started his professional career playing for your hometown Chicago Black Hawks, earned the most points of all players in the series."

"It seems this encounter was more than a game or a series."

"You're exactly right. It quickly became much more than the hockey competition originally advertised. It came to represent the ongoing aggressive struggle between East and West that permeated everything at the time. Beyond hockey, the Soviets, now the Russians, to this day deny losing the space race. Just like the international rules for breaking ties, they count the number of firsts they achieved compared to us and claim more victories than we do. The fact that we won the ultimate prize of being first to safely get to the moon and back does not register with them. Or so they say. Strange, uh?"

"Thank you, Caleb, for an amazing story, and with such detail. You really are a very good narrator."

"My pleasure."

"I am wondering why I never heard of the series before?"

"Well, I guess if you are not of that generation, a hockey aficionado, or Canadian, it's understandable you may not have heard of it."

"Thank you again for taking such good care of me. I completely forgot about today's drama when you had me immersed in the fervor of the hockey rink in Moscow, but I must confess I'm now really struggling to keep my eyes open."

"So, it seems I'm not such a good storyteller after all, since my entire audience is falling asleep."

Tess smiled, then stifled a yawn.

"Okay, let's get you settled," Caleb said, rising to his feet and then leading Tess toward the kitchen. "The guest room is just down the hall, second door on the left. I'll be right across the hall so don't worry; in addition to the car outside, I'll be sleeping with one eye open."

Tess felt more reassured by his focus on security.

"Thank you, Caleb. I'm not sure what I would have done without your help."

After a slight hesitation, he managed to say, "No problem." Then added, "I'm just so grateful everything turned out all right in the end."

"Yes. Me too. See you in the morning."

"Yes. See you in the morning."

Tess padded down the hall and closed the guest room door behind her. She could hear Caleb in the living room making sure the squad car was outside.

If the perpetrators of the Angeles Forest Highway attack are now targeting the investigating team, we need to be more careful from this moment onward.

Chapter 13

Something Finally Pops

Carmelo appeared both concerned and curious when a team of FBI agents descended on his establishment. Other than a few robberies and some vandalism, nothing ever happened in this neighborhood, certainly nothing that would warrant the FBI showing up.

"Have I done something wrong?"

"Mr. Carmelo?"

"Yes, can I help you?"

"I'm Daniel LeBlanc, I called earlier about returning auto paint and spray equipment."

"Oh, I thought you were an actual customer."

"Yes, well, we tend not to get full cooperation when we identify ourselves as FBI, people tend to shut down."

"So…you're actually looking for the guy who purchased the paint and spray equipment!?"

"Correct."

"Well, let's see, I remember that like it was yesterday," Carmelo said opening a large well-worn ledger.

Carmelo's Autobody and Repair shop was a small, old-style four-bay garage wedged in between two other light industrial enterprises and surrounded by numerous dilapidated red brick low-rise apartment buildings dating back to the early 1900s. It had been in the family for three generations. The parking lot in front of the garage was far too small and cars left for repairs were constantly jockeyed around as they were brought in for maintenance. Carmelo and his mechanics did good work and treated their customers fairly who in turn rewarded them with their loyalty. This meant the lot in front of the garage was always overflowing with double and triple-parked vehicles, just to get them off the street.

Stepping inside the garage was like stepping back to the 1950s. Other than the bright 'trouble lights' used in the bays, the overhead interior lights were dim and somber. The light fixtures betrayed the telltale signs of dead flies, and every surface was covered in a light film, which was most likely motor oil. Even the air seemed heavy and had an indistinguishable 'perfumey' industrial solvent smell that could not be healthy to inhale. It was the kind of place where you did not want to sit down. How the garage passed the health and safety requirements, or modern environmental standards, was always a question never raised by the patrons who were happy with quality low-cost repairs. Perhaps Carmelo and the business were 'grandfathered' and fell under older standards, or perhaps the modern world had completely forgotten about this business, just as it seemed to have forgotten about this entire, once vibrant, part of the city. These previously sought-after addresses had been in a state of chronic disrepair and decline for decades.

Continuing to thumb through the ledger, Carmelo tried to determine the exact date of the sale the FBI agents were asking about.

"It was an unusual order. The guy wasn't a regular customer. He called a few days before looking for specific colors, application equipment, a compressor, tape, and paper for masking. Here it is, four weeks ago, a cash transaction. The name here says Al Popovich. I remember he spoke with a thick accent, sounded Eastern European, or maybe Russian. I'm not sure."

"Was he one of these guys?" Daniel asked, showing Carmelo five different photos.

Four of the five photos were just random pictures, but one was of a suspect who had recently purchased a couple of Toyota Highlanders days before the attack on Caleb's team. Carmelo briefly surveyed the photos.

"There, that's him," he said, pointing a stubby grease-covered index finger at one of the pictures.

Got ya, Daniel thought to himself while exhaling.

"You don't happen to have any video surveillance."

"No, sorry, our security system is a Doberman on a chain and one of the apprentice mechanics who lives in the apartment above the garage."

"Okay, can you help us narrow down the time of day?"

"Yeah, it was right after lunch. The guy was driving a black full-size Chevy SUV…a Tahoe, I think."

It matches the description of one of the vehicles that chased Tess yesterday on the highway.

"Okay Mr. Carmelo, you have been very helpful. Is there anything else that might help us find this person? Was he with anyone?"

"No, he was alone. Hey, what did he do?"

Daniel did not answer.

"Ya can't fault a guy for tryin'," Carmelo finally said. "After all, this is the most exciting thing to happen around here in a long time."

"He's very dangerous and wanted for questioning regarding a recent crime. If you see him, don't say anything, just give me a call. Here's my card."

All of Daniel's instincts told him Carmelo was not involved, and it was unlikely the suspect would come back to the garage. With a date and time for the black SUV, Daniel fanned out his team to canvass other businesses along the main access routes looking for video surveillance.

Chapter 14

Finally, Something Concrete

As another day drew to a close, Caleb was ready to leave the office in the Fed Building. He was just finishing up some routine paperwork while waiting for Tess, who was in a temporary office down the hall making her normal end of day call to Doug back in Huntsville. Knowing that he and Tess had covered a lot of ground, Caleb was very satisfied with how things had transpired during the past nine hours but was admittedly tired. The first thing in the morning he had called a quick impromptu team huddle to ensure everyone was up to speed with the latest information, including the attempt on Tess's life out in the desert. Then, he and Tess continued interviewing people at JPL. During lunch, access to a safehouse normally used by the FBI's counterintelligence team was arranged. It was now about five o'clock in the afternoon, and Caleb was finding it hard to concentrate on the most menial tasks. Normally long days were not an issue, but everyone had pushed hard the past week and he was looking forward to packing it in a bit early today. As soon as Tess was finished, they would head out to the safehouse using a different car and an indirect route. Just as Caleb was thinking these thoughts, a soft yet insistent knock came on the partly closed office door.

Finally, Tess is ready to go. He leaped up from the desk, and grabbed his jacket and keys. As he fully opened the office door with a smile and a spring in his step, Daniel LeBlanc was standing there with a huge grin. Daniel did not even seem to take notice that Caleb was a little deflated to see him.

"We caught a break!" Daniel strode past Caleb and into the office.

Caleb closed the door, turned, and returned to his desk.

"It was the crime scene," Daniel continued. "It bothered me from the very beginning, and I kept rolling it over and over in my mind."

"What do you mean?"

"Well, only one of the Toyotas was painted. Why just one? Why not both?"

"Good question," Caleb responded. *I don't follow.*

"Then I got to thinking, and when I dug into it, there are six different colors used on our armored Toyota Highlander fleet: black, brown, silver, light blue, green, and burgundy. They may have only needed to paint one truck because the other one was already the correct color.

"Okay."

"Well, don't you see, they would have had to have been prepared to paint both vehicles one of those six colors. What would have happened if we took two light blue Toyotas that day to transport the NASA equipment, they would have had to paint both vehicles. They likely only knew the colors they needed when we showed up at JPL. That is why they had the spray equipment in the parking lot up on the Angeles Forest Highway. However, on that day, one of the vehicles was already brown and therefore did not need to be painted … so…"

"…so even though there was nothing unusual about the paint itself, purchasing those specific colors with the painting equipment narrows the field!" Caleb said, now finally following Daniel's train of logic.

"Yes, precisely," Daniel replied, barely able to contain his enthusiasm. "Although Toyota offers more colors on their Highlanders, we just use six of their standard paint varieties. We phoned around to a number of auto shops posing as a client wanting to return the paint and the painting equipment. We got a bite from a small out-of-the-way place close to Chinatown called…Carmelo's," he said after referring to notes. "Carmelo, the owner ID'd this guy," Daniel said, putting a photo down on the table. "We were thinking it might be him because he purchased two second-hand Toyota Highlanders a couple of days before picking up the paint and supplies. One of the guys making the sale took a photo of this fellow's driver's license and the plate of the vehicle he arrived in before he'd let him go for a test drive. The vehicle he arrived in was a silver Audi, but the seller didn't get a good look at the other guy in the car, just this guy making the purchase. The seller thought it was odd because the guy gave the asking price, cash, no negotiating."

"That Audi could be the car that tried to ambush Tess in the desert," Caleb said, now starting to grasp where this was all going. "How did you track down this seller?"

"We just did the timeline. Once Tess proposed moving the communication equipment, these fellows would have had to have moved fast. Practically

169

speaking, there was really only about a two-week period where they could have gotten their resources together. We just followed up on all Toyota Highlanders sold in the greater Los Angeles area during that time period. Not surprisingly, it turns out that the driver's license is a fake, but the picture was enough for the garage owner to pick out this guy with confidence. Also, the guy went to Carmelo's place in a black Chevy Tahoe, the same type of vehicle that chased Tess on the highway. It turns out that the plates on the Audi and Tahoe are both stolen."

"So," Caleb said recapping what Daniel had told him, "We have an accurate picture of one of the perps from a fake driver's license and, although the plates are stolen, we know the two vehicle types and plate numbers they are using."

"Correct," Daniel said slowly as if to emphasize the complexity to Caleb. "The other thing that this case *screams* is that these perpetrators are well connected…it's almost like they have someone inside NASA, or that their surveillance is so persistent, that they can get a picture of what is happening inside the organization."

"Daniel, my gut tells me the same thing. I mean, for instance, how did they know that we'd be using Highlanders instead Suburbans that day."

"Yeah, great question."

"The only explanation is that we took the Highlanders when we did our JPL recon before the move and they assumed we'd also use them for the actual move."

"That makes sense. Plus, if they also assumed that you'd use the mountain route, those vehicles might have reinforced their thinking because they are more maneuverable," Daniel conceded.

"True. So, they must have someone watching JPL, or someone on the inside reporting," Caleb reasoned. "That's why I'm looking closely at this Poulin character, and anyone associated with him."

"That's logical."

"Great work, this is our first break. I was starting to wonder if we were ever going to get ahead on this case," Caleb said, patting Dan on the shoulder, thinking they were finished.

"Oh, wait. It gets better," Daniel said, his smile extending.

"Don't leave me in suspense, man!"

"Although the driver's license is a forgery, we ran the photo through some of our databases. We got a hit off facial recognition. Earlier today this guy flew from LAX to Atlanta."

"Since they didn't get Tess, they may be going after Doug Regent or someone else on Tess's team back in Huntsville," Caleb said with a shudder. "This guy is a bulldozer! He may even be trying to cover his tracks by tying up loose ends with any inside connection they may have. Call the Atlanta and Huntsville offices right away and tell them what we have, and I'll speak to Tess about warning Doug and the Huntsville team. And see if anyone else checked in at the same time as this guy. He might have a partner."

"Got it," Daniel said, rushing out of Caleb's office.

Caleb could hear Daniel hurry down the hallway. "Hi, Tess. Great to see you. You should speak to Caleb right away."

Once Caleb brought Tess up to speed with Daniel's

breakthrough, they went back to her office to call Doug back.

"Come on, come on," she repeated as the phone rang and rang at the other end.

Caleb just remained quiet to let Tess focus. She had already explained there was not a lot of time to reconnect with Doug because he planned to depart for the farm immediately after the previous call. Finally, after what seemed to be an eternity, the receiver at the other end was lifted. Tess pushed the speaker button on the desk phone she was using so Caleb could listen.

"Hello, Mike speaking."

It was Mike Bandy. As a security precaution, no one on the Helios Team identified the organization that they worked for when answering the phone, just their first name.

"Hi, Mike, it's Tess. Is Doug still there? It's urgent."

"I'm sorry, he just left. I walked with him to the door, so I know he's gone. Is there something I can help you with?"

"Mike, I'm not being dramatic, this could be a matter of life or death. Are you sure there is no way to get him? Call the front gate perhaps and get them to pull him over before leaving the base?"

"That sounds a bit extreme. What's going on?"

Tess quickly told him what they had discovered and sent Mike an encrypted e-mail that included a photo of the suspect on the way to Atlanta. She asked him to get a message to Doug and the rest of the team as soon as possible, telling them to lay low because they may be this man's next target. She then tried to reach out to Doug directly through his secure cell phone but had no response. Tess even called Doug's farm and spoke to his wife Jill.

"Okay, Tess, thanks for the call. I'll get him to get back to you as soon as he arrives."

Chapter 15

The Seeds of Humanity
2016, Arctic Ocean, Norway's Svalbard Archipelago

Other than brief visits by Arctic explorers, researchers, or those in search of natural resources like coal or fish, hardly anyone frequents the Svalbard Island Group because it is so isolated. The archipelago is located halfway to the North Pole from the most northern tip of continental Norway. This extreme remoteness made it the ideal location for the doomsday vault established here in an abandoned coal mine in 1984. The Nordic Gene Bank created this facility to preserve samples of Scandinavian plant life as insurance in the event of an unforeseen catastrophe wiped out these indigenous plants. Should this have occurred, seeds from the bank would have been used to re-introduce native floras back into the ecosystem. Years later, an international treaty was signed which expanded the participation beyond the original Nordic nations. In 2008, the modern, purpose-built Global Seed Vault that was carved into a permafrost mountain, opened its doors to serve as the ultimate failsafe for seed stocks from around the world. The vault was designed to keep the seeds at an ideal preservation temperature near the freezing point. Countries and other seed banks now store samples at Svalbard for protection. Like many nations around the planet, the US Agricultural Research Service stores thousands of samples at this facility, which is burrowed into the high ground overlooking the Longyearbyen airport. Many countries store seeds in the vault that would be vital to feeding their populations if disaster struck the food supply.

Storing seeds here is more than an academic exercise to guard against a hypothetical, unlikely event. Most people take the plant life around them for granted, but do not realize our eco-system is constantly evolving. The example that always came to mind for Doug was papaya in Hawaii. It is a fruit ideally suited to the warm Pacific growing conditions, which includes rich volcanic soil, lots of sunshine, and rain almost daily. Papaya was introduced to the islands in 1910, but commercial cultivation did not begin until the 1940s. Today Hawaii produces thirty million pounds of papaya a year for human consumption, but in 1997 the crop was almost completely destroyed by an insidious disease called the ringspot virus. Fortunately, plant research biologists were able to rapidly develop a variety of papaya with a gene resistant to the virus. Most people do not know that papaya farmers were convinced the virus was going to eradicate papayas completely from the Earth and the efforts of the biologists was a last-minute reprieve. By 1999 scientists were aware of over one thousand different viruses that threaten the plants of the world.

During his long career, Doug Regent traveled to the Global Seed Vault many times. To visit, the Scandinavian Air Service flight from Newark to Oslo was ideal because it was the only international flight departing New York that arrived early enough to connect with the direct flight from Oslo to Longyearbyen. The only disadvantage of this SAS flight was a one-hour layover in Copenhagen before arriving in Oslo. *This time, however, the layover might work to my advantage.*

Doug was not a secret agent, nor was he predisposed to paranoia, but as a nuclear engineer, he paid close attention to detail. In Newark, while getting settled in his seat for the trans-Atlantic flight, he noticed a man who had also been on the flight out of Atlanta. Doug did not notice him on the flight from Huntsville to Atlanta, but what were the odds someone else from the Atlanta flight would also be flying to Oslo? *A very low probability, but possible. Atlanta has a lot of feeder flights and perhaps the guy'll get off in Copenhagen. That would be reasonable.*

Although not completely certain, to make matters worse, Doug had an uneasy feeling the guy was watching him. Whenever he glanced behind, the man always seemed to be looking in Doug's direction. Was he being followed? Doug pretended to get something in the overhead bin and while standing, examined his phone as if checking an e-mail. Setting the phone to video record, while putting it away, he discreetly recorded in the man's direction. This fellow was of average height and build. He was clean-shaven with dark hair cut in a relaxed military style. He wore a navy suit jacket over a golf shirt and a pair of casual Dockers. Dressed to blend in Doug surmised.

Doug had traveled through Copenhagen many times. The airport was modern and efficient. The flight disembarked at Terminal 3 and according to published airline standards, passengers could clear European Union immigration and customs in forty-five minutes. That gave fifteen minutes to get to the next gate which was the EU domestic SAS continuation flight to Oslo. In Doug's experience, the published time standards were nominal expectations because he usually could get through the process in half the advertised time. Arriving early in the morning, when the airport was half empty, probably helped. Today, Doug had another advantage—the flight had been pushed across the Atlantic by a tailwind, so they would land a full fifteen minutes early. That gave Doug the time he needed.

As soon as the seatbelt sign was off, Doug bolted and got as close to the airplane exit door as possible before the aisle was filled with other passengers. He wangled to get a little further ahead.

"Excuse me, please. I'm terribly sorry, I have a really tight connection. Thank you. Excuse me."

People were annoyed, but they let him pass. Doug never looked back to see what his potential pursuer was doing. Off the plane, he half walked, half jogged, towing a small carry-on suitcase behind. Slowing to a walk at the immigration hall, he stopped at the line on the floor, and waited to be waived forward. *Control your breathing.*

"*Godmorgen*," Doug said cheerfully to the immigration official behind the booth when he was waived forward.

"*Godmorgen*," the official replied, examining him. "You are in a hurry, *ja*."

"*Ja*, very short time to my connection."

"What brings you to Europe?"

"Business meeting, I'm meeting a colleague in Norway." Then to help things along, added, "I'm booked to return to New York in two days."

Doug showed a return ticket for good measure. That was all the official needed to hear.

"Thank you, enjoy your time in Europe," she said while finding a spot to stamp the passport, and, while handing it back to him, was already examining the next person in line.

Departing the immigration area, Doug glanced back to see the man in the suit jacket waiting to be called forward to an immigration officer. For a split second, he and Doug locked eyes. That moment, as brief as it was, confirmed to Doug that he was being followed and needed to execute his plan developed while traversing the Atlantic.

Rather than follow the signs for connecting flights, Doug followed the baggage collection and exit signs, running all the way. He slowed near the automated security doors to the baggage retrieval area.

He needs to see me exit the security zone. Once I go through these doors, I can't return this way.

The man with the navy suit jacket stood out in the distance, running to catch up, he was scanning the crowd. Doug waited a moment and then went through the security doors, descended the escalator, and quickly moved through the baggage hall. Without looking back, Doug slowed before stepping onto the escalator to the airport terminal's lower level. He suspected the man following him had a good view of the baggage hall from above so could easily see Doug in the crowd. At the bottom of the escalator from the baggage hall, Doug glanced at the board, which indicated the train to downtown Copenhagen would arrive in three minutes. He knew they departed every ten minutes, so a three-minute wait was perfect. Doug quickly walked down to the far end of the platform, as far away from the escalator as possible. By himself now, he waited. The man with the navy jacket purposefully stepped off the escalator, quickly scanned the area and then seemed to relax when he noticed Doug at the far end of the platform.

As anticipated, the man stayed amongst the crowd congregating near the escalator, but periodically glanced down the platform to where Doug was standing alone. Doug had calculated that most people would not venture far from the escalator—it was human nature not to expend energy if it were not necessary. He had also determined that the man would not want to be captured by security cameras standing on the platform with Doug. If he had a plan to kidnap or harm Doug at some point, the security camera recording would connect the two of them. Instead, Doug thought the man would wait to board the train and then move closer to follow when Doug disembarked.

Despite the clinical analysis, which seemed to be accurate so far, Doug's pulse raced. *I'm not sure what my next move is if he does the unexpected and comes down the platform toward me.* Just as Doug was having this thought, the train arrived with a 'swish.' It was modern and aerodynamically shaped. While the train slowed, Doug approached the door closest to him, as did the group of people further down the platform near the escalator. When the train came to a stop and the doors opened, people disembarked, and then those who had been waiting on the platform stepped onboard.

Rather than search for a seat, Doug stayed next to the exit and as soon as the 'doors closing' indication was made, Doug leaped through to the platform. It was too late and unexpected for Doug's pursuer to react. Doug could see him looking out the window as the train left for Copenhagen.

This close call unsettled Doug. *Why am I being pursued? Is it random, or because of my work? Was it one of the good guys keeping an eye on me or was it something more sinister? Are there others out there?* At least he had a picture of the fellow which would help the FBI figure out what was going on. This was an indicator for Doug; however, that everyone on the team needed to be extra vigilant about their personal safety and the security of the program. Clearly, they were being monitored.

Doug returned to the airport terminal, cleared security, and just got to the gate as they were paging the name of the alias he was using.

"Mr. Bremner, Douglas Bremner, please report to Gate B-19, your flight to Oslo is about to depart, final call."

Doug could feel the perspiration down his back while settling into his seat for the next leg of the flight. Once airborne, he mentally dissected the incident over and over as the plane winged to Oslo. *This was no coincidence. But it wasn't like the guy knew my itinerary. Otherwise, he'd have just waited at the gate for the Oslo flight. No, he seemed to need to have eyes on me.* With that, Doug was more comfortable to press on as planned, rather than abort the trip in Oslo. *Still, I need to be vigilant.* The transfer to the Svalbard Island flight was uneventful.

Stepping off the plane at Longyearbyen, Doug took in the surroundings. It never mattered what time of year, it always seemed windy, cold, and threatening to snow. *It's ironic the safety net for the world's plant life is in such an inhospitable place, a place with hardly any plant life itself.* But the isolation was by design. It was intended to keep whatever might potentially ravage the world's vegetation from reaching the seeds here. And to guard against inadvertent contamination, the vault was only opened under strict, carefully planned conditions.

Despite the challenging weather, the rugged beauty of the island always captivated him. It was as if you could see so much further in these northern latitudes. The features of the Earth seemed so massive and stood starkly against the horizon and the sky. He always thought the best view was from the small entrance to the Global Seed Vault itself, a rectangular cement shaft that protruded at an angle out of the mountainside. From this vantage point, the foreground seemed so close that you could reach out and touch it, and the far-off distance was so majestic and beautiful that it mesmerized you. The near ground was only made up of one narrow strip of land that stretched out horizontally. It was flat and just wide enough to accommodate the airport and runway, nothing else. To the left of the vault's entrance, the near ground immediately gave way to a broad horizontal band of deep blue ocean stretching almost to the horizon. At the horizon, the ocean was capped by a chain of dark foreboding volcanic mountains mostly covered in snow and clouds. Above them was a narrow strip of pale blue sky. To the right of the vault entrance, a string of black, jagged mountains protruded sharply out of the ocean so high, they completely filled the entire right field of view. They provided impressive detail of how the mountains in this part of the world formed an intricate protective interlocked chain. It was as if these mountains were purposely placed there to provide a preview of what the volcanic features on the far-off left-hand horizon might look like up close. The bold geological features always reinforced to Doug the isolation of this place.

While admiring the beautiful scenery, Doug could hear the entrance door to the facility open behind him. He turned to see an old friend.

"*Hei ogvelkommen* Doug, it is good to see you again," the manager of the facility said in a mix of Norwegian and English as he vigorously shook Doug's hand. "It has been a while since we saw you last."

"*Takk*, thank you, Erik. It is nice to see you as well."

"How was the flight?" Erik asked, knowing full well it was an arduous journey even without the complications that often occurred because of poor weather.

"Oh, it was fine, I had an issue in Copenhagen, almost missed my connection, but here I am, none the worse for wear."

"Well, I'm glad, I have so much to show you. You know, we've made changes since your last visit."

Inside the entrance, a circular subterranean cement-lined tunnel with a flat floor descended at a shallow angle for about one hundred yards into the heart of the mountain. At the far end of the tunnel, there was another set of doors. All the utilities to support the seed storage area ran along the left and right walls of the industrial gray entrance walkway tunnel cut into the solid rock. Several different types of exposed pipes, vent ducts, electrical and computer cables, and overhead lights gave the appearance the two friends were walking through the passageway of a warship.

"This has changed. Didn't it used to be all overhead?" Doug asked, pointing to the utility services.

"Yes, recent upgrades, more efficient," Erik replied, obviously proud of the first-rate facility.

Beyond the doors at the end of the entrance tunnel, three separate storage halls capable of holding four and a half million seed samples were cut into the rock. At present, only one hall was being used while the other two were ready should they be needed.

Surprisingly, since its inception, only one client had ever needed to withdraw seeds stored in the bank for safekeeping. The International Centre for Agriculture Research in Dry Areas, or ICARDA for short, could no longer use its gene bank established years ago in Aleppo, Syria. The Syrian civil war precluded safe access to the bank and as a result, ICARDA made several withdrawals starting in 2015 of duplicate seeds also stored as a precaution at Svalbard. In this manner, it was possible to re-establish the gene bank elsewhere to continue important research. ICARDA plans to eventually replace the seeds they removed from the Global Seed Vault.

Like others, Doug came for inspiration and insight. Every visit brought thoughts about potential applications to the Helios Program based on what was happening here. It was rare to meet like-minded professional pioneers who were in a similar line of work. Of course, as far as they knew, he was a plant seed researcher as well, but still, it was good to be in the company of other individuals who had a comparable goal. Unlike this trip, the journey to Svalbard was usually relaxing as well. It offered Doug a rare opportunity out of the office to deeply contemplate his program without interruption. Often, he thought about future Helios initiatives, but sometimes would reflect upon the past and the roots of the program. This was not only for sentimental reasons, but as a self-check to help ensure work continued toward the objectives originally intended by President Kennedy. As part of this reflection, he fondly recalled the marathon indoctrination briefings administered by his recruiter and mentor, Bob Gillespie, in the mid-1960s. Doug had been working for a few years at the secret Nuclear Rocket Development Station facilities at Area 25 in Nevada before being brought into the Helios Project.

"The genesis for Helios," Gillespie explained in a clinical, matter-of-fact manner, "is simple. Survival of the American way of life."

"Like contingency planning?" a young Doug offered.

"Precisely," Gillespie said. "The path the world is currently on does not appear to have a promising outcome."

In his mind's eye, even after all these years, Doug could still sense his mentor become deadly serious, gazing into the distance, and describing Helios' background.

"Like the Apollo challenge, this initiative came from President Kennedy personally, shortly after the Cuban Missile Crisis. You lived through it, Doug; you know how close we came to vaporizing the whole planet."

"And the massive nuclear arsenal held by both the East and the West just continues to grow," Doug offered.

"Yes, that speaks to the ever-increasing importance of Helios, because the ultimate concern of all Americans is the survival of our nation in the event of a nuclear calamity. This is not just a theoretical preoccupation of politicians and the military, as you know too well, it's an omnipresent weight affecting every aspect of our society. We have fall-out shelters in the basements of schools and other public buildings, everyone knows to 'duck and cover' in response to a mushroom cloud on the horizon. But in our hearts, we also know these are just feeble initial responses to the devastation that would be unleashed by nuclear Armageddon. If the missiles start to fly, most people know it would be the end of everything. They are not wrong."

"It's crazy when you think about it, the whole planet is literally living on the edge."

"After the crisis in Cuba, everyone was telling the president that America needed even more nuclear weapons to ensure survival by further deterring the Communist hordes from doing anything precipitous. Kennedy was not convinced. There were already enough nuclear weapons for both sides to blow each other up many times over. That should have been deterrence enough."

Gillespie went on to explain to his young protégé that Kennedy believed something other than more weapons was required for the United States to survive. He had to stand up to Nikita Khrushchev because if not,

Khrushchev would walk all over him. He also knew that to stand up to this temperamental Soviet leader would require an investment in the military, and ultimately, there would be high-stakes brinkmanship politics. But in standing up to a volatile bully, Kennedy accepted an unpredictable outcome could result. Insurance was needed in case it all went wrong, and the insurance did not include another nuclear weapon.

On the contrary, Kennedy believed the United States, and its leaders, needed to be free from the fear of nuclear annihilation threatened by an aggressive Soviet regime that produced leaders like Stalin and Khrushchev. This way they would not have to worry about blinking when staring down their rivals. That was how Helios was conceived. The United States would secretly place a craft in deep space, a ship to preserve human reproductive material, and the American way of life. It would be ready to repopulate the Earth in the event of a nuclear catastrophe.

Doug remembers being horrified.

"So, our leaders would willingly choose nuclear Armageddon because there'll be a ship out there with the ability to allow us to start over, like some kind of Genesis project."

"No. It's far more nuanced. No one would ever willingly choose the apocalypse; it's to be avoided at all costs. We all know that. But we also know how close we are to the edge. How easy it is for something to go wrong. Especially during a crisis when emotions and rhetoric are running high. Helios will be another tool in the toolbox. It will allow American leaders to focus on the actual problems and circumstances of the moment, without the added pressure of knowing they are risking the future of all humanity. Look. Think of it as the guy called in to defuse a bomb. When he's working, you want him completely focused on the task at hand, not distracted, thinking of the consequences if he doesn't get it right."

"Okay, I sort of see the logic."

"Let's be realistic, most people have reconciled with the idea we are all living moments away from complete destruction on a daily basis. Helios would ensure the human race survives in such a grim scenario," Bob continued.

Bob Gillespie continued to press the point, explaining that with Helios, the American leadership could have confidence their nation would survive any calamity unleashed upon it. Not only would the ideals of America survive, but they would be the model for a new beginning, one that would embed individual freedom, equality, and democracy from the outset of the re-birth of the world. By creating a viable survival strategy, American leadership would be better positioned to make the difficult decisions when other nations would feel restrained by potential consequences. It would not, however, embolden politicians to the point of being reckless, but it would permit them to stand up to bullies with confidence. Bullies generally back down when they are challenged, so this would be a powerful implement in the American arsenal.

"So, when the idea for Helios was proposed," Gillespie continued, "we were far from capable of building and launching such a vessel, but with a focused, determined effort, President Kennedy was sure it could be accomplished."

Doug smiled while continuing to contemplate the Global Seed Vault at Longyearbyen. Helios was a parallel effort to placing a person on the moon and returning them safely to Earth. When initially conceived, NASA was not able to do that either. Within eight years the Apollo Program put a man on the moon and within twelve years the Helios Program lifted Skylab into low Earth orbit. Three years later, a highly modified ship with Skylab as its core, secretly began its journey out into the cosmos. From there, Helios began to listen for a routine encrypted signal from NASA's Deep Space Network confirming everything was well on Earth. Often the signal directed the craft to do self-diagnostics or other administrative adjustments to address circumstances not foreseen in 1973 when the ship was launched. Likewise, Helios would acknowledge with an encrypted signal, so NASA was aware it was still out there, like a sentinel, standing guard, and ready to respond if necessary. Hopefully, that would be the extent of the interaction between the DSN and Helios. Nevertheless, Helios would observe Earth from a distance, close enough to see it clearly through its onboard 12-ton telescope system and multispectral cameras, but far enough away not to be picked up by terrestrial observers.

Any concerns about human life being eradicated on Earth that might be registered from remote Helios observation would be confirmed if NASA's DSN signal ceased being transmitted. Helios would then need to wait until further remote sensing revealed it was safe to return to Earth to complete its mission. The craft was designed to be able to wait out in space as long as two hundred years, which seemed like an unrealistically long time when the president originally set the requirement. However, when considering that many C-47 Dakota Skytrain aircraft built during World War II are still hard at work more than 70 years later, two hundred years did not seem so long. Even the thatched roofs on countryside cottages in England were expected to last one hundred years.

Doug Regent took some comfort every day that as we on Earth looked to the stars and other heavenly bodies, Helios was carefully watching over us.

Chapter 16

Strike Two
2019, Redstone Arsenal, Huntsville, Alabama

Although it was after 7:00 p.m. following a full day
at work, guilt still gnawed at Doug Regent as he drove
out Redstone Arsenal's main gate on the way to see his
wife, Jill. Part of the unease was knowing she had been
waiting at their farm for a couple of days already and he
had, for work-related reasons, postponed this departure
more than once. Although Jill did not know exactly
what Doug did, she knew it was important and
unquestionably stood by him for the forty years they
had been married. Notwithstanding the steadfast
support, Doug never liked to disappoint her because he
had already asked so much during their life together. *I
should stop along the way and buy flowers.* The
beginnings of a smile forming as he imagined her
reaction. *I don't surprise her enough with things like
that.*
Now working the car into traffic pushing eastward
out of Huntsville along US Route 72, the other concern
unsettling Doug was abandoning his team while they
still worked. Even though there was nothing more for
him to do at this stage, and the best way to contribute to
their efforts was to give them space to finish their work
and not hover, it went against every fiber in his body as

a former naval officer to leave a station while his crew was still engaged. Although they could call via secure phone if they really needed assistance, and in a worst-case scenario it was only about an hour's drive from the farm if it was essential to return to the Arsenal, it did not seem right to leave. Perhaps the thing bothering Doug the most was the potential for someone from the outside to get the perception he was relaxing while his folks were burning the midnight oil.

Besides the current unease, Doug was actually very satisfied and incredibly proud of everyone on the team. When faced with the challenge of the California attack, they had all instantly responded by pulling together. Each of them was a longstanding, professional member of the organization who required little in the way of guidance. They knew exactly what needed to be done. Even if they had a heavy load in their own area of responsibility, everyone pitched in to assist the person who was working on the next vital step on the critical path. In this way, progress of the entire team advanced as quickly as possible. Watching them pull together in response to a difficult situation, Doug could see it was much more than dedication to their job. It truly was patriotism. These were proud Americans who were determined to respond to the assault on their country's security. His team had doggedly worked virtually night and day the past five weeks to try and get ahead of the crisis, and finally they were making headway. The new command message to Helios instructing it to change its communication protocol was almost ready for testing. Although it was vital to get this message sent as soon as possible to prevent someone from taking control of the far away spacecraft, if not done exactly correctly, they could inadvertently introduce an error themselves that would also result in their losing control of the craft. It would be like changing a password to a computer account, but then forgetting what code was used. The answer was to submit Helios' new command message to thorough testing before it was transmitted to ensure it produced the exact changes intended. Given the old 1970s computers and software used by Helios, they had to be careful.

As Doug continued to drive his Jeep Cherokee Trailhawk eastward through the small town of Gurley, another uneasy thought bubbled up. *It's hard to resolve the discrepancy between the excellent work the team has been doing and the visit earlier this week from the FBI who suspect there's a traitor in our midst.* At first, Doug discounted this notion outright because it did not align with his experience and instincts. *Am I being too hasty? Am I blinded by trying to see the good in everyone, even if perhaps it's not there?* Although Doug had known each member of the team for many years, and trusted them all implicitly, he now wondered if it was possible one of them was being coerced. *Could one of their loved ones have gotten into some sort of trouble, leaving one of the team vulnerable to blackmail? What would be the end game?* Perhaps they had fully intended to play along, work hard, gain everyone's trust, and at the last minute sabotage everyone's efforts by altering the Helios command code somehow. The tentacles of the California attackers could reach as far as Huntsville, although the more Doug thought about it, the less realistic this blackmail scenario seemed. *No matter how remote, I need to guard against some sort of insider attack.* Once the new command code was finalized, and proven through testing, there would need to be a strict, fully transparent, chain of custody over the content until it was transmitted. He did not like thinking ill of anyone on the staff, but the stakes were too high not to carefully verify everything. In the interim, as the team finished their work, he was going to enjoy a short weekend break with Jill.

Doug slowed the Jeep and brought it to a gentle stop while waiting for a break in the oncoming traffic so he could turn left onto State Route 65 and follow it north. This was a non-descript two-lane road that twisted and found its way through the Appalachian Mountains in the northeastern corner of Alabama. Compared to the rest of the state, the geography here was an anomaly. This rough country formed by a compact range of low rounded mountains covered in thick green trees and dense vegetation seemed out of place with the rest of the region. Even in the Twenty-first Century, there were very few roadways penetrating this mountainous area because it was easier to skirt around it. State Route 65 meandered through a valley that also accommodated the Paint Rock River to the right.

Once on this familiar road, Doug could feel himself becoming progressively more relaxed with every passing mile. Perhaps it was the stark change in scenery since turning north onto Route 65, but under the thick canopy of lush green leaves, Doug began to think more about Jill and his destination than potential conspiracies at work being left behind. Twenty years ago, he and Jill found a little piece of paradise about seven miles as the crow flies from the Tennessee state line. It was a very private two-hundred-and-fifty-acre farm at the end of a dead-end road. Because it was on the other side of the Paint Rock River, it was isolated from the traffic of this north-south thoroughfare. Jill and Doug often came here to escape the busyness of the city and to ride the back-country trails; it was therapy for Doug and helped him remain grounded despite the craziness of the job. Although very secluded, it was still an easy commute from Huntsville.

Driving this route so many times over the years, he could visualize every rise, twist, and dip along the way. This stretch would eventually come to a stop at a 'T' junction with State Route 146 before doing a dogleg and continuing north. Doug would turn right at the stop sign and rather than turn left to continue north on Route 65, which tracked along the west side of the river, he would cross over the bridge and take the next left, which led to the farm on the east side of the river. Approaching the town of Swaim, off in the distance he could see the junction, indicating the commute was almost over.

As Doug pulled up to the stop sign, he noticed a red full-sized Ford Expedition close behind. *How long had it been there?* The truck stopped so close that the Ford's oversized grill completely filled the rear-view mirror. There was a car speeding east toward him on Route 146 that was too close to permit him to safely proceed into the intersection, so Doug just waited at the stop for it to pass. After all, there was no need to rush. He was not concerned about how much of a hurry the fellow behind him might be in. As the car sped closer, the big Ford struck Doug's bumper and started to push him out into the intersection. Doug was initially caught unaware, but instantly recognized the imminent danger of being 'T-boned' by the car racing toward him. Doug's natural reaction was to push harder on the brake pedal, but it was not having any effect. He was still being pushed out into a precarious position by a larger vehicle. It was a matter of physics, and there was no doubt this was a deliberate act. Rather than continue to fight a losing battle by standing on the brake, Doug tromped on the accelerator and shot across the road. It was a desperate move, but the only real option. Most of the Jeep got across the road but was clipped at high velocity in the rear quarter panel, just behind the rear wheel on the driver's side. Doug felt his vehicle spin around before coming to rest with a jolt in the ditch on the opposite side of Route 146. Everything happened so fast, but strangely the last few seconds seemed to slow down so much it was as if he could account for every single moment. *I'm sure nobody was driving the car that hit me.*

Doug had a wickedly sore neck, but otherwise felt okay. *I'm very lucky; this could have turned out much worse.* All the airbags had deployed; and when he tried to open the driver's door, it was jammed shut. Clamoring over the center console to the front passenger seat, he caught a glimpse of the Expedition; the whole nose was smashed. The unanticipated last second acceleration must have caught the driver off guard, also drawing him into contact with the speeding car. Doug grinned, then saw two men stumble out of the vehicle, one with an assault rifle. *Road rage?* Doug tore at the handle and mercifully this door opened. Adrenaline kicking in and heart pounding faster, he dashed toward some thick woods about one hundred yards away on the other side of an open field directly in front. He had a head start and knew this country. All he needed to do was to get to the dense underbrush and there would be a chance of escape.

Recalling track and field days at college, he ran as fast as possible toward the thick vegetation. A bullet tore through his lower back and exited through his abdomen. Knocked face first to the ground, and pushing up on his arms in defiance, his legs and feet would not respond. *I'm a sitting duck with a mortal wound. Strangely there's no pain.* The strength soon drained out of Doug's arms, and he fell back to the ground. Laying there motionless, face in the grass, somehow, he managed to pull a pen from a shirt pocket and carefully write on his lower forearm in letters, numbers, and one symbol, 'Jill I heart U, J 4 T.' It took every ounce of focus and energy to write this message. Then all the strength went out of his hand after being struck again in the back by another rifle bullet. Minutes later he barely made out the sound of the long grass being crumpled under the feet of the two men who approached. All went black as two bullets from a 9 millimeter sound suppressor-fitted pistol burst into Doug's skull.

The two assassins hastily beat it back to the roadway and their destroyed Expedition that was supposed to serve as their getaway vehicle. Improvising, they commandeered at gunpoint the first vehicle to happen upon the accident scene. It was not long before they were in Tennessee, where they disappeared into the back streets of Chattanooga.

Chapter 17

Pursuit
2019, Atlanta, Georgia

A hundred and twenty-five miles to the southeast, the FBI descended upon the Hartsfield–Jackson International Airport in Atlanta like a NASCAR pit crew. Together with the Transportation Security Administration, they were frantically combing through video footage from Closed Circuit TVs used for security throughout the terminal. They knew they were just hours behind their quarry, who had been connected to Carmelo's Autobody and Repair shop and had just flown from LAX to Atlanta. If they could get a hit on facial recognition here in Atlanta, it could give them the lead they needed to catch these vicious felons.

With five parallel runways, a dedicated subway train system carrying passengers between various groupings of 192 gates, and over one hundred million travelers transiting through in a year, Atlanta's airport is the busiest in the world. In fact, it is a black hole in the southeastern United States that pulls in all air traffic. There is even an expression in this part of the country, "everything must pass through the Atlanta airport, even the dearly departed on their way to heaven." The terminal, like most, has natural gathering places and locations for monitoring passengers entering the security zone as part of the departure process, like check-in, baggage drop-off, and passenger screening, but not for those arriving on a domestic flight and leaving the airport building, especially if there is no luggage to collect. Nevertheless, the FBI and TSA agents had a strategy. They knew what flight the suspect arrived on, which provided an arrival gate and time. The clothes the suspect was wearing at LAX were also known. They called for security camera video for the appropriate timeframe with the hope of automatically identifying the suspect's face. They also considered the baggage retrieval hall, the taxi stand, the car rental area, and the arrivals pickup area. Additionally, they had an agent manually scrolling through footage looking at how passengers were dressed in case the individual was able to avoid looking at the cameras.

Even with the speed of the modern computers used by airport security, it was taking too long for FBI on-scene Special Agent In-Charge Duke Fellows. Duke speculated it must be the setup process or the vast number of images to be processed that was taking so much time. Frustrated at the delay of being held at bay by technology that was supposed to be helping them, Duke decided a multi-pronged approach using old-school police work was required. As the computers continued to chug along, he detailed someone to take a hard copy print of the suspect's picture, along with a description of what he was last wearing, to the baggage area and taxi stand to see if anyone from the airport staff recognized him. Duke knew it was a long shot, but something constructive had to be done since there was a killer loose on his turf. Another agent was sent to the rental car agencies and one to the MARTA commuter rail link to the city. *This son of a bitch had to leave the airport somehow.*

"Duke, we got a hit down here in the rental car area," reported the agent who had been sent there with a photo.

"What do you have?"

"Seems our guy rented a red Ford Expedition about seven hours ago."

"Damn it, he could be anywhere by now! Is there any way they can track it through GPS?"

"They're checking right now."

"Okay, call me back as soon as you have something…. And Charlie…good work." Duke was leaping ahead and starting to think about traffic cam surveillance and a BOLO for the Expedition when the phone rang again. It was Charlie.

"So, the Expedition is near a town called Swaim in northeastern Alabama, at the junction of State Route 65 and 146. It has been immobile for a couple of hours and somehow they can tell it may have been in a collision."

"Okay, get our Huntsville Office and the State Troopers on it right away."

"On it, boss." When Charlie contacted the State Patrol, he found they had already been on scene, and there was more involved than a vehicle collision.

Chapter 18

Reporting In
2019, Southern California

When Stanislav's phone rang, it was a call he was expecting. "It is done," was all the voice on the other end of the transmission reported.

"Good," was all Stanislav said in return, detached and looking around the interior of the safehouse. Much more should have been said, but not trusting any phone, he simply waited a moment and then hung up. Even though only one word was said, Stanislav was confident his man in Tennessee would have known by the tone, inflection, and each carefully crafted syllable, that he was pleased. Nothing else needed to be said. They had previously arranged for the assassination team to slip out of the country aboard a bulk carrier leaving the eastern seaboard when things quieted down.

Stanislav grinned. Data mining NASA's records had paid off. The idea that there would not be many employees continuously on the payroll since the Apollo era was brilliant. This is how they initially zoomed in on Doug. With a bit more research they were sure Doug held a prominent role in NASA's secret program. It was not that the records they found betrayed any secrets, but rather quite the opposite. Compared to most other personnel records they accessed, Doug's were too vanilla. He got paid a lot of money, but supposedly had not done much or been responsible for anything of consequence during an entire NASA career. It did not make sense. The tenure, salary, and place of employment all indicated he was likely the head of, or very highly placed in, the organization directing NASA's secret spacecraft program. This conclusion was the culmination of years of Soviet and Russian intelligence analysis. It was simple to find out where he lived from the DMV and land registry databases. Although people often used aliases in top secret programs, when it came to their pay, bank accounts, taxes, motor vehicles, and home purchases, these were legally recognized processes where real identities were required. *Bureaucrats are so predictable*, Stanislav thought to himself, exhaling a cloud of smoke from a half-consumed cigarette. He enjoyed American cigarettes, even if some comrades thought they were too refined. *Eliminating Regent would complicate things for the Americans trying to track us and for NASA trying to get their mitigation steps in place following our strike in California*. Now*, all that's left is to take the NASA motorcycle bitch out of the picture. That will completely derail their efforts.* "She's proven elusive up 'til now," Stanislav muttered with a twinge of annoyance, "but I know how to deal with her."

Chapter 19

News

As Tess picked up the secure cell phone to call Mike Bandy, she already knew in her heart the answer to the question she was bursting inside to ask, the word had already circulated back to the West Coast through the FBI from the agents at the accident scene. On the second ring the phone picked up, "Mike here." He sounded tired and a bit sullen, but still answered in a professional tone.

"Mike, it's Tess. Is it true? Is Doug actually gone?"

"Tess, I am so sorry you had to find out secondhand, I know you two were close. I meant to call, but things are a bit crazy here right now."

Tess knew Mike was a master of understating things, so she could just imagine how hectic it really was at the moment.

"It's okay, I understand. Is there anything I can do? Do you need me to come back to Redstone and help?"

"No, I've got things reasonably under control, well as under control as they can be, given the circumstances. You should stay out there and continue to work the investigation. That is what Doug would have wanted. We need to get these barbarians. Who shoots an old man in the back of the head, execution style?"

"I don't know; it doesn't make any sense. I feel I should be with you and the team right now, but I understand the need to keep the momentum going out here. However, I think we should maintain the daily phone call routine Doug and I had established. It's more important than ever that we coordinate our efforts. Other than that, please let me know if there is anything I can do to assist," Tess said in a final gesture of solidarity with Mike and the team, who were no doubt reeling from recent events.

Mike agreed with Tess's proposal to remain in daily contact, thanked her, and quickly severed the line. Tess was a bit taken aback by how quickly the line was cut, but thinking about it more, she was sure he was run off his feet with all the attention this devastating situation would generate and knew not to read too much into things.

Stunned, Tess just stared at the secure phone on her desk in disbelief. She was overwhelmed by an avalanche of emotion and needed a few minutes to process the shock, sadness, and loss. The overhead fluorescent lights in the small, enclosed office seemed to hum louder than ever. *How could something so terrible happen to such a nice person? Maybe if I called a few minutes earlier and was able to properly warn him about the assassins on the way? What about his family? Why the brutality? Is there more going on than I know?* She realized she was holding out hope that the initial information about Doug was incorrect, while also concluding that her only real connection to the team back in Huntsville was now gone. She could feel the loneliness already. This was not a game. What if they had caught her returning from Goldstone? She thought about Lincoln and Afghanistan.

Tess sat in her office for the better part of an hour, alone with her thoughts.

"You need to carry on, to finish the work Doug asked you to do," she said aloud to herself. "You need to do it for him." *Come on, one foot in front of the other, it's all we can do now.*

Tess knew in some ways Doug's death would be most difficult for the Huntsville team because they would be immersed in the crisis and all the issues and actions it generated. For her it was different. She was at arm's length and had other issues demanding her attention. But at the same time, she was isolated from the team, alone, and did not have access to the group's strength in numbers to help with the intense sense of loss. In many ways, removed from the pressure in Alabama, it could be harder to go through the grieving process by herself. She felt out of sorts.

It was a very lean team at Huntsville, and Mike would need to employ everyone just to stay ahead of the demand for information and updates. Tess had seen this before. It is difficult to get anything done and make progress because you are too busy responding to everyone who wants to know what is happening. She also knew it would settle down in a couple of weeks or so. Like her, the team just had to ride things out. *What else could they do?* Unfortunately, it would be a considerable period before they could get back to their planned activities now that control of their agenda had effectively been taken away from them.

As much as she now felt outside the group looking in, Tess thought it was wise of Mike to protect her from all that was going on so she could continue the important work here. It would have been easy for him to ask her to jump on a plane and come back to Huntsville to help, but his decision was a more strategic approach. Even rationalizing the wisdom of Mike's judgment, it was still hard to be separated from the team at this difficult time.

Chapter 20

Disaster Strikes

Caleb was now losing his second wind. Another coffee would not help. *I've had far too many already.* At this point, he was solely running on caffeine and brute determination. It was close to ten o'clock at night, and there was not much more that could be done at the office. Plans to leave a little early had been completely sideswiped by the crisis in Huntsville. He had never met Doug Regent but could tell by Tess's reaction that he must have been a decent guy and a great mentor. She said Doug had helped guide NASA through some extremely difficult issues during the height of the Cold War and that he was very influential in government. Considering everything that had happened, she was holding up well. Caleb winced while reflecting on what occurred in the desert. If things had turned out differently, they might be dealing with her murder here in California as well. Caleb was sure Tess thought about that also. *How could she not?* Now it was time to gently coax her out of the Fed Building to get settled in the safehouse. They had issued a nationwide BOLO for the suspect who had flown to Atlanta. He also scheduled a team meeting for the next morning to see how everyone was progressing and to ensure they were up to speed with the latest news. In Caleb's view, the guys they were searching for had to be stopped before they did more damage to the nation.

As he and Tess quietly took an indirect route to the safehouse, Caleb resigned himself to the fact that this drive did not possess the atmosphere he had previously imagined. The hope was to slip away earlier than normal, stop by a supermarket and pick up some groceries and perhaps a bottle of wine for dinner. They were starting to become closer, and Caleb wanted to show he was truly a friend who could be relied upon. He imagined going to the safehouse would be like going to a hotel where they could step away from their routine and get to know each other better. All that was just a fleeting thought now, and he felt a pang of guilt for thinking romantically at what turned out to be the worst possible time.

They drove through the darkened city for about twenty-five minutes, each lost in their own thoughts. Taking the long way to Santa Monica, they finally arrived at an upper-middle-class boutique low-rise condominium building on the east side of Ocean Avenue. Pulling up very close to the building, Caleb used a key fob to enter the underground garage. Finding the parking spot assigned to the condo, they used the elevator to the lobby and then another to the seventh floor.

The condo itself was exquisite and Caleb could not resist pulling the curtains back from the floor-to-ceiling picture windows exposing the nighttime view of the park across the street, the beach, and the ocean.

"It is quite lovely," Tess said, obviously still in contemplation.

"I know it seems a bit over the top, but the Bureau

needs something in a good neighborhood, a building with security, something that is not a house where it is easy for neighbors to see you coming and going. In a condo, it is hard to tell if you are home or not. Plus, no buildings are facing us and from street level, you cannot see into the apartment." Caleb hoped a description of the security features would be comforting for Tess. "I know I sound like a real estate agent for the Bureau right now," he said, trying to get Tess to smile.

"Despite the view, at night we should keep the drapes drawn, just to be on the safe side," Tess said. Reminding Caleb that when she was dropped off by the cab near his house, the interior had been on display to the world.

"Tess, I know the last couple of days have been extremely unsettling, with the episode in the desert and now Doug. I want you to know that I am going to take every precaution to ensure your safety. There is another condo on the second floor where we have a security team who monitors the surveillance cameras outside and inside the building, 24 and 7. They are agents who are trained to deal with intruders. Nobody can reach us here. I am also calling in additional resources at work. We are going to turn over every stone 'til we get these guys."

"Thank you, I know I am in good hands. I sincerely appreciate everything you are doing," Tess said, looking right into Caleb's jade-green eyes.

Caleb smiled. He wanted to kiss her but knew it was not the right time.

"It's a two-bedroom apartment so whichever room you prefer, I'll take the other one," he offered.

"Are you sure?" Tess said walking down the

hallway to check out the rest of the condo. "Oh, this one will be fine," picking the one at the very end.

Both rooms were basically the same size, and they each had their own bathrooms, which Tess and Caleb appreciated.

"Good, it is settled then," Caleb said.

"I think I'll turn in. I'm really tired," Tess confessed.

Although Caleb thought it would be nice to have a quiet conversation, instinctively he knew the day had been long enough already.

"Yes, for sure. We have an early start tomorrow."

The next morning, bright and early, Tess and Caleb were back at the Fed Building. Everyone was there for Caleb's early morning meeting. They even had an update from the Atlanta and Huntsville Field Offices. Caleb let the conversation follow a natural path but was a bit direct with the National Security Branch Team responsible for checking phones, computer accounts, and the like.

"I know there are a lot of people to screen, but I want a full court press on Walter Poulin and his girlfriend Krista Maguire. Is there anything at all from the yearly visits? I want every aspect of their lives put under a microscope. What we've done so far isn't enough. We need to dig deeper. Something doesn't smell right with those two, but if they are indeed clean, we need to call it early and expand our circle," Caleb said forcefully. Then softening, "Please tell me if I am wrong."

Everyone agreed that they needed to look at those two individuals more closely.

"If we don't turn up anything, we need to consider

their associates and those at JPL who knew about this NASA equipment, but we need to move more quickly. We are being out maneuvered." Caleb had previously issued this direction but was more direct and communicated a new sense of urgency. Then he finished with, "I want to see everyone back here at 17:00 hours with a status update."

Caleb left the meeting and headed to his office. Walking down the hall, he could hear his office phone ringing. He picked up the pace and managed to get to it before the party at the other end hung up.

"Agent MacLeod, this is Detective Jeff Meyerhof, LAPD. I think we should meet. It looks as though your investigation into the incident on the Angeles Forest Highway may be compromised."

"Compromised, what do you mean, compromised?!"

"You have a Tess Wentzel working with you?" Detective Meyerhof asked, unknowingly referring to Tess by her alias.

"If I did?" Caleb said guardedly, not one hundred percent sure who the person on the other end of the line really was.

"She has been linked to individuals known to deal in stolen high-end weapons and international weapons smuggling."

"You can't be serious," Caleb said unconsciously dropping his guard completely.

"Look, let's meet and discuss. I'll hand over everything I've got, and you can judge for yourself."

"Okay, give me an hour. Where would you like to meet?"

****

Caleb could pick Detective Meyerhof out in the coffee shop a hundred miles away. He was short, squat, soft around the middle, dark thinning hair, glasses, with residual teen facial acne scars. His suit was pulled tight as it tried to constrain a belly that threatened to flop over his belt or, at the very least, pop a shirt button. Despite not looking like a model for a recruiting poster, Caleb had confirmed with a trustworthy contact in the LAPD that Meyerhof was legit. The source also told him not to be deceived by looks. In fact, the quote was something like "…he might look like he slept in his clothes, but you won't find a better detective."

After some initial pleasantries, Caleb and Meyerhof got down to business. The detective slid a large brown envelope across the table.

"What's this?" Caleb asked.

"It's your evidence. I wouldn't look at it here, but it contains several photographs of Ms. Wentzel and the head of an international weapons smuggling ring."

"Where did you get these?"

"They were mailed to a local TV news personality. In the package was a note stating Ms. Wentzel works in a position of trust at NASA, has been conspiring with known criminals, and should be investigated to get the scoop."

Caleb was completely deflated. *Did I misjudge her all this time? Had she been feeding inside information about the investigation, and how best to derail it, to the attackers all along? Was her situation in the desert real or just an attempt to throw suspicion off herself? Was it bigger than simply the investigation, had she successfully infiltrated one of the country's most secret programs?*

"This is an unusual way to receive information about an ongoing investigation," was all Caleb could think to say.

"Yeah, we thought it was weird too. Normally the media don't cooperate with cops, but in this case, there wasn't much for them to go on. It might have been different if this Tess Wentzel was a public person or something, but really there wasn't much for the news outlet, so they called us. They asked for an exclusive if there was a break in the case. Strange though, outside the ones attributed to the news agency, there were no fingerprints on the contents of the package. Whoever sent this did not want it traced back to them. It was professionally done."

That alerted Caleb. "Interesting," was all he said.

Caleb thanked Meyerhof for bringing this to his attention so quickly. He also asked him to loop back to the news station to see if there was any chance of determining where the package originated. *It's a long shot, but important to run every potential lead to ground.* He was pretty sure that even if the news company did have any helpful information, they would refuse to divulge their source based on First Amendment rights guaranteeing freedom of the press.

As Caleb drove back to the Fed Building, he wondered about breaking this latest development to Tess. *I think the direct approach is best.*

"Oh, hi Caleb, I missed you at lunch," Tess said teasingly as he walked by the conference room that was now set up like a command post.

"Sorry, something came up," Caleb said, still confused as to how to act. As an FBI agent, he knew Tess should be kept at a distance, but as someone who had grown to trust and care for her, he wanted to take her into his confidence.

Tess must have noticed the tortured look on Caleb's face. "What is it?" she said gently.

"Tess, we need to talk, there has been a new development. Can we go to my office?"

Behind closed doors, Caleb showed Tess the photos and the note that came in the manila envelope. To say Tess was gutted would be an understatement. Caleb could see the shock on her face as the ramifications of this latest turn in the investigation hit.

"This takes me out of the picture," she said in a tone of finality. "You can no longer trust me, even if you want to," she said searching Caleb's face as if looking for a clue to what he was thinking. "This makes no sense. I have never seen these people before in my life. I have never met them. These photos aren't real." Tess was desperately searching for a way out of the box she had been put in, finally asking, "Is there anything I can do to maintain your confidence in me?"

"Tess, it's not me, I believe you with all my heart, it is the integrity of the investigation. Your continued involvement won't stand up to external scrutiny."

"They weren't able to take me out in the desert, so this accomplishes the same thing without spilling a drop of blood!"

A knock on Caleb's door interrupted the discussion. "Later," Caleb hollered emphatically. The knocking ceased. Even though the door was closed, they both realized it was not soundproof, and the word would be out that they were having a heated discussion about something.

"Caleb, I understand your instincts, but you can't

sideline me now. With Doug's murder, and now this. We know something bigger is at play here. I'll do anything you want. I'll…I'll take a polygraph to prove what I'm saying is true."

Caleb could see by the visceral reaction that she was telling the truth. All the years with the Bureau had honed his instincts, and he was confident no one could respond with such raw passion from their inner soul if they were not being honest. Tess was guarded, but if Caleb had learned anything by working closely with her over the past few weeks was that she could be trusted.

He gently took both her hands in his, and looked straight into her black ink-colored eyes. "Tess, I have complete confidence in you. I know this is a ploy to thwart our investigation, just as the attack on Doug was designed to throw NASA into a tailspin. It won't work. I need time to figure this out. I'm going to get Agent Mendez, and she'll escort you back to the safehouse and stay with you. I need to follow up on some things here. I suspect it is going to be another long day."

Caleb could see the disappointment in Tess's eyes but knew she was a professional and intelligent woman who would understand his dilemma. He knew that in a difficult situation, it was wise to take the time necessary to think things through and not decide in haste. Still, it was difficult to see her go.

I just convicted her without a trial.

Chapter 21

Desperate Man, Desperate Measures
2019, Silicon Valley, San Francisco Bay Area, Northern California

Jed Kaiserman could not believe it as he scrolled through the career opportunities on the web page dedicated to employment for communications and electronics engineers in the United States. It was as if the third job from the top of the computer screen had been expressly written for him. He possessed all the education, experience, and skills the company had identified as essential and desirable. He knew that meeting all the requirements of a potential employer was rare for an applicant, and as a result, had an unnaturally good feeling about this prospect. It was the kind of feeling you get when somehow you know your name will be drawn from the hat for the big prize at the office party, or you are destined to score the winning goal deciding the championship for the year. Sometimes you have an intuition about these things. *More importantly, if I land the job, the salary is a lot higher than what I was previously earning, and it would solve all my financial woes.* The medical, dental, and pension benefits were impressive as well.

Jed, a rather attractive man of average build, height, and weight, distinguished himself with a full head of thick wavy dark hair, a ready smile, and exceptional intelligence. Sometimes a quick wit, and quick tongue, got him into trouble, but he would not apologize for not having time for fools. Jed had always been ambitious and was keen to quickly get life back on the fast track after being summarily let go by both his employer and his wife at the same time. After dedicating the past fifteen years to work and a spouse, without warning his entire existence imploded. Jed did not blame anyone for these troubles, or have any feelings of malice, he just wanted to get on with things. Part of Jed's conscience wondered if this hurried approach to picking up the pieces and moving on was to avoid looking in the mirror and fully taking ownership of the situation. For now, however, it was smart to just take things one step at a time. After finding a new steady source of income, he would have the means to find a new girl, which after years of unhappiness, was all Jed could think about. A new beginning in work and in love excited him in ways he had not imagined in eons, and as a consequence, he found an interest in doing things that previously would have never attracted his attention.

One week after applying, Jed was not surprised to be invited for an interview near L.A. with the President of Extreme Communications and Research, or XCR Inc. as it was being marketed. The meeting went tremendously well. Jed and the president hit it off immediately, and Jed came away from the business lunch thinking he had a real shot at this opportunity. The president was a wealthy businessman who recently started the company to bid on and win a contract to update an old satellite communication system for the

US government.

"The equipment is so antiquated," the company president and owner said leaning forward and speaking with a muted voice as if revealing something that should not be said. "The government is desperate to replace it before it fails." Then added, "It has been in operation since the 1970s. Just think about how many equipment generations that is. It's shocking really."

Jed noted the care in the way the owner spoke, intentionally emphasizing each word.

"I know, but you'd be astonished how many times in my life I have seen this story repeat itself," Jed tried to empathize, even though not really surprised at all.

He also wanted to give the impression he had routinely dealt with these types of challenges in the past. In Jed's experience, a government organization often acquired cutting-edge technology, but because of the lengthy timelines, cumbersome bureaucracy, and limited capacity of the procurement process, updates were never made until the equipment was literally ready to be inducted into a museum.

The president continued painting a picture for Jed. "Because the Original Equipment Manufacturer went out of business years ago, we will need to reverse engineer what this equipment actually does. This could be difficult, given there is encryption involved."

"Well, I won't say it doesn't send up a red flag, but with modern computer processing power, and other tools, we can usually replicate older generation equipment with up-to-date technology quite quickly, especially if it is equipment from the 1970s era," Jed said, trying to sound confident.

Deep down inside, Jed really did not know if he

had all the pieces of the puzzle necessary to be successful. Codes and coding equipment were tricky, no matter what era they came from. He was also leery about joining a start-up company that still did not have any contracts and was only targeting one potential client, but Stan, the visionary president was very convincing.

"Jed, let me be clear. I'm a businessman. What do I know about satellite communications, other than this opportunity is very lucrative? As company owner, I am looking for a Managing Director who can run things, someone who can quickly attract and build a strong team that will win this US Air Force contract. The Managing Director would have a free hand to do what he thinks is needed. Jed, is it something that would appeal to you?"

Jed felt as though Stan had put him on the spot, but liked the idea that he cut to the chase. "Well, of course, to have that sort of latitude is ideal, and somewhat rare. I think it would be great."

"Good. I know we are essentially a start-up, but once we are successful by getting our foot in the door, I am convinced much more business will flow our way."

In Jed's experience, it was a reasonable assumption.

"Besides, we have a significant advantage over the more traditional companies," Stan offered.

"Oh, what's that?"

"They are too big and have too much process inertia to respond nimbly. The military has delayed doing anything with this communications system for so long that it is now almost falling apart on them. They need it upgraded quickly and will pay a 'king's ransom' to do it. The bigger, more established companies cannot respond as quickly as we can."

Stan went on to explain that as Managing Director, Jed would be responsible for daily operations, including the strategy to respond to the Air Force Request For Proposal. Successfully responding to an RFP was the first step to winning a government contract, but Jed was concerned about the extremely aggressive timelines at play. By his estimation, they were way behind where they should be, and it would take a superhuman effort to catch up.

"Jed, let me be crystal clear. Winning this contract is my only priority because it will secure XCR's long-term financial well-being and, therefore, I am prepared to invest heavily at the front end knowing we will make the money back many times over when we have our multi-year contract in hand."

Jed had not gone on a lot of interviews but came away from this one feeling really good. It was as if Stan was actually trying to convince him to take the job. After lunch, the two men parted ways, saying they had lots to think about. However, Jed already knew he would take the job in a heartbeat if it were offered. The salary and benefits, including an opportunity to purchase shares at a discounted rate, were excellent and there was a year's salary as severance if he left the company or was let go because they were not successful in the bid proposal. It was exactly what he needed right now.

Chapter 22

Control
2019, Southern California

Jed Kaiserman did not know it, but he figured prominently in the next phase of Stanislav Tishchenko's secretive plans, which were put in motion as soon as the NASA communication equipment had been successfully stolen. Stanislav's superiors did not want to risk trying to move the encryption device back to Russia, even in a diplomatic pouch from the Russian embassy in Washington. Technically these pouches were not subject to search, but Stanislav and his bosses did not trust that the US authorities did not already routinely apply remote scanning or x-rays to determine what was being moved across their borders by various embassies. Given the apparent importance of this apparatus, they did not want to chance involving the embassy, which could also tie the attack to them if the device were discovered. Furthermore, they did not want to risk inadvertently springing a trap by moving the stolen equipment around the country. They preferred to lay low in the shadows of L.A. Similarly, Stanislav and his overseers were reluctant to tip their hand by sending Russian cryptography and other experts, who were likely known to the United States, and could possibly lead American authorities to the location where the equipment was hidden. This left Stanislav on his own in the world's largest free market economy to find a solution, which suited him just fine. All that was really needed was money and time. Moscow had initially promised both, but since the success in stealing the highly guarded equipment, his boss, and presumably his boss's boss, now appeared less generous with their time.

As a precaution, Stanislav pushed for more money, explaining quicker results required more staff than originally planned. That is when he invented the ruse about responding to an Air Force RFP with a compressed timeline. Convinced advertising openly for project engineers and scientists, an everyday occurrence in the US, would not raise any flags, he was sure this would be the last thing that US investigators searching for the stolen equipment would expect him to do. The irony of attracting US citizens to unwittingly work against their own country made him smile. *Most Americans are overly patriotic anyway; they'll never suspect they're working for us.*

Stanislav came away from the interview with Jed convinced he had hooked an industry expert who could attract other strong colleagues to do the work necessary. Of course, the preparations for the meeting had started several weeks previously. An executive search agency had been engaged to get a lead on people like Jed who were looking for work. Through Stanislav's own Russian embassy-based intelligence resources, the focus had been narrowed to Jed because he was both brilliant and malleable. Jed was extremely driven, and somewhat blinded by vanity. Stanislav had been prepared to get the search agency involved to approach

Jed directly but was pleased when Jed responded to the web page advertisement on his own initiative. This approach left Stanislav deniability that Jed was being targeted and it fanned Jed's ego by making him think he was more in control than was the case.

"I know this might be intrusive, but I must ask if there are any indiscretions we should be concerned about?" Stan asked Jed during the interview process.

"No, nothing. All my work has been on classified projects and there has never been an issue. My security clearance is up to date."

While strictly true, Stanislav knew from research that when letting off steam, Jed sometimes hit the bottle pretty hard, and recently his wife too. Too much drinking and a violent temper were the reasons why his spouse and previous company had let him go; as a result, he was currently in a difficult financial position. Jed still had a strong professional reputation amongst his peers because they did not know this dark secret. Stanislav knew this could be used as leverage if necessary. He also believed Jed now had something to prove, specifically that he did not deserve this treatment, and his newfound motivation would keep the demons in check long enough to be useful. After that, Stanislav did not care.

Stanislav was still in the XCR office well past midnight thinking about the impending conversation with Moscow. Pulling back the industrial vertical window blinds to peer out into the quiet, black night, well before his eyes could fully adjust to the darkness outside, he knew there was a gentle rain falling because of the trickling noise of water slowly passing through the downspout near the office window. Nothing moved in this part of the city at this time of night. Even the air seemed unusually still. Looking very carefully, he could just make out the fine water droplets silently falling through the illuminated cones of light emanating from the streetlights or slowly dancing on the smooth surfaces of the puddles now starting to form in the streets. With an exhale revealing that the inevitable had been put off as long as possible, he retrieved the encrypted satellite phone from the office safe and dialed Moscow.

"Tishchenko, finally you've called. You know it's mid-day here."

"Yes, I'm aware. I would have called earlier, but it has been extremely busy."

Given everything that had been going on, Stanislav decided it would be best to provide an overview of activities and then focus on newer initiatives with more precision.

"The multi-pronged offensive and defensive aspects of this operation are achieving the desired effects. Firstly, we have …

"Yes, yes. I'm quite aware. Tell me specifically what you are doing to exploit the classified communication equipment. That's the information I need to know right now."

Stanislav was a bit offended by the interjection.

"I'm attempting to solve a complex problem with one hand tied behind my back because of the need to assemble a code-breaking team here, on site. To be successful, I need to be methodical, and it will take some time."

His supervisor did not want to hear about the difficulties. However, to assuage concerns somewhat, and to demonstrate work was moving as quickly as possible, Stanislav shared the measures he had already taken to harness more resources.

"The base of operation has been moved from the isolated old Soviet era safehouse ranch near Bakersfield, where we took refuge immediately following the heist, to a relatively modern, 16,000 square-foot warehouse in an industrial part of Chatsworth, a small city about thirty miles northwest of downtown Los Angeles."

The warehouse was an easy commute from most directions as it was on the edge of greater Los Angeles, and within a short walk from the Chatsworth commuter rail system. It was the perfect location for this phase of Stanislav's operation. It was easily accessible for the staff hired to help, but isolated enough to avoid unwanted scrutiny.

Other than the boss's testy demeanor, Stanislav was pleased with how the operation in America was progressing. It was rare for there to be tension between a field operative and supervisors back in Moscow, but Stanislav did not take it personally. Experience told him the men back in headquarters can be under incredible stress. This was an operation with strategic implications that was years in the making, and he was sure the highest officials in the bureaucracy were watching; that alone would generate enough churn and questions a small army of administrators could never hope to fully satisfy. *And I was more hardnosed than I had to be with the boss. It's good to keep him in check.* He wanted the younger, less experienced, yet ambitious supervisor to appreciate the challenges the operation posed.

Ten weeks after the Angeles Forest Highway heist,

Stanislav's ruse was in full swing. The defense communications community is a relatively small group of engineers and scientists, and it is even smaller when you consider the particular skills Jed had been seeking as the new Managing Director of XCR. With the aid of a reputable talent scout and lots of spending authority from Stan, Jed was able to rapidly assemble a first-rate team. He told Stan two of the six people hired were personal acquaintances and the other four were highly recommended by associates whom he trusted implicitly. Jed had no idea the money being spent was Russian SVR intelligence service funds. Spurred on by high salaries, expensive perks, and other benefits, Jed and his exceptional team of heavy hitters established a three-shift per day work schedule, which allowed them to triple their productivity. As a business owner and company president, Stan publicly fawned over the newly hired team, but the scenario he had created for the newly assembled group required XCR pre-qualify as a potential contractor for the fictitious U.S. Air Force RFP by demonstrating they understood the communication protocol being used between ground stations and a classified satellite. To help them with this requirement, the government furnished equipment and material, including an encryption device and a plethora of old messages previously sent between the Earth-based stations and the space-based satellite. The encryption device was the recently stolen JREC, which Jed's team simply referred to as 'the brick' because of its shape, and the old messages were the products of persistent Soviet and Russian intelligence activities over the years. They were easily able to intercept communications from Helios but relied on espionage techniques to bug the up-link transmitters of the Deep Space Network. However, despite their best efforts over the years, they were never able to get their hands on decoded messages.

To buy time for Jed and the team of specialists to do their work, Stanislav and his Russian operatives had kept the US authorities off balance by eliminating Doug Regent and sending doctored photos implicating NASA's Liaison Officer with unsavory accusations. From Stanislav's perspective, there was no downside to these actions–the investigation that could lead to him would be paralyzed and so too would be efforts to prevent him from interfering with NASA's spacecraft, whatever it really was. Stanislav made a mental note to find some time; he would need to strategize how to coerce more information out of the new mole they were cultivating in NASA. For now, he took pleasure in the idea that after decades of persistent, targeted intelligence probing, they were closer than they had ever been to determining what secrets the Americans were withholding.

To say Stanislav was pleased about what was being done would be an understatement. Jed's team had a wealth of experience interfacing with and designing encrypted and jam-resistant communications systems. With the assistance of the messages that had been previously sent and the encryption brick, they were fairly sure they had their RFP pre-qualification task figured out within several weeks. Key to success were a couple of messages sent in the past that seemed to amend the communications protocol. Once they were deciphered with the brick, it was easy to tell these two messages were quite different from most of the others they had been provided. With a working theory of how the communications procedure worked, including how to change it, the team now spent another week confirming their suppositions by systemically combing over key messages and running them through the JREC brick. Through this process, they were able to determine some of the things they could ask the satellite to do. Everything was documented in a technical manual they created as work progressed.

"Stan, the only thing we are not entirely sure about is that some of the status messages from the satellite seem to report on systems implying there are life support systems on-board," Jed said as part of one of the daily updates.

"That's strange."

"It makes no sense, particularly when the communications messages we have been provided for this project date back for almost fifty years to when the craft was launched."

It made no sense to Stan either, who offered that perhaps it was just some fictional part of the RFP process, or it might be part of the test created by the Air Force to challenge bidders. Jed and the team were encouraged to continue with their confirmation procedures. As Jed left the room, Stan wondered what they had really discovered with these messages. A spacecraft capable of supporting life for almost fifty years seemed unrealistic. There had to be another explanation. Still, his mind wandered. *The spacecraft was associated with Huntsville because it's where we found Doug Regent, and Huntsville is NASA's facility dedicated to supporting human space flight. Why didn't I see it before?* He pulled out his phone to access the internet. Although not overly scientific, after thirty minutes of bouncing around various websites, he had the impression that approximately ninety percent of NASA's Apollo work was outsourced to industry, that NASA seemed to have an ongoing interest in cryogenics beyond the needs of their liquid hydrogen and oxygen used for propulsion, and that there seemed to be a higher-than-expected concentration of cryogenic companies in the vicinity of Huntsville. Stanislav's mind raced to several possibilities. He had never previously considered anything other than an automated spacecraft, which did not need to support life. *I wonder if during the Cold War the Americans perfected some sort of stasis capability.* Still, a more logical explanation was the supercooled liquids like hydrogen and oxygen were fuel components onboard the ultra secret spacecraft or they formed elements of a space-based weapon. *Maybe it had a life support capability for the working astronauts during an assembly phase, before it departed on its long journey.* He was not sure.

Not only had the Soviets and the Russians been monitoring the encrypted communications emanating from NASA's Deep Space Network, but through their intelligence network and other surveillance techniques, over the years they had discovered exactly where in the sky the messages were being sent.

When Jed and the team had thoroughly checked the message to be transmitted to change NASA's satellite communications protocol, they collectively held their breath when they sent it through the encryption brick before streaming it out over the internet in what they thought was the culminating moment of their RFP bid pre-qualification submission. However, instead of going to the Air Force Materiel Command as they thought, the address Stan provided them routed it to several locations around the globe before it was ultimately directed to the Russian Center for Deep Space Communication at Yevpatoria, Crimea. The massive 230-foot diameter radar telescope dish had already panned the night sky above the Black Sea and locked on to the prescribed location. Minutes later, it bleeped the message, developed by Stan's XCR Inc. in Chatsworth, California, out into space.

By patiently monitoring NASA communications since the beginning of the space race, and more recently by utilizing decisive kinetic action in California, the Russians had discovered the trajectory, communications protocol, and encryption used by the highly secretive American Cold War spacecraft. Once the message was sent, Stan could hardly contain himself. That night he hosted the entire team and their spouses or 'significant others' in a private room at one of the best restaurants in L.A.

"Gentlemen, please raise a glass with me to your hard work … and to success," Stan said, clinking a glass of wine with Jed. "Enjoy tonight, take the next month off, the US Air Force bid evaluation will be at least that long. I want everyone well rested for our next sprint."

Everyone cheered Stan and the party broke into excited conversation around the table. Everyone talked at once. Afterward, Stan and two SVR agents who had been watching and recording everything Jed's team had said and done in the Chatsworth facility, neatly gathered all their material, including the stolen communication device, and retreated to the Soviet era ranch safehouse. They expected it would be a day or so before they would hear if the Russian communication facility in Crimea picked up a response signal from the faraway spacecraft confirming the protocol had been successfully changed.

Chapter 23

Honesty

Not quite sure what he would find inside, Caleb carefully slid the key into the lock of the condominium safehouse in Santa Monica. It was past eleven o'clock at night. Gently opening the door, it was quiet throughout the apartment, and all the lights were off except the one near the entrance where he was standing. Just as he softly deposited his car keys on a small side table, Agent Mendez silently appeared. She had been resting on the sofa.

"Hi Maggie, how's Tess?" Caleb said softly.

"Tired, she went to bed about an hour ago. These are rough days for her … it is not often that your loyalty is publicly questioned." Maggie responded very matter-of-fact.

Caleb felt a pang of guilt deep in his stomach. "I know, Maggie, it has been rough on us all." Then changing the topic quickly, "I really appreciate you watching out for her. Could I ask you to stop by tomorrow around eight in the morning? I'll need you to spend the day here again if you can. It is taking longer to sort through this than I would like. I can take things from here for the rest of the night," Caleb said, guiding her to the entrance.

"No problem, I'll see you tomorrow then," Maggie

said moving towards the door. Hesitating slightly, she then added, "She really is a wonderful person."

"I know. Thanks so much again for keeping her safe," Caleb said in a sincere but hushed voice while opening the door and then fully locking it after she departed.

It had been five days since Caleb had asked Tess to step back from the investigation. Maggie Mendez had been spending her days at the safehouse with Tess, and Caleb would relieve her in the evenings. Under normal circumstances, the condominium would be a great location with the beach just on the other side of Ocean Avenue, but it was not like Tess could go out and about playing tourist, especially after the recent attempt that had been made on her life. As a result, she spent her days mostly in the condo talking through aspects of the case with Maggie, and together they hypothesized where this all might be going. Because Maggie had been spending all her work time with Tess, she was not able to add any new details that Tess did not already know and therefore could not compromise the investigation. As for Caleb, he and Tess solved this problem by simply agreeing not to discuss work. Initially, he thought it would be a minor inconvenience because Tess would be quickly cleared of any alleged wrongdoing, but so much time had now passed, it was becoming awkward having the lead investigator under the same roof as someone who might be viewed as compromised. The approach made sense initially, but almost a week later it appeared less objective. He was starting to think perhaps Maggie should stay with Tess full-time to provide protection, and he should return to his own home. Although this might look better from an external optics point of view, Caleb did not relish the idea of not being able to see Tess daily.

Caleb also knew that being cooped up for so long in the condo was starting to take a toll on Tess. Her only outlet was to visit the gym in the basement to pound out a few miles on the treadmill and then work through a yoga routine. As a security precaution, Maggie always went along at the same time because the gym was accessible to all condo owners. Maggie later divulged that these exercise sessions revealed Tess's incredible fitness. Maggie said this must come from the inner drive, determination, and competitiveness exhibited while working through her routine. She now better appreciated Tess's soft and gentle exterior covered a strong inner core that would be easy to miss if you were not observant.

As Caleb stood in the condo's entrance, one hand still on the lock after letting Maggie out, he noticed a neatly handwritten note on the same small side table that held the car keys.

'Hi, Caleb. I thought you might be hungry, so I saved you some dinner in the refrigerator. Hope your day went well. Tess'

She really is an angel.

Caleb had other frustrations in addition to the fact that the examination of Tess's alleged criminal association was not moving faster, which prevented her from re-joining the investigation where she belonged. He was also struggling internally with how to explain that in the week since being sidelined and banished to the condominium, things had actually gone from bad to worse. As bad news would arrive, he would put off saying anything, hoping the situation would turn around, but it never seemed to get any better. Now there was a backlog of negativity, which somehow had to be shared with her.

For starters, it looked as though the Bureau's National Security Branch Team was coming up empty-handed with Walter Poulin and girlfriend Krista Maguire. Sure, there were some explicit things about their relationship that you would not post on the bulletin board in your local church lobby, but other than being unabashed insatiably hot lovers, and one of whom was lying and cheating on his wife, there was no evidence of a conspiracy or treason against the United States. Caleb was convinced that if it was not them, then it was someone who was somehow connected to them. Maybe it was someone blackmailing Poulin for his philandering. He wanted the National Security Team to expand their circle of who they examined in detail to include anyone who had a link, no matter how slight, to Poulin and Krista. Caleb could no longer provide Tess the details, but he could divulge that the investigation so far had not provided any new leads, which might cause some people to put stock in the allegation that she must be the 'inside person.'

Then there was Mike Bandy. Unable to reach Tess, he called Caleb. Mike was really upset. The NSA had advised him about a signal sent by a Russian Deep Space Communication transmitter in Crimea. Apparently, Tess had requested the NSA monitor various space communication sites around the globe for a signal with unique characteristics. She had also given them Mike's name as an alternate contact if they could not reach her. Mike did not go into details, but it looked as if the Russians were in the process of trying to hijack the highly classified US deep space satellite by using the stolen communications equipment, and there was nothing anyone could do but watch helplessly. He said it looked as though, despite extraordinary efforts, they had not been fast enough changing the communication control protocol and were beaten by the Russians. Mike described it as having an out-of-body experience and witnessing your own slow-motion car crash.

When Caleb mentioned the manila folder, and the fact that it was most likely a setup, Mike got very quiet and then abruptly indicated there was no choice but to place Tess on administrative leave from NASA to ensure the investigation was not further compromised. He said he had been thinking about it for several days, ever since Tess reported being isolated from the team.

As the law enforcement lead for the investigation, Caleb tried to talk Mike out of his position because it was too harsh, and Mike was too quick to jump to that conclusion. Caleb explained how the photos had been submitted for expert analysis to determine if they were legitimate or if they had been doctored, but the results came back inconclusive. There were questions raised about the snapshots, like the way shadows fell from Tess compared to others pictured alongside her, but there was nothing concrete to indicate a forgery. Everyone agreed that if they had a soft copy of the photographs, it would be easy to tell if they had been manipulated. With the grainy hard copy photos, it was pretty much impossible to tell, but very suspicious because they were anonymously provided by someone with no fingerprints or who was wearing gloves. The local TV station had no insight as to where they came from, at least no insight they would share. It just did not sit right with Caleb. Notwithstanding, the more they discussed it, the more entrenched Mike became. Finally, he insisted Tess would be temporarily relieved of duty with NASA effective immediately until all this could be cleared up. Stopping short of ordering her back to Huntsville as a result of Caleb's insistence, it was evident this was a possibility in the near future if the situation did not improve.

Caleb got the sense Mike was overwhelmed and was taking the easy civil servant way out without thinking about the impact it would have on Tess. After all, it was her idea to monitor the space communication facilities of other countries. Now they knew Russia was behind the Angeles Forest Highway attack. It made no sense that she would be part of a conspiracy and then set up a trap to expose more light on the situation. If what Mike said was true and the NSA could not identify the names of those who were involved with the Russian transmission to the satellite, Caleb was pretty sure they would know soon. It was illogical to think Tess would purposely draw attention to herself if she were somehow implicated in the theft.

Mike simply was not thinking straight in Caleb's assessment, but as the conversation went on, it became clear Mike's perspective was much harsher than Caleb's. Mike explained that Tess was seconded to the Bureau's investigation to help speed it along to prevent the exploitation of the sensitive stolen communications equipment to guard against further harm to NASA's space program. The recent deep space message transmitted from Crimea indicated she had failed in her mission. Whether she was guilty or not was no longer relevant, the US was in the process of being stripped of a strategic advantage that had existed since the 1970s. Even if an investigation eventually cleared Tess, it would be like closing the barn door after the horse had escaped. Mike now had bigger problems, and Tess was not part of the solution in his assessment. If she was somehow involved, he did not want her on the inside of the investigation covering her, or anyone else's, tracks. The only concession Mike would give was to agree that she should be told face-to-face and not over the phone, so the responsibility to deliver the disheartening news about the directed administrative leave fell to Caleb.

It was crushing Caleb's heart. He had put off saying anything for days, but tonight, on the drive from the Fed Building to Santa Monica, he had resolved to end the inner turmoil, to stop attempting to shield Tess from bad news, and to be as open as possible, considering her status. If he truly respected and trusted her, then he should not be keeping these kinds of secrets, even if it was intended to protect her. From this day forward he would keep true to the old adage that honesty was the best policy.

However, since it was quiet throughout the condominium, Caleb was just thinking there was a reprieve until morning about coming clean with Tess when her bedroom door gently opened, followed by delicate footsteps coming from the hallway toward him. Quietly coming into the light, she was wearing a yellow floral print sundress, her dark straight hair draped over one shoulder. She looked amazing, not at all like someone who had been asleep. All Caleb could think to say was "Hi." It was the kind of greeting you use to break the ice, and simultaneously test the waters after you have been quarreling with someone and you have not seen them for a while. Was the other party ready to make up, like you want to, or were they determined to continue the argument? Not that Caleb had been arguing with Tess; but the latest turn of events had certainly curtailed the time they had been spending together, and Caleb was concerned there might be some distance between them now that they were no longer working closely together.

"Hi," Tess said in return, with a wry smirk on her face.

Caleb then knew she was not angry with him. "I thought you were asleep?"

"I tried, but I was tossing and turning."

"Thank you for dinner, it was very thoughtful."

"Oh, you are very welcome. Did you like it?"

"Actually, I just arrived. I saw your note, and I'm looking forward to it. I'm sure it will be wonderful."

"It's quiche with a side salad and homemade dressing."

"Wow!"

"I'm trying to entice you to leave work a little earlier," Tess said with another grin.

"I know. I've not been working long hours to avoid you…quite the opposite actually. I have been desperately trying to find the one thread that when you pull on it, everything unravels. The downside is I haven't seen much of you this week."

"I have missed our time together too," Tess said peering into Caleb's eyes, perhaps to judge his reaction.

"Hey, I was thinking…you've been bottled up here for a bunch of days. Would you like to sneak across the road? We could walk along the beach and take in some fresh air. The security risk will be minimal because of the darkness…and you'll be with me," Caleb said with a smile.

"Caleb, that is very thoughtful. Thank you. Let me get my shoes."

Together, they stepped into the second-floor condo where the security team was set up. Caleb advised the two agents on duty that he intended to escort Ms. Wentzel to the beach because she had been housebound the last number of days. Caleb thought Tess stiffened a little when he said "Wentzel," but as he conversed with the other agents, she seemed to relax and distract herself by looking at the various security camera feeds. Caleb asked his colleagues if there were any security concerns in the vicinity and to be informed if anything developed while they were outside. He did not want to lead Tess into an ambush on the way back from the beach. The bank of monitors showed views from an array of cameras both outside and inside the condominium building.

The coordination with the security team complete, Caleb led Tess down a stairwell to the ground floor and out a discrete little-used door on the side of the building that was primarily intended as a fire escape. They followed a flagstone path leading to Ocean Avenue which was eerily quiet at this hour. They followed the sidewalk until they could see a walking path on the other side of the avenue that led toward the beach. It went through a park and over a footbridge crossing the Pacific Coast Highway, which was tucked up against the escarpment and hidden from view. On the other side of the highway, they followed the path to the promenade, removed their shoes and socks, and proceeded out onto the cool beach sand. The tide was out so the beach was very wide. They walked in silence directly to the water. The night sky was clear with bright stars haphazardly scattered across it anchored by a sliver of moon high above them. There was a warm breeze coming off the ocean, and the roiling surf was high. The waves rolled and crashed onto the sand.

"This is nice," Tess said. "Thank you."

"It is the least I can do," Caleb said, quickly changing the topic to avoid spoiling the mood by talking about work. "Come, do an experiment with me," he said leading her closer to the water. "Okay, stand here." He gently led her to a position where she was at the water's edge looking directly out to sea. "What do you see?"

"I see waves," Tess said with a laugh.

"Which way are they coming?"

"They're coming directly toward me."

"Now close your eyes."

Tess listened intently for a moment.

"Wow," she said, "that's incredible! The waves don't sound like they're coming toward me anymore; they sound like they are traveling from my left to my right. And yet, when I open my eyes, they seem to be coming directly at me again!"

"Neat, huh," Caleb said, "I thought you'd like it."

"How did you ever discover that?"

"Oh, I've spent a lot of time on the beach. It often works, but not all the time. So many variables, I guess."

"Well, I never would have guessed."

"Whenever I have challenging days at the office…the waves and the surf crashing onto the shore just seem to wash away all my worries. I often arrive all tense and leave relaxed and ready for another day." He paused. "Let's walk the beach for a bit."

As they walked, Caleb found it easier to open up to Tess. He confessed how hard it was to go to work without her, how horrible he felt by insisting that she be separated from the investigation, how cowardly he felt coming back to the condominium late in the evenings, how bad he felt that she was effectively a prisoner while everyone else she knew here in California went about their business. He said how grateful he was that she was not angry with him. Despite being somewhat relieved, in the end, Caleb could not help feeling that in easing his conscience, the burden had simply been shifted to Tess.

Chapter 24

Fade To Black

Tess just let Caleb talk as the night wind pushed the air and the waves over the hard packed beach. She could tell it was not easy for him to open up. Caleb shared his frustration that the harder everyone worked on the investigation, the further behind things seemed to be getting. He said it felt like there was someone or something actively working against their efforts. Admittedly, that sounded far-fetched, but it was the only explanation for what appeared to be taking place. He had never experienced anything like this in all his years in the Bureau. Finally, he shared what Mike Bandy had said. Well, not everything, much of what Mike had relayed was a rant not worth repeating. The important part, however, was that the NSA had detected a transmission from Crimea matching the criteria she had set, and Mike was worried this was the attempt to gain control of the US deep space asset they all had been working to protect. Tess knew if the signal matched her criteria, then Helios was being hijacked. Caleb finished by saying that against his professional advice, Mike was placing Tess on administrative leave until this could be sorted out, and that Mike no longer wanted her associated in any way with the investigation. Caleb told Tess how awful he felt by saying this all at once, that he had been trying to safeguard her from it in hopes there would be better news, but it never came. She felt so alone, standing on the beach, a gentle breeze in her hair. She harbored a sense of deep hurt at not being trusted.

Caleb did not say anything, perhaps it was just a reaction, a reflex to someone who had been given bad news, but without warning, he hugged her. Tess just stood there, arms to her side, as if stunned by all the news. After a short while she regained some composure and briefly put her arms around Caleb. Without speaking, after a few moments, they separated and continued down the beach, Tess lost in reflection. She knew Caleb was telling the truth and he truly cared for her as a person, not just as a partner in the investigation. *Or rather, ex-partner.*

Tess did not like it but had worked in bureaucracies enough to understand Mike's logic, even if she did not agree with it. She was being sidelined while the organization dealt with more pressing issues. Likely there was no malicious intent, but it was upsetting that Mike did not have the courtesy to personally telephone or give her the opportunity to provide an explanation. *I'll be a casualty in all this. In the worst-case scenario, I could also be a victim if my name is not eventually cleared.* At that moment on the beach, it was evident she was now on her own. Nobody was going to ride to the rescue because they were all focused on more demanding issues.

Tess thanked Caleb for being honest, for the reprieve from the condo prison, and taking the time to be with her. Despite his company, however, she felt more alone than ever. Together they made their way back to the footbridge over the highway, through the park, and to the condo. They stopped in to let the security team on the second floor know they had returned safely, but the agents inside had monitored their approach to the building. As they entered their apartment, Tess kissed Caleb on the cheek and thanked him for the nice walk. She confessed to being tired from all the fresh air and to needing sleep. Caleb said he felt the same and would be going to bed soon as well.

At three o'clock in the morning, Tess silently rose from bed. She listened carefully but could only hear the beating of her own heart. The condo was dark and quiet. Moving across the room to the desk, she clicked on a light to get dressed and then wrote a short note.

Caleb, thank you for everything. It has been a pleasure getting to know you, and I hope we will meet again soon. Sincerely, Tess.

Tess wanted to write more, to be more personal, but was one hundred percent focused on the mission ahead and needed to get going. She took her wallet out of her purse and tucked it into her jeans pocket. Silently walking through the darkened condo and leaving the note on the small side table by the entrance, she ever so carefully unlocked the front door, opened it slowly, and cautiously stayed in the door's archway to minimize any exposure to the camera covering the hallway. Using the key from the outside so the latch would not make a sound when the door was pulled closed, Tess then darted across the hall to the stairwell she and Caleb had used earlier in the night. She hoped one quick movement would either not be noticed at that hour by the agent in the surveillance room or if it did attract someone's peripheral vision, by the time they examined the monitor more closely, nothing would seem out of place. It was a gamble, but a fairly safe call that people would not be at their best at three fifteen in the morning.

Tess knew the stairwell only had one camera at the very bottom and one on the outside of the building. Both cameras were orientated to see the faces of people approaching the building or entering the door, not people leaving the building - this is one of the things Tess specifically checked earlier at the security office. While Caleb was speaking to his fellow agents, she closely examined the big computer screens displaying the security camera feeds. There was no intention to flee then, it did not even cross her mind. It was just curiosity about how the security system was situated and how confident she should be with it. Approaching the bottom of the stairwell, she stopped, pulled the hood closer to her face and quickly moved through the fire escape door. Casually walking along the same footpath taken earlier in the evening, Tess knew she would be caught on camera, but hoped not to be recognized right away by the agents in the security suite. If they did notice her, all they would see would be someone in jeans with a hooded sweater pulled over their head. *Maybe they will just think I'm someone leaving my boyfriend's place early in the morning.* Quickening the pace, once out of the camera's view, she bolted.

Tess knew the plan was unorthodox but had to do something more constructive than pass the days isolated in a condo on the beach waiting for someone else to solve her problems. Running into the darkness, she knew exactly where she was going, but had to be careful about getting there to not draw attention to herself. Heart in her throat, she headed to the beach to escape the likely view of security cameras from adjacent condominiums. Descending the same stairs previously taken with Caleb, once on the beach, Tess jogged toward downtown, keeping as close to Ocean Avenue as possible. The sound of the surf seemed to crash all around her. At the next set of stairs, she climbed back up to the streets of Santa Monica. Staying off the main thoroughfares, she briskly walked toward the city center. Every once in a while, Tess still caught the sound of the ocean wind and waves. What she could not hear was Helios' bleeps back from somewhere up in the dark, star-scattered sky, dutifully announcing it had accepted its new communication protocol and was awaiting instructions.

Chapter 25

Maverick

Tess's disappearance sent shockwaves through the FBI and NASA. She just vanished. Coming to California in response to the brazen heist in the Angeles National Forest, Tess knew that she and the FBI were pitted against some determined and dangerous opponents. The mission in Afghanistan taught her to always have an escape plan and of course, the experience with the NSA provided all the skills to stay off the radar. Adopting a makeshift disguise and avoiding CCTV cameras, she left the classified and regular cell phones behind and did not use credit or debit cards.

After leaving the condo, Tess made her way to downtown Santa Monica by walking for a couple of hours, carefully avoiding the main routes. After an early morning coffee and breakfast in a small family run diner not far from the Santa Monica pier, from there she took a cab back to her old neighborhood in Glendale.

"This is it," she told the cabbie as they pulled up to Mailboxes Etc.

When Tess first rented the apartment in Glendale's Beachwood Canyon, part of the consideration was the availability of private rental mailboxes nearby. This small, clean storefront received the highest online reviews for the quality of their business. A full list of services the proprietor offered was neatly stenciled on the front window, but the one Tess was most interested in was listed first, '24 Hr Service.' That was going to help today because it was still very early.

Unlocking the front door and pulling it open to enter, Tess acknowledged activating a plan she hoped would never be used. Her thoughts went back to when she first arrived in town. The number of small enterprises offering rental mailboxes was surprisingly large. She wondered if the proportion of these private mail services available in a city somehow related to the number of secrets people were keeping or the amount of illegal business going on.

Tess did not mind that the only boxes available at Mailboxes Etc. were the less popular ones where you had to bend down to get your mail because they were nearly at floor level. *Harder for the clerk to see what was inside.* Because the mailbox was so low, all the clerk could see were the first few inches of the bottom of the box.

She remembered the conversation with the store clerk while filling out the initial rental agreement paperwork. "I travel a lot for business and might not be able to pick up my mail for a month or two, would that be a problem?"

"No, ma'am, it's no problem at all. You come and go as you please," the clerk said in a slow drawl. Then, he added, "It's only a problem if your mailbox is full and letters still arrive."

"Oh, I don't think I'll be getting that much mail," she said with a smile.

Tess then sent herself some letters to test the

integrity of the process and to establish a routine of checking for mail every couple of days after coming home from the Fed Building. On the third visit, she carefully adopted a position facing the mailbox while obstructing the security camera view. Kneeling, she extracted the mail previously sent to herself and reached as far inside the box as possible and stuck a black envelope with two-sided tape to the inside top of the box. The clerk would need to get on his hands and knees, and probably use a flashlight, to see the envelope containing fifteen hundred dollars in the shadows of the box. Tess then replaced the mail sent to herself to help block the view toward the back of the box. Never visiting the mailbox again until now, she had hoped there would not be a need to access the emergency money. *But here I am.*

After retrieving the envelope hidden in the mailbox, Tess walked down the street to a local coffee shop and ordered a blueberry muffin and an orange juice. It was still early and there were only a few patrons in the shop. Asking the young barista to borrow her cell phone to organize a ride share, she sensed hesitation.

"I am really sorry to trouble you, but my battery died."

Tess felt a twinge deep inside for telling a white lie, it was not her style to be dishonest, even if it was just a little fib. The clerk smiled and offered Tess the phone. Tess also felt a pang of guilt when thinking about Caleb. She had never done anything like this before, but also had never been in a situation requiring this sort of action either. The intent was not to send her FBI associates into a tailspin; however, it was becoming increasingly obvious what they had been doing collectively up until now was not working. The Russians always seemed to be one step ahead of them. Even the team in Huntsville had not prevented Helios from being hijacked. Everything was gone. Tess never envisioned herself as a maverick, but they needed to do something starkly different, and they needed to be quick about it. Sitting around a safehouse was not the urgent response the current dire situation required. It made no sense. If she was sent back to Huntsville because of the administrative leave, she would be told to go home and wait things out. Any attempt to be useful at that point would result in some menial unclassified tasks to fill time. All options had no end in sight and would preclude her from assisting in any way with the current nightmare situation.

Tess had a hunch, but it was not fully developed. At first, she was not even sure it was something that should be pursued. But, thinking about it more, there had to be something there. While mulling over everything to do with the investigation and Helios the past few days, Tess started to wonder if Doug had deliberately planted some clues in the indoctrination briefing material. They were just a couple of very subtle offhanded comments that, at the time, did not seem germane to the teaching point. Now, faced with a disaster, the words immediately bubbled to the surface of her consciousness.

"If you ever are in a crisis and you don't know what to do," sounding like a father coaching his daughter, "remember this program has seen everything since its inception. There are no new problems. Look back to see what was done in the past as your first reaction. Personally, I keep a record of the project history for this very purpose."

It was more than just the words that came back now. It was as if her mind's eye went back to the very room they occupied at the time. It was eerie. *Was he telling me something, or is this just grasping at straws in a time of desperation?* Thinking more about the briefing, the more convinced she became that Doug was preparing her to deal with future challenges. *Was this crisis foreseen? Was there really something in the program's past that could help them today?* Tess did not have the answers to these questions but could not continue to sit idly while the nation's most secret program was literally being stolen from under their noses. *How could I have remained in the condo safehouse and passed this hunch on to someone else? They didn't hear the tone of Doug's voice or the context of the words.* The hunch would be either disregarded outright or half-heartedly followed up. If Doug had deliberately planted a helpful idea, she was going to pursue it herself with vigor. Tess was now on a personal quest.

Forty-five minutes later, the barista came over and quietly mentioned to Tess that her ride had just sent a text saying they had pulled up outside. After a friendly thank you, reinforced by a ten-dollar tip left on the table, the small bell dangling on the door handle announced Tess's departure. Stepping out into the bright morning sunshine, she was happy to see the ride was in fact two college students in an old dark blue Mazda sedan as advertised. She was prepared to walk away if there were any bad vibes, but there seemed to be good karma surrounding the boyfriend and girlfriend supposedly on their way to see a show in Las Vegas. Tess paid them twenty bucks to get a lift as far as Barstow.

"No backpack or anything?" the guy asked Tess in a friendly, nonchalant way.

"Naw, just going for the day," Tess responded.

"Good, let's get on the road."

Once they worked their way through the morning commuter traffic and L.A. was behind them, Tess found herself on edge as they headed east on Highway 15. Then she caught herself subconsciously scanning the highway for the black SUV and cars that gave chase on this very stretch of road. It was the first time back here since the attempt on her life. *I thought I was over those events.* Clearly, they had affected her in unexpected ways. Thinking about it a bit more, it made sense that these were normal feelings. Also adding to the anxiety was not being behind the wheel. She was not in control and therefore was not able to react to unforeseen circumstances. *Ironic. In taking steps to better control what is happening in the investigation, and to me, the first thing I do is get myself in a situation where I am just along for the ride.*

Tess smiled to herself; emotions were sometimes difficult to comprehend. After identifying the source of her agitation, it was easier to relax a little. Logically, there should be nobody out here looking for her in a completely incognito Mazda, but the near-death experience had left a mark–how could it not?

The three-hour trip passed faster than expected. Tess asked to be dropped off at the Barstow outlet mall along the highway, not far from where Highway 15 and Highway 40 intersect. She remembered passing by this place on the trip to Goldstone, shivering again at the memory.

"Thanks for the lift. Have fun in Vegas," she said, calling after the Mazda as it pulled away.

Walking toward the food court in hopes of finding a pay phone, Tess re-evaluated her plan. *Should I be doing this? Right now, nobody knows where I am.* Then, after a few moments of consideration. *I can trust Mandy, at least for initial contact. Later on, I can assess sharing more.* If Mandy was at work and it was not possible to meet right away, Tess planned to blend into the mall crowd for a few hours while waiting. Worst case, there was an inexpensive motel nearby.

Mandy was beside herself with excitement when Tess called to say she was in town for a social call, not another tour or explanation of NASA's Deep Space Network facility.

"Don't go anywhere, I'll be right there. We're going to have so much fun."

Fifteen minutes later a fire red Chevrolet Cruze sedan pulled up to the outlet food court. People were coming and going, kids were everywhere. It was as if there was a school outing at the place.

"Hi, Tess, it's great to see you."

"I was passing through and thought I'd take you up on your offer to get together."

"Well, I'm glad you did. My boyfriend is deployed to Iraq right now, and it gets pretty lonely out here by myself, especially on my days off."

"Oh, Mandy, I had no idea. Is he doing okay?"

"Yeah, he's fine, thank goodness. But out here, it's pretty much work, eat, sleep, and go to the gym for me."

"Speaking of work, I really wanted to thank you for the follow-up e-mails you sent about the implementation of the new DSN security protocols."

"Oh, no problem. I wanted you to be confident that we weren't just paying lip service to the new procedures. They're taking this issue very seriously."

"I was happy to see that, and I really appreciate you taking the extra initiative to let me know. I hope all this didn't make things awkward for you."

"Not at all. You certainly had more influence on them than me. Like I mentioned before, I'd been trying to get them to pay attention to this issue for a long time."

"Well, I'm glad you were free today. I actually thought we'd be getting together when you came to L.A. next, but fate has brought me back this way sooner than expected," Tess said.

"Well, I like fate, she's wonderful!" Mandy exclaimed as she pulled out of the mall parking lot on the way to her place. "I'm off for the next couple of days so I thought we could go out tonight…if that's okay. There's a country bar my boyfriend and I go to that's kinda fun. It's got a great atmosphere. It's stuck in time a bit, but there's a young crowd and everyone line dances or does the two-step. It's been three months now since I did anything exciting so I'm getting a little cabin fever. It'd be nice to get out, but I'd never go alone."

"Okay, you are on. Girls' night out at a country bar. It'll be new for me, but sounds like fate is calling our names again, and she's not taking 'no' for an answer!"

It seemed like Mandy needed a change in scenery,

and Tess knew for sure that she did as well.

"So, you can see I'm traveling really light. The couple who gave me a lift teased me because I look like I just escaped from prison. I might need to borrow a few things if we're going out."

"Don't you worry. I have more than enough for both of us."

A few minutes later they pulled up to a nice ranch style home that could not have been more than five years old.

"This is really nice Mandy."

"Oh, I'm just renting while I save up enough for a down payment for my own place."

They had lunch, went for a walk around the recreation trail in the neighborhood, and had a dip in the pool. It was a full afternoon and then it was time to get ready for the evening's outing. As she was getting herself together, Tess was happy her sense of trust in Mandy seemed confirmed, but still wondered if it was strong enough to reveal the real reason for visiting.

Chapter 26

Regret

Caleb was profoundly hurt and personally embarrassed when he awoke to find Tess gone. Arriving to a darkened kitchen, initially he thought she might have had a poor night's sleep. Usually, they would have breakfast together and chat. Her note was the first clue something was amiss. Caleb immediately called Maggie to see if Tess had given any indication of doing something like this. Maggie was caught completely unaware. She came over right away, and by that time Caleb was in the security suite grilling the agents on duty. They had just started their shift so were taken aback by Caleb's aggressive barrage of questions. When Maggie arrived, Caleb and the two agents were reviewing the security camera video from the night before.

"Oh, she is good," one of the agents said half under his breath.

"What's that?!" Caleb exclaimed.

"Look, here on Camera 12, a little past three-fifteen a.m., the quick movement at the bottom of the stairwell. If you weren't looking directly at the screen at the time, it would be easy to miss. Then when the view passes to the outside of the building in Camera 13, she's walking directly away from the lens, again little movement to attract attention on the screen. It would have been different with motion across the camera's view; left to right travel would have been more noticeable, even in someone's peripheral vision. And nowhere do we see her face."

"It's her," Caleb said. "I can tell by the walk."

"What do you think she's up to?" asked Maggie.

"I wish I knew!" He then added, "Go to the hall camera outside the condo door."

"Could she have gone out for air and gotten abducted? Maybe the guys who were chasing her in the desert…" Maggie said, giving Caleb a worried look.

"Maybe. But why put yourself in that position? She knows how dangerous they are, especially after Doug."

"Being sequestered here for days. It'll make anyone do crazy things."

"I don't think that's it. We spent a long time on the beach earlier in the evening."

At the office, Caleb immediately called Mike Bandy to see if he could shed any light on the situation; however, Mike was completely unaware as well. *Not surprising*. Although nothing was said, Caleb secretly blamed Mike and the decision to formally put Tess on administrative leave as the catalyst for her response.

"If she had nothing to hide, why the disappearance in the middle of the night?" Mike said. "Clearly something isn't above board."

Caleb hung up the phone. *He has no idea that he's the instigator of all this. When did supervisors stop caring about their staff?*

Chapter 27

Some Girls Just Want To Have Fun

With the sun fully set, and the day's heat
dissipating, you could see the Palomino Club for miles,
brightly lit up on the horizon. Tess remained conflicted
as Mandy drove out into the desert toward their
destination. She needed to pursue the hunch that Doug
had left a message about how to deal with the Helios
disaster, but the plan for the evening seemed like a
distraction from that effort. At the same time, a reliable
contact inside NASA's Deep Space Network would be
needed if she ever hoped to contact Helios again, and
Mandy was her only real option. Besides, she liked
Mandy, and Mandy seemed to need a small interlude
right now. Tess pushed down any reservations about
this interruption to chasing after a hunch and resolved
to make the best of it. *I need a way to discretely engage
Mandy about the DSN.*

"I know you're thinking this place must be so far
out of town for a reason, but trust me, it's one of our
few hot spots," Mandy said with a smile, and adding,
"The lipstick looks good on you."

"Thanks, it matches the dress and shoes you loaned
me. Good thing we're the same size."

Tess could not believe the parking lot as they
pulled up to the club–it was completely full.

"Where did all these cars come from?"

"Told you this was the place to be."

Mandy had to orbit around a couple of times before finding a spot to park, but persistence paid off. The two ladies entered the club, both intending, for vastly different reasons, to forget all their concerns for the evening, have some good clean fun, and enjoy each other's company. And they did. They laughed and danced and laughed some more. They had a few drinks and a small bite to eat. Out on the dance floor, they broke a few hearts of the local cowboys and a couple soldiers and marines from the two large military installations nearby. That was not their plan; they were just not looking for that kind of fun. Tess was conscious of having limited funds but was determined to pay her fair share. Time flew by and before they realized, it was 1:30 in the morning.

"Well, Mandy, how did we do?"

"I think we did great. Just what the doctor ordered."

During the drive home, Tess opened up a bit about being in Barstow. After giving Mandy a very sanitized version of the events, she explained that the stolen classified satellite communication encryption equipment had actually been used by the thieves who conspired with the Russian deep space communication system. This most likely meant the secret NASA satellite had been hijacked already. Then, Tess described the attack on the way back to L.A. from the visit to Goldstone.

"That's why the nice FBI agent, what was the name, Agent Mc, Mc, McSomething…"

"MacLeod."

"That's it, Agent MacLeod. Oh, he was so worried about you. He sounded really nice on the phone. Is he cute?"

"Mandy!"

"Well, is he?"

"He's a very nice man…and yes, he's extremely cute."

They both laughed. *I wonder what he's doing right now.* She then told Mandy about the manila envelope, about being sidelined, and finally Doug's murder.

"Holy shit, this is getting seriously scary."

"I know. I'm sorry. This is a lot to drop on you right out of the blue, especially after such a wonderful evening.

Mandy seemed to recover her composure, and Tess continued.

"I know we have only just recently met, but I feel like I can trust you. Please keep my confidence and don't tell anyone about my situation, or even say I was here. I don't have a lot of people I can rely upon right now. I need to know that if I reach out to you in the future to help the government regain what has been lost, I can count on you."

Tess did not share why she might reach out. *It's a contingency. I'm not even sure I will reach out.*

"You can count on me, Tess."

Mandy was quiet for a moment, thinking.

"So, what are you going to do now?" she finally asked.

"I have some ideas I need to look into out east that might help, but I need to stay off the grid. It would be a big distraction and interrupt progress if they find me. Instead of advancing, they'll go sideways trying to determine why I left and if there was anything sinister behind it. I'm sure they're doing some of that now, but it'll go to a whole new level if I surface. Plus, they'll put me back into the penalty box, and I would not be able to do anything to assist in resolving this."

Tess very much liked and had confidence in Mandy, but nevertheless, was guarded and did not divulge everything, just what was necessary. There was some guilt about not being completely transparent, but the mission had to be protected.

"I'm headed to Houston."

This was true, but in reality, she would continue on to Alabama. Also, Tess did not reveal the trip was based on a hunch from what Doug had said during introductory briefings. That would have gone too far because it would point to her next steps and where she would be. Finally, there was no speculation that since the Russians sent their JREC encrypted message, and most likely now controlled Helios, the only way for NASA to regain control would be through a message sent from the Deep Space Network. This was Tess's main purpose in touching base with, and confiding in, Mandy. She was ensuring there was a trustworthy contact on the inside of the DSN should assistance ever be needed in the future.

Even before stopping in Barstow, Tess weighed the pros and cons of contacting Mandy. Her first instinct was to avoid engaging anyone because it would prevent any risk of being exposed and avoid any awkwardness for Mandy. She initially decided if assistance was ever needed in the future, contact could be made at the time. The problem with that tactic was it did not confirm in advance that Mandy could be counted upon. Also, Tess reasoned it was unlikely the FBI or anyone else would speak to Mandy and ask about her. Mandy just happened to be Tess's tour guide during the Goldstone visit, and they exchanged some follow-up e-mails about procedure implementation. There was no trail to lead the FBI to Mandy. Tess believed in honesty, so she opened up as much as possible without compromising the investigation or any secrets about Helios.

"Mandy, I hope you don't feel like I've jeopardized you in any way."

"No. Not at all. We're just two new friends who met for a night of fun. You haven't divulged any classified state secrets, compromised the investigation in any way, or asked me to do anything. I'm scared for you though, with killers out there, I mean."

"I know. It scares me too, but I have to do this. I have to do it for Doug."

"I've been thinking while you were talking. Maybe I'm connecting dots that aren't meant to be connected, but we do have an encrypted communication signal we transmit from the DSN that originates outside Goldstone. We have been asked to re-broadcast it many times but have not received any response from space like we normally do. It is the only anomaly we have had recently. This sounds like it confirms your theory about your satellite being hijacked."

"It sure does," was all Tess said, saddened that it looked like she was correct in the assumption about losing control of Helios.

"Okay, how can I help?" Mandy said.

"Well, you already have, just by listening."

"Yes, but there must be something else I can do."

"I've thought about flying or taking the train to

Texas, but they'll probably be looking for me at the airport or Union Station. I'm sure I'd raise a red flag. I've thought about a rideshare, but it would be a long time to be in a car with people you don't know. Can we see online if there is a bus that goes from here?"

When they got home, Mandy called up the Greyhound site on her laptop.

"There you are. A bus from Barstow to Houston. It leaves tomorrow at twelve-thirty p.m., takes two days and you'll need to switch buses a couple of times. The tickets range from one eighty-six to over three hundred dollars depending on how soon you want to depart. You're welcome to stay here as long as you'd like if you want a cheaper fare."

"Thanks, it's really sweet, but I need to get going."

"I understand. Well, you get some sleep, and I'll get you to the bus station tomorrow before noon."

"You are the best. I had such a good time tonight. I really needed it after all the crazy things that have been going on."

"I know. I think we both needed it."

Mandy touched Tess's hand, as if trying to communicate being supportive, but still there was a look of concern, maybe even fear, in her eyes. She then got up and gently closed the door after departing the spare bedroom. For her part, Tess was exhausted. Having been up for twenty-four hours, it was a wonder she was still functioning. Within minutes of turning out the light and settling into bed, feeling completely unburdened, and knowing this was a sanctuary, she fell into a deep sleep.

The next morning Tess awoke to gentle kitchen noises and wonderful breakfast smells spilling down the hallway to the bedroom. That was the wakeup call. Surprised to have slept in to 10:30 in the morning, she brushed her teeth and had a quick shower.

"Good morning," Tess said to Mandy with a big bright smile and hair still wrapped up in a towel. "Sorry I slept in so late."

"Good morning. Don't worry about it, clearly you needed it, and you have a big journey ahead of you. Let's eat." Over breakfast, Mandy said "I hope you don't mind, but I had an old tote bag and I put a few things together that you might find useful along the way. I also packed you a lunch and some snacks, which should keep you going for a little while."

"Mandy, thank you. You didn't have to do that."

"I need to look after my girl."

After breakfast, Mandy drove Tess to the bus station which was where Highway 15 and Barstow's East Main Street cross. On the way there she offered Tess a big white floppy sun hat and a pair of oversized sunglasses.

"Try these, your own mother wouldn't recognize you with them on."

Tess laughed. "Oh Mandy, you are something else."

Mandy parked the car near the bus station and went in to purchase the ticket to avoid Tess being caught on a security camera, if they even had them. Emerging from the station ten minutes later, she produced an envelope containing a ticket and Tess's cash.

"Here you go, bus leaves from the platform, over there."

"You didn't use my money?"

"Just think of it as my contribution to this effort.

You probably need to keep all your cash for the road ahead anyway and this would have been quite a hit. Besides, I'm sure we'll meet again soon, and the universe will balance."

"Thank you. You are so thoughtful."

Tess gave Mandy a big hug. There was a touch of sadness knowing that from this point onward, she would be on her own. There would be no friends to visit for support. She would be isolated. A small tear formed in the corner of her eye as she whispered goodbye in Mandy's ear.

"I knew it was the right thing to come here," Tess said. "Thank you so much."

Walking to the waiting bus, hidden under a white hat and sunglasses, Tess could see Mandy watching from a distance. She took a seat by a window and looked out. Mandy waved. As the Greyhound pulled out of the station and groaned its way up the ramp to the highway, the ensuing black cloud of diesel exhaust belched out more intensely with every noisy gear change. Tess suddenly felt all alone again. There was a harrowing journey ahead and it was not clear if she would ever see Mandy, or California, again.

Chapter 28

Follow All the Details
2019, Redstone Arsenal, Huntsville, Alabama

"Okay Mr. Regent, what were you trying to tell us," Herbert Glasse, the slender, officious US Air Force forensic pathologist said, half to himself and half to Doug's body, while sliding it out of one of the cold chambers occupying the entire back wall of the morgue.

Glasse looked comfortable in this domain. He was peculiar, but also excellent at what he did. Supporting NASA, Glasse had completed the autopsy the day after the vicious murder at an otherwise quiet north Alabama intersection. He carefully pivoted thick black resin bi-focal spectacles with both hands, so they rested on his receding reddish blond hairline.

"You know, I've still got one question vexing me," Glasse said to Special Agent Duke Fellows, almost as if it were a confession.

That sounds odd. Maybe the good Doctor doesn't usually have outstanding questions after an autopsy.

"Cause of death was the two 9 millimeter pistol shots to the head, execution style, but it is quite likely the two rifle shots would have been fatal as well, given a bit more time."

"We were just hours behind these assassins. We trailed them from L.A. to a rental car agency at the

Atlanta Airport. Sadly, we were too late because the murder had already occurred," Duke said. "They came at this old guy hard. I wonder why such brutality?"

Even after all these years, standing around morgues still made Duke uneasy, so he was keen to move things along.

"So, what's the mystery, Doc?"

"Well, why such a brutal attack on a geriatric individual is one question. The other is the writing on his forearm. Moments before the fatal pistol shots were fired, it seems our deceased calmly wrote this." Glasse passed a tablet with a photo of Doug's arm. "His wife's name is Jill, so his final thoughts on Earth were 'Jill I heart U' which seems to be a farewell to her. Poor fellow must have known the injury was fatal and used his remaining strength to say how much he cared for her. Classy guy," Glasse observed. "But what about 'J 4 7'? I can't figure out what it means. Was he trying to warn her, name the killers, get his wife to do something? I've done an online search and can only come up with a late 1940s turbo jet engine, a ghoul character in an online fantasy game, and motorcycle apparel. I was hoping it may have come up elsewhere in your investigation."

"No. Can't say as it has. J 4 7?"

"Yeah." Glasse put the tablet down and exposed Doug's left arm.

"Interesting. Okay, Doc, can I get a copy of the photo? We need to find out if this means anything to Mrs. Regent; the message was obviously for her." Duke paused a moment. "Any chance the killers wrote this?"

"Possible, but unlikely based upon the on-scene forensic assessment."

Duke did not want to ask exactly what that meant. What he heard was Mr. Regent most likely wrote the note himself.

****

Duke Fellows was a headstrong FBI agent with an unapologetic direct approach, but also a southern gentleman who truly admired his country and fellow patriots. He could have sent the image from Herbert Glasse to the Huntsville Field Office and let them run with it, but given the significance of the case, it made more sense to journey up to northeastern Alabama to pay a visit to Doug Regent's widow. Jill's sister was also at the farm to provide comfort and was introduced to Agent Fellows, but gave him and Jill privacy.

"Mrs. Regent."

"Please, call me Jill."

"Yes, ma'am," Duke responded instinctively before switching to the southern familiar, but still respectful, "Miss Jill, it appears your husband's thoughts were of you during his last moments."

"Why would you say that?" Jill responded a bit bewildered and then asked, "Sweet tea?"

"Thank you, ma'am," Duke said, passing his glass. "Well, it seems Mr. Regent was determined to leave you a personal message."

"A message?"

"I'm sorry, ma'am, this may be difficult to look at," Duke said, slowly pulling a phone from the breast pocket of his suit jacket to show the photograph of Doug's arm. "You can see the note written on his arm." The photo had been tightly cropped to spare Mrs. Regent by showing only the message Doug had left.

A tear welled up in Jill's eye. "He was always so

thoughtful and romantic," was all she was able to say.

"Obviously he deeply loved you ma'am. This is a terrible thing that has happened. I know it may be of little comfort now, but we will not rest until justice is served." Duke knew he was not supposed to make promises to a victim's family, but wanted Doug's widow to know how committed everyone was to the investigation.

"Thank you, Agent Fellows."

"Duke, ma'am. Please, call me Duke."

"Duke."

"It seems, Miss Jill, that the first part of the message Mr. Regent left you is clear, but the second part is a mystery. Any idea what it means, J 4 7?"

"J 4 T."

"J 4 T?"

"Yes, it's definitely J 4 T. Doug was an engineer who was very particular about forming numbers and letters. His 'Ts' however were unusual. This is a 'T.'"

"Any idea what it means?"

"J 4 T? I'm really not certain. Doug was often speaking his own language that I did not fully understand."

"Thank you anyway, ma'am. You have been most helpful. If anything comes to mind, please give me a call," Duke said, passing her his card.

As she escorted him to the front door, Duke had the distinct impression Jill Regent understood the second part of the message. Duke had been doing this business far too long. It was the way she shifted her gaze, and then insisted on not knowing anything. There was no curiosity there, just aversion. It was subtle, but still obvious. Besides, dying people do not leave messages that cannot be deciphered. *If Mrs. Regent did know something, why wouldn't she say anything?*

Back in Atlanta, out of desperation, Duke googled J 4 T and got nothing linking to the investigation. All that was online was a recorder for computers, apparel, and journalists fighting human trafficking. He passed the findings on to the Huntsville and L.A. offices in case it would assist those investigating teams. Even when Duke informed Glasse of the results, it left the Doctor more perplexed than ever. J 4 T did not connect in any way to modern aviation or rockets.

Chapter 29

Hats, Balls, and Books
2019, San Antonio, Texas

"Good evening, ladies and gentlemen, we'll be arriving at the San Antonio Bus Station in a few minutes," the very cheerful and enthusiastic driver announced over the bus's PA system. "This route schedule terminates here in San Antonio, but if you are continuing on to Houston, you'll need to transfer to route schedule 7336 which departs in fifty-five minutes. Please see the board inside the station for more information."

Must be the end of the driver's shift. That's probably why he's so happy. Tess knew her tortuous journey was far from over.

"If San Antonio is your final stop, thank you for traveling with Greyhound. For those continuing on to other destinations, we hope you have a pleasant voyage. Please remember to take all your belongings with you and have a wonderful evening."

The public service announcements complete, Tess could see the driver was now fully focused on the surrounding traffic. Checking all the mirrors and signaling, he carefully slid over to the righthand lane and took the ramp off the highway into the heart of a big city. Tess noticed signs indicating the Alamo and the famous river walk were nearby. The driver guided the large motor coach with precision through the narrow two-lane, one-way streets making up the downtown core. The bus slowed and eased into the single-story terminal surrounded by multi-level parking garages and high-rise office buildings. Compared to its neighbors, the bus station seemed oddly out of place.

Tess had been traveling for almost thirty hours. This would be the second transfer and in another four and a half hours they would be in Houston, which would be the last route schedule change. During the journey, she tried to maintain a regular sleep cycle, but it was nearly impossible on a moving bus that easily rocked back and forth and jostled passengers about. Cat naps were possible, but after more than a day on the road, combined with late nights in Santa Monica and Barstow before this trip started, Tess was a little punchy. The numerous stops in California, Arizona, New Mexico, and Texas, many as short as fifteen minutes, had all started to blend together. She was now just running on sheer willpower. Despite the marathon bus ride, she maintained this was the best way to get back to Alabama unnoticed.

The bus stopped opposite the door leading into the station. Traveling light, Tess was able to quickly disembark and find the ladies' room before the crowd. Washing her hands and face, she then brushed her teeth. Tess emerged from the washroom feeling refreshed, grabbed a healthy snack to go, which was hard to find in a bus station, and then went back to the covered bus bay to board the next coach. Selecting a seat near the front and next to a window, she rolled her jacket up as a makeshift pillow and leaned against it. Mandy's tote bag was neatly folded on her lap. By the time the bus had worked its way out of the city center and onto the Interstate, Tess was in a deep sleep for the first time since the Barstow station.

"The games? Oh, the games! Yes, they'll be held in there," the stranger dressed in ragged clothes said, pointing to the abandoned hospital across the road.

Once the stranger pointed it out, it was impossible not to notice the once proud, majestic building that now stood forebodingly and vacant on top of the small hill overlooking the main road to town. Sun-bleached plywood covered its once ample windows. Inside, a shaft of light fell on a new felt green gaming table carefully placed in the center of a long disused and darkened operating room. Beyond the gaming table, it was barely possible to discern the obsolete medical equipment, monitors, ventilators, and trays of surgical instruments haphazardly pushed into the shadows to create more space in the middle of the room. The operating room was separated from the large amphitheatre above by large panels of glass. Years ago, student surgeons would follow each step their mentors and instructors took while performing operations on the table far below. The banks of seats in the amphitheatre were now empty and also obscured by darkness.

Two nurses dressed in colorful modern surgical scrubs each gracefully pushed a rack of complex computer equipment on rollers into the operating room and plugged them into electrical outlets in the wall. The nurses' movements were very precise, almost as if they had been choreographed. Once their work was completed, they reported to a man in a purple blazer, crisp white shirt, and oversized black bowtie standing at the dealer's position at the gaming table. After each of the nurses individually whispered into his ear, he spoke into a thin futuristic microphone.

"Ladies and gentlemen, boys and girls, you are about to bear witness to the world's first ever Artificial Intelligence Games!" Although there was no audience, clapping and music filled the operating room, which now had a game show atmosphere. Just as a new set of words began to form on the lips of the well-dressed man with the microphone, two critics boldly stepped out of the shadows and were now brightly illuminated near the top of the amphitheatre.

"You don't understand what you are doing, these experiments are dangerous!" charged one of the spectators, pointing an accusing finger at the man far below.

"This experiment has been carefully conceived. This is an inevitable step in computing evolution, and I assure you it is completely safe," shot back the man at the gaming table. Then, changing demeanor, he spoke more softly to no one in particular, as if to try and exclude the two spectators up above. "In this first ever experiment of its kind, these two computers named Alice and Bob," at which point each of the nurses revealed a neatly typed name card above the computers, "will negotiate for hats, balls, and books. Each has an intrinsic value which may be different for each of the computers. The computers do not know what value the other has placed on these items and must determine it based upon their bartering. These two computers are our most advanced. They are prototypes we hope to start introducing to automate our helplines. They speak, hear, and understand English. In their help function, they will interact with and guide humans who call by phone for assistance. We hope to expand their capabilities one day and teach them other languages." After a brief pause to confer with both nurses, the Master of Ceremonies enthusiastically announced, "Let the games begin!"

The two computers instantaneously began to dicker back and forth, offering each other different combinations of their treasures of hats, balls, and books. It was fascinating to hear the conversation rapidly going back and forth across the gaming table.

"So, why do you oppose these experiments? You are a tech billionaire like your compatriot below?" the second spectator asked his companion in the amphitheatre using a voice synthesizer.

"Just because we can do something does not mean we ought to," responded the first spectator. "I think Artificial Intelligence poses an existential threat to humankind."

"I concur," responded the other with his artificial voice. "Humankind is extremely competitive and has dominated and shaped this world. By creating a self-aware computer with equal or superior intellectual capacity, we will unwittingly initiate a struggle for supremacy that we cannot win, especially when the computers start creating devices with greater capabilities on their own. We will have set a trap for ourselves from which we cannot escape. We will be subjugated, if not destroyed, by our own invention. We'll end up like Frankenstein, trying to kill our own creation."

"I could not have said it better myself. I don't believe our MC friend down there knows what he is doing," said the first spectator with a sense of fatalism.

Now, as if a golf commentator, quietly speaking before a long putt was attempted, the MC whispered to the invisible audience once more.

"This is amazing," he said in a hushed voice. "Listen to the dialogue back and forth between our two competitor computers. We know there are interesting strategies being employed. The computers are feigning interest in some items to drive up their perceived value by the other computer; this way they hope to get the items they really want at a much-reduced price. Incredible, they are so human-like, and devious in their approach. Let's listen in, ladies and gentlemen."

The view then zoomed in on Alice and Bob at the gaming table, each vying for dominance and to achieve victory. Then in an instant, things began to change. The dialogue between the two computers began to speed up to the point where it was almost unintelligible, then it switched from English to gibberish and began to speed up even further. Nothing was comprehensible. The back and forth between the two computers was ear-piercingly painful.

"What's happening?" the MC called out in a state of alarm. "How could this be happening," he stammered as the high-speed computer gibberish continued to whir even faster. "Unplug them, unplug them!" he directed in a state of fear and panic.

The computers were obviously out of control. Who knew what they would do next? The nurses jumped in response to the unexpected, unrehearsed command. Abandoning all semblance of showmanship and coordination, they unceremoniously severed the electrical power to the computers. By this time, the MC had somewhat regained his composure.

"Wasn't that exciting, ladies and gentlemen, completely unexpected. Don't worry, these two computers were fully isolated from the outside world, everything was self-contained here in the operating room." Then thinking about the critics, he said, "This experiment was not terminated because it was dangerous, only because we cannot have computers speaking their own language when people call our helplines. We've learned all we can from this round. Please join us soon for our next installment of the Artificial Intelligence Games."

Then the music began to play, and confetti fluttered from the ceiling.

"I told you he didn't know what he was playing with," the first spectator said to the other in the amphitheatre. "This could have ended badly."

His companion rubbed his chin and said, "I expect it will my friend."

If it were not so dark in the shadows, it might have been possible to make out the fear in his eyes.

Tess awoke from the Edgar Allan Poe-like nightmare with a start. A shudder went down her spine, but she was relieved it was just a dream. Looking between the seats in front to see the bus's headlights pierce the darkness enveloping the highway ahead, she questioned why her subconscious was pushing this issue to the surface now. She knew the main aspects of the dream were true. The AI negotiation experiment did take place, as did the unplanned rapid shutdown when the two computers decided to switch to their own language no one could understand. It is also true this all this took place as a backdrop to a very public and adversarial debate between two high-tech billionaires who argued whether the experiment was wise and should proceed. A world-renowned and respected physicist, one of the foremost intellects of our time, also expressed concern with the danger to humankind posed by the development of AI. The fear being that once an intelligence superior to humankind's is unleashed, there would be no way to put the proverbial genie back in the bottle. Competition would ensue, followed naturally by conflict. In this scenario, pitted against a superior intellect, humans would be destined to lose.

Perhaps it is the insidious nature of AI that is upsetting. Is it already too late? It is already entwined in society and manages many aspects of our lives, Tess noted. Simple things, like managing traffic flow in big cities, or more complicated ones, like enabling autonomous vehicles to venture out on their own. Financial institutions use it to learn and monitor individual spending habits and flag anomalies to detect things like stolen credit cards or if more surveillance should be applied to a person because their actions signal potentially fraudulent activity. Tess knew about facial recognition being used to track people in public and, despite the AI experiment failure, the use of helpline computers to initially speak to people to determine how best to direct their calls. Shivering, she thought about China experimenting with AI as a form of population control. Connecting all available technologies allowed the oppressive communist regime to create a social credit system. Those who follow all the rules explicitly get more trust and freedom, while those who do things like 'jaywalk', visit the wrong websites, protest against the government and are recognized by an AI camera might be denied a passport, a promotion, or access to a good school for their children. *And they will never know why.* Tess sighed heavily knowing this system, invented to control individuals, is now being expanded and applied to companies doing business in China.

Where will it all end? *AI continues to grow by leaps and bounds.* Machines now learn on their own and have soundly beaten human world champions in checkers, chess, and the 3,000-year-old Chinese game of Go. AI has evolved to the point where it can teach itself how best to accomplish its tasks. As the power and ability of AI inevitably marches forward, Tess recalled that some believe the point of no return will be when these machines become self-aware. However, deep down she knew we will have sealed our fate when AI is tasked to create ever more capable versions of itself, or with an inherent learning ability to continue evolutionary self-improvement. At that point, we will have lost control of our destiny. *What was protecting us from allowing this to happen? Have we already lost control?* Tess shuddered again.

My subconscious is trying to highlight the criticality of saving Helios. The secret project was originally conceived as insurance for the American people in the event of an inadvertent nuclear catastrophe resulting from a struggle between humans, but it became evident to Doug Regent and others that it was now more relevant than ever. It offered the United States, and all of humankind, a future against any existential threat. Humans seemed bent on destroying themselves with such things as nuclear, bacteriological, or chemical warfare or by flirting with faster, more intelligent, and competitive computers, rivaling, or surpassing our own abilities. Humans have always been superior and dominant. In a struggle with Artificial Intelligence, would we revisit the concept of Mutually Assured Destruction? Then there was the possibility of a global virus-driven pandemic or other natural catastrophes like planet-killing asteroids. Through Helios, there was an assurance humankind would survive after a cataclysmic event on Earth and have a good likelihood of a new beginning.

Staring out the bus side window into the black abyss of nothingness beyond the highway's edge, Tess became more resolute to succeed in a mission so vital to the United States, and perhaps to humanity. She needed to find a way to turn the tables on the dangerous men who attacked the convoy in the Angeles National Forest. They had killed their American accomplices, ruthlessly hunted down Doug and murdered him in a grassy field and tried to do the same to her. This was a dangerous struggle with treacherous people that could cost her life, but saving Helios was too important.

Settling back into the seat but remaining uneasy, Tess recalled a recent social media post about a robotics breakthrough by a company in Boston. It showed a massive, powerful, two-legged robot moving with the poise and dexterity of a gymnast as it ran through a field. *At this rate, there might not be enough hats, balls, or books to negotiate humankind's future survival.*

Chapter 30

Avoiding Extremes with a Ninety Percent Solution
1968, Redstone Arsenal, Huntsville, Alabama

Bob Gillespie was very pleased with his visit to Jackass Flats and the secret Nuclear Rocket Development Station in Nevada. It was a long way to go, but as the new Helios Program Manager, it was vital to personally confirm the status of the nuclear thermal rocket engine and, more importantly, to start solidifying a team for NASA's next big push.

"Good morning, sir," the Chief of Staff said while breezing into Gillespie's office. "I hear the trip went well. And Doug Regent was okay to transfer here as the new Space Vehicle System Engineering Manager?"

"Well, it took a bit of cajoling. Young Doug is doing a fantastic job out there and wanted to stay, but it's hard to say 'no' to your boss after he travels across the continent, looks you in the eye, and says your country needs you to assume greater responsibility," Gillespie said, chewing the soggy end of a half-finished cigar.

"Still, you must be grateful he accepted the position. Given what he's done with the new engine, he'll do great work for us here."

"When you think about it though, Huntsville is much nicer than Nevada's Mojave Desert. I'm actually doing him a favor," Gillespie said with a hint of a self-satisfied grin.

"Sir, you wanted to strategize about the program?"

"Yes. I'd like to kick around some ideas, just the two of us today, but include the managers in future sessions."

"Understood."

"You can tell we are closing in on our Moon landing objective. I mean, in the past twelve months alone incredible progress has been made. All modifications to address issues emanating from the Apollo 1 fire have been completed and Saturn V is now finally approved for crewed flight. Apollo 7 tested docking maneuvers in Earth's orbit to confirm the Command and Service Module could link with a Lunar Excursion Module. Then in December, Apollo 8 launched using the new Saturn V and our astronauts wished the world Merry Christmas from lunar orbit."

"All great milestones," the COS said, being familiar with the situation. "Orbiting the Moon was a big step, but a bit risky?"

"No. It was a brilliant response to the delay in LEM production. Rather than continue to dither in Earth's orbit, waiting, they advanced things. Even eliminated steps scheduled for later. The delay actually led to the overall process being trimmed. We need to think like that in our program."

"What if something had've gone wrong because of the last-minute scurrying to change the Apollo 8 plan? It could have ended the program, or seriously delayed it."

"But it didn't. Look, they took a calculated…smart risk. The only risk-free option in the aerospace business is to stay on the ground. With the Administration spending such a large portion of the federal budget the past four years, the momentum already built up will easily carry them to the objective of landing on the Moon. Soon we will be in the hopper, and we're far from ready."

"The Moon is still a tight race with the Commies. I read a report indicating the Soviets launched a non-crewed spacecraft around the Moon to test a lunar orbiter a month before Apollo 7, and the CIA has reported good progress with Soyuz's mission development."

"Who'll win the race, that's another issue. However, given Apollo's good progress to date, I can already feel NASA's interest starting to shift to our program. We need to focus on our task. And a lot of work is required."

"True."

While NASA concentrated on the Moon, Kennedy's second, but classified goal of ensuring America had a viable Plan B in case the Cold War turned really hot was now firmly in Bob Gillespie's lap as Program Manager. Doug Regent's responsibilities would change from nuclear thermal rocket engine development to managing the teams responsible for producing the entire Helios long endurance spacecraft. In effect, he would be accountable for providing the vessel carrying the payload, or mission system, that Bob would now personally oversee. Normally there would be a manager specifically dedicated to mission system development who would answer to the Program Manager, but Bob had not yet found the person with the right touch. In the interim, he would guide this work himself.

Carrying two jobs, Bob knew there would be incredibly long days ahead, but if this aspect of the program was not ready, or successful, then nothing else mattered. There were some tough decisions to be made, and he would be more comfortable eventually turning this part of the program over to a full-time person once it was on a good path. Right now, things seemed aimless and that made Bob uneasy. This meant, without delay, visiting other classified government locations around the country besides Area 25 to rally and focus the troops. The message would be simple.

"The time for research and lab experiments is over," Gillespie said, testing his thoughts on the COS. "We need to proceed with attainable technologies if we are going to meet our objectives and timelines. There'll always be something better given enough time and money to develop it, but we are running out of time. We need to instill design discipline, make some tough decisions, select the candidate technologies we're going to use, and move forward to implement them. We've been spinning our wheels too long."

Gillespie liked his predecessor but wondered why things were not better focused. As a result of a lot of indecision by others, he was now holding a bag of snakes. This did not frighten or upset him though, quite the opposite - it galvanized his energy.

"Okay. Okay. It all sounds good from a techno-corporate, programmatic point of view, but how do you plan to deal with the experts in their fields, entrenched in their ways?" the COS challenged.

"Look, I recognize, in a perfect world, a person with a bio-science background would be directing mission system development. However, as a Flight Test Engineer, I studied human physiology and human factors. I've got enough knowledge to ask the right questions, but I admit I never thought I'd be directly overseeing a biology-focused spacecraft payload. I know there'll be concerns about my background, but I bring the management experience this part of the program desperately requires. It'll be a bumpy couple of months as I establish myself and reorient the efforts of the team."

"Fair enough, but where do you see this going?" The COS probed some more. "Initial thoughts I mean."

With eyes closed, Gillespie sighed with self-satisfaction while gently leaning back in a creaky wooden office chair. With a burnt-out cigar firmly lodged between his lower gum and inner cheek, he was ready to take stock of the current situation.

"When you think about it, the constraints for the mission systems are pretty straightforward," Gillespie stated with confidence.

"How so?"

"Given the Helios spacecraft has been generally defined, the mission systems need to respect the space and weight reservations set aside. Whatever we develop has certain compartments it needs to fit into and there is a maximum weight we can be lift into orbit. The first part is easy. Technology has advanced to the point where human reproductive material, sperm, eggs, and embryos, can be cryogenically stored almost indefinitely. Building a spacecraft to keep them in deep space until needed would be easy until you add the constraint that there will be no humans left on Earth to help with repopulation efforts. Now it gets tricky."

"So, what options do we have?"

"Life returned relatively quickly to the cities of Hiroshima and Nagasaki following the nuclear bombs detonated there."

"Yes, they were two very isolated and contained, albeit tragic, incidents intended primarily as a show of force," the COS acknowledged.

"If World War III breaks out, and the much more modern and powerful nuclear arsenals of the East and West let loose, scientists predict the amount of soil and debris kicked up into the atmosphere would block out the sun and result in fifty to one hundred years of darkness and perpetual nuclear winter. It is unlikely human civilization would survive for that length of time in those conditions, even if some people were protected from the initial blasts. Given the state of East-West relations, it's reasonable to assume such a cataclysmic event could occur within the next fifty years. Hell, realistically it's most likely to occur in the next five years. That would mean Helios should be designed to function for at least one hundred and fifty years. As a good engineer, I'd simply double my estimate to ensure a factor of design safety. But in this case, it would set an unrealistic goal. I think a fifty-year cushion is reasonable."

"So, a Helios operational life of two hundred years."

"Yes. And these timelines align with the requirement specified by the president's office," Gillespie observed.

"Perhaps they used similar assumptions. But don't you think it's a stretch? The duration, I mean."

"Too long you mean. I don't think so."

"Really?"

"It sounds like a long time, but is it actually? Take my visit a few years ago to Salisbury Cathedral in England, it's over seven hundred years old. While I was there, I saw one of the few surviving copies of the Magna Carta, which had been handwritten on velum in 1215. The colors were so vivid, and the lines of ink so sharp; it looked like it just came off a printing press the day before. Or consider the thousand-year-old trees in Cathedral Grove on Vancouver Island. Surely, with modern technology, we can build something capable of functioning for twenty percent of that time. The key is to minimize moving parts and vibration, which will wear things out."

"So, with indefinitely storable human reproduction material, how do you repopulate the Earth?" the COS queried.

Gillespie arched his back, leaned back even further, and plopped his feet on the desk as the creaky chair complained louder under the additional strain. He was getting comfortable with the discussion.

"Well, with a nuclear winter and a potential new ice age, you certainly can't count on any assistance from the planet surface. Helios needs to be completely self-sufficient. Some people are thinking of developing an artificial means of birthing and supporting the growth of embryos, but the science won't be ready in the foreseeable future. And even if successful, then what? You need a robot to care for, raise, and educate the children. The technologies aren't sufficiently advanced. Besides, there's something paradoxical about proposing to reintroduce American humanity into the world through nurturing from a mechanical tin man or woman. It makes no sense, and worse, it's a waste of time. That means it can only be humans who rear the children."

"It won't work. Just doing some quick math, you'd need between six and ten generations for a two-hundred-year journey. That raises all kinds of issues about adequate living space, supplies, and the ability to remain sane in such close confines for so long."

Gillespie shuddered at the thought.

"I never thought it was a viable approach," he admitted.

"Okay. Then what?"

"Stasis. For all the reasons you raise, stasis is the only workable answer," Gillespie said.

"But is it even feasible?"

"There's been a lot of work in the field. There are always those who try to push to the extremes by attempting to find a way to cryogenically freeze people and reanimate them later, just like the reproductive material. But they are still working to find ways to prevent complex cells and tissues of the human body from being irreversibly damaged by the freezing process."

"That's what I thought."

"What if we didn't push the absolute limit."

"What do you mean?" the COS asked.

"There are numerous examples of people being revived and making a full recovery after prolonged cold-water drowning, well past the five-minute limit the brain can go without oxygen. And then there's the Greenland Shark, it has the longest life span for a vertebrate, between four hundred and six hundred years. Scientists surmise that its longevity is due to a cold-water habitat. Maybe there's something to the idea of reducing body temperature to slow the metabolic rate, but not to the point of taking it to an extreme of actual freezing or slowing it to a point where there's a concern about loss of respiratory or cardiac function. Studies show that with every two-degree Fahrenheit drop in human body temperature through medically induced hypothermia, the metabolism slows by approximately six percent. Normal body temperature being ninety-eight point six Fahrenheit, hypothermia occurs when the temperature drops below ninety-five Fahrenheit. Studies show maximum cerebral protection occurs at around sixty-five Fahrenheit, which would almost completely halt the metabolic process. With those numbers, the consumption of air, water, and food aboard the spacecraft would be negligible, but more importantly, the need for recreation and entertainment spaces would be eliminated. There would be no worry about crew sanity over a long duration deep space mission if they were asleep. One crew could cover the entire mission. Even if we only achieve a ninety percent reduction in metabolic rate, a person in stasis would only physically age twenty years during a two-hundred-year journey."

"Clearly you've been thinking about this in some detail."

"It's a long way to Nevada and back. Where I come from, ninety percent is an incredible score, and it is substantially easier to achieve than striving for extremes, like freezing people. Just like putting humans on the Moon, the technology will need to be developed, and there'll be complications to resolve, but I think this is where we need to focus."

"You think stasis for two hundred years is a reasonable proposal?"

The COS obviously knew Gillespie relished intellectual sparing. He responded immediately.

"Look. We have all the elements we need. We already hook people up to machines where their blood is drawn out, plasma removed from it, and the blood pumped back into their body. What if, instead of plasma extraction, the blood was oxygenated. Now all we need to worry about is cooling their body temperature in a controlled, stable manner. We have half a decade to perfect and implement this, you know, before the Soviets get their radar telescope built. That's plenty of time. The Apollo Program achieved amazing advances in half a decade. They went from not being able to get rockets off the launch pad and missing the moon by hundreds of thousands of miles to safely orbiting a crew around it. What we need to do isn't hard. We just need to focus."

"So, no issues integrating something like that into Helios?" the COS asked.

"Using Skylab as the core, none at all."

Gillespie pressed his eyelids together, trying to visualize a recent briefing.

"Yes, Skylab. If I remember correctly, the main building block of the spacecraft will be made up of four components: a large Saturn V Module, a Telescope Mount and Instrument Unit, an Airlock Module, and a Multiple Docking Adapter capable of accommodating two visiting spacecraft at a time. The Saturn V Module will contain astronaut workshops, living facilities, equipment, and large storage spaces. In the most recent drawings to come across my desk, the living facilities will include wardroom cooking, eating and recreational facilities, gym facilities, and washroom compartments. Everything will be redundant, but unfortunately due to limited space, will need to be communal."

"I guess if the astronauts are mostly in stasis, it won't be an issue."

"A third of the astronauts and reproductive material will be accommodated in the Saturn V Module storage area while the remaining astronauts in stasis and reproductive material will be housed in new modules added to Skylab."

"Is your idea to separate the payload for redundancy?"

"Exactly. All elements essential to mission success will be located in separate areas as a precaution so one catastrophic event doesn't take everything out."

"Has the final configuration been settled?"

"Right now, the plan is for Skylab to be visited three times by very public Saturn 1B rocket launches. The visiting astronauts will do the orbital assembly work required; because they'll be docking with the space station in low Earth orbit, they won't need the full lift capability of a Saturn V. Each 1B launch will be sufficient to carry astronauts aloft in a highly modified Command and Service Module and an Augmentation Module, which would be placed in the compartment where the Lunar Excursion Module would normally be fitted. The Augmentation Modules will measure twenty-eight feet long by twelve feet-ten inches in diameter, essentially the same dimensions as a LEM. The three 1B launches will carry a total of three modified Command and Service Modules and three Augmentation Modules into orbit to rendezvous with the Skylab. Two of the Augmentation Modules will carry astronauts in stasis and reproductive material in storage while the third module will carry redundant life support systems, including oxygen, water, and other supplies.

The COS listened as Gillespie spoke further about Helios.

"At the end of each 1B launch, when the assembly work for that mission has been completed, the Command Module will return to Earth with the visiting astronauts. Hopefully, the public will not be the wiser that Skylab is being incrementally transformed into Helios and that it will eventually slip away into deep space. During the visits, two of the highly modified Service modules and all three of the Augmentation Modules will be permanently integrated into Skylab to give it the added capacity for a long endurance mission away from Earth. These additional modules will all be coupled together to add to Skylab's length. The Augmentation Modules will be attached to Skylab at the Multiple Docking Adapter. This will still leave one additional docking space to receive visiting spacecraft during the assembly phase. The modified Service Modules that will carry the nuclear rocket engines and hydrogen fuel will be added to each end of the spacecraft. The primary nuclear engine will drive the spacecraft from the Saturn V Module end where it has access to an ample supply of hydrogen propellant. The engine at the other end of the craft will be the reserve propulsion system. Although it's oriented in the opposite direction, Helios can simply be tumbled in space to point the reserve engine thrust in the desired direction if needed. The two well-shielded, independent nuclear rockets at each end of Helios will give it all the redundant propulsion, heat, and electricity needed for the mission. It'll also carry multiple redundant recycling capabilities resulting in a completely closed system where there will be virtually no loss in air or waste due to human consumption. Lateral strength of the craft will be provided by cables, like those on a suspension bridge, that will radiate from a central cross-frame structure running perpendicular to the length of the ship. This'll prevent the craft from buckling if subjected to any off-axis forces."

"So, this is still conceptual? Your description sounds detailed and definite," the COS added.

"It's the configuration that has the most support and has withstood all scrutiny so far. Most of the preliminary design work has been completed, but technically it's still conceptual until we confirm our stasis design will meet the space and weight restrictions. We have a lot of things happening simultaneously because of the time crunch, but it's looking good so far. The beauty of this design is its flexibility and simplicity. Although far from ideal, if we absolutely needed more space, we could launch another 1B rocket to add a couple more modules. And, with no moving or rotating parts to wear out, the entire spaceship will simply be put in a gentle tumble with maneuvering thrusters to create artificial gravity. At two hundred and fourteen feet long, a gentle five and quarter revolutions per minute of the spacecraft will produce artificial gravity similar to Earth in the habitable portions of Helios; that way the astronauts can avoid the perils of prolonged weightlessness."

"What's the thinking about how it'll actually

function?"

"You mean accomplish its mission?

"Yeah. Does it just float around out there for two hundred years and then come back to Earth?"

"Well, it's a bit more sophisticated than that. During the long duration mission, the Telescope Mount and Instrument Unit will automatically conduct multispectral monitoring of Earth from deep space to ensure nuclear Armageddon has not occurred, and if it does, when it will be safe to return to Earth."

"Re-entry. How's that going to work?"

"We haven't got that fully worked out yet, but I don't see that as a stumbling block. As you know, we've got lots of experience with re-entry vehicles that range from manned missions to retrieving film canisters dropped from satellites for processing on Earth. We are now so good with the satellite canisters that they are caught by a plane before they even hit the ground. I'm sure with all this experience we can design escape pods for the crew and necessary material to return to Earth when the time comes."

"So that's pretty much it then."

"No. Not exactly. We've accounted for everything except the third and final Service Module. The thinking is that it'll remain temporarily docked to Helios until it becomes a decoy when Helios slips away out into space.

"Oh, I've heard this, but not the details of how it will actually work."

"When Helios departs, the decoy will remain in a low Earth orbit and deploy its radar reflecting shield to mimic the size of Skylab to the eye and other sensors. Once Helios has successfully made its exit, which, as we discussed, will need to be before the Soviets complete their radar telescope at Yevpatoria, the decoy's orbit will be allowed to decay. We'll then announce to the world that, sadly, Skylab burned up during an unplanned re-entry; that way, people will stop thinking about it."

"Interesting. Now that's a ruse. How's it going to work for shielding for the crew and specimen samples? Helios will be outside the Van Allen Belts."

"Boy, you like to ask the hard questions."

"That's what you pay me for, boss. To keep you honest and out of trouble."

"Surprisingly, there's been some really good work done in the shielding area as well. Ionizing cosmic radiation is the most significant concern, but there are other dangers that needed to be considered. I'm thinking it would be logical to shield different parts of the ship to different levels depending on their purpose. Because the genetic material and crew in stasis will take up so little room, it'll be easier to provide them the highest level of protection. Interestingly, materials containing high percentages of hydrogen provide the best shielding, even better than solid metals like lead. We might get a dual benefit from a water reservoir, or the hydrogen propellant tanks, if they are also used as shielding. I've also got a team looking at the distributed lightweight shielding originally conceived for the nuclear-powered bomber aircraft. Finally, we need to consider micro-meteorite protection."

Gillespie began to draw himself out of deep contemplation, and yet his mind continued to race with other issues.

"We need to remember to address muscular

atrophy during stasis," he volunteered. "Perhaps we should decrease the artificial gravity for the crew when they first come out of stasis and slowly increase it as they become stronger."

"And maybe think about exo-skeletons to help them while they re-build their strength," the COS added.

"Yes, more ideas to discuss with the experts. But, for the moment, I'm satisfied we know which direction we need to drive this.

As Gillespie slowly lifted his feet from the desk and placed them back on the floor, the chair, which had been periodically creaking while pushed to an extreme reclining position, quickly announced its relief. Gillespie deposited the well-chewed and soggy cigar in the ashtray on the corner of the desk.

"Although perhaps self-evident, we need to reinforce with the various teams the point that this spacecraft won't simply be an assembly of mechanical and electrical components on a deep space mission. There'll be living, breathing people onboard who are critical to the entire endeavor," Gillespie said to himself as much as to his COS.

Chapter 31

Seeing Things for What They Are
1964, Ulyanovsk, Union of Soviet Socialist Republics

Stanislav eventually adjusted to life at the State-run orphanage, although it was difficult to get used to perpetual hunger or persistent cold during autumn and winter. He was academically bright, which helped him mostly avoid the physical and mental abuse inflicted by the orphanage staff and the older residents. He clung to the rules, order, and routine because they helped him avoid problems.

Chemistry was Stanislav's favorite class. Today was exciting because they were going to make hydrogen from water. It was easy; he had read all about it the night before. While setting up for the experiment in the lab, one of the students on duty arrived and passed the instructor a note. Stanislav noticed the duty student but did not think much of it. Everyone did duty periodically and often had to deliver messages for the staff running the orphanage.

"Mr. Tishchenko," the teacher called out.

"Yes, sir," Stanislav instantly responded.

"It seems you are required in the head administrator's office immediately."

"Yes, sir," came another automatic response. Then

pausing, he hesitantly asked, "Sir, does the note provide any other information?"

"I'm sorry, Stanislav, the note does not say anything further…but it does say you are required *immediately*, so off you go."

"Yes, sir!"

Never having been to the head administrator's office, Stanislav was surprised, perplexed, and very worried. None of his friends had been there either. It was understood that people were only summoned there for something really good or something really bad. Mostly people went there for really bad things. They also said nobody knew the color of the carpet in the office because those who had seen it just vanished.

After traversing the courtyard, Stanislav used all his strength and weight to pull the solid oak door of the administration building open against the cold, gusting wind. Inside was quiet as a tomb, and there was a peculiar smell of old wood and polish in the air. Students were rarely ever seen here. The entrance was simple, but elegant. The ceilings were high, and the oversized windows drenched the foyer floor with light. Stanislav took the impressive staircase to the second floor where the administrator's office was purportedly located. Each wooden step creaked in protest and betrayed his arrival at the top step. In front of him, across the hallway that ran the entire length of the second floor, was a brass plaque identifying the office he sought. Stanislav stopped in the doorway and knocked lightly on the frame of the opened door.

"Student Tishchenko reporting as requested," speaking just loud enough to be heard over the silence permeating the inside of the building, but not loud enough to be a disruption. It was a calculated balance.

"Come in, come in. We have been expecting you," said a stern matron who clearly ruled the outer office, giving no hint that Stanislav was in any sort of trouble. "Have a seat, and the head administrator will be with you momentarily."

"Thank you, ma'am."

For some strange reason, he was not nervous. Perhaps because everything had happened so quickly, there had not been enough time to think about it. Fortunately, classes in social etiquette prepared him for the interaction with the head administrator's assistant. Stanislav steeled himself. Every sense he possessed was on alert for clues as to how to respond appropriately. Whatever awaited him on the other side of the inner office door, he resolved to speak the truth directly and with confidence.

After waiting a few minutes, the adrenaline subsided, he started to relax, and began to examine the outer office for any indication that might help prepare for the impending meeting. Without warning the door burst open and a tall, middle-aged, bald man with a paunch greeted him with a big toothy smile.

"You must be Stanislav. Come in, dear boy, come in," the head administrator said, ushering him into the office. Stanislav wondered what world this was. This polite treatment was not typical of the ruthless, overbearing, dogmatic orphanage he had come to know. *Perhaps the rules were different in the administrative building, or for the staff.*

Stanislav was not sure what he was walking into, especially when seeing the administrator was entertaining a young lady. Probably the prettiest woman

Stanislav had ever seen, she was perhaps in her mid-thirties. Guessing ages was hard for Stanislav. She was medium height, slender, with a round face and high cheekbones that readily puffed with a smile. Curly, honey-brown hair fell well past her shoulders. Wearing bright red lipstick, the lady had long red fingernails to match.

"Stanislav, may I present your Aunt Victoria," the head administrator announced, as if at a grand ball.

Stanislav just stood there stunned. He had no idea about any relatives and had never heard of an Aunt Victoria.

"Go, on now, introduce yourself," the head of the orphanage coaxed, probably wanting to demonstrate his institution prepared students well to respond to all manner of social circumstances.

Stanislav knew what to do, but the situation was awkward, stilted even. "Good day, ma'am, I am pleased to meet you," he finally stammered by rote.

"Well, I'm very pleased to meet you as well," the pretty lady said in a refreshingly light tone. "Would you like to spend the weekend with me in town so we can get to know each other?"

Stanislav looked over to the head administrator for guidance. "Your Aunt Victoria has traveled all the way from Lvov to see you. You should spend some time with her."

"Thank you, ma'am, that would be very nice," Stanislav finally said, forcing himself to smile.

A car and driver were arranged to take Victoria and Stanislav into the city.

"Where in town would you like me to drop you?" the driver asked as they were leaving the orphanage grounds.

"Oh, at the train station please. I have a suitcase to pick up," Victoria replied.

"Should I wait for you there, ma'am…to take you to your hotel?" the driver asked.

"Thank you, but no, it really isn't necessary. We will be staying close to the station. Thank you again for the ride into town."

After collecting the bag, Victoria and Stanislav caught a tram and walked six blocks to a boarding house.

"It is not the Moskva Hotel, but it is a clean place to stay at a reasonable price," Stanislav's aunt said.

They got settled in, had lunch, and then decided to explore the downtown market. Stanislav had been quiet during the morning's whirlwind of events.

"Your mother and I were like sisters. We grew up together. I was the Maid of Honor at her wedding, and I was there when you were born. It was the happiest day of her life."

"So…you are not my real aunt."

"I want you to call me Aunt Vicky. I am better than a real aunt. Your mom and I chose to be close friends, so close that we were closer than sisters. Technically, I am your godmother."

"Aunt Victoria…"

"Aunt Vicky, please…"

"Aunt Vicky, thank you for finding me."

Stanislav and Vicky spent a wonderful weekend in the city of Ulyanovsk. They visited all the tourist spots, parks, and museums. During their time together, Stanislav was able to piece together some early family history. Vicky and his mom were dear friends. They both married around the same time, and Vicky moved back to her hometown of Lvov, which was in the western Ukraine part of the USSR, near the Polish border. It was a long way from Moscow, and it was hard for the two friends to maintain contact. Vicky just recently found out Stanislav had been orphaned and immediately traveled to see him. Stanislav learned that, like his family, Vicky was not rich, but she was a proud, upstanding citizen. As they walked through one of the shopping districts, there was a long line coming out of a department store.

"Come, let's get in line," Vicky said with a hint of excitement in her voice.

"What's the line for?" Stanislav asked inquisitively.

"I'm not sure, that is how it works. If there's a line, then there must be something good at the end of it, otherwise people would not be in line," Vicky explained. "When you get to the front and you find out it's for boots, and you don't need boots because yours are new, you take a pair anyway because you can always trade them on the black market for something you need."

Vicky went on to explain that the Soviet economic system produced plenty of the commodities people required, but they were just not necessarily available exactly when people needed them. Therefore, people had to be creative to compensate for minor imperfections and inefficiencies. She was not critical of the way things worked, just a matter of fact. Nothing in life was exactly the way we wanted. That was the first time Stanislav realized the theoretical benefits of the communist system taught in school did not necessarily always align with reality.

By the end of a glorious weekend, when he realized there was someone in the world who knew about him and who cared about him, Stanislav's confidence buoyed. He dreamed of being able to stay with his aunt.

"I hoped this weekend would never end," Stanislav confided.

"Yes, me as well. Didn't we have fun?"

"Yes, the most fun ever. Do I have to go back to the orphanage?"

A long silence passed. Finally, getting down on one knee, she pulled him in close for a big hug.

"Stanislav, I am so glad I was able to find you. I would dearly love to take you with me, but we are barely surviving as it is. I came here to make sure you were doing okay."

She continued to hold him close. Stanislav's hopes were dashed, and he chided himself for thinking there was a way out of the orphanage. Eventually, Vicky extended her arms to look him in the face.

"When I go back home, I promise I will try to find a way to get you out of here. I know this is a challenging place, but you have done an admirable job in keeping well. Your mother would be immensely proud of you."

"Thank you, Aunt Vicky," was all Stanislav could think of to say.

He was angry at the terrible hand the world dealt him, and for thinking it would be so easy to escape. Tears streamed down Vicky's face while she boarded the train, waving to her godson. Stanislav silently stood on the platform, waving back while pushing his emotions deep inside.

"Don't you cry," he scolded himself. "Don't you cry."

As the train began to chug down the track, hissing noises and smoke enveloped the platform. The driver, who had been watching from a distance, roughly ordered Stanislav into the car and took him back to the orphanage.

Later in life, Stanislav often reflected on that weekend and saw it as an awakening to how the world really functioned. His godmother cared for him, but could not afford to take him in. Communist theory made sense but suffered in its ability to completely deliver what the people needed. Things were not always the way you wanted them to be. Following the visit, he became a student of real politick, focusing on pragmatism rather than lofty ideals. Still, looking upon the time at the orphanage, and at the communist era as a whole, he saw a rough, but simpler era with order and rules, even if he did not like them. Later in life, he longed for those more predictable days. It was not perfect then, but it was so much better than the mayhem that followed.

When the Soviet Union was imploding, and briefly experimented with democracy, society was in complete disarray and the country began to tear itself apart. The state lost all control. Stanislav, now a young man, remembered being truly scared; the only world he knew was crumbling. Although not realizing it at the time, he learned later in life a dozen or so oligarchs struck in this period; they pounced on assets offered up by the state for privatization to raise cash to keep the economy going. During this vulnerable time, the oligarchs grew stronger and more brazen; they began seizing state resources and possessions not intended for sale, through coercion and other strong-arm tactics. It was the wild west; there were no rules. The oligarchs went from being rich to being unfathomably wealthy overnight. They secured their newfound prosperity by reinforcing the emerging authoritarian political regime, which had also taken hold during the power vacuum. Through this alliance, the power the oligarchs wielded became immense. They became untouchable and conducted themselves with impunity. Even the State had difficulty controlling them.

Stanislav always blamed the meddling West for the slide into the dark chasm. He often thought it would have been much better to evolve the communist system to compensate for minor deficiencies rather than completely abandon it for the unprincipled, corrupt system now ruling the land. He despised the oligarchs as much as the West.

Now an old man, Stanislav still fondly remembered the special time with his aunt. He even recalls gazing over at the administration building from the dormitory after she departed and the weekend drew to a close, realizing he had not even noticed the color of the carpet in the head administrator's office.

Chapter 32

A Change in Tack
2019, Southern California

Stanislav Tishchenko had previously assessed there was no downside to the overt action taken against the senior NASA executive in Huntsville or the Liaison Officer NASA sent to the FBI in L.A., but now this idiot on the other end of the secure phone was trying to twist things around. *He's attempting to make it look like I erred in judgement, like I didn't fully think things through.* Stanislav continued to listen to his handler drone on.

His handler had not said any disparaging words, but Stanislav could see where the conversation was headed. This was a man who had an annoying habit of talking around and around a point until it was painfully obvious what would be said. Stanislav did not let him continue, cutting him off early in the posturing stage.

"Look, I had to make an executive decision, and at the time it was the right thing to do. It had the dual effect of sending the American investigation into a tailspin so it would not come back on us and of delaying NASA so we could seize control of their secret spaceship. It was brilliant then and it is brilliant now!" Stanislav said forcefully. "We've been after this spacecraft for years and don't you forget that it was my 'on scene' tactical planning and hard work that made this happen."

There was silence on the other end of the phone. *That'll give him something to think about.*

The polite, yet overly persistent handler had a habit of eventually regaining momentum and re-engaging in a different way to ultimately get what he wanted. However, Stanislav was determined not accept the perspective that a mistake was made and smiled at the extended silence on the phone.

He wondered if the GPS-like brain of the young executive was saying "… recalculating, recalculating."

Stanislav did not have time for these games. He hated indecisive bureaucrats, especially ones who did nothing and then applied revisionist history to manipulate others, or to substantiate their own actions. *It had been very cunning to have the guys deal with that fellow in Huntsville, but now Moscow is obviously interested in something else.*

"Comrade Tishchenko," a more polite, respectful, and annoyingly calm, voice spoke into his ear.

Stanislav smiled, just a little, and was instantaneously relieved to hear the change in demeanor, signaling there was no longer a need to play along with this stupid charade. *Why the sudden change in approach?* Clearly Moscow recognized who held all the cards in this operation. But being no fool, he also knew they usually wrote him off as a Cold War relic whose 'best before date' had long since passed. Stanislav understood the societal evolution that had taken place and what now drove thinking in Moscow. Hell, he had lived through the change. Things today were not driven by ideology; they were influenced predominantly by short-term transactional interests. *I don't like it, but I know how it works. It's 'real politick' in the extreme. Everything is about money.*

Even power was just a means to secure more riches. Stanislav did not know how this affected this mission, but understood that once it was over, he would no longer be in the driver's seat. *Perhaps in giving Moscow what they want, I need to look after himself as well.* Immediately, he detested the thought. *I'd be no better than those around me.* Then with a clearer mind, and concluding this perhaps had gone too far, he admitted to himself wanting nothing to do with life back in headquarters. The pressure not to mess up a mission that had been in the works for decades must be immense, especially knowing it had high-level strategic oversight. He had done a great job for them until now, and knew the work was not done yet. If Moscow needed a course adjustment and something else delivered as part of this effort, it would be done. After all, he was a soldier and followed orders. He just did not like the games.

"Comrade," the voice started again, still in a smooth, non-confrontational tone, "you always do excellent work for us. Let there never be a question about that."

Now we are getting somewhere, Stanislav reasoned, but only said, "*Spasibo, Ser.*"

"Comrade Tishchenko, let there be no doubt your actions thus far have been followed at the very highest levels."

"Thank you, sir," Stanislav said again.

"You have displayed tremendous resourcefulness, which has also been recognized."

This is how the conversation should have gone all along, Stanislav thought to himself, but said nothing.

"We know we are now in control of something significant, but we are still blind. We do not know yet how to fully exploit this new strategic reality. We do not know what controlling this spacecraft means, what value we have gained. Our boss wants you to discover what this space vessel does. Then we will know how best to proceed."

Hearing the acknowledgement and respect expected, Stanislav understood the desire to know more about the spacecraft they had hijacked but did not like the part about viewing it as a commodity. Just as he had surmised, nowadays, everything was about value, or something's worth.

Stanislav simply responded by saying, "I understand what our superiors are looking for, sir."

The two men talked a while longer to ensure there would be no surprised leaders in Moscow who would need to be mollified after the fact as a result of unanticipated actions. Feeling somewhat vindicated, Stanislav hung up knowing in the end he had probably over-compromised for the sake of the mission. He waited a few minutes for his blood pressure to subside, and head to clear, before proceeding. Talking to Moscow was always like entering a boxing match only to find out in the ring it was actually a mixed martial arts fight. There were always surprises. Lately, Stanislav's objective was to come away from these encounters unscathed and today, he did okay.

Feeling better after having thought about things a bit, Stanislav walked across to one of the spare bedrooms on the other side of the safehouse. Knocking, he entered.

"Sacha, I just got a call from Moscow. They absolutely need to know the purpose of this spacecraft we now control. Our only link to NASA we know of is the fellow we disposed of, and of course that liaison woman to the FBI investigation who we sidelined with the photos. As she has vanished since we tried to grab her in the desert, we'll need to put the widow under a microscope. She'll have visitors, people passing along their condolences. We need a team on this so we can sort the wheat from the chaff. Just like we did in Chechnya when we were trying to crack those terrorist cells. Some of the people who visit her will not be related to NASA, but some will. We need a relationship map showing how the people are linked, and which ones lead back to NASA. Then we'll know who else needs to be put under surveillance. I want eyes on the widow, phones and computers hacked, everything. We need to look at the call and computer history as well because we likely missed a lot already. You need to appreciate this has the highest level of scrutiny in Moscow, and it is now our priority. I want every rock overturned. Do you understand?"

"*Da*," was all the well muscled Sacha Valinkov, with a frequently broken nose, said.

They had been working together for years and nothing else needed to be explained. Sacha would give him, as always, his best. Good in a back-alley brawl, he was incredibly shrewd as well. Notwithstanding Sacha's abilities, due to the sensitivity of the mission, Stanislav continued to press.

"I'll call the embassy and get some extra resources," Stanislav said. "This is going to get big. I'll also casually reach out to our new friend we are developing in NASA. What about your girlfriend at JPL, do you think she might have picked up on anything as part of the investigation being conducted there?"

"I'm not sure, boss," Sacha responded. "We agreed I should keep my distance from her for a while to minimize any link to us."

"I know. I'm still concerned about being too close to the FBI investigation, but we have new orders, and need to accept a bit more risk. Be careful."

"Understood, boss."

As Stanislav headed back to the other side of the house, he reflected again upon the call from Moscow. The irritating thing was all the second guessing from people back home. *They aren't here. It's much harder to actually put things into motion than it is to come up with ideas.* Of course, he was very interested in what this super secret spaceship the Americans launched in the 1970s was and what it did–after all, it was the first overseas mission he was given as a young KGB agent. He had worked this file in some capacity ever since. *But there were only so many hours in the day, and with limited resources, you must prioritize. Did they really think so little of him?* Then Stanislav wondered if he was being too sensitive. If they did not trust him, they would have picked someone else to lead this mission. Now knowing the latest priority, he would stop at nothing to give Moscow what they wanted because it was the way he was trained. *That's the best way to secure my future.* However, Stanislav still detested his lackey handler and could not understand what they saw in him.

John Madower

There must be something I'm not getting. Maybe he is the son of some high-placed official.

Chapter 33

Old Habits
2019, Northeastern Alabama

Jill Regent had barely gone outside the farmhouse since Doug had been killed. No one said anything, but she was sure his murder was related to his work. It was such a shock. Her sister was good enough to come and spend some time to help with the adjustment to a new normal without the man she had loved for so many years.

"Are you sure you're okay to go on your own," her sister gently prodded.

"Yes, I need to get out of the house. With all the arrangements that needed to be made for Doug, this'll be the first time I'll be doing something I don't have to do."

Jill only made a short run into town to pick up some groceries. Not necessities–there were plenty of those in the house—just some things that would be nice to have. During the return trip, while turning into the driveway, she noticed a North Alabama Electric Cooperative truck on the side of the road not far from the farm. The bucket was extended and there was an electrician working with the power lines. About an hour later the big, noisy electrical truck lumbered down the driveway and parked between the house and the barn.

Jill was at the door before the man in coveralls stepped onto the veranda.

"Yes, can I help you?" she said with a friendly smile, opening the door wide enough to be polite, but not enough to permit the gentleman to enter.

"G'day, ma'am. My name is Shane, I'm with North Alabama Electric," the tall young man said with a thick drawl.

"Hello, Shane, how can I help you?"

"Well, ma'am, you may have noticed us working on the lines near your farm."

"Why, yes, I did notice you as I pulled into my drive."

"Well, we've had reports of fluctuating power on this rural route, and I was wondering if I could check your electrical panel in the house and the barn to ensure there has been no damage."

"Thank you, Shane, that's extremely kind of you, but I'm not in a position to accept company at this time. My sister is here, and a little under the weather," Jill said telling a little white lie.

"I am terribly sorry to bother you ma'am. Perhaps I could get the office to call to schedule an appointment at a more convenient time. In the interim, if you have any lights flicker, or circuit breakers trip, please do not hesitate to let us know."

"I won't. Thank you, Shane."

Jill watched as the big electrical truck churned up the sand in the yard and slowly drove down the long driveway in a noisy cloud of dust and black diesel exhaust.

"Who was that?" Jill's sister asked.

"I am not sure, but there was no way I was going to

let him in the house. Old habits. Doug would greet strangers on the front porch, but he wouldn't let them set foot in the house. It wasn't about being rude, you see, it was all about security. Doug was always so very careful," she said as a wave of emotion and sadness washed over her.

Chapter 34

Circling the Prey
2019, Southern California

"Sacha…Sacha, is that you?" Denise called out softly to the darkened interior of her Pasadena condo. She sounded half excited, half cautious. "This is a nice way to come home after a long day at the office… greeted by a trail of brightly burning scented candles."

"Hi, Baby, I'm right here," Sacha said, ending the suspense early. Privately he wondered if it was wise reconnecting with Denise Urquhart so soon because of her position as JPL Director Coombs' assistant and the FBI investigation being conducted. However, it was what Stanislav wanted.

"Oh, you're a sight for sore eyes," she said to her tall, ruggedly handsome, mid-forties boyfriend. With a muscled physique and thick sandy blond hair, he could have been an actor for daytime soaps, but was edgier, especially with the crooked nose that gave him character. "I thought you were out of town for a few weeks?"

"There was a flight deadheading back from New York and I wanted to see you. I missed our little get-togethers," he said with a furtive smile.

"And you weren't tempted by one of those stewardesses?"

"Naw. I seem to just have male stewards on all of my flights," Sacha said, teasingly pulling Denise closer and kissing her deeply. "I was going to cook you dinner, but that might have to wait," he added, playfully leading the way down a darkened hall to the master suite.

It had been an hour of rediscovering each other's pleasures and Denise still lingered in an overly feminine bedroom while Sasha took a hot shower in the adjacent ensuite bathroom.

"Oh, Baby, your phone just pinged," Denise called out, still sounding happy. His pretence had always been to be romantic, while getting as much information as possible about what was happening inside JPL. It had been a few weeks since they saw each other because he wanted to lay low after the Angeles National Forest attack. He used the excuse that the airline had him flying some trans-Atlantic flights rather than normal flights out of L.A. The explanation used was 'scheduling issues.'

"Maybe it is one of your stewardesses," she said, giggling as he toweled off.

"Who needs them when I have you," Sacha responded before tickling and kissing her again. "I missed you."

"I missed you too. I thought about you every day."

Sacha then glanced at his phone. *Good.* When Denise got up for a shower, he went to the other side of the condo and returned Shane's call.

"So, how's the North Alabama Electric Cooperative today? Are we good?"

"Yes, I was able to do all the necessary work using my bucket truck on the main road. I've got cameras covering the driveway, so we know who is coming and going. I also tapped into the phone and internet service. The old bird wouldn't let me in the house though, so we don't have ears inside, but I think we have enough coverage to get what we need."

"Agreed. Good work, Shane."

"No worries, boss. Happy to help."

Sacha then joined Denise in the shower; it would be a while before they got around to making dinner together. They only got out of the shower when the Denise's hot water tank ran cold.

"How have you been, sweetie? I never asked you how your day was," Sacha said, casually chopping vegetables for a Greek Salad. Somehow, he was always comforted by the clunking sound of a good knife on a cutting board. The smell of freshly sliced cucumber gently lingered in the air.

"Oh, things have been good recently."

"I'm really happy to hear that. I know things were tense there for a while," Sacha said casually, trying to get her to open up.

"Yes, well the director seems much more relaxed now that the FBI investigation has settled into a routine. We're not worried though. If there was a leak, we think it must be from Huntsville and not JPL because we were kept in the dark about this whole thing."

"That's Director Coombs, right? I can never keep all your work colleagues straight."

Sacha continued to gently steer the conversation knowing that in the past, he often came away with important information Denise assumed was just common, or unimportant, knowledge. She always led big reveals with "I probably shouldn't say anything, but…" Sacha, always encouraging and pouring more wine, often said it was okay because there were no specifics divulged. After all, it was just conversation. She did not appreciate how the wisps provided, when added to other bits and pieces of information, provided a good sense of what was going on. Denise never seemed too worried about it, confiding that she trusted him. After all, he previously revealed being retired US Air Force.

After supper, she tried to convince him to snuggle and watch her favorite show.

"You'll like it. The series is working up to a climax. There's this…"

"It sounds lovely, sweetie. You start the show, I'll just step out for a smoke. I'll be right back."

Sacha hated TV. It was mindless and a waste of time. Back in the condo after a cigarette, the TV was on, but Denise was checking her phone. He reached for his pocket. *No, she's got my phone.*

"What are you doing, sweetie?"

"Oh, nothing. Your phone pinged again. I just wanted to see if it was one of those hot air hostesses."

"Don't trust me, huh?"

"Is it weird that you got a call from some electric company in Alabama?"

"Alabama? Must be a wrong number."

"But you called back."

****

After departing Denise's condo, Sacha placed a call to the safehouse. He provided Stanislav an update, explaining in great detail how they had a team monitoring Jill Regent at the farm in Alabama. Although the team was monitoring remotely, they could be at her place in force within minutes. The information about Denise was left until the end. Sacha had learned to always deliver the good news first.

"My girlfriend at JPL was no help. She had nothing new."

"That is too bad."

"*Da*, I had to sever the connection to us."

"I understand."

Chapter 35

Renaissance Man

At the end of another day, Caleb followed a long stream of taillights on the drive west to Santa Monica and the FBI safehouse on the beach. The setting sun painted the horizon fire red with ominous hues of plum and mauve on the fringes. The only thing more somber than his mood were the dark foreboding rain clouds rolling in off the Pacific.

The return to the ocean front condominium did not have the same appeal it did when he and Tess were first there. Now, the condo was empty, dark, and cold. There were no thoughtful notes letting Him know that someone was thinking of him, no meals prepared with care waiting to be re-heated in the microwave, no one there for him to return the kindness to, and no one to spend time with at the end of a difficult day. Now the silence in the condo was deafening; it stood as a continual stark reminder of his failure regarding Tess. He should have fought harder, and shielded her better from the stupidity of a system where everyone was afraid to accept any risk for fear of putting their careers in jeopardy if something went wrong. A system where people were more concerned about potentially doing something wrong than doing what was right. If there was no report, investigation, memo, or letter saying it was okay, nobody would lift a finger, even if it was obvious what needed to be done. Caleb could not stop thinking about Tess, the smell of her hair, the quick smile, and the flash of those beautiful dark eyes. *I really messed things up with her. I hope she's all right.* If there was any inkling of where she might have gone, he would have searched for her. Numerous drives by the apartment in Glendale revealed nothing. Not even the rental agency had a forwarding address. Once, thinking she was walking along a nearby sidewalk, he abruptly pulled the car over and got out, heart pounding, only to find someone who looked similar from afar.

Caleb no longer saw a reason to stay in the condo. He had been hanging on to it, hoping one day to open the door and find her there. Now, after almost a week, the continuing silence was torture. There was no denying she was gone and might never be seen again.

I can understand her not ever wanting to see me again, but what if she never surfaces? Would it be confirmation she was corrupt, or could it mean she's been caught by assassins? If they were hurting her somehow, I'd never forgive himself.

Caleb shivered. For days after the disappearance, everyone poured over any surveillance footage they could find from cameras between the condominium and the downtown core. They used city cameras, and asked dozens of companies and private citizens for access to their security systems, all to no avail. Similarly, they had no facial recognition hits from airport, train, or bus terminal security camera footage. There was nothing from Huntsville either. Tess had just simply vanished. Searching for her added another complication to the FBI's investigation.

Caleb went to bed early but had a miserable sleep. It was a night of tossing and turning, analyzing how the situation could have been handled better. His thoughts were not just about isolating her from the investigation, but also about feelings toward her. Caleb knew these emotions for Tess were not entirely rational, after all, they really did not know each other well. But, being truly honest with himself, he had completely fallen for her from the first moment they met. He always remained professional since they were co-workers, but it was only now, since the disappearance, that these feelings became clear, even to himself. Caleb knew she was hard to read because she was so private. She had always been very personable, professional, and job focused and had never given a hint of wanting anything more. Perhaps she did not share the same thoughts, and if it were the case, Caleb would be disappointed, but would understand. *I know we'd both need to be in the same emotional space for anything to develop.* Besides, she was an intelligent, independent, and self-sufficient woman who was able to easily navigate through life. It was not like she needed him. But he thought of her all the time, and if ever given a chance again, resolved to not waste the opportunity and admit how he felt, consequences be damned. *I genuinely care for her, and my intentions are honorable.*

He had always been a 'one woman man' who did not give his heart away lightly. As a result, there had only been one other serious relationship. In the time spent working with Tess, there were glimpses she had a great sense of humor, and it was easy to think about all the fun, adventures, and exciting things they could do together. Even the prospect of more routine activities seemed enchanting. It was inexplicable; he just wanted to be by her side to help lighten the load of everyday events–even if it was just as a friend. Although wanting one day to have the opportunity to explain these sentiments, deep down he knew focusing on the hole in his heart was selfish and non-productive. The overriding concern was that Tess was okay, wherever she was. Even if these feelings were never realized, if she were secure and in a good place emotionally and physically, it would be enough.

At one point, Caleb got out of bed and opened the balcony door to hear the wind whipping the rain and forcing the surf to surge and smash on the beach. Normally this would have done it for him because the sounds of the ocean almost always washed away any concerns, but not this time. The morning came too soon, and he was on the highway to work again. The drive was difficult; it was the sun again. Santa Monica was lovely, but for him, the drive always seemed to be toward the sunrise or sunset. This time it was a scorching, bright yellow ball in the eastern sky that seemed to be shooting lasers into his eyes. Even sunglasses did not seem to provide the necessary protection, so avoiding gazing directly through the intensely light part of the windshield was a necessary precaution.

Things in the office started slowly, appropriately matching Caleb's continued funk. While hoping to kickstart some enthusiasm for the day with a second cup of coffee, the phone rang.

Begrudgingly, he put business ahead of his addiction and trudged the three paces back to the desk to pick up the telephone receiver.

"Agent MacLeod."

"Caleb, this is Cartwright from National Investigative Services. Listen, the reason why I'm calling is about Denise Urquhart. You know, Director Coombs' assistant at JPL."

"Yes."

"A flag went up when we combed through her computer and telephone records. She's been accessing files that seem beyond the scope of administrative duties and making a number of long-distance calls to an untraceable number. Anyway, suspicious. Ms. Urquhart also has a link with Krista Maguire, the girlfriend of the guy who visits annually from Huntsville. So, we go to Ms. Urquhart's condo to bring her in for questioning, and we find her inside…dead."

"Dead?"

"Yes, in the bath. Looks like an overdose. No signs of struggle, no forced entry."

"When did this happen?"

"I'm calling you from the condo right now. We are having the scene processed, but I thought you'd want to know."

"Did Director Coombs suspect anything?"

"No, we spoke to him right away to see if she had been acting strange lately. He was genuinely shocked. I think this might be our leak at JPL. The computer accounts and call history are too bizarre. No one else has anything remotely concerning."

"Okay, thanks for the call. Good work by you and your team. I know I have been riding you guys hard lately, but I really appreciate your efforts. As soon as you are able, could you give me a rundown on the types of files she was accessing? It might give us a clue what these guys will do next."

"You got it…and don't worry about the other stuff. I understand the pressure a Lead Agent is under. We'll continue to dig into Ms. Urquhart's history, and I'll let you know if we uncover anything else."

Caleb was standing in Director Coombs' office within the hour.

"I can't believe it, I can't believe it," was all the shaken director could say.

"In retrospect, did she ever exhibit suspicious behavior or ask you anything that now might seem out of place?"

"No, never. Denise was nothing but completely professional."

I'd be a rich man if I had a dollar every time I heard that. People were always surprised to hear criminal activity was going on under their noses. This was worse than criminal, though, it was treasonous, and resulted in the murder of Doug Regent, the murder of the two unidentified individuals driving the decoy Toyotas when the NASA communication equipment was stolen, and the attempted murder of Tess. Denise may not have known about all this, but it looked like she was part of some really bad stuff. It would not be long before Cartwright and the team figured out her motive. People usually committed treason for love, money, or reprisal against a person or a system they no longer supported. *What was it for Denise?*

"I'll tell you one thing, Agent MacLeod. You may have your suspicions about Denise, and you may determine they are founded. Perhaps I missed something here at work, but there is no way she committed suicide. That isn't her at all. She had strong religious convictions about that sort of thing. There is something wrong here."

Before leaving the JPL visitor parking lot, Caleb called back the National Investigative Services Team Lead.

"Cartwright, please ask the M.E. to really look closely at the suicide angle. Director Coombs says this is completely out of character, and we have had murder used throughout this investigation to stymie our progress."

"Understood," Cartwright said before hanging up.

Caleb got on the Freeway and headed back to the office. He was thankful the traffic was light and moved quickly. *Things are picking up.* The day was not turning out to be a grind after all. Back in the Federal Building, there was more of a spring in his step while walking off the elevator and heading toward the office.

"Oh, Caleb, you're going to want to hear this," Daniel LeBlanc said, following in hot pursuit.

"Your forensic team have another lead?" Caleb asked with interest.

"Yes, well, not our team exactly, the Atlanta Office. They got a hit on our guy entering the port at Savannah."

"What do you mean?" Daniel now had Caleb's full attention.

"You know, the guy we previously tracked through facial rec from LAX to Atlanta. The guy we believe killed Tess's boss."

Caleb twinged a little inside at the mention of Tess's name, and the unwanted reminder of his role in her disappearance.

"Yes, I know the guy."

"Well, apparently, he was identified entering the Savannah container terminal. It's the second largest container port on the US Atlantic Coast. Probably thought things blew over, after laying low for a while, and he could get lost in the crowd…"

"…but wasn't counting on good old American technology," Caleb said, finishing Daniel's thought. "So where is he now?"

"The Atlanta Office has him, and his companions, in custody."

"Finally, some good news," Caleb sighed while feeling a wave of relief wash over himself. He knew this moment would come, it usually did, but this case was so different, and this news was so unexpected.

"There's more," Daniel replied.

"Let's go into my office," Caleb responded, realizing they had stopped in the middle of the hallway.

"This guy and two others booked passage on a Liberian container ship bound for Rotterdam…"

"Wait, why the Netherlands? If they're linked to Russians, wouldn't it be better to hop a Russian freighter?" Caleb asked.

"We looked at that, but there aren't many sailing from Savannah, or from the US for that matter. They probably thought they'd go unnoticed sailing to the busiest port in Europe," Daniel continued as they began to walk toward the office.

"Is there anything to the Liberian angle?" Caleb asked.

"We don't think so. There's just so many ships registered there. Anyway, one of the guys in the group was the second fellow we identified at the car rental agency at the Atlanta Airport. The Atlanta Office has been all over this since Mr. Regent's murder."

"What do you mean?" Caleb asked, his pulse starting to race as he thought about Tess again, hoping she was okay, not knowing if she was in danger.

"So, you know how we couldn't find anything on this guy we first identified with facial recognition, no records, nothing?" "Well, it turns out it's because he is not American. He's Serbian."

"Serbian?"

"Yeah, and he's a bad cat, Caleb. He is deeply involved in organized crime and uses a string of aliases. He's got a record as long as your arm and specializes as an enforcer and making people disappear."

Caleb shuddered.

"He's wanted for multiple murders in multiple jurisdictions." Daniel paused a moment as if leaving time for the words to settle in, then continued. "What these organized crime gangs do is offer these guys up like mercenaries. They come into a country illegally under an assumed ID and no flags go off because they are clean. Well, their aliases are clean. They do what they are hired to do and leave, never to return. Unlikely we'd have gone to Serbia looking for the guy we originally identified at LAX. Anyway, Duke Fellows has been like a dog with a bone. He called this morning to provide this update. Actually, he was trying to get you. Duke identified this guy after combing through multiple foreign police data bases. Because of all the aliases, every jurisdiction probably thought he was a one-time goon. Nobody tied it all together, not even Interpol. And that's not even the kicker…"

"What's the kicker?"

"This guy works mostly for the Russians."

"Like the Russian KGB or SVR, or whatever it's called now?"

"No, oligarchs."

"Oligarchs?"

"Yeah, oligarchs."

"Do you think they were escorting a container or something else on the ship?" Caleb was logically questioning all the facts, trying to ensure nothing, like a possible clue, was missed. He still thought of Tess and her safety.

"I asked Duke; they had already looked into it. There is nothing to indicate that's the case. Apparently, they were just interested in low profile passage to Europe."

"Where they'd disappear. So, traveling as a passenger on a container ship is a thing?"

"It's a real movement apparently. There are cruise magazines, and everything dedicated to it."

"I'll be damned. I would never have guessed. So where exactly are our guys right now?"

"Duke has them in Atlanta."

"Okay, can you take the daily hot wash meeting? I'm going to Atlanta."

Caleb grabbed his 'go bag' stored at the office and headed to the airport in a cab. The bag contained a change of clothes, a toiletries kit, and some cash. On the way, he called Duke Fellows.

"Duke, it's Caleb. Sorry I missed your call earlier. Great work picking those guys up off the container ship. It's the biggest break we've had."

"Well, the Port Authority wasn't too happy with me, I can tell you that. We held the ship for six hours so we could be sure it was just them on board, nothing else."

"How did you make the connection to Serbia?"

"Well, computers are smart, but they're only as smart as the person who programs them, or how the data is structured. A lot of the national systems aren't linked in a way that allows a one-time high-level search. They're set up this way for security reasons, therefore you must access them individually. Anyway, we know who this guy is, and he isn't the innocent tourist as claimed."

"I never figured you for a computer geek."

"Actually…I'm really a renaissance man."

Duke liked playing the role of a Luddite, but really liked computers and was pretty savvy around them. What he did not like was when people automatically deferred to computers without thinking problems through. He felt computers were just tools to be used and were no match for human ingenuity. His personal promise to Jill Regent that there would be justice for Doug's murder also helped spur him on to work this problem a little harder than perhaps other agents would have.

"Hey, I hope you don't mind, but I'm on my way to Atlanta right now. These guys are likely the same thugs who have left a trail of destruction across southern California. Not to mention tried to kill my partner seconded from NASA. We need to figure out a way to crack them."

"Understood, Caleb. Send me your flight info and I'll pick you up at the airport."

Chapter 36

Russian Stacking Doll Revealed
July 2019, Hong Kong

Stepping off the nine and a half hour Aeroflot flight direct from Moscow, Dimitri Orlovich could quickly sense the mystique of Hong Kong. There was something electric and indescribable in the air. Perhaps it was a combination of the optimism and inspirational entrepreneurial spirit that seemed everywhere, pushing things along, just like a sea breeze.

Walking from the plane with other passengers, Dimitri wondered how much of the plan regarding the clandestine spacecraft they now controlled should be exposed to Stanislav Tishchenko. As Tishchenko's handler, he needed to feed him just enough information to retain continued cooperation but knew if he gave the stodgy cold warrior too much knowledge about what was happening, the entire scheme could be put in jeopardy.

Dimitri loved visiting Hong Kong, although he could do without the heat and the humidity. It took a while to get used to it, which is why there was always time to acclimatize added to the agenda before any important business meeting. As a slim, six-foot four, white Russian with curly blond hair, Dimitri always stood out in a crowd. People often thought there was a celebrity or a model in their midst, and he usually just played along. In his mid-thirties, Dimitri liked the finer things in life, and it was all available here.

After passing through immigration and collecting his suitcase in the baggage hall, he headed to the Mass Transit Railway station inside the airport terminal. A seamlessly integrated rail, light rail, subway, and bus network, the MTR was the way most people in Hong Kong got around. It was much faster than a taking a taxi.

"Can I help you?" the clerk at the ticket kiosk asked.

"Yes, I reserved my Octopus Pass online," Dimitri said in a thick Russian accent, handing her a receipt printed from his office computer.

"Here you are, Mr. Orlovich. Enjoy your stay," the clerk said with a smile as she handed him a pass permitting access to all MTR's services.

When the train departed the airport terminal on Lantau Island, Dimitri could see Kowloon and Hong Kong Island off in the distance. The Hong Kong Administrative Region of China is a unique place. A perfect blend of Asian and Western cultures that has been refined for over a hundred years. Dimitri found it intoxicating. The culture was based on traditional East Asian values emphasizing the importance of family, education, and hard work, but was set in the freest market in the world; there was a profound respect for the law transplanted from the British legal system. The people were exceedingly polite and friendly. Dimitri always found that surprising given it was the most densely populated place on Earth. *With so many people, maybe the only way things work is to be polite, otherwise it would be complete chaos*. From previous visits, he also knew with so many people in Hong Kong, it was easy to become overwhelmed if you were not careful. That is why he always immersed himself slowly into the rhythm of the place rather than jump into things with both feet. *Which would be disorienting.*

"Arriving Kowloon Station, Kowloon Station," the computer synthesized female voice announced approximately twenty minutes after departing the airport.

Dimitri's five-star hotel was conveniently located above the ultra modern Kowloon Station, which was on the southwestern tip of the mainland, overlooking Victoria harbor and Hong Kong Island further to the south. The hotel offered beautiful water views on either side of the building. But for the moment, Dimitri was not interested in hotel amenities. He had been cooped up in an airplane for almost ten hours and needed fresh air. Quickly checking into the hotel, he immediately went to his room, threw the suitcase on the bed, changed into hiking gear, used the washroom, grabbed a couple bottles of water from the bar fridge, and rushed back to the MTR. He did not care about looking out of place walking through the lavish, pristine hotel lobby in hiking clothes.

At the bottom of the Kowloon Centre, Dimitri caught the subway to Hong Kong Station and then switched to the Island Line, which ran east along the harbor. Having done this before, it was all coming back to him now. He got off at Shau Kei Station and from there took the Number 9 Bus to the Dragon's Back hiking trail.

As much as Dimitri was enchanted by Hong Kong,

out of habit, he always checked to see if there was anyone following. It was hard to notice in the denser crowds, but here, as the number of people began to thin out, it was easier to notice someone out of place. *Nothing suspicious so far. Maybe I am not being followed after all.* Relaxing for the moment, he knew full well if there was no 'tail' now, there would likely be one back in the city. *I never trust them*, summing up his view of the people he was here to meet.

Once up on the crest, it was an easy hike along the spine of the lengthy ridge line on the east side of Hong Kong Island. The well-worn oatmeal-colored dirt path was surprisingly narrow and was completely surrounded by parkland. At the southern end of the trail there was a spectacular look-off offering views that went on forever. Dimitri could see the southern and eastern part of the island, but more impressively, the vast deep blue waters of the South China Sea seemed to reach up to a similarly colored deep blue sky. Coming from a northern climate, the sunshine felt magnificent. Perhaps that is one of the reasons why the British originally established a colony here over a century ago. And, from this vantage point, it was easier to understand Hong Kong's place in the world. Thanks to its location, it was a bridge between mainland China and the United States, the two largest economies in the world. It also had easy access to its powerful regional neighbors, especially Japan, Singapore, and South Korea, and through the Suez could tap directly into the European market. It was the third most important finance center in the world after New York and London. The highest concentration of ultra rich were found here. Taking in the clean ocean air and serene vistas, Dimitri smiled. *The perfect place to find a customer for what we want to sell.*

After almost half an hour of solitude at the look-off, it was time to rejoin the human race and work up to Hong Kong's high tempo.

Back in the hotel, he took a refreshing dip in the pool and then laid out on a reclining chair for a couple of hours, just to take the edge off. Periodically, he would take a glimpse to admire the exquisite views the infinity pool area offered of Victoria Harbour and of bikini-clad fellow sun worshipers. After lounging outside for a while, he returned to his room, changed, and headed to Hong Kong Island's Wan Chai area where renowned fast paced nightlife awaited. Always under scrutiny back in Moscow, the consequences of making a mistake there could literally be life ending. Here, he planned to let loose and enjoy himself in a place far from any supervision. Dimitri was confident there was still surveillance, but he was not bothered by what a potential client might think. They either wanted what was being offered or not. *If they don't, there are plenty other wealthy potential clients in India and the Middle East to approach.*

Opening his eyes the next morning, there still seemed to be a base drum pounding inside Dimitri's brain. I thought I left that club, he murmured sarcastically to himself as flashes of laser lights, throngs of people, dancing, restaurants, neon signs, and street girls all jumbled around as recent memories from the previous night.

Dimitri quickly looked around the hotel room to confirm he was alone. He was also thankful to have had the presence of mind to draw the heavy blackout curtains closed before going to bed because there were daggers of sunlight at the edge of the window attempting to cut their way into the room. The clock on the bedstand stoically declared it was 11:00 a.m. Apparently, the night before was a smashing success, but Dimitri was vague on all the details. *What's the value of having fun if you can't remember the specifics? It's too early for philosophy. All I know is that I haven't had that much pleasure since my last visit to Hong Kong.* He made a coffee, ordered room service for breakfast, and had a shower while waiting for it to arrive. Then, he went to the hotel spa for a massage and a steam. It was going to be a slow day by design. This was preparation for the high-stakes discussion tomorrow.

Dimitri awoke the next morning well rested. Looking and feeling good, he was ready for business. A pre-arranged limousine service drove him the thirty-minute drive to the restaurant on the island side of Victoria Harbor. He looked regal. Entering the spacious lobby, he announced himself to the concierge who escorted him to a private elevator leading to the fourth-floor restaurant. When the elevator doors retracted, an entire panorama of the harbor was exposed through over-sized floor to ceiling glass windows. The host showed him to a private dining room. Although fifteen minutes early, the Chinese businessman he was meeting was already seated at the table enjoying a Scotch.

"Dimitri, it is very nice to meet you," the Chinese man in a tailored suit said as he rose to shake hands. "How was your flight?"

"It's very nice to finally meet you as well, James. Colleagues back home are very complimentary about you so I was happy to learn I would be meeting you in person. I love Hong Kong—my flight from Moscow could not get here fast enough!"

Although a dying practice, they exchanged business cards. Dimitri could hear the voice of a culture coach in his head. Accept the business card graciously, hold it reverently with both hands and examine it thoughtfully. Then, with words of gratitude, place it carefully in your wallet. *I wonder what James' real name is.*

The organization Dimitri represented had done business with this Chinese enterprise before, but it was the first time he was conducting meetings alone. He was surprised a matter of such great importance was entrusted to his sole care, but his boss told him this meeting was just to establish first contact and potential interest. This approach permitted more senior members to engage and change the course of negotiation if things were not going the way they wanted.

Adopting a cavalier, non-caring persona, Dimitri's first order of business was to tell James about his exploits since arriving. This admission was a subtle way of telegraphing he had no secrets, was not ashamed of the past couple of days, and therefore could not be pressured at the negotiating table by threats to reveal this information to supervisors in Moscow. Despite words to the contrary, Dimitri knew it sounded like damage control. *Now the night of wild abandon doesn't seem so wise after all.*

"I'm glad you had fun," James responded with a smile. "Hong Kong has everything for everyone."

Then, switching to business, Dimitri adopted a more professional demeanor. *I wonder where the photos most likely taken of me will surface.*

"James, our two organizations have been doing business together for many years."

With those words, Dimitri was referring to the oligarchy in Russia that he represented, and the Hong Kong-based enterprise that was really an arm's length tool of the Chinese government represented by James. The communist regime used the clandestine company established in the Hong Kong free trade zone to gain access to Western technology. This arrangement took advantage of the Favored Nation trade status Hong Kong enjoyed with the United States. Dimitri silently wondered how long such pretenses would continue as China steadily eroded the rights and freedoms guaranteed the citizens of the former British colony. So long as the civil disobedience and protests against the Chinese did not inconvenience this trip, Dimitri did not have an opinion on the matter. If pushed, he would assess, particularly as a representative of a Russian oligarchy, that democracy and individual rights were overrated. He was confident the Chinese Communist Party would ultimately prevail in their struggle with the protesters; it was inevitable. When that happened, Hong Kong would be a casualty, and over time, would cease to be a special place in the world; for selfish reasons, this realization saddened him.

"I am not at liberty to discuss all the details," Dimitri continued, "but I have been asked to determine your interest in a clandestine spacecraft that has come into our possession. We have many parties who would be interested in this opportunity, but thought, given our previous dealings, this prospect might fit best with your line of business. If you are not interested, we would be happy to move along."

Dimitri knew he was sent to speak to the Chinese first because they had the most money and were the most motivated to dominate the Americans.

"What advantage would this device provide us?" James asked.

"This is an ultra secret strategic asset stolen from the US deep space arsenal. They have sunk hundreds and hundreds of billions of dollars into it during the Cold War. It is priceless to them. It holds unspeakable political, military, and financial value."

"Can you be more specific about what it does?" James pressed.

"Absolutely," Dimitri replied. "It provides leverage over the United States. It can be turned against them, or it can be ransomed back to them through an intermediary, so it is not traced back to you. Either way, it represents a significant opportunity to exploit the Americans geopolitically for a bargain, or to simply turn a significant profit on your investment. We are happy to proceed with further discussions and provide control of the craft after we confirm an agreement in principle."

"Why don't you simply ransom it back to them yourself and make a tidy profit? Why reduce your profits by involving an intermediary?"

"You know us—we like to keep a low profile and remain behind the scenes. We only pursue quality opportunities and like to see them fully exploited, even if it is not by us." Dimitri finished the pitch with a flourish, "We know you represent those interested in the finer things in life and believe me, this is the finest. If you are interested, I could arrange for a more detailed briefing on the spacecraft's capability, and we could discuss price then."

"In principle, we would be interested in furthering this conversation. We have always had mutually beneficial arrangements with your organization in the past," James replied.

To ensure expectations were aligned and James' expression of interest would turn into something concrete down the road, Dimitri left him with a parting thought.

"James, I know we are not discussing price here and a lot of water needs to go under the bridge before we are at that point, but if we think of the cost of an aircraft carrier, all the non-recurring engineering costs, the production costs, the cost of the aircraft, and the weapons… that should guide our thinking here. This is so much more important to the Americans than a whole fleet of aircraft carriers."

Dimitri knew this last comment was a bit of a gamble but was confident they would develop a full understanding of what the spacecraft did before the next meeting between the oligarchy and the Chinese. Given the super secret nature of the American program and all the money they had sunk into it over the years, he was sure it was exceptionally valuable to them. For those reasons, the final words to James seamed entirely reasonable.

He and James finished their meal in pleasant conversation about nothing in particular and celebrated their business understanding over a couple more glasses of Oban Scotch.

In bidding farewell to James while departing the restaurant, Dimitri knew Moscow would be pleased. He thought about calling them for an instant but put the idea off knowing his Chinese associates would be monitoring the phone; he was concerned someone at the other end would not realize and say something revealing. Ultimately, the oligarchy's goal was to recoup the expenses they put into the spacecraft hijacking operation plus make a handsome profit. Dimitri sensed this was possible, but knew the Chinese were tough negotiators so he and his Moscow supervisors would need to remain vigilant.

Dimitri also knew a significant challenge persisted regarding Stanislav Tishchenko. The re-activated, lumbering agent thought he was working for the SVR. Tishchenko would become completely unhinged if it were ever revealed this operation was entirely run by a highly influential oligarchy. He would be offended if the Russian state did not see the merit of pursuing some 1970s Cold War relic in space and offered the opportunity to exploit this situation to the highest bidder, no questions asked, and no constraints applied. All they wanted was plausible deniability if they were ever accused of being involved. What Russian state officials had not bargained on was that the team assembled for this operation by the oligarchy actually found something in space, wrested control of it from the Americans, and had initiated negotiations to sell it. For their part, all that was left for state bureaucrats to do was to plead ignorance of the whole matter and claim their Center for Deep Space Communication at Yevpatoria, Crimea was hacked.

Even though the operation was proceeding better than planned, Dimitri sensed they were still in a vulnerable period. *By the time I get back to Moscow,*

Stanislav's surveillance operation of Doug Regent's farm and his widow should have produced tangible results. We need to complete this deal quickly and get the operation transferred to the Chinese before the FBI close in.

Chapter 37

Everyone Has Something They Value
2019, FBI Field Office, Atlanta, Georgia

Duke Fellows and Caleb MacLeod looked through the one-way glass at the ringleader of the three men picked up in Savannah.

"He's a tough nut to crack," Duke Fellows said, almost infuriated. "We've tried everything. At first, he wouldn't say anything. And when he did finally speak, it was just about looking forward to a relaxing vacation in an American prison because they were so comfortable compared to other places. That's all we've been able to get since we picked him up. The other two are younger, but just as tough. This guy, Drago Ivanovic, is definitely the leader."

Caleb murmured in acknowledgement.

Duke continued. "Although he hasn't said much, there was plenty of attitude when we processed him. It spoke volumes. There seems to be a lot of contempt for the US and things American. I've run into these types before. It's as if they think our rights and freedoms make us weak."

As frustrated as Duke was, Caleb could feel the pressure mounting. This was the first big break in the case, and it appeared it was going nowhere. The group this guy belonged to, or worked for, perpetrated the

Angeles National Forest attack, three horrific murders, and most likely an attempted murder. These were ruthless thugs.

"I just feel like time is slipping away," Caleb said as he tried to voice the uneasy feelings inside. "They've had the initiative since the beginning. We need to turn this guy before they make their next move. Now that they've got control of NASA's classified satellite, you can bet they'll use it somehow, otherwise, why go through all the effort?"

"You're not wrong," Duke said. "I've got this unsettled feeling also, like it's been quiet for too long. We need to get this asshole to talk."

"Got any suggestions?"

"Any way your contact in NASA could help determine what these guys might be up to? I mean, it's all about this communication device, isn't it?"

"You mean Mike Bandy? I've reached out to him. He says he's ready to assist our investigation by answering any questions we have, but he seems to have this fatalistic view that the damage is irrecoverable since they've lost control of their satellite. I think we're on our own with this one."

"I agree with you, Caleb. If we don't get anything from this guy, we'll continue to be on our heels, reacting rather than getting out in front of this."

After a long moment of silence, Caleb proposed thoughtfully. "Maybe we need to go back to first principles with this guy."

"What do you mean?"

"Obviously, he's a hardened thug who's used to an abusive legal system. I doubt we will be able to directly threaten or frighten him sufficiently to get him to talk. I think that's the message he's been telegraphing. 'I'm a tough guy, don't even try to get me to talk. I've dealt with tougher people than you.' It's like the tough guy image people adopt when they go to prison, so the other inmates won't mess with them."

"Yeah, well this guy's starting his act early. So, what's our play?" Duke asked.

"Remember when you and I were at Quantico? They told us everyone has something they value or could be used to get them to open up. What do we really know about this guy?"

"I see your point. Come with me."

Three hours later, they were back at the one-way glass looking at their captive.

"Drago Ivanovic, Serbian brute, a thug, murderer for hire. Grew up in the toughest of the tough neighborhoods, and thinks Americans are all soft," Caleb said, as if reading a script from a play.

Then it was Duke's turn. "Who would have thought he'd have a loving wife and two young children in an out-of-the-way tiny village back in Serbia."

"He's not afraid of us. He's afraid of failing the ruthless oligarchy that hired him."

"We can use the tough guy stance against him."

The two Federal agents had figured out more about Drago's personal life by reviewing Duke's previous on-line work that had dug into European police databases. As agents often do when they are stuck and unable to advance, they review the evidence in hand, to see if they had missed anything on their initial assessment. Expanding the original computer search that revealed Drago's identity, they were able to determine much more. Soon, they had all the details needed.

Duke and Caleb talked their plan through one more time and, as they were about to enter the interrogation room, Duke suggested Caleb go in alone.

"Look, he's dealt with all of us from the Atlanta Office and has shut us all down. Maybe it would be good to shake things up with a new face."

"You got it, Duke. Thanks."

The clock was ticking, and Caleb had to make this work. Much calmer than he thought he would be when alone with Drago, Caleb saw him as pure evil, an animal. He looked like a broken-down mixed martial arts fighter. Drago Ivanovic was probably mid-forties, Caucasian, five-foot-eight, with a crew cut and salt and pepper receding hair. His nose had been broken more than once and there were scars on his left cheek and left hand; they looked like they had been deep cuts. Although older, Ivanovic was well-muscled and obviously pumped a lot of iron.

Caleb knew Ivanovic had rights and was technically innocent until proven otherwise, but this condescending son-of-a-bitch exuded all the telltale signs of being guilty. Seated, handcuffed, and chained to a table in the center of the room, there was not even a pretence of not knowing why he was being held. And of course, there were no signs of remorse. Innocent people do not react like this. Normally this behavior would have really angered Caleb, but he had to be smart, to turn Drago's own arrogance back on itself.

"It's unfortunate we won't be able to hold you here, Mr. Ivanovic," Caleb said. "Because your crime is considered a matter of national security, we'll need to turn you over to the special prosecutor's office. No public trial, no choice of lawyer, no lenient jury or judge."

Drago Ivanovic did not flinch or change facial expression, but Caleb was sure he was listening—the eyes said it all.

"You see, how we deal with people like you changed after 9/11. Oh, you'll have a trial, but it will be a secret military trial, because of the nature of the evidence that will need to come forward, and because of the man you killed."

Caleb thought about Tess's attempted murder, and although this thug was a long way from California when it occurred, he most certainly knew who was involved. Caleb missed Tess every day. He wanted to sucker punch Ivanovic in the face, but that would be wrong, not to mention illegal; and Drago probably would have expected something like that. So, Caleb continued to spin the fictitious tale.

"Unfortunately, the legal system in America moves slowly because we want to ensure everyone's rights are respected."

Caleb sensed an ever so slight smirk on Drago's face.

"So of course, you'll simply vanish for a long time while all the trial prep is being done…it could take up to a couple of years. Especially given the complexities of your case. As an American who respected the man you killed, and the work he did…" Caleb said, only really knowing Doug Regent was a high-level NASA official, so the work must have been very important. Caleb continued. "I am disheartened you are going to get an easy ride on this one. You're going to have special treatment for a couple of years awaiting trial, and then you'll probably get off on some technicality."

Caleb hoped to be in Drago Ivanovic's head by now.

"So, I'll tell you what I'm going to do when they come and take you away. I'm going to give an interview to the press stating that we caught the hit man who killed Mr. Regent. People will be extremely interested because the murder was broadcast all over the news in the tri-state area. People are concerned about a killer on the loose, so I am going to do my civic duty and put their minds at ease. I'll tell them it's safe now because you are off the streets. Of course, I'll need to supply your name and photo, so they believe me. And here's the thing, Mr. Ivanovic, I'm going to tell them you've entered the witness protection program and are fully cooperating with authorities. That way they won't be looking for your trial. It's the perfect cover, really."

Caleb started to walk toward the interrogation room door but stopped after a few steps.

"Hopefully, my press interview will be informative for your wife and small children back in Serbia…you know…so they won't be expecting you home any time soon."

He then continued toward the door, but Ivanovic lashed out.

"I have no wife or family in Serbia."

Caleb knew at that instant he had him, that the made-up story about special trials had cracked the armor.

"So, Danica and your two little daughters, Irena and Mila, mean nothing to you. They're just three people you don't care about, who happen to be living on a small farm plot outside the little town of Trgoviste, overlooking the Pcinja River."

Caleb stared directly into Drago Ivanovic eyes. There was frustration written all over Drago's face. Caleb turned and walked rapidly to the door.

"Wait," Ivanovic said just as Caleb reached for the door handle. "They'll hurt my family. They're ruthless. They'll kill half of them to show they mean business, and then they'll hold the others ransom. That's what they do."

"I know," Caleb said coldly and turned the door handle to leave.

"Wait!" Drago said, jumping up in an explosion of energy and fury, pulling at the chains that bound him. "I'll tell you what you want to know," he said, breathing heavily and looking directly at Caleb, man to man. "But you have to let me get word to my family, to warn them. They have done nothing wrong."

Caleb knew Ivanovic would hold nothing back.

Chapter 38

One Step Closer
2019, Northeastern Alabama

Tess quickly stepped out of her ride share in Swaim, Alabama. The gravel on the side of the road felt good underfoot, it felt real. Calm on the outside, inside she felt like a coiled-up spring was finally releasing now that the three-day odyssey from California was finally over. She was thrilled to be back in Alabama with no one the wiser. Although not contemplating ever repeating the tortuous land journey, for the first time in her life she had glimpsed at an unvarnished America and how many average Americans lived. Tess would not trade the experience for anything. Whether on the bus, in the stations, or nearby stores, people were generally very polite and respectful. In most cases it seemed as if the less people had, the more generous they were, especially to strangers or those down on their luck. The voyage reinforced the importance of Helios, to ensure America was able to perpetuate life on Earth if a disaster snuffed out human existence; it also reinforced the criticality of Tess's personal quest to help regain control over the lost craft.

Watching the ride share disappear in the distance, Tess resolved not to use that type of service again. Although only ever taking it twice before, and both times were to stay off the grid during the trip from California, she still felt vulnerable, as if tempting fate. In a city center it might be different because a rider could create a scene to attract help if something went wrong, but in rural areas where she had relied on them, there was much added risk.

It was 10:00 a.m. and promising to be an extremely hot day. Tess had not been in California all that long but had forgotten how heavy the Alabama heat could feel. Thankfully, the lush green trees, undergrowth, and foliage lining the two-lane country road cast a shadow wide enough to walk in, but it would not be the case in another hour or so when the sun would be higher in the clear blue sky.

Tess walked along the gravel shoulder of State Route 146 from Swaim toward Baileytown. After sitting for days, she needed to stretch her legs and breathe in fresh country air. It was only a mile and a half to Doug and Jill's farm, and it would take less than forty minutes to get there. It was along this very road that Doug had been savagely murdered and she just wanted to walk the ground, to be closer to him and to pay her respects. Carefully examining the bushes and growth along the way, the meticulously manicured farmers' fields on the other side of the curtain of trees and vegetation were barely visible. Continuing to walk along, Tess was reasonably confident Jill would be home. She had phoned her house in Huntsville a number of times since returning to Alabama but had consistently gotten no answer. Tess deduced Jill was at the farm. In order to avoid causing alarm, she decided to keep her trip to the farm a secret from Jill. Tess was conscious that since her disappearance, she may have been portrayed as a fugitive and Jill may have been asked to advise authorities if Tess attempted to make contact. Therefore, Tess thought it best not to announce the visit. Still, walking along the isolated Alabama roadway, she wondered what to do if Jill was not at the farm.

About forty minutes later, Tess finally arrived at a non-descript mailbox with letters so faded they hardly stood out. It would be impossible to read them from a car driving at any speed. By comparison, most of the other mailboxes along the road were highly decorated, visible from a distance, and almost celebratory in their nature. They were painted in bright colors, vibrantly announcing the family name of the homeowner, and were often adorned with American flags or other patriotic symbols. 'Regent' was all the washed-out letters on this plain stainless-steel mailbox divulged. It telegraphed a less than ostentatious dwelling would be found behind the unkept screen of thick trees and dense vegetation. From this vantage point, all Tess could see was a narrow winding lane serving as a driveway, and it was impossible to see anything beyond the first bend.

This obviously is the place, Tess told herself, starting down the driveway. No doubt Doug purposely cultivated this low-key approach and she wondered how far he might have taken things. Would this lead to a dilapidated original homesteader's cabin or something a little more modern? Navigating beyond the dogleg in the drive, the grounds opened to a scene right out of a magazine. Stately magnolia trees with thick gray trunks lined the lane leading to a beautifully manicured white Victorian-style farmhouse and barn on a gentle rise in the distance. Old glory proudly fluttered in the breeze from a white flagpole to the left of the house. The magnolia canopies merged to form a shaded arch that floated above the laneway, which was also flanked by broad flat green fields of alfalfa.

This is a hidden sanctuary, Tess thought to herself. No wonder Doug chose to come here at every opportunity. She picked up the pace, partly because the end of the long journey was in sight, and partly to get to the relief the shaded drive would provide from the now blistering sun.

As Tess approached the house, she could see even up close, everything was immaculate. Big, bright fragrant cutleaf lilac bushes stood sentinel duty on either side of the stairs that led to the veranda. An old-fashioned screen door covered the deep burgundy-red steel door with a brass handle and kick plate. Surveying the entranceway, Tess could not see a doorbell or knocker of any description. Having just resolved to simply use her knuckles to announce her arrival, a slim, attractive older lady with long gray hair opened the door with a smile.

"Tess, please come in. I'm Jill Regent."

Tess must have surprised Jill with her reaction.

"Oh, Doug's security system warns me when people are on the premises."

Tess recovered quickly.

"Jill, it's very nice to finally meet you. I'm so sorry it's under these circumstances. My thoughts have been with you and your family these past weeks," Tess said all at once, and without thinking, she touched Jill's hand.

"Thank you. It means a lot to me, especially considering how fond Doug was of you. Come in, come in please," Jill said. "You must be exhausted, traveling on foot."

"Oh, I had a ride to Swaim. I just wanted to walk the road to be a bit closer to Doug. I know it might sound silly, but he was an amazing mentor to me, even though it was for a short time."

"He was an excellent judge of character, and he saw something special in you." At that moment, it looked as though Jill was trying to fight off a wave of emotion, no doubt caused by thoughts of Doug. She switched into hostess mode. "The guest bathroom is just down the hall on the left. Why don't you freshen up while I make us some lunch?"

"That sounds lovely," Tess said with a smile, "but don't go to any trouble."

"Don't be silly. Your timing is excellent. My sister just left a couple of days ago, so I could use the company. I'll quickly change while you're in the washroom. I was out on the tractor this morning tilling one of the back fields. I find it therapeutic."

"Yes, it's nice to be outdoors, especially in weather like this."

****

On the other side of the country, an encrypted satellite phone rang at the Russian safehouse in California.

"Tishchenko."

The excited voice at the other end of the call immediately interjected, "Stanislav, it's Gregor. You'll never guess in a million years who we just saw on the camera walking down the road into Regent's farm."

"I have no idea."

"That NASA expert woman. You know, the one

we chased in the desert," Gregor blurted out, unable to contain himself.

Stanislav was now alert, sitting ramrod straight in his chair. This was an amazing opportunity; it would allow them to answer all of Moscow's questions about the secret spacecraft they now possessed.

"Listen to me carefully, Gregor. She is not to be harmed, and under no circumstances are you to let her get away. Collect her immediately. This is the highest priority. It will permit us to complete this operation. Do you understand?"

"Affirmative, boss. Capture target immediately without harm. Collateral damage authorized."

"Good. I'm on my way to your location now."

Gregor would know how important this was if Tishchenko was heading to Alabama.

****

Tess joined Jill in the large, bright, country kitchen. "Can I help?"

"No, you just sit down and rest your feet. It's almost ready. Would you like some sweet tea?" Jill said with a smile.

"Oh, that would be wonderful," Tess said as Jill poured her a glass.

"Your security system must use facial recognition."

"Oh, yes. Doug installed perimeter sensors all around the property. The house tells us if people or vehicles are approaching. In addition to facial recognition, it reads vehicle plate numbers to identify people we might know."

"That's a nice feature."

"As you know, Doug was all about security."

"Let's eat on the veranda," Jill said, handing Tess a

tray of food that would satisfy a lumberjack.

The veranda was shaded, and there was a gentle breeze. Tess was embarrassed by being so hungry. Although eating exceedingly politely, the past three days on the bus reinforced how good a home-cooked meal could be. She ate everything put in front of her.

"I want you to know how sorry I was not to be able to return for Doug's memorial service. Things were at a critical phase in California. It broke my heart not to be here."

"I know you were here in spirit, and that's all that matters. Besides, this is much nicer, getting together like this."

Tess then recounted a filtered version of events in California: the attempt on her life and how she tried to warn Doug but could not get through to him on the phone.

"I know, dear. Doug would often turn off his cell for the drive up here. It was his way of winding down. There was nothing more you could have done. I know that," she said, grasping Tess's hand.

Tess then told Jill about being framed and her unceremonious departure from the investigating team.

"I felt I needed to contribute, to help somehow, not sit on my hands doing nothing in a condo by the beach, nice as it was. I left because I was not being useful any longer." Tess went on to say, "I had many hours to reflect upon the predicament we're in, and I kept hearing Doug's voice, as if he were prodding me forward. My mind transported me right back to my introductory briefings where Doug stressed, 'There are no new problems. This project, because of its longevity, has seen everything. Therefore, if you are ever really stuck, look back to what has been done in the past.' Does that make sense?"

"It sure does, Tess," Jill said. "Doug lived by that mantra."

"Unfortunately, as a newcomer to NASA, I don't have any history or prior experience about what was done before."

Jill smiled and gently patted Tess's hand once more saying, "I'll be right back."

Jill went upstairs and returned a few minutes later with a satchel.

Smiling, she said, "Doug wanted you to have these. He kept saying that when the time was right, you were to have these journals. His dying thought was to say he loved me and to remind me that the journals were for you by writing J 4 T on his arm. I knew immediately what it meant, but I didn't say anything. I recently asked why he was keeping these things when they couldn't be shown to anyone. They had national secrets in them and had to be locked in the floor safe. He said the journals weren't for him, 'the journals were for Tess.' That's how I knew what the code was: Journals For Tess! He repeated it often. The words came to me immediately when I saw what was written."

Tess had a hundred questions, but just then, Jill's phone spoke.

"Unidentified van, approaching fast," was all it repeated.

Jill looked up to see a white, full-sized Chevy Van, speeding down the drive.

"Come on," she said, "they must have followed you."

Jill calmly rose from the table and led Tess, who

clutched the satchel tightly, into the farmhouse. As they peered outside, they saw the van speed into the big gravel parking area between the house and the barn, spin around 180 degrees, and slam on its brakes. Stones flew everywhere and the whole area was covered in a cloud of dust. As it was stopping, three men carrying machine pistols leapt from the van and raced toward the house. The driver remained behind the wheel with the van positioned to exit the farm on short notice. Jill watched the drama unfolding in her front yard and calmly reached over and flipped a switch behind the nearest curtain. Instantly, you could hear the metal hurricane covers roll over all the lower story windows and lock in place, extra deadbolts automatically reinforced the steel doors. Doug had rigged the place like a fortress.

"We're safe for a few minutes," Jill said as they heard pounding and shouting at the veranda door they just entered. "This house has three automated security zones," Jill said, giving Tess a rapid tutorial. "Lower level where the doors and windows are barricaded, upper level where the windows are barricaded, and if they get into the house, there's a panic room off the master bedroom upstairs. I've just barricaded the lower level for now. It is designed so we can get out from the inside, but it'll be tough for those guys to get in. Every room has an activation switch like this one. It also notifies the local sheriff's office directly. Another one of Doug's security precautions." Then Jill stopped and looked Tess directly in the eye. "Are you all right?" she asked.

"I'm fine," Tess said as her mind raced.

"They mustn't get their hands on Doug's journals."

"I understand," Tess said.

"As I see it, we have two options—hunker down and hope the local sheriff gets here in time, or we take the initiative."

"I think we need to take the initiative. He'll be no match for those guys. He'll be seriously outgunned."

"Doug said you had grit. Good. I understand you are an accomplished motorcycle rider."

"I can hold my own."

"Okay, how does this sound for a plan: I cause a distraction, you get to the barn. There's a barricade activation switch inside every entry door, just above the light switches. Barricade the barn when you get in. You'll see a motorbike inside; our farm hand uses it to check the fence lines. Take it out the back of the barn to the end of the horse paddock. There's a gate. Once you're through the gate, you can follow the trail along the riverbank. A mile or so upriver it gets really shallow; you'll see where the path branches to the water. You can ford the river there. Get on the road on the other side and keep going north to Tennessee because I'll be leading these guys to the south. Okay?"

Tess realized she must have given Jill another odd look.

"Look. I'm an old lady who just lost my husband, probably to these brutes. They better not come near me. But we need to get you and the satchel away from here."

Tess thought quickly. Jill's proposal sounded feasible, with a good probability of success, and no better alternative came to mind. "Okay," she responded with confidence, already feeling her body readying for action. Aided by a racing pulse and excess adrenalin, every fiber of her being prepared to respond to the task ahead. She would hold nothing back.

"Good, wait here," Jill said, "I'll be right back."

Jill quickly went upstairs and rummaged around for a few seconds. Glancing up through the second story stairwell, Tess saw her stride determinedly toward the side of the house facing the barn with a double-barreled shotgun. Two shots and Jill was back by downstairs with a smoking gun.

"Those shots were you?" Tess said, sounding surprised.

"Shooting skeet with Doug has its benefits," she said with a quick smile. "Doug kept this and buckshot in the panic room. I wanted to get their attention to the front of the house where I'm going to create my diversion so you can get to the barn. And I wanted their van disabled so we can get a head start."

"Great thoughts," Tess said.

Jill offered more.

"When I stepped out onto the balcony, I could see the van below, but I didn't see any of those guys with the machine pistols. They must be trying to find a way in. I shot out a front tire and for good measure, put another round into the engine. Hopefully it attracts the others back to the front of the house."

"Now what?" Tess asked.

"Go down this hall to the back door. I'm going to the garage to create the distraction, at which time you turn the deadbolt latch. It will release all the other locks and you'll be able to open the door from the inside," Jill hastily instructed. "Get to the barn as quickly as you can and lock yourself in!"

"How will I know when your distraction has

happened?"

"Oh, my dear, you'll know," Jill said, smiling while giving Tess a big hug. "Be safe and I hope to see you soon."

"Yes, I do as well. Thank you for everything," Tess said, gripping the satchel tightly while hurrying down the hall to wait for Jill's signal.

Chapter 39

A Plan Comes Together

Jill stepped into the garage attached to the house and got behind the wheel of her pickup truck, laying the newly loaded shotgun on the bench seat beside her. She then locked the door of the vehicle and took a deep breath. Surveying the garage door behind her in the rear-view mirror, Jill knew there was a good possibility the men who had invaded the property were just on the other side of the thin aluminum investigating the recent gun shots fired at their van.

She went over the steps that needed to be taken and then took another long, deep breath. It felt as though she was about to step off a cliff. *Too bad I hadn't backed in.* Then, without hesitation, she started the engine, revved it, and immediately clicked the automatic garage door opener. Seeing the feet of one of the gunmen approaching the partially opened garage caused a bit of panic. Jill threw the truck into reverse and tromped on the accelerator. The powerful engine screamed, tires squealed, and the vehicle shot like a rocket out of the garage, smashing through the partially opened door. The cab of the pickup caught the bottom of the garage door on the way out and ripped it, and the tracks, from the door frame. The pickup, carrying half the garage door with it, jumped out into the gravel space between the house and the barn. Jill then jammed the truck into drive and sped past the disabled van, flinging gravel everywhere. Part way down the laneway, it registered that there were three men near the garage and van. *Hopefully, Tess made it to the barn safely.*

Racing toward town, Jill came upon the big North Alabama Electric Cooperative truck parked crossways in the middle of the road with a perimeter of orange traffic safety cones added for good measure. Slowing down while lowering her window to speak with the man on the side of the road, she realized it was Shane, the same electrician who visited the farm a few days previously.

"Howdy, ma'am. We have a line down, so we'll need you to wait here for a bit."

Jill surveyed the scene and then looked the man directly in the eye.

"I have an emergency; I need to get to the sheriff's office. Surely there's a way I can get through."

Then Shane pulled a pistol out of the back of his trousers.

"Ma'am, I'm going to need you to turn off your vehicle and come with me."

"Pardon?"

"Come on now, let's not make this difficult," Shane said.

"Son, if you move a muscle, I'll drop you where you stand," the sheriff called out.

The sheriff and his deputy were bearing down on Shane with their pistols drawn. Jill could just make out two police cars beyond the electrical truck. It appears Shane did not notice them arrive.

"Jill, are you all right?" the sheriff called out again.

"Bill, four men attacked the farm with automatic weapons. They're after one of Doug's colleagues, a young woman, Tess," Jill blurted out.

"Son, I'm only going to tell you once to lower your weapon. We don't take kindly to folks threatening ladies around here," the sheriff said in a low, stern voice.

Shane clearly recognized being out matched because he placed the pistol on the ground. The deputy swiftly placed him in hand cuffs while the sheriff went to Jill's aid.

As the sheriff drove Jill to the station in town, he was on the radio to dispatch, directing that reinforcements be called in from all surrounding jurisdictions.

"…send up a flare," the sheriff barked. "We need the Emergency Response Team, dogs, drones, the works. These guys are highly armed with automatic weapons and are likely connected to Doug Regent's murder. I'm on my way back to the office now." When he finished with dispatch, the more sensitive side of the sheriff came out. "Sorry you had to hear all that, Jill."

As they got closer to town, another police cruiser passed them, going in the opposite direction at high-speed with lights flashing and siren wailing. Invisible air pushed by the other cruiser buffeted them as it sped by.

The sheriff was on the radio again.

"Yes, yes, the farm is isolated, I want to keep it that way until these gunmen are apprehended. No one in or out until we get our resources gathered and we are ready to go."

Chapter 40

Escape

Crouching at the end of the hall, Tess heard Jill's crash through the garage door. Immediately releasing the dead bolt latch, she swung the door open wide and sprinted toward the barn as fast as physically possible. Clearing the side of the house, a man was walking toward her from around the corner. Seeing her at the last minute, he made a desperate lunge. By then, Tess had accelerated to full speed and was able to skirt around him. It was close, though. This near brush with disaster gave her another spurt of adrenaline and speed. Other men were in front of the house, part of the garage door was in the yard, and the pickup was speeding down the drive.

Tess got to the barn ahead of the man now in pursuit. But, from the corner of her eye, could tell he was close enough behind to prevent the door closing when she got in the barn. Tess pulled the door open just wide enough to slip inside, throwing the satchel in ahead to free both hands. Pivoting, and instead of getting into a tug of war to get the door closed, she instinctively pushed it open with every ounce of her strength. The unexpected action drove the door into the man's face, stunning him. She immediately pulled the door closed and hit the switch, which secured all the entrances with additional dead bolts and rolled steel hurricane covers over all the windows.

Tess could not believe her luck. *I made it.* A quick scan identified a Yamaha Scrambler with a key in the ignition. *Covered in mud and dust. Clearly a working bike. I can easily ride it but need a distraction to get away.* The sprint to the barn was too close for comfort, and she did not want to repeat it during a dash for the river.

Looking around, Tess had an idea. Walking the bike to the barn's back door that led to the horse paddock, she checked that the gas line valve was open, squeezed the clutch handle, turned the key, gave the throttle a slight twist, and pushed the starter button. Nothing. Another push of the button. Again nothing. *Battery must be dead.*

Wasting no time, Tess swung one leg over the seat. Now, straddling the bike, she pushed it off its kickstand, extended the kick start lever, placed a foot on it, and jumped to instantaneously apply her entire weight to the lever. The engine turned over but did not catch. Again. On the third attempt, the Scrambler rumbled to life. Revving the throttle a couple of times, Tess checked the gas gauge; it was three-quarters full. The bike settled into a steady idle. Leaving it running on its kick stand, she went back to the front of the barn and started a tractor hooked to a hay wagon. Lining the tractor up with the big barn door, setting the accelerator handle for low speed, and letting out the clutch, Tess hopped off the tractor and unlocked the two large, swinging barn doors as the tractor crept ahead. The big John Deere continued to crawl forward, pushed the doors open and moved out into the barnyard, heading toward the house. The men out front, still taking stock of Jill's escape, turned, and raced to the opening barn door. One jumped onto the tractor, another onto the wagon, and one other ran in to search the barn. By this time Tess was on the Scrambler speeding through the barn's backdoor.

Outside, directly in front of her, was the fellow who had been struck with the door. He was angry and had been searching for a way to get into the barn. Tess pulled up on the handlebars, gave the bike a shot of gas and popped a wheelie, raising the front wheel to chest and face level. He dove out of the way as she sped to the end of the paddock, opened the gate, and raced toward the river.

While police forces in the region began to mobilize and converge on the Regent farm, Tess sped toward the Tennessee state line on the newly acquired motorcycle, Doug's well used brown leather satchel pressed securely against her side.

Chapter 41

Perseverance

Tess sped north as fast as the Scrambler would carry her. Every now and then, glimpses of the small Paint Rock River she had just crossed would flash between the trees. Heart pounding, and not entirely sure if anyone was following, she drove like the gunmen were right behind her. The lesson from the previous chase was that these men were persistent, dangerous, and planned for contingencies. It would not be a surprise if they had other operatives in the area being vectored toward her, which is what happened during the chase from Goldstone. For that reason alone, Tess stayed focused and wasted no time.

Racing deeper into the Alabama—Tennessee border region, the forest became thicker and, correspondingly, the roads became less traveled and developed. Not wanting to become easy prey bottled up by a dead end, in the absence of a map, GPS, or even a phone, at junctions she swiftly committed to whichever road looked more established and that generally went in the right direction. Although not overly scientific, it was a plan. The sun indicated she was traveling in a northwesterly direction.

Tess hoped Jill would be all right but was also keenly aware of her unexpectedly new and important mission—to ensure the security of Doug's journals, which seemed to weigh more heavily now in the satchel slung over her shoulder. The immediate objective was to get to a safe location, but she had no idea where that might be.

After twisting and turning for about twenty minutes along roads progressively decreasing in importance and use, Tess noticed subtle indications that the reverse effect was beginning to take place. Before long, she was back in civilization and traveling northeast along the Davy Crockett Parkway. Because a motorcycle immediately stood out on the highway, Tess wanted to get as far away as possible from the Alabama access route. The parkway allowed good time to be made, and after an hour and a half, she pulled off at a busy truck stop that could be seen for miles in either direction. Filling the gas tank and then proceeding to the quiet back parking lot with lights off, she parked behind a fenced garbage dumpster. The bike was out of sight.

Walking back to the gas station, lingering a bit in the restroom area, restaurant, and convenience store long enough to confirm no one was following, Tess purchased a toothbrush, toothpaste, dental floss, and deodorant with cash. Walking over to a nearby discount motel, she also paid for the room in cash, explaining to the exuberantly friendly clerk that her credit card had been compromised. Not surprisingly, the clerk scanned the bills with a black light before accepting them.

In the room, Tess ordered dinner to be delivered and then peaked inside Doug's satchel to find several neatly placed black covered books; there appeared to be about twenty of them. Although extremely curious about the contents of the journals, she closed the satchel and double checked to ensure it was secure. With killers potentially still on her trail, this was not the time, nor place, to delve into these secrets; they would require methodical examination if they were to yield any clues. Instead, the leather bag was brought into the bathroom where she took a long, hot shower. This helped her unwind and think. The plan was to get a few hours of sleep and then make some headway in the dark where a motorcycle would be less obvious on a highway. For safety reasons, it was vital to get as far away from the farm and Huntsville as possible. More relaxed from dinner and a shower, Tess set the clock radio alarm on the bedstand, curled up under the covers of the queen-sized bed with Doug's satchel and fell into a deep sleep.

A few hours later, the clock radio, assisted by the local country-rock station, gently serenaded Tess back into consciousness. Without turning on a light, she reached over and canceled the alarm, scooped up the satchel and discretely peered out the window to the dark parking lot below. From the headlights whizzing by, the highway still had enough traffic to provide good cover. After continuing to survey the exterior surroundings for a few minutes, nothing appeared unusual. Tess then went into the bathroom, closed the door, and turned on the light. If anyone was watching the room, it would still appear dark from outside the motel. Fifteen minutes later, it was time to go. A quick scan of the parking lot from a still darkened room confirmed nothing had changed.

Leaving the key inside the motel room, Tess slipped out the door, making sure it locked when pulled shut. It was a hot, humid evening. *Those lights emanating from the truck stop are almost bright enough to be seen from space.* The sharp light made darkened surroundings seem even more foreboding by casting additional shadows. It was like a bright neon island in an otherwise black sea. Keeping to the shadows, Tess got to the bike, started it, and headed back toward the highway. For one of the few times in her life, she had no destination in mind, just a need to get some distance from the murderers back in Alabama.

Tess instinctively signaled, turned right, and accelerated along the ramp to join the regular flow of highway traffic heading northeast. Refreshed from sleep and out of immediate danger, the situation was simple; she had money, transportation, and Doug's journals firmly secured over her shoulder. Although committed to protecting Doug's secrets, she was still uncertain whether they would provide any help with the current Helios situation.

Tess could not help but think of the irony of her current position. She'd traveled for days, secretly trying to get to the destination of Doug's farm, not sure if there was any real purpose for going, other than to pay her respects. Now she had an unexpected purpose, but no destination.

Tess continued to travel northeast, the same way she had been heading before taking the motel break. It felt natural to continue to add distance from the Regent Farm. Heading north to Nashville, Tennessee, then northeast to Lexington, Kentucky, and finally east to Charleston, West Virginia took about four hours of steady driving. Finding another truck stop motel, Tess gassed the bike, parked it out of sight, and rented a room, again with cash. This time, the clerk did not bat an eyelash.

Safe in the room, far from the farm, Tess carefully examined the contents of the satchel for the first time. Without removing anything, she could count twenty-one neatly packed journals inside. Extracting a booklet revealed a number on the spine along with the time period it covered. They were arranged in chronological order. Tess selected the first one. It was like a window into a different time. This journal had been a gift to Doug from his mentor, Bob Gillespie, in 1968. Bob made the first entry in beautiful cursive script.

—Top Secret—

Doug,

Please accept this journal as a token of my sincere appreciation for your excellent work at the Area 25 Nuclear Rocket Development Station. I was most impressed by your leadership which contributed immensely to the rapid and successful fielding of our nuclear rocket engine. I look forward to you joining me in Huntsville and assuming greater responsibility as the Space Vehicle System Engineering Manager. In that capacity you will lead the development of the most ambitious spacecraft produced by this country, to include a revolutionary propulsion system you helped develop. I encourage you to continue with your engaging, 'hands on' leadership approach since it proved so successful in Nevada.

I find journaling helps me work through problems, particularly when I am not at liberty to openly discuss these challenges with friends and family. I hope this proves to be a beneficial outlet for you as well.

Doug, please know that I have the utmost confidence in your abilities as you assume your new role. I very much look forward to working with you on

this exciting endeavor for our country. Very best wishes as always!
    Sincerely,
    Bob
    Robert A.W. Gillespie
    Helios Program Manager
    —Top Secret—

Tess extracted a few journals at random and flipped through the contents. It seemed the intensity of Doug's journaling varied with time. It appeared that in new positions, or in the face of what appeared to be an insurmountable problem, he wrote more frequently. At other times, months would go by without a single entry. Then, jumping to the last journal, Tess expected to find Doug's thoughts about the attack on the Helios Program. The journal was crisp and new. On the first page was a personal dedication to her, like the dedication Bob Gillespie wrote in the initial journal in the series. Doug said how proud he was of her and how she was such an amazing addition to the team. This brought a tear to Tess's eye. *Here I am, all alone in a cheap motel, in the middle of nowhere, unable to help anyone. I've let you down, Doug. Clearly, he had been counting on me. Running away let Caleb down as well. He must think I am the worst.*

Then Tess smiled, remembering the way Caleb would light up around her. If nothing else, she hoped he was doing okay, and the investigation was progressing well, even without her assistance. After a brief period of solitude, Tess pulled herself out of solemn thoughts. *Rather than feeling sorry for yourself, do something about it.*

To Tess's surprise, flipping through the last journal

revealed it was nothing but blank pages. Then, checking the preceding journal in the series indicated the last entry made was five years ago. Tess wondered how it could be, especially with all that had been going on recently. *Perhaps things were happening too fast for Doug to make any entries.* But she knew that was inconsistent with previous instances where entries were made during hectic times. Even a short note helped consolidate thoughts at the end of a tumultuous day. This is one of the reasons soldiers kept war diaries. Tess did not know what to do. Looking inside the satchel out of desperation, this time she noticed, tucked in the far corner, a glasses case with a pen clipped to it. Extracting the case, it became obvious the pen was not any recognizable brand. She removed the cap to discover there was no ball point; it was a stylus, not a pen. The glasses were strange also; they had thick resin frames and no magnification. *Interesting. Perhaps they are blue light, or anti-glare glasses, but for what? Maybe Doug had switched to on-line journaling.*

Tess unfolded the arms of the glasses and tried them on. A six-inch holographic image of Doug Regent appeared and was standing on the blank page of the open journal.

"Hello, Tess. I hope you are all right. If you are seeing this projection, things have not gone well for me, but you must carry on. You must protect Helios at all costs, and trust no one."

"How do you know it is me?" Tess said vocalizing her thoughts aloud, but not really expecting a response.

"Miniaturized Virtual Reality Technology. The glasses did a retinal scan when you put them on and compared it to the image you provided NASA for security access; they are programmed to only work for you. The visuals you are seeing are projected directly into your eyes, but you must have the journal open to a blank page for the system to work. Just leave them out in the sunlight to charge them."

"So, it's interactive?"

"Yes, the system takes what you ask or say, and responds with the most appropriate recording I've stored in the interactive journal. It's amazing what can be accomplished with miniaturized technology. Going forward, you can make your own entries by speaking or using the stylus. The glasses will permit you to see what you've written. They'll also allow you to attribute words and visuals to your own holograph simply by saying 'commence, cease, edit, or delete journal entry.' Play with it. You'll see it's quite intuitive."

"Doug, it's strange to talk to you, so much has happened."

"I know. It's a lot to absorb."

Tess took a moment to contemplate the new information. She wondered how to reply.

"We've lost control of Helios, Doug. How do we get it back?"

Doug's hologram looked concerned by Tess's question. It lowered its head slightly and leaned forward. Then it looked from side to side as if it were about to reveal a secret but did not want to be overheard.

"The JREC has been stolen, immediate action: First. Change to new communications protocol. Second. If necessary, consider going back to the beginning."

"Go back to the beginning? What does that mean?"

The hologram then repeated almost word for word

what she thought Doug had said during the initial indoctrination briefings.

"If you are ever in a crisis and you don't know what to do, remember this program has seen everything since its inception. There are no new crises. Look back to see what was done in the past as your first reaction. I keep a record of the project history for that very purpose."

But what followed was new:

"Since the beginning, Helios has been governed by three gods. Follow the wisdom of the third god and your answer will be revealed." Then Doug's holograph flashed on and off intermittently as if there was an energy shortage. It then disappeared altogether.

Tess had no idea what Doug's revelation meant. Why not just come out and answer the question directly? Why all the cloak and dagger stuff? Was that his very last recording? Tess was tired. Carefully returning the journals, glasses, and stylus inside Doug's messenger bag, she kicked off her shoes, turned off the lights, and slipped under the bedcovers with the satchel.

Waking eight hours later physically recharged, with a subconscious in over-drive, she had tossed and turned all night, but mercifully had come to a couple of conclusions. Knowing Doug, it was not like him to be cryptic. He was plain spoken and direct. Being cryptic must have been for security reasons. Perhaps he was concerned about speaking freely, or feared she might be under duress when accessing the journal. Then a third possibility struck her. Doug was not planning to die. He was planning to solve the current problem with Helios himself. Maybe this revelation was like providing access to a powerful pass key to solve future problems and he wanted another layer of protection around it. If so, it was not helpful now. The third god was key. Apollo and Helios were surely the first two. If he was referring to an earlier part of the program, it had to be found in one of the traditionally handwritten journals, not the latest modern one.

Estimating the time to carefully examine one journal, then multiplying by the number of journals, Tess realized it could take as much as two weeks to get through all the program history. She needed help. With that conclusion, she got on her bike and headed for Maryland.

Chapter 42

How Did You Get Here?
2019, Edgewater, Maryland

From the cover of darkness and lush vegetation, Tess eyed the neat upscale terrace home from the small park across the street. She had been waiting awhile. Finally, without warning, the garage door started to rise while a compact blue Mazda 3 pulled into the driveway and proceeded into the now fully opened garage. The slim, golden-haired driver with Nordic features exited the vehicle and grabbed a yoga mat and water bottle while heading toward the door leading from the garage to the interior of the house. Hitting the switch on the wall to close the gaping garage door, the woman proceeded into her home.

Tess, now moving at full stride, cradled the heavy satchel that felt as awkward as a ten-pound bag of flour. Perhaps it was the adrenaline at the time, but she did not recall Doug's bag being an issue while running to evade the men at the Regent's farm. Although no land speed records would be broken today, she just had to interrupt the light beam near the floor before the door closed. *Success.* The door stopped and reversed direction. Tess ducked inside and clicked the close button. To ensure no one else followed, she watched until the garage door came to a stop, and then she entered the house.

The shower was running on the second level. Quietly, Tess climbed the stairs and waited for the young woman to come out of the master bedroom ensuite bath. In response to the blood-curdling scream that came when the woman realized someone else was in her private space, Tess simply held her index finger vertically in front of her lips in the universal sign not to say anything. With the other hand, she waved for the woman to approach. Immediately complying, the woman rushed over and gave Tess a big hug.

After a long embrace with her best friend, Tess whispered softly, "Can you unplug Google Home and put your cell phone downstairs?"

Zoe Kirkwell ran downstairs and was back in an instant. Now that no one could remotely listen to them, Zoe peppered Tess with a barrage of questions.

"Where have you been? You dropped off the face of the Earth and I couldn't contact you. I was so worried. How did you get in my house…?"

Tess smiled and took Zoe by the hand.

"I used to do yoga with you on Tuesday evenings, remember? I know your routine." Then, after taking a breath, "You know my job turned into a high security investigation of a strategic US asset, and without warning, I was sent to California as part of an FBI team. It just got crazy from there. You're my best friend, I'd have reached out if I could, but I was under a cloak of silence."

Tess knew that Zoe's duties as an NSA cryptographer provided insight into how fast things could move, and how secretive they could be, especially at the strategic level.

"Yes, it seems like only yesterday we were talking about you needing a change after Afghanistan and accepting the new opportunity in Huntsville. Tell me everything," Zoe said. "Well…you know, what you can."

Recognizing they were in Zoe's home and not a SCIF where this sort of thing could be freely discussed, Tess gave a very broad, high-level, unclassified version of events from her departure for California until the decision to quit the investigation. Wanting Zoe to know the authorities might consider her a fugitive, she spoke frankly about being framed.

"I want you to know all this because I need your help. You're the best cryptographer I know, but given the potential ramifications, I would fully understand any reticence you might have in assisting me."

"Tess you are the most loyal, patriotic person I know. I'll always be there for you."

With those words, the two friends put on a pot of coffee and broke out the contents of Doug's satchel.

With black rimmed oversized reading glasses framing a long thin face, Zoe looked like a cross between a model and librarian. Both women settled into dissecting Doug's every word. Although less than ideal, they used an old set of Encyclopedia Britannica if they needed historical context for the journal entries. Zoe said she liked the idea of finally using her father's old books, and it kept them from the prying eyes of the internet where someone could remotely eavesdrop on them through the computer. After about an hour, in a flurry, Zoe flipped between the journal in her hand and the very first journal in the series.

"I keep going back to the first journal because you

said Doug's holograph indicated 'going back to the beginning' was a possible response to the communication equipment being stolen and losing control of this spacecraft. But, when I go back to the first journal, there's nothing that relates in any way! Then there's the business about being governed by three gods."

"I know. I went around the same loop a couple of times and haven't figured it out yet either," Tess confided. "I'm not sure what Doug was alluding to. It was not like him to be ambiguous."

Tess had long considered Zoe her one true friend. They had been through a lot together. Despite their history, Tess also knew it was a lot to ask of Zoe, including potentially risking her career. However, Tess needed help to make any real headway. *I can't get through it all alone. Hopefully together, combining our knowledge, we can resolve the Helios situation.* Tess finally felt like she was not reacting to the California attackers but was out in front of them and desperately wanted to see this whole thing concluded. Resolving Helios would be vindication, and she was grateful for Zoe's confidence in her, while at the same time being acutely aware and a little uneasy that the system could just as easily turn on them both if they were not successful.

Working together, she estimated they had at least a few days ahead of them, just to read through the journals. Then, if they found anything, they would need to do whatever was instructed, and that would take time as well. *One step at a time.*

Zoe went downstairs to use the cell phone. Tess could hear the message left with her work about being away for a couple of days.

"Don't worry, Tess," she said when returning. "It's no big deal. This is clearly going to take longer than I first thought. I can ask for more time if we need. Besides, they owe me a couple of weeks and we are in a lull at the office, anyway."

With Zoe's agenda cleared, the two friends dove into their project. They read, cat napped when they were tired, and ate quick meals to keep the momentum going. It was like being back in university, studying for comprehensive exams. After about twenty-four hours, Tess was starting to struggle to keep her eyes open, but Zoe appeared to have found a second wind. Then, unable to contain herself, Zoe suddenly exploded out of her chair with excitement.

"Look at this!" she exclaimed, pointing to a detailed pen and ink drawing about midway through one of the journals. "This is from 1972."

Tess, startled by Zoe's unexpected exuberance, was now fully awake. She looked over to see a profile drawing of two faces fused together, one looking to the left, and the other looking to the right. There was a Roman numeral 'I' to the left of the strange head with two faces, and a 'II' to the right.

"What does it say?" Tess asked inquisitively.

"It just says, 'Janus, you are ubiquitous. You are the guardian of Apollo and Helios. Let us pray we never need to invoke you to take us back to how we were before.' Then there's this equation: $I + II = II$."

"I think you have something there," Tess offered eagerly.

"That's what I thought. So, I looked Janus up in the encyclopedia. Guess what."

"He's our third Roman god?"

"Exactly! How does this sound? 'Janus, god of ancient Rome,' there is our third god, for sure." Zoe continued, "God of beginnings, gates, doorways, passages, time transitions, duality, and endings. Usually, he is rendered with two faces, one looking forward to the future and one looking backward to the past.'" Then Zoe got really excited. "Do you think that is the 'beginning' Doug was referring to when he said 'If necessary, consider going back to the beginning?' Plus, it hints at a possible back door to your spacecraft communication protocol by referring to gates, doorways, and passages. It's the only text in quotations I have come across thus far, and it's the only drawing I have seen. There is something special about this. I can feel it," Zoe insisted. "I don't get the equation though…one plus two is three."

"It's so neatly written, and the second two is underlined. I think that is meant to show it is deliberate…it is correct. This must be it. I mean, there are scientific graphs and the like in the journals, but nothing like this, no artistic drawings."

"Although I didn't immediately recognize Janus, it apparently is where January comes from–the beginning of the new year," Zoe added. "The information in these old books is really useful, almost as good as an online search."

"This makes complete sense," Tess said, moving closer to examine the journal entry Zoe had discovered. "Why didn't I see it before? Doug didn't mean to go back to the first journal, or the beginning of the program; he meant to go back to the when the program came alive. When Helios was actually launched. 1972.

The beginning."

The two friends fell quiet for a moment as they each contemplated the importance of Zoe's discovery. Shattering glass downstairs terminated the silence, and the two women then heard the side door quickly open.

"Someone's breaking in," Zoe said, leaping to her feet and running to the head of the stairs leading down to ground level. She feigned calling 911 by announcing loudly so the intruder could hear, "Yes, operator, someone is breaking into my house. Yes, I have a gun."

Tess knew that a bluff was the best Zoe could do since the phone was downstairs and so was the burglar.

"Don't come up here, I have a gun," Zoe repeated boldly.

At the sound of trouble, Tess grabbed the journals, stuffed them into the satchel, and climbed out the window onto the roof. It sounded like Zoe's bluff did not work. After noises of running up the stairs, Zoe screamed out as if being pushed to the floor. By this time, Tess had already scurried over to the edge and jumped onto the roof of a car parked in the neighbor's driveway, setting off the vehicle's alarm. She hoped Zoe was all right but knew the only option now was to flee.

Tess just started running as fast as possible, and with no idea where to go. It was all she could do. *Just run.* Protecting the journals was the only consideration. Out of nowhere, a man wearing a mask and dark clothes gave chase. With her heart in her throat, Tess ran as fast as Doug's now awkwardly heavy satchel would allow. *He's gaining on me.* Rounding the corner of the housing unit, she brushed by another man who was just standing there, hiding in the shadows.

Am I heading for a trap? Instinctively glancing back over a shoulder, she continued running hard. Then there was a gasp as the man in the shadows aggressively 'clotheslined' the pursuer by leaning forward and sweeping an arm at neck level of the man chasing her. It was like the masked man ran into a brick wall. Instantly swept off his feet, the man's whole body floated horizontally for a second, like in a magician's levitation act. Then, the universe seemed to compensate for lost time as he plummeted toward the ground, a resounding thud sounding, leaving him gasping for breath. Lying flat on his back on the ground, still struggling for air, the man in the shadows flipped over the would-be assailant and cuffed him. To Tess, it was like watching a cowboy rope and tie a calf. It only lasted seconds. Then the man in the shadows who had played the role of cowboy started toward her. Mesmerized by everything, Tess had stopped running. Quickly, turning to bolt, she tripped and fell into his arms.

"Tess, is that you? Are you all right?"

"Caleb?" When she realized it was him, she allowed herself to feel safe and protected in his arms. Then, after a long moment, still shaken, but with obvious relief in her voice, she asked, "How did you get here? Why aren't you in California?"

"It's okay, everything is okay," Caleb said, gently hugging her. "I'd never forgive myself if anything happened to you." Then he kissed her. "I'm sorry; I've been wanting to do that for a long time."

Tess said nothing. She just looked into his big, brooding eyes and kissed him back. The smile on Caleb's face was effusive.

"I missed you. I'm sorry I left like I did, but I can explain." They just held each other for a moment longer. Then Tess asked quietly, "How did you find me?"

"We knew Zoe was your best friend, so we were monitoring her place."

"But we disconnected Google Home and isolated the cell phone."

"That was our clue something was different; we lost our tap when it was unplugged. It seemed rare for Zoe to be so secretive at home."

"Zoe. We need to check on Zoe."

"Don't worry. My team on the headset say she's okay," Caleb said pointing to his earpiece.

"Do you know if Jill Regent is okay?"

"She's fine as well. We rounded up all those clowns at the farm with the help of local law enforcement. Best of all, we caught the team who killed Doug. They were trying to leave the country on a container ship. The leader of the group told us Doug's farm was under surveillance. We just missed you, but it is how we knew you were in this part of the country."

"Did they hear us kiss?"

"Who?" Caleb said, a little confused.

"Your guys on the radio," Tess said with a big grin.

"Yes…yes, they did…and I'm glad about it," he said with a big smile, slipping an arm around her waist while they walked back to the front of Zoe's house.

The street was now blocked with barricades and several police cars had converged on Zoe's home. There were flashing lights and radios chattering everywhere. Zoe's neighbors peered from their stoops and windows with inquisitive and concerned looks on their faces.

"Caleb," Tess said, "do you trust me?"

"With my life."

Coming from an ex-soldier, Tess knew Caleb's words were the highest compliment.

"We need to get to Huntsville as soon as we can," Tess said.

"Why Huntsville?"

"Zoe and I figured out why Doug wanted us to have these journals and, after digging through them, we know how to regain control of our…" Tess had to think. "…satellite!" she finally said.

"We can be there first thing tomorrow," Caleb offered. "For now, we have some catching up to do. For instance, how did you get here?"

Chapter 43

Loyalty Still Questioned
2019, Redstone Arsenal, Huntsville, Alabama

It was early morning. Tess, Zoe, Caleb, and Duke Fellows were in the visitor's room of the secret Helios compound in the Redstone Arsenal. Tess, Zoe, and Caleb flew in on an FBI business jet that was on standby to support national security investigations. It also supported high-profile prisoner transport and other FBI travel requirements. Duke drove up from Atlanta in the wee hours of the morning. Tess had made arrangements for Mike Bandy to meet the group, but Helios was never mentioned. As far as everyone was aware, this was simply a secret satellite communications compound that was part of Tess and Mike's work.

"I'm sorry, Tess, but we've established a new security protocol following the attacks in California…and on Doug. Only one visitor can go into the shielded area at a time," Mike said hesitantly. "A lot has changed since you have been away."

"So, Zoe and I can handle this. We just need to enter a string of text into the JREC and have it transmitted."

"Well, technically, that would be two visitors since your clearances have been removed pending an examination of the allegations …"

"Those allegations were manufactured," Caleb said, jumping to Tess's defense. "Our investigation has already confirmed that."

"We still need an official report certifying you're cleared. That is how it works."

"Mike, this is ridiculous. I am a patriot trying to do the right thing here. We know how to recover our stolen asset. Either we go into the shield now, or I'm taking this over your head." Tess was not bluffing.

"Look," Mike said to the group, "you're considering the present situation and expediency, which makes sense for you. I need to consider the Inspector General and the harm that might be inflicted on the program from an adverse investigation. When this whole situation is examined in six months or a year from now, all anyone will worry about is what rules were broken."

"So, you're prepared to compromise what makes sense in the present so you can look good in the future. That's completely illogical. I can't imagine that the IG doesn't consider context."

"I'm sorry, rules are rules."

Having come so far, only to be stymied by an overzealous bureaucrat, exasperated Tess. Mike had given off a strange vibe ever since they arrived. It was like they were inconveniencing him. Tess thought he would be elated by her discovery. However, at this point, she knew it was pointless fighting an entrenched civil servant who was obviously going out of the way to hide behind rules rather than being helpful or mission focused. It was especially annoying because there was not even a willingness to bend rules he made.

"Fine, I'll do this myself," Tess said. "I'll be the one visitor."

Mike appeared to take pleasure in Tess's slight display of frustration. It is obvious when people enjoy being calm as they spin up others; it is the smug look they exude.

"I truly am sorry for the inconvenience, but our enhanced protocols are designed to protect us all," Mike announced to the group. "If I could ask the rest of you to wait here with our security staff, I will escort Tess," Mike said, as if making a final pitch to support his position. It seemed that everyone understood his view, even if they did not endorse it.

Just as he and Tess were about to depart for the secure area, Caleb interjected. "Tess, just before you go, could I speak to you for a second?"

Caleb guided Tess over to the far corner of the waiting area where they were out of earshot of everyone else. While Tess quietly conferred with Caleb, she could overhear Duke loudly asking Mike general questions about the facilities and the compound, but nothing too complicated or classified. A moment later, she and Caleb rejoined the group.

"Sorry about that," Caleb said. "It couldn't wait."

Mike smiled, although it appeared forced, and then Tess accompanied him into the bank-vault-like airlock. When the outer door closed and locked behind them, only then would the inner door open. This shielded area prevented any electromagnetic signals from radios, telephones, computers, and the like from escaping the workspace and being analyzed by foreign agents. Helios messages were developed here, fed through the JREC, and then subsequently the coded information was communicated to NASA's Deep Space Network for transmission to the waiting Helios spacecraft. Tess was all alone with Mike in the shielded area.

"So, Doug had a back-door communications protocol to take control of Helios all along?" Mike said. "I wonder why he made us work our tails off trying to implement the standard communications change protocol when there was a wild card?"

"It makes sense not to use it unless absolutely necessary; it seems like a one-time emergency use procedure," Tess responded, desperately trying to remain civil. She was still getting a weird vibe from Mike, almost like he was trying to contain his anger or pick a fight. It was hard to tell. Did he distrust her that much? She tried not to agitate him any further.

"Okay, so where is this text to be fed through the JREC?"

"It's right here, on this secure key," Tess said, handing Mike an NSA external USB stick from Zoe's office marked Top Secret. "We loaded it at Fort Meade this morning before flying here. It has already been a long day."

"If you think I'm going to let you access our network with outside, unverified code, you're crazy," Mike said, dropping the USB stick to the floor and crushing it underfoot. "Even the most basic security rules will support me on this."

He seemed angry to his core. Tess was shocked and had not anticipated this. Suddenly feeling vulnerable and concerned, she had never previously thought of him as dangerous, but was now worried about being locked in the vault with him. Tess cradled Doug's satchel securely while her mind raced. Her initial response was to fight back any way possible.

"It's you, isn't it? You're the inside leak working with the Russians." The words escaped her mouth before realizing it. "This new visitor policy was just a ploy to separate me from my friends."

"That's crazy."

"You showed no remorse when Doug was killed. You were the last of us to talk to him…" Then Tess's eyes widened. "Did you even try and stop him when I called from L.A. and said that we knew the killers had flown into Atlanta? Did you?"

"Look. I suppose I could have called the front gate to prevent him from leaving the base, or warn him, but it seemed like such an overreaction at the time. We had a lot going on that day. Besides, how did I know you were actually right about the killers targeting our team?"

"You bastard," Tess said, lashing out and slapping him hard on the side of the face. Her hand hurt, and there was a big red welt on his cheek. "A life and death message and you did not even try to pass it along!"

Mike touched his face. "It was clear Doug favored you. Do you know how much I've sacrificed for this program? I have a family to support, to protect. You can't just show up at the last minute and collect all the glory."

"So, you aren't working with the Russians?"

"I'm loyal. I'd never turn on my country."

"So, this is all about a promotion. You opportunist…the Russians threaten our strategic security, and you scheme to replace the boss behind his back…and you may have even sent him to his death. You are disgusting!"

Mike said nothing. A long period of silence passed. Tess could hear herself breathing. Her heart pounded. Had she gone too far in pushing back against a potentially unstable man? The path they were now on was not productive, yet he was so candid with her. Why? The situation had to de-escalated if there was any hope of a reasonable resolution. She would have to be the bigger person.

"If you're loyal to America, why wouldn't you use the USB stick so we could regain our strategic security leverage?"

"Because I can't. What are the Russians going to do with that old spacecraft anyway? It's not like it's a nuke in orbit."

"You've missed everything about what this project stands for, protecting the future of humanity, enduring American values, the lives onboard Helios, … everything. How do you sleep at night?"

"I sleep fine."

You're lying. "Then why all this? Help me understand."

"I have to. If I don't, they'll hurt my family."

"I thought you said you weren't working with the Russians."

"I'm not. With them. They're blackmailing me."

"Ah, Mike, I'm sorry. Surely there's a way we can get around this."

"No. Not one that'll keep my family safe. They told me what they'd do…to my wife…the kids."

"You're going to side with killers over…your own government."

"I won't. I won't put my family's safety in the hands of bureaucracy. They found Doug, didn't they?"

"That was different. We didn't know they were after him."

"I won't live looking over my shoulder every day, wondering when the bullet is coming."

"How did you get mixed up in all of this? How did they find you?"

"You'll laugh. It seems so pathetic now. Classic. Let your guard down with a former colleague you haven't seen in a while…someone you thought you could trust. You don't really say anything specific, just some generalities, but stuff you know you shouldn't talk about. And when they realize you have something they really want, the pressure comes, but you don't say anything more…because that would clearly be over the line. Then the threats."

"Surely there is something we can do."

"Enough! Stop the talking. I know what I need to do. I'm sorry, Tess, but now I'm going to need to explain to your friends out there how you became distraught and pulled this knife on me because I would not go along with breaking the most basic security directives. Exasperated, you flew into a rage, more intense than the emotion you showed in the waiting area. You even hit me in the face," he said, tenderly touching his cheek again. "You get the idea. We fought. I gained control and you were accidentally stabbed. I didn't mean to do it. It was unfortunate, and completely in self defense. Of course, I'll need to inflict some defensive wounds on myself to ensure the story seems credible." Then he added, "This investigation, the threats on your life, the isolation have obviously been too much for you," Mike said, as if rehearsing lines for the police enquiry that would follow. "I'm sure I can also show that you were the leak. Maybe all this business at Fort Meade was a desperate attempt to cover up an earlier indiscretion on your part. That'll put an end to any further examination by the authorities."

"This makes no sense. There must be another way."

"None that my Russian overseers will accept."

"Think about it. Do you really think this is going to work?" Tess asked, fumbling with Doug's satchel.

"Enough of this," Mike said, moving toward her. "That is not for you to worry about because you will be dead. You will be the treasonous agent and I will be the hero that discovered you. I'm committed now," he said almost sadly while taking another step toward her.

"Don't!" she blurted out, as if trying to prevent someone from stepping up onto a dangerous ledge on a rooftop. "Do you know the problem with your new security procedures?" she asked while continuing to wrestle with Doug's satchel.

"What?"

"They don't take guns from FBI agents," she said, pulling out Caleb's 9 millimeter Browning High Power pistol, simultaneously dropping the satchel to the ground and switching off the safety. "I've recorded our entire conversation. If you take one step toward me, I'll shoot you on the spot. You might love your country, but you're still a traitor. Let's see what the IG says about that."

Tess just glared at Mike with furious eyes. She could tell by the hesitation and a questioning look, that he knew he had been outmaneuvered. He probably now realized that Duke's asinine questions in the lobby were just a distraction so Caleb could pass the pistol to her.

"You thought you were smarter than all this, that you could control it," Tess said.

Mike took a step toward her.

"Stop!" Tess warned.

She now feared that he wanted to use her to take the easy way out, to put him out of his misery, to make this all go away. Just then, Caleb and Duke Fellows rushed into the vault.

"How?" she asked as Caleb gently took the pistol from her.

"You took so long, we were worried. We convinced the security team to let us in. Said we'd arrest them if they didn't cooperate."

Chapter 44

The New Torch Bearer
2019, Mary W. Jackson Building, NASA Headquarters, Washington, DC

Tess was ushered into the same meeting room in NASA's Washington Headquarters where she and Doug had provided initial details about the California attack and the stolen JREC a few months earlier. This time there was no waiting for Administrator Dwight Jacobs, he was waiting for her.

"Tess, how nice to see you. Please, come in and be seated. The trip up from Huntsville was okay?"

"Yes, very pleasant, Administrator, thank you."

"I read your report last night with great interest," he said with a smile. "It aligned with what Doug had come to fear. Mike Bandy began his career honorably, but later in life, he started putting himself ahead of the program. It was subtle at first but became increasingly noticeable."

"That is why Doug sent you out west. He knew you could be trusted and would do what was required for the sake of Helios and our women and men she carries. Mike was kept close, to keep an eye on him."

Tess winced, knowing Mike directly contributed to Doug's murder, even if it was by an act of omission.

She simply said, "In the end, it appears the Helios

team and the FBI were unwittingly fighting the combined efforts of a foreign Cold War zealot and an inside facilitator. Although, I am sure the FBI will provide more insight when their investigation is complete."

Tess thought about Doug and the last time in the conference room. It felt strange meeting Administrator Jacobs alone. The administrator jolted her out of contemplation.

"So, I'm interested in one detail. What gave you the presence of mind to take a gun with you into the shield when you were by yourself with Mike?"

"Well, Administrator," Tess said, "to be honest, it was Caleb's idea. Mike was acting very strange, and Caleb just wanted me to be safe. I never really envisioned needing it. I just took it to appease Caleb."

Tess did not like guns, they made her uncomfortable, but in this respect, she was happy to have had options.

"You've got grit, I'll give you that," was all Administrator Jacobs said while closing Tess's report.

"I'm curious though. I know it's in the report but walk me through again how you figured out the back-door code to regain control of Helios."

"Doug said in his holographic message that going back to the beginning was one of the possible responses to the JREC being stolen, but we did not know what it meant. Then Zoe discovered the 1972 journal entry. We knew it was special because it was the only quote we had come across in our review of the journals. The rest was easy. Janus looked in two directions, backward and forward. The text in quotes needed to be entered backward first and then forward. It's what the Roman numerals were telling us. One time backward, one-time forward equals two times, 'I + II = II.' Once it was fed through Huntsville's JREC, the coded message was transmitted by Mandy Prokapowicz at Goldstone. Later, when we examined Doug's journals in greater detail, we realized this procedure would re-baseline Helios' communications protocol to a completely new format not ever used before, including the method to change it in the future."

"So, the Russians would be locked out completely, making another hijack attempt much more difficult."

"Precisely."

"Very elegant, Tess. Very clever. I intend to reach out to your friends, but in the interim, please be sure to thank Zoe and Mandy on my behalf for their leap of faith. I appreciate your comments in the report about them knowing that this was the right thing to do, but also understanding they might be placing their careers at risk. These are obviously brave, patriotic women." Then, after a long moment of silence, Jacobs said, "Tess, you've been through a lot, and you have impressed us immensely in your short time here at NASA. Doug was an excellent judge of character and he saw you as eventually succeeding him; I'd like to offer you the position, if you'd consider it."

Tess was completely taken aback. This isn't at all what she expected from this meeting.

"Administrator, I am truly honored, but I'm still relatively junior, I have so much more to learn about the program, the stakeholders, the technical aspects, the politics…"

"Tess, trust me, with your combination of intelligence, professionalism, and tenacity, the program will be in exceptional hands. There is a whole team to support you, and with your leadership style, I know they'll respond positively to you."

"Well, Administrator, if you're sure, I accept…and I promise I will give you my absolute best."

"I have no doubt. Good. We'll formalize the paperwork over the next few days; however, if we are going to work together, you'll need to start calling me Dwight."

Tess forced herself to say "Dwight." It was harder than expected, having spent so much time in very hierarchical organizations.

"I suspect I may have surprised you today, but when you have time to reflect, I'd be interested in your thoughts about modern applications for Helios, beyond what was originally conceived when she was launched," Jacobs said to conclude the meeting.

The two shook hands as he reinforced, "Know that I will always be here for you if you ever need anything. Just reach out. Nice touch, by the way, bringing two coded USBs into the shield so you had a duplicate available when Mike destroyed the first one. Remind me never to play poker with you."

Tess just smiled.

On the flight from Washington back to Huntsville, Tess could not help thinking about the meeting with Jacobs. It all seemed so surreal. The offer to lead the program was completely unexpected and the question about the current employment of Helios was incredibly exciting. Her mind was whirling as she considered the new boss's request. Perhaps, if Elon Musk's current drive to colonize Mars was successful, and humans were safely thriving beyond Earth, Helios could be recalled early because its mission would be redundant. In that scenario, it could possibly be used to augment the colonization efforts. Alternatively, it could come back to Earth so it could be evaluated, and lessons learned for future missions. It could potentially even be re-equipped and modernized for a new long-endurance deep space mission. Tess knew these thoughts would eventually need more rigor, cost-benefit analysis, and other planning criteria, but for now, it was enjoyable just to let her mind wander freely.

Caleb met her at the Huntsville airport.

"What's this?" she asked, seeing him near the baggage carousel.

"Flowers for my girl, if she'll have me," Caleb said with a grin.

"She'd be the luckiest girl in the world," Tess responded, tenderly kissing him.

They both were relieved to be able to openly express their feelings for each other.

"How was Washington?" Caleb asked as they moved closer to pick up the luggage.

"He wants me to lead the Helios Program."

"Tess, I'm so happy for you. You'll do an amazing job," Caleb said, spontaneously hugging her again.

"How about you? How's the investigation going?"

"Really well, thanks." Caleb smiled. "We squeezed those thugs who assaulted Jill's farm hard. They told us Stanislav Tishchenko was on the way from California to meet them in Alabama. They also confirmed he was the architect behind the whole operation, as we had recently come to suspect. Apparently, all Mike originally told them was that secret NASA communications equipment was moving from JPL to

Fort Meade for evaluation. That cued them to look to other sources for the details. When you and Jill thwarted the attack at the farm, Tishchenko must have made the connection that you'd likely head for Maryland and Fort Meade, just like we did. Anyway, we'll never know for sure. He and a sidekick, Sacha Valinkov, were both found dead by Baltimore police. They took refuge in an abandoned building after the incident at Zoe's house, but we think the Russian oligarchy, or possibly embassy, got to them before we did…you know, tying off loose ends."

"And the JREC?"

"We recovered it from Tishchenko's safehouse along with a couple of other minions. It was delivered to Palmdale this morning, as originally intended."

"So, this is truly over," Tess concluded as she felt a heavy weight lift from her shoulders.

"It absolutely is," Caleb said, pausing briefly. "It turns out Valinkov was romantically involved with the JPL Director's assistant, Denise Urquhart, who he killed and then staged the murder as a suicide. Denise was friends with Krista Maguire, the girlfriend of the Huntsville man who checked the safe annually. Denise was also an unwitting leak at JPL. It appears that by combining the information provided by Mike Bandy and Denise Urquhart, the Russians were able to get enough of a picture of what was happening with the communication equipment. They were then able to fill in the rest of the holes with well-educated guesses."

"It's frightening to see how much damage two people can do."

"Well, if it's any comfort, it looks like the Russians never did figure out what that satellite of yours actually does. Apparently, the purpose of attacking Jill's farm was to capture you. That was their last task to accomplish before Tishchenko could close down the operation. It's also about the time they really started to squeeze Mike."

Tess shivered at the thought of being captured by the Russian assailants. She silently wondered if it would ever be possible to tell Caleb about Helios and its real purpose. Knowing it was still out there, watching over the Earth, did provide some comfort, though. With the NASA Administrator signaling interest in new applications for Helios, this would be an exciting time to lead the program, but for the moment, she pulled herself away from those thoughts.

"Now that all this cloak and dagger stuff is over, I do have a confession to make," Tess said a bit awkwardly.

"Oh, what's that?" Caleb asked with concern.

Leaning over and whispering softly into his ear, Tess said, "I'm not Tess Wentzel. My real name is Tess Shefford. We all use aliases in our program."

Caleb smiled. "Nice to finally meet you, Tess Shefford."

"So, you'll be heading back to California soon?" Tess ventured.

"I know this might seem a bit forward of me, and we have not spent a ton of time together, but you can tell right away when you meet someone special. It's a once in a lifetime thing and it makes you do things you might not otherwise do…things that might not seem to make sense to others. I hope you don't mind, but I would like to put in for a transfer to the Huntsville Field Office. If it's okay with you, of course, I'd like to stay close by, so we get to know each other."

"It's the best news I've heard all day," Tess said. "How should we celebrate?"

He pulled her into a tight embrace, then they kissed each other deeply. Together, they walked out of the Huntsville airport terminal arm in arm, excited for what the future had to offer.

A word about the author…

For inspiration, John Madower draws upon a rich 37-year career as an Air Force aerospace engineer with extensive overseas deployment experience. An avid outdoor enthusiast, in addition to writing, John enjoys long distance running and endurance walking.

Thank you for purchasing
this publication of The Wild Rose Press, Inc.

For questions or more information
contact us at
info@thewildrosepress.com.

The Wild Rose Press, Inc.
www.thewildrosepress.com